HONEYSUCKLE SONG

LYDIA BROWNE

JOVE BOOKS, NEW YORK

HONEYSUCKLE SONG

A Jove Book / published by arrangement with
the author

PRINTING HISTORY
Jove edition / January 1996

ISBN: 0-515-11786-2

A JOVE BOOK®
Jove Books are published by The Berkley Publishing Group,
200 Madison Avenue, New York, New York 10016.
JOVE and the "J" design are trademarks
belonging to Jove Publications, Inc.

PRINTED IN THE UNITED STATES OF AMERICA

10 9 8 7 6 5 4 3 2 1

HIGHEST PRAISE FOR
JOVE HOMESPUN ROMANCES:

HONEYSUCKLE SONG
by Lydia Browne

To my mother,
SUE ANN BAILEY,
with love

Chapter One

"Defendant's name?"

"I don't know, Your Honor."

The defendant stood before the bench, grubby, his beard snarled and tangled. Every time he blinked, sand seemed to rub against his eyes. A large bruise on his right cheek tightened painfully when he spoke.

"Huh," the judge said, disbelief crossing his mature face. "Doc says you're in reasonable shape for a drifter. How come you don't know who you are? Hiding from something maybe?"

"Maybe, Your Honor. I don't know."

"The marshal says you were sleeping in Casey's alley last night. That true?"

"I don't have any money."

"No money, no place to stay. Sounds pretty low to me."

The judge tilted back his chair, rocking it with the slow movements of his big feet. He wore his black silk hat at an angle on his graying hair and pushed his hands, with some difficulty, into the waistband of his checkered pants. "Seems to me I got two choices. Let Reg run you out of town, or throw you in the hoosegow for a couple days while we dig through wanted posters."

The defendant glanced at the marshal, who grinned back at him as if relishing both prospects equally. Reg Wyman wasn't a tall man, but the defendant realized that his own exhausted condition made him no match for the burly marshal. Give him a few decent meals and a couple of nights' rest, though, and he'd soon learn whether the marshal was as tough as he looked.

From the back of the empty courtroom came a clear, confident, *woman's* voice. "Maybe there's a third way."

All five men in the court turned to look at the woman who came in. The marshal, who hadn't uncovered in the presence of justice, took his derby off. The defending attorney, who'd hardly looked up from his yellow-back novel during the judge's questions, rose to his feet. So did the judge. The bailiff grinned, then coughed.

She walked down the aisle, holding her full calico skirt slightly up to keep it out of the tobacco juice and dust. Under her dark blue bonnet, her face seemed to glow with good health. Though the bonnet hid every vestige of her hair, the defendant had no doubt of her essential feminity. Her full mouth belied the severity of her expression and the cold reason of her smooth forehead. Her shawl, crisscrossed over the shoulders of her high-necked white blouse, made more display of her proud bust than would a low-cut satin gown.

The defendant's mouth went dry. She was as lovely as a mirage and completely out of place. She glanced at him with cool gray eyes as she walked up to the judge's table.

"I'd be pleased to hear what you're thinking, Mrs. Landers."

Mrs? Some men were born lucky. The defendant could remember nothing about himself, which led him to think his luck couldn't be very good.

When Judge Sterling heard what she said, he nodded. "I don't see why not. Better that than having him eating and drinking at the town's expense."

"I object."

The lawman and the defendant glanced at each other, stunned to hear the same words from each other's mouth. The defendant's lawyer said in an agitated whisper, "Don't be an idiot!"

Marshal Wyman said, "Your Honor, you can't allow Mrs. Landers to do this! A woman all alone, nobody around but a vagrant who can't even give his name . . ."

"Don't tell me what I can't do," Judge Sterling said, with a disapproving glare over the top of his glasses.

"No, Your Honor. But look at Mrs. Landers. Two

young kids, nobody for miles. For all we know this man's a wanted criminal."

"That's true, Mrs. Landers," the judge said. "Have you thought about that?"

Firmly, she said, "Of course I have, Judge. I don't require the marshal to point out the dangers. However, I do need someone to work around my place and I can't afford to pay wages." Now she glanced at him, briefly, as if she had already weighed his worthiness and didn't need to do it again.

"I guess I could order a man to watch him," the judge said hesitantly.

"It won't be necessary to take the marshal or his deputy from their duties," Mrs. Landers answered, grateful that the judge at least was treating her with respect. Prepared to argue her points against confirmed opposition, Grace was glad to see she wouldn't have to fight as hard as she had feared.

Reg fixed his big brown eyes on Grace, putting into them the soulful expression she'd begun to dread. He never made an obvious advance, but he made it very clear he admired her with more than friendship. She didn't allow his pleading gaze to affect her decision.

"You there," Grace said, realizing how wrong it was to discuss the stranger as if he had no more understanding than a bull for sale. "What's your objection?"

"I don't care for the idea of being bought and sold," he said, meeting her steady gaze.

Behind all the brush of beard and long curling hair, his blue eyes gleamed unexpectedly alert and brilliant. She thought of foxes, half-glimpsed in the twilight woods, stopping to return her wondering stare with preternatural assurance. Grace looked away first.

The judge stepped in before she could speak. "It ain't a matter of buying and selling. The town has an interest in keeping you out of trouble. Mrs. Landers has offered to spare the town the expense of feeding and housing you. On the other hand, the marshal here has a perfectly legitimate reason for not wanting you to go off with Mrs. Landers. Hang on a minute while I puzzle some."

With a lazy hand, Judge Sterling reached into the deep drawer of his desk. He tilted an amber bottle against his lips. The level of liquid in the bottle had sunk considerably before he lowered it.

"Okay," he said, patting his mouth with his handkerchief. "Here's my decision. This John Doe'll work off his sentence at Mrs. Landers's place. She in turn will be responsible for feeding him. At night, he'll come on back to the jailhouse. That answer you, Marshal?"

He lifted the bottle to use as a gavel without waiting for Marshal Wyman's answer. "Okay. Any other business?"

"You haven't given the sentence yet, Your Honor," the defendant's attorney said as he turned another page.

"Oh, yeah. Thirty days or thirty dollars." The bottle came down with a bang that woke the bailiff from his nodding sleep. "Any other gol-durned business? Good, I'm goin' go drown me some worms."

That was as close as Judge Sterling ever came to saying "Court adjourned." Grace didn't wait for the judge to leave before facing the defendant. Now that she had him, what was she going to do with him?

He was taller than she by several inches. She could no longer see into his eyes. Behind the tangled beard and long hair, she could see the end of his nose. She found it hard to tell his age or indeed anything about him from the suntanned tip. His black hair curled over the edge of his splayed collar, both that of his head and that of his chest. He had a wide chest with good shoulders.

Grace jerked her gaze back to his face, not wanting to offend him by seeming to look him over as she would a prize-winning bull. "I'm Mrs. Landers," she said.

"I'm glad you know who you are. I'm sorry I can't introduce myself." He had a deep voice, low but clear. He made all the other men sound like whiny children.

Remembering that she had just acquired the rights to his services, Grace asked more confidently, "Did you know who you were yesterday? I mean, is it because of that bump on your head that you can't recall anything?"

"I haven't been able to—"

Marshal Wyman swaggered up to them. He didn't seem

to realize that he'd broken in rudely, saying, "Come on, you."

"Just a moment, Marshal," Grace said. "Shouldn't I be taking him home now?"

"Sounds good to me," the defendant said.

"Gotta fill out some paperwork on him first, ma'am. Can't just let him go. Tell you what. I'll bring him by your place in about an hour. Come on." He locked his fingers about the other man's elbow and led him away. Grace saw that the defendant looked over his shoulder at her for as long as he could. She couldn't tell whether he was puzzled, angry or pleased.

"You're sure you want him?"

"It's not as though he's done anything violent," Grace said wearily. How many times would the marshal take her over the same territory? "It's good of you to worry. But . . ."

"I can't help but worry, ma'am. You're all alone out here. And if it's just a matter of charity, I know ol' Mr. Boz'll take him in. He needs a new hired man after his run off with that lady whiskey drummer that come through last month."

Grace wiped her hands on her faded calico apron. The June sun gilded everything with hope, even the man sitting in the saddle of the marshal's second-best horse. He hadn't dismounted when Reg had, but sat there still, looking around him with half-opened eyes.

He wore no hat. The sun brought out reddish gleams in his black hair and beard. His bruised cheek looked much worse in the full light of day than it had in the courtroom.

"Once again, Marshal, thank you for your concern. Now, if you don't mind . . ." She fixed her gaze on Reg Wyman, willing him to stop debating with her. He shuffled his feet like a schoolboy, then turned toward his prisoner.

"Okay, you. Git down."

Her new hired man dismounted heavily. As he swung his leg over, Grace saw a worn spot in the bottom of his boot. His clothes were stained, and there were tears in the

knees of his jeans and at the elbow bends of his worn
flannel coat. The stranger made a strong contrast to the
marshal, who kept himself as neat as a new pin.

The stranger looked past her toward the house. Grace
knew what he saw. A sagging roofline, mere flecks of
paint clinging to the weathered gray clapboards, a broken
porch step; beyond the house, a half-weeded garden beneath a straggling apple tree with wormy fruit. A lean
hound dog sat on the porch, panting good-naturedly and
kicking every now and then at his ear. It all looked, she
knew with a pang that never dulled, run-down and seedy.
But the barn at least had been painted within the last two
years and the animals were healthy.

Reg spat, a long stream of tobacco juice zipping
through the dust at their feet. He said, "There's plenty to
do, all right. A widow can't run a farm as well as a man
and that's fact. It's not like your young'uns are big enough
to be much help to you."

Grace stiffened. She'd like Reg a lot more if he'd stop
dwelling on how alone she was. "We get along," she said.
"We've managed to get along so far and, if the Lord is
willing, we'll go on that way."

The stranger started to speak, then cleared his throat.
"Water, ma'am?"

"Pump's round in back."

Despite the hole in his boot, the stranger walked tall,
with an easy swing to his stride. His shoulders were set as
straight as if he wore a fancy suit and a high silk hat.
Suddenly, the marshal looked *too* neat, even overdressed
for what promised to be another scorching day.

Her hound dog, Toby, stretched and yawned, his long
red tongue lolling, then followed the stranger, sniffing
along at his heels. Grace watched the man and the dog,
then turned back when the marshal spoke.

"You sure you don't want me to wait around?"

"No." She softened the monosyllable with a late smile.
"Thank you for thinking of me, Marshal."

"You know I always do." He gave her that crooked
smile all the women in Ogden thought was so wonderful.
Unmoved, Grace watched him mount up.

"See if you can find out his name," he said. "I need it for the records. We've been callin' him John Doe, but that don't look so good. Gotta earn my pay, after all."

"I'll try."

"Thanks. Listen, I'll come back out 'bout suppertime to get him. I'm not sure I trust him to come back on his ownsome."

"As you like. And . . . thanks again."

Grace sighed when Reg rode off, leading his second horse behind him. The marshal's interest added a complication she didn't need. She wished she could think he was just being neighborly when he showed up so often. *Stop flattering yourself,* she thought. *Unmarried women are far and few between in this neck of the woods. Even the scrawniest old maid's got a beau nowadays.*

She bent to pick up the swill bucket and tipped out the last of the table scrapings into the trough. The mellow old sow grunted gratefully as she chomped into half a potato.

Brushing fallen wisps of hair out of her eyes, Grace tramped up the slight hill that climbed from the road to her house. Had she done the right thing in taking on a vagrant, and a forgetful one at that? Only there was the garden to be weeded and the cultivator to drive and the shutters needed repairing and . . .

She knew that once she started thinking about all that needed doing she'd never stop. Even if he didn't know who he was, he could swing a paintbrush. That would be one less chore on her shoulders. Maybe this man would turn out to be a blessing in disguise.

As she came around the corner of the house, she heard her son's high voice. "An' I like apples better than pears. But our apples don't never get big and fat like Mr. Kennedy's. Why do his get so big and ours don't?"

"I don't know," said the stranger. "What do you think?"

"I figure he must be doing something we're not doing, but I don't know what."

"Now, Bart," Grace said. "Don't bother him."

"It's no bother, ma'am. Your son's very interesting to listen to. And I owe him quite a debt. Both of you."

"He's the one, Ma. The one in the alley."

"Yes, I know."

He'd laid his brown coat on the stump of the old oak. Grace noticed that he'd folded it carefully, shoulder to shoulder. The worn lining gleamed in the sunlight. He'd turned back his sleeves too, when he'd washed his hands with the rough yellow soap she kept for the children. His forearms were strewn with black hair. As he moved, she could see the muscles flex and relax under his skin.

Telling herself she liked what she saw only because strength was desirable in a hired hand, Grace said, "I've got a razor in the house if you'd like a shave."

He ran his hand through his beard in wonder. "I guess it's been a while, hasn't it? You'll never know how itchy a beard can be from the inside."

Working the pump, he splashed water on his face. Grace knew the underground spring kept that water icy year-round. He gasped and laughed, shaking his head so the water droplets flew from his long hair. Meeting Grace's gaze, he grinned. "You wouldn't happen to have a bathtub too? I could do with a soak."

Bart asked, "Didn't they give you a bath at the jail? I thought that was the first thing they did."

"Bart!" Trust her son to know all the sordid details. "Where's your sister?"

"I dunno. Henhouse, most likely."

"You're supposed to be watching her. Go find her."

"Aw . . . Come on, Toby."

As he walked away, dragging his bare feet in the dirt, Grace saw with a pang that his bony ankles were protruding from the legs of his overalls. There wasn't another spare inch to let out, either. He was growing so fast. . . .

"He's a smart youngster," the stranger said. "And brave."

"Why didn't . . . ?" she began, then stopped. It was none of her business really.

"Why didn't I fight yesterday?" He frowned and flexed his broad fingers. "I was asleep when those boys appeared. Then . . ." Gingerly, he touched the bruise on his cheek. "One of them is an excellent shot with a rock."

He'd combed his wet hair back from his forehead with his fingers. Crystal beads clung to his skin until he wiped them away. Some fell and spread on his once-white shirt.

"You're sure you don't remember who you are?"

His white teeth flashed for a moment in the depths of his beard. "No, ma'am. I haven't known who I am for . . . a long time."

"Then what am I supposed to call you?" she asked.

His broad shoulders lifted in an uncaring shrug. "I hate to keep saying this, but I don't know. I do know that even an anonymous man may be grateful, Mrs. Landers. I'm very grateful. Your town jail isn't built for comfort."

"I'm sure it's not supposed to be." Absently, she picked up his jacket. "I'll mend this for you. And your trousers too. We've already got a scarecrow."

He chuckled. Grace glanced up. She hadn't meant to be funny.

About to turn the jacket right side out, a word caught Grace's eye. She read the name stitched in maroon thread on the brown lining. "Lucas . . ."

"What?" The stranger snatched the coat from her hand. He read the name out loud, as if he were testing the taste of it. "Lucas. Lucas."

"Is that your name?"

"Lucas." He shut his eyes and rubbed his forehead. Then he admitted bitterly, "It doesn't mean a thing to me."

"Where did you get this coat?"

"Ma'am, I don't remember a damned thing beyond six months ago and even that's foggy. For all I know, I stole this coat. I certainly never noticed a name in it before."

Standing this close to him, Grace saw there were a few flecks of gray in the thick black hair. The corners of his eyes were creased. She didn't know why he thought he needed a bath; he smelled of honest sweat that reminded her of all she'd lost, as well as of strong yellow soap.

"Well," she said. "It's a name, anyhow. I'll call you Lucas. Mr. Lucas, if you like."

"No need for such formality, ma'am. Lucas is fine." He

stared down at the name. "It's better than nothing. I wonder if that really is . . ."

"Also, I want to tell you that I don't tolerate swearing. My children aren't going to learn foul language the way their friends do."

"If their friends say 'damn,' then they surely will."

"At least they won't learn it at home." She turned to go into the house. "I'll bring out that razor for you."

"Ma'am," he said, touching her arm.

Grace stopped. When had a man last touched her? The day of the funeral, probably, when Brother Marill had put a comforting arm about her shoulders. She'd been so cold inside and out that she hadn't been able to feel it.

Lucas's touch sent a flutter through her, a faint, unwanted reminder that she was still a woman though her husband was dead. She stepped away, drawing herself up coldly. "What is it?"

"I want to thank you, ma'am. Not only for today in court, but for yesterday. It was you in the alley, wasn't it?"

"No thanks are necessary. My son came to get me when he realized those boys were hurting you. They left the moment that the marshal appeared. You really owe your thanks to him."

She shied away from the memory of the ugly moment when those hardened faces, their expressions of hungry hatred belying their youth, had turned to examine her and Bart. When Mr. Kent, the banker, had turned up with the marshal, the young toughs had run away. She'd been secretly relieved as she went to the aid of the wounded man.

"I thought I dreamed it. Not the attack, but the ministering angel who came afterwards."

Grace stepped back farther. She didn't care for such fulsome praise. Time to get this conversation back to a commonplace level. "Have you ever done any farm work?"

"You're asking the wrong person. There's no way to tell what I've done. But I have calluses, whatever that means."

He held out his hands, palms up. There were rough patches on the outside of his thumbs, and the heels. But the most noticeable mark was a rough bump on the last joint of his right middle finger. He had good hands, with long, strong-looking fingers. The nails were broken short.

"Yes," Grace said, "you've got some calluses. But they're not farmer's calluses. You'll get those soon enough, I reckon."

"I hope so, ma'am. It'll be a way to repay you for your kindness. Not everyone would help a drifter like me."

"People can't help being suspicious of strangers. But it was wrong for those boys to try to hurt you just because you didn't have a place to sleep."

"Wrong but typical," he said, his mouth twisting.

Grace wondered how many places had run him off, how many distrustful and hostile glances he'd had to suffer. "I'll get you that razor," she said. "Maybe if you looked less like a Union general, folks would treat you with more respect."

"They were a rascally bunch, weren't they?" he said, his powerful voice lightening as he rubbed the bristles.

While she was gone, he sat carefully on the bottom porch step, testing it to be certain it would bear his weight. The place was run-down to the point of ruination. He wondered how long she'd been a widow. He wondered if somewhere his wife asked the sky what had become of her husband.

To himself, he said his new name. It still meant nothing, but he supposed he could learn to answer to it in the same way a stray dog learned to come to "Here, Rover" instead of "Here, Prince."

Lucas yawned and probed delicately at the other bump on the back of his head. His old hat had cushioned that particular rock or he might never have awakened. The hat was now ruined beyond hope, though it had served him well. He still had a headache that the bright sun intensified. At least they'd fed him reasonably well at the jail, his first meal in two days.

He looked toward the house, wondering how soon she'd come out. He wouldn't have guessed her hair would be honey-blond, but it suited her so well he couldn't think of a color that would be better. It complemented her sea-gray eyes, hard when speaking to a man, soft when dwelling on her child.

Lucas guessed that the marshal admired Mrs. Landers as well. His eyes had passed more than once over her womanly figure, lingering on her slim waist and full breasts. Lucas couldn't blame him. If he'd had a name, he might have made an effort in that direction himself. But he was no one. He wished the marshal the best of luck in his wooing, though he didn't like him at all.

As they rode out to this farm, Wyman had spoken of retribution, in violent detail, if anything happened to Mrs. Landers while he was working here. Lucas wasn't sure, but he felt that no one had cause to fear him. Had he ever done harm to another person?

That is something you should know about yourself, he thought. *What am I capable of?*

When Grace came out, carrying a looking glass with awkward care, she saw him sitting on the bottom step, his head in his hands. His fingers dug deeply into his hair, as though he were about to rip it out in handfuls. She asked herself again if she'd done the right thing in taking him on.

As she propped the glass up on the railing of the porch, she decided that she'd see how he worked today. If he turned out to be lazy or handless, she'd tell Reg Wyman to take him away. She had enough trouble keeping the farm going without some ham-handed drifter helping time tear it all down.

Glancing down at the straight razor in her hand, the shining steel and mother-of-pearl handle reflecting back the sunlight, she asked herself whether she should let him have it. That would be all a man needed to . . .

She closed her mind to the ghastly images. "I'm afraid it hasn't been sharpened in two years."

He laid his clean hand, chilled from the water, over hers to take the razor. Grace resisted the urge to wipe her hand on her apron, to rub away the tingling sensation he left behind. It must be the cold water, she thought.

"Your husband's?"

"Yes. He . . . he won it at a fair."

"Good steel," Lucas said, testing the blade on his thumb. "No rust."

Grace stepped out of his way as he approached the mirror. She saw a frown creep onto his brow as he looked at himself, turning his face this way and that. "I can't get used to it," he said. "It's a strange feeling. I know that's my face because when I touch it, I can see and feel my hand on my cheek."

He ran his palm over his cheek, the beard rustling beneath his hand. "But it's like passing a stranger on the street. Maybe he looks a little familiar, but you know it's no one you've ever met before."

"I can't imagine that, not about my own face," Grace said, fascinated despite the hundred things she should be doing.

"Sometimes I think if I stared hard enough into a mirror, it would all come back." He gazed into the spotted silver of the mirror. "Do you have any scissors? This beard of mine is long enough to need trimming before I try to shave. And some shaving soap would be great, if you have any?"

"I . . . think so. I'm not sure."

"And hot water makes it easier to scrape the bristles off."

"Yes, my husband used to . . . The kettle's heating up. I'll bring you some."

"You don't have to go to all that trouble, Mrs. Landers. I'll come in."

"No." Grace planted her feet firmly on the weathered boards of the back porch. "That has to be clearly understood, Mr. Lucas. You are not to come into the house. Not ever."

"But . . ."

"I have to think of my reputation. The marshal's right about one thing. I am alone. And you don't know how people talk."

"I understand."

"I don't mean to be inhospitable. Though lots of people have hired hands, it's best if—"

"I said, I understand." He smiled at her. "I won't come in even if you ask me to."

"Oh." Grace, all wound up to argue her point, felt her unspoken words build up inside her like steam pressure. "All right. So long as we understand each other."

"Yes, ma'am. We do."

Grace tried to keep away from the windows while Lucas shaved. She found it surprisingly difficult. What was behind that black beard? Not flab, or dangling dewlaps—she'd stake her last penny on that. She'd guess he was about forty, though a beard always made a man look older. Maybe he had a cleft in his chin, or a dimple.

Grabbing the broom from behind the kitchen door, Grace marched off to do battle with the dust rats lurking under her son's bed. Cleaning house always worked off her brief angers or lingering fears. With any luck, a good dusting would clear her head as well as the floor. The first thing she brought out was their tabby cat, who began at once to rearrange disordered fur.

"Georgette, you know you're not supposed to be in the house." The cat blinked at her, her great golden eyes outlined in black, as carefully applied as an actress's.

Grace went back to digging with her broom under Bart's bed. Coughing from the dust cloud she'd raised, she opened the window and took some deep breaths. A picture of her new hired man's chest appeared in her thoughts. Naked, it would surely be covered with the same black hair that flourished over—Finding she needed more oxygen yet, she inhaled even more deeply and broke out coughing anew.

She leaped when the back door slammed.

"Ma! We're hungry!"

Nothing new in that. Her children were a pair of bottomless pits. Between them, they'd shame turkey buzzards the way they picked a chicken clean down to the bones and dug to the bottom of the potato bowl almost as soon as it landed on the table. She had enough trouble filling them up at mealtimes, but it was the snacks the rest of the time that stretched her imagination and her limited budget.

As she cut thick slices off the loaf she'd baked early that morning, she heard Callie whispering to her doll. That was a habit Grace had yet to be able to break the little girl of. Her mother, with a sniff, had suggested Grace be more relentless. But Grace herself had so often wished for someone to tell her troubles to that she wouldn't begrudge her daughter one confidante, even if it had a rag body and yellow yarn hair.

"Plowdy wants to know who that man is." Callie's voice could rise as high as a bat's, impossible for even her mother to understand. But her doll's questions were always clear.

"I told you," Bart said, mumbling around his mouthful of bread and damson jam. "He's a criminal and if you're not real careful, he'll—"

Grace interrupted him and said simply, "He's come to work for us, for a while."

"Doesn't he want something to eat?" the doll whispered to her mistress. Callie duly repeated the question.

"I'll take it to him," Bart volunteered. "An' if he don't want it, that's more for me."

"No, you've had enough," Grace answered, lifting the other piece of bread out of reach of her son's grubby hands. "You two go clean your rooms. A wild boar would be ashamed to live in such a mess."

Over her shoulder, as she went outside, she said, "Callie, finish every drop of that milk. Mind me, now!"

"Yes'm."

Chapter
Two

Stepping outside, Grace looked around for Lucas. Except for a quantity of black hair drifting on the ground in the slight breeze, there was no sign of him. Had he taken this chance to flee her and his sentence?

The razor and scissors sat on the porch rail beside the mirror. She picked them up and slipped the bright utensils into her apron pocket. At least he hadn't stolen the razor. She didn't have many things left of Chick's, not since the creditors came calling after his death. Most of his clothes were gone, though his good suit had served to bury him in. She would have given the rest to Lucas, if he'd stuck around.

"Oh, well," she said out loud. "His loss."

A two-inch-long curl of his hair drifted against her skirt. She brushed it off at once, surprised to find that it wasn't coarse, but soft and silky. It clung to her fingers, rolling around them. She had to shake it off forcefully.

Turning to go into the house, she trod hard on the curl. *Best just to forget about him,* she thought. *Though I guess Marshal Wyman will have to know Lucas has taken off. He probably wouldn't have worked out anyway. Though it would have been nice to have a grown-up around to talk to. . . .*

A whistle floated down to her from the front of the house. Grace darted around the corner to catch her last glimpse of Lucas, for no doubt he was strolling along the road, free as a bird. The sun struck her full in the face as she came around the corner. Blinking blindly, she nearly stumbled over him.

He knelt by the front steps, examining the warped

board that had lifted from the riser. As he tried to force it down, the whistling faded. When he saw he couldn't fix the step by merely adding new nails, the whistle broke out again, a danceable little tune that Grace did not remember ever hearing before.

"Oh, you're still . . ." But she couldn't say what she was thinking. She didn't want him to think she mistrusted him.

"I thought I should get right to work." He sat back on his heels and lifted his face.

Grace swayed as a wash of hot color rose in her cheeks. Dropping her eyes as soon as she realized she was staring, she said, "I think . . . there are most likely some boards in the barn you can use to repair that step. The nails are on a shelf above the hammer and saws and such."

She quickly walked away, but her pulse wasn't racing because of her speed. And it wasn't the bright sun that made her feel so hot. She walked to the well, winched up the bucket, and let the frigid water run over her hands. Patting her cheeks in the hope of cooling them, she tried to catch her breath.

With a slight shake of her head, she declared that he couldn't be *that* good-looking. She'd been dazzled by the sun, blinded by the little red dots floating before her eyes. No man could have chiseled features, black wavy hair falling a little over his forehead, *and* deep lines carved in his cheeks when he smiled, a feature she'd always been partial to.

She'd made it all up, no doubt about it, out of a half-glimpsed image and her imagination. An experienced woman like herself ought to know better than to delude herself the way the young girls did.

Grace went inside and crept through the hall that led from the kitchen to the seldom-used front door. The children didn't see her. Warily, she pushed aside the white lace curtain that hung over the glass panel beside the door.

Peering out, she saw only the top of Lucas's head. His hair was the color of a black cat's pelt, and now that it was cut, it did indeed lie in deep waves.

He lifted his head. Grace shrank out of sight. Then, cautiously, she peered out again.

The sun had turned his skin very brown, so that his blue eyes shone out all the brighter for the contrast. Though his nose couldn't be called small, it fit his square face. His chin was firm, though the skin was paler because of the beard. The beard had also hidden his well-cut mouth and his strong neck. Only the purple bruise marred his looks, swelling one cheek.

The beard had added ten years at least. She now guessed him to be no more than thirty. She didn't have to guess to know that he was cataclysmically attractive. Not with the evidence right before her eyes.

Goodness and mercy, what would everybody think of her when Lucas appeared in town tonight? Bad enough that Reg Wyman had made all those hints about farm folk and drifters. Let the women get a glimpse of Lucas's face and no one would believe that she was utterly uninterested in a new man, let alone the one who would be spending every day with her. Before the sun rose tomorrow, she'd be the best grist the gossip mill had seen in months.

Lucas stood up and dusted off his hands on his pants. Grace chewed her lower lip. His broad shoulders led her eyes down his flat waist to his hips, enticingly narrow in the torn, faded—

"Ma!"

With great presence of mind, she ran her finger along the lip of wood between the two panes of glass. "Dusty," she murmured, letting the curtain fall. "What is it, Bart?"

"Can I go watch the hired man now? I finished my room."

"I don't want you bothering Mr. Lucas. He has a great deal to do. And I'll see your room before you can do anything."

As she guessed, the drawers of his single dresser were crammed with all the multitude that had been scattered on his floor. She didn't need to say a word, a simple chastising, if amused, glance did the trick. With an abashed saunter, Bart went to begin his chore again.

Grace put her hand on his shoulder. "Why not go see if our lines have caught any fish?"

A man freed from prison could not have shown more joy than a boy let off cleaning his room. Bart took off like a bullet from a gun, not even pausing to holler his thanks. The back door closed with a bang. "Come on, Toby!"

Grace knew that Callie would work without complaint until her little room was as neat as could be. Nevertheless, it wasn't fair that Bart should be excused and not her. Grace glanced in. The room was tiny, a former pantry left over when the new kitchen had been added on before they'd bought the place. The room was also spotless, everything in proper order.

Her little daughter slept on her bed, her doll tucked up close beside the thin ribs. Her shoes lay neatly under the edge of the quilt. Callie's long eyelashes cast tender shadows over her pink cheeks. She looked completely innocent and heartbreakingly sweet. Grace sighed, reproving herself.

A mother with two children should not be peeping through the curtains at a man. She certainly should not be admiring his build, or his face. Lurid thoughts of naked chests should never occur to her. Motherhood should fulfill all her needs—or at least that is what her mother would say. Ever since Chick had died, her mother had dwelled repeatedly on the joys of motherhood making up for the loss of a husband. Of course, Grace's father was still alive, so Grace couldn't be sure where her mother was getting her information.

But it was a scandal that Grace should think of a man she'd just met in that way. Actually, come to think of it, she hadn't really met him, not formally. You couldn't meet someone whose identity had been lost. She should keep that mystery in mind and quit mooning over the way he looked.

When he came back from the barn, a board under his arm and a few nails held between his lips, she was waiting for him on the porch. "You'll have to hold off on that," she called softly. "My daughter's asleep."

"Oh! Well, I guess I could fix your gate instead. I see the hinges are broken. I bet your son was swinging on it."

"I told him he was too heavy."

Grace realized it hadn't been the sun that had dazzled her before, but his smile. He had the whitest teeth she'd ever seen. The few drifters she'd seen before had nothing but black stumps, which made them no different from some of the established people she knew. But Lucas's were clean. She ran her tongue around her own, inside, promising herself to scrub extra hard with the salt tonight.

"Would you like something to eat, Mr. Lucas? I baked this morning."

"I haven't done anything to earn your hospitality yet, Mrs. Landers. Though I thank you for the shave." He rubbed the exposed back of his neck. It was whiter than his face. She wondered how long it had been since he'd cut his hair last.

"I see you cut your hair too."

"After the shave, I felt I had to. I was no sight for a lady, that's for certain."

"My husband had a beard," she said. "Just a little one." She ran her finger from her jaw to under her chin to show him. "I never liked it. It looked . . . absentminded. Like he was careful with his face and then forgot the rest."

Grace took herself in hand. This was no time to indulge in reminiscences. "If you want to make yourself useful, you can stack that firewood. Though they were kind enough to split it for me, Mr. Hopton's boys just dumped it in the yard."

She waved at the pile of wood thrown down higgledy-piggledy about fifty feet from the back door. The whole yard had an slovenly, unthrifty appearance that tormented Grace. But, between farming and keeping the house, she hadn't a moment for anything but vegetable gardening. And even that sprawled and looked scruffy. At least it was green, not hard-packed earth or burned grass like much of the yard.

"Okay," he said. "Where do you want it? Beside the house in that lean-to?"

"That's right."

He nodded and walked out to pick up the first log. Grace called out a belated thank-you. He waved in answer. She watched while he piled four pieces of wood onto his outstretched arm. He staggered awkwardly, around to the side of the house.

Grace considered telling him there was a wheelbarrow in the barn. But most men, all she knew as a matter of fact, would be more antagonistic when told they were doing something the hard way than they would if they found out an easier way on their own.

On the other hand, what did it matter to her if his feelings were a little wounded? He was her employee, and she really couldn't afford to have him strain his back on the first day.

"Um, Mr. Lucas!" she called when he reappeared. "I'm sorry to ask. . . . You must feel like a pea on a hot shovel the way I've got you jumping from one thing to the next . . . but would you go up to the barn and bring me the hoe? I can get started on the weeds in the garden while you stack the wood."

He must have wondered why she didn't go herself. That was the interpretation Grace put on the sideways glance he gave her as he straightened up from picking up more wood. "Certainly, Mrs. Landers. Glad to."

He returned quickly, pushing the wheelbarrow. Running it to where she knelt among the rutabagas, he said, "I brought you your trowel and rake too."

Tipping up the barrow, he dumped it all on the ground. The clatter startled her. Grace jumped up clumsily. She caught her foot on the trailing honeysuckle vine she'd come to uproot. Stumbling, she fell toward Lucas. He steadied her with his arm.

Pleasure shot through her at his touch, stronger than before. It scared her. Grace skipped away almost before she'd gained her balance. She saw a flash of hurt cross Lucas's face, extinguishing all the laughter. "I . . ."

"Are you afraid of me, Mrs. Landers?"

She'd never admit it. "Of course not. Should I be?" Against her will, her voice quavered.

"I don't think so," he said seriously. "But I could be wrong."

"That's comforting," she muttered.

"But you don't have to worry that I'll fly off the handle if you tell me there's a wheelbarrow in the barn. I'm not such a brute that I'd snap your head off for saving me from carrying all that wood in my hands."

How odd that he'd guessed she'd been trying to save his pride as well as his hands. "At least, you don't think you're that kind of a brute," Grace said seriously. "I don't envy you anymore, Mr. Lucas. It must be a scary thing, not knowing who you are."

"You envied me before?"

"We'd better get to work." She met his eyes, though she knew her color had risen again.

Lucas let her change the subject. For a woman who stood up to bullies and judges with equal firmness, she seemed strangely skittish where he was concerned. Thinking back, he realized it was only after he'd shaved that she had changed. When she had told him not to go into the house, she'd been as strict as a schoolteacher.

Was there something so frightful about his face that she couldn't bring herself to look at him? He'd noticed she tried so hard not to stare that her gaze stayed mostly on the ground when he spoke to her. Lucas wished he could sneak a second glance in her mirror. He hadn't noticed any particular scars or an evil expression when he looked at himself before.

And why, he wondered, trundling the wood around the house, why would a woman with nice kids and her own house envy a drifter like him for even one second? The envy should all be on his side. As a matter of fact, it was all on his side.

After a while, he came over to where she worked. A trickle of sweat ran icily down the middle of his back. He wiped his beaded forehead with the inside of his wrist. Mrs. Landers didn't seem to notice him; she was intent on cutting up honeysuckle roots with her hoe. She raised it over her head and brought it down on a twisted, fibrous root with a thwack that made Lucas move out of range.

He wondered how she could appear so cool even while doing the backbreaking labor of a man.

"All done?" she asked after a few more strikes.

"Yes, ma'am. Would you like"—*Thwack!*—"me to do that?"

"No, thanks." *Thwack!* Grace pushed the hoe handle away and used it as a support as she bent down to tug the yellow-gray root out of the ground. "Thought I had it," she panted as she exerted all her strength.

She let the hoe fall and used both hands to tug, her back curved. "Come on," she pleaded to the root as she struggled with it. "Give in."

"Here," Lucas wrapped his hand around hers and exerted his power as well. She felt cool to his touch.

"Must be rooted clear to China," Grace said. His breath tickled her ear, unnerving her. "I'll cut at it some more."

"No, it's coming. Another try and—"

The root let go just then, with the ill-natured willfulness of things in general. They tumbled down, the tension that was holding them up gone from the other end.

Grace found herself practically sitting in Lucas's lap. His arm was around her waist, pressing her back into his chest. If she'd turned her head, her lips would have brushed his cheek. She managed to fight down the temptation, though the very fact that she felt there was a temptation to fight alarmed her.

"I beg your pardon!" Yanking at the edge of her skirt, trapped beneath him, she tried to get to her feet. Irritatingly, Lucas began to chuckle.

"What is so funny?" she demanded.

He raised his hand, showing her the tiny piece of root they'd managed to dislodge. "Whoever coined the phrase 'a hard row to hoe' must have lived in the Dakota Territories."

"Dakota?" Grace turned her head and stared at him. She forgot her unfortunate position, even forgot that they could be seen from the road if anyone happened to pass.

Lucas saw the surprise and fear in her eyes. When she moved to stand up, he helped her with a hand under her elbow. She took herself out of range of his touch as quickly as she could.

"Isn't this the Dakotas?"

"No. This is Missouri. Odgen, Missouri. Didn't you hear the bailiff announce it?"

"My lawyer was talking to me then." He put his hand up to his head, rubbing his right eye with the heel. "Missouri? You're sure?" A smile flickered across his mouth, humorlessly. "Course you're sure. I'm sorry."

"The Dakotas are hundreds of miles from here. Almost due north. You must have been walking for months! Unless . . . Did you have a horse?"

The pain behind his right eye was growing, a rising tide that brought fire instead of coolness in its wake. "I don't know! How would I know!"

Grace shrank back. In an instant, he had changed from a friendly new hired hand into a man whose face was lined in torment. "Not the Dakota Territory," he said, almost to himself. "*Not* the Dakota Territory. But I know . . . I could have sworn . . ."

Grace saw him clutch his head as though in agony. Hardly knowing what she did, only that she wanted to help him, she grabbed his hands, forcing them down. Holding on tight, she gripped them between her own. "It's all right," she whispered, as though comforting one of her children. "It's all right."

His breath came in great gulps, as if he were choking. He stared around as though scenting ambush, his eyes rolling like a wild horse's. She could feel his heartbeat drumming in his hands.

Then she saw him gain mastery over himself. He drew a breath without shuddering, swallowed normally. The glint of irrepressible humor reappeared in his indigo eyes. Suddenly, she was no longer holding his hands. He was holding hers. Little flickers of awareness danced up and down her arms.

"You're sure you want to keep me around?"

"I don't know," she said honestly, pulling gently away. He released her hands. "I can't blame you."

"Not that I think you'll do us any harm. You don't *seem* dangerous."

"Thank you for that at any rate," he said, a tiny smile twitching the corner of his mouth.

"What *do* you remember about yourself, Mr. Lucas?"

"That's the question, isn't it?" He tossed the piece of honeysuckle root carelessly away.

"No!" Grace yelped, racing after it. It landed in some tall grass at the edge of a ditch.

"What's wrong?" he asked, following.

"Do you see it anywhere? We've got to find it. All it needs to do is lie out for a couple of days and I'll have a whole new vine taking over. Half my day is spent rooting honeysuckle out. At least, that's how it seems."

"Here it is." He bent and picked up the tiny piece, hardly as long as his middle finger. He eyed it with respect. "I didn't realize it was such powerful stuff."

"You don't know, Mr. Lucas. I wouldn't dare take my eyes off a vine for fear it would have me half-strangled before I knew what was what."

"What do you do with it, then? Obviously you can't bury it."

"I burn it. I put all the pieces in a pile and burn it down to ashes. Honeysuckle won't take over *my* place. Not while I have my strength."

He smiled at her vehemence. "I'll be more careful in future."

"Please do," she said solemnly. She couldn't afford to let him turn a pernicious weed into a joke. "Of course, some people think a fence all overgrown with the stuff looks pretty. And I admit there's something nice about the way they smell. The children always protest when I prune it. They like to strip the flowers and sip the honey. . . ."

"They do what?"

"Why, didn't you ever . . . Oh, I forgot!"

"Isn't that what I'm supposed to say?"

Try as she might to hold it in, a smile escaped her. "I guess it is at that, Mr. Lucas. If you really want to try . . ."

She led him across the hard-packed dirt road to a small tree overgrown with the sprawling vine. Among the heart-shaped, glossy green leaves, delicate yellow flowers grew lushly. A dizzyingly sweet scent arose from the plant, befuddling him more thoroughly than had the rock that landed on his head. He heard the throbbing drone of many bees, bustling among the flowers.

"Look there," Grace said, pointing to the branch of the host tree. "You see how it's all twisted round and scarred? That's from the honeysuckle."

The vine had contorted the branch, digging in as it curled and twined until the vine and the branch were virtually one. "Give it another year or two and this tree will be completely dead. It's hardly got any leaves of its own as it is."

She reached out and picked one of the blossoms. Grasping the green stem firmly, she gently drew out the yellow flower with her other hand. A trailing white thread hung from it. Grace put it to her lips.

"Go on, it's sweet," she said, showing him again with another blossom.

He jerked his gaze away from her mouth. Maybe it was his bad memory, but Lucas could have sworn he'd never seen lips so soft and naturally pink. Especially now, when she forgot to be stern and cold, her mouth had a fullness that seemed to beg for kisses.

He coughed, knowing these were not the thoughts a hired man should have about his brand new employer, especially one who could put him back in jail if she decided she didn't like him. Lucas concentrated on picking a honeysuckle blossom.

Like a sugared sigh, the sweetness dissolved on his tongue. Without thinking, only knowing he liked the taste, Lucas reached for another.

"Sometimes if the kids are really pestering me for something sweet, I send them out here."

"The bees must hate that."

"There's plenty for them. The woods is chock-full of honeysuckle. Too much. And the wisteria is almost as bad.

A couple of weeks ago, this whole place was hung with purple."

She frowned at the wall of green on the other side of the road. It was as if her enemy had put on armor and sent forth a challenge. Lucas could almost hear the bugles calling the trees to arms. The honeysuckle was the scout, sent to test her will to resist. Soon would come seedlings of the sycamores and oaks as the vanguard, while the clandestine assaults of carpenter ants and termites weakened the enemy's morale. He saw that the price of freedom was eternal vigilance. A wildflower left to flourish for its beauty might be the infiltrator that would bring Mrs. Landers's farm down.

Lucas looked across the road at the farmhouse. "Why do you live here?"

"Where else should we live?"

"Well, in town, I guess." He followed her as she returned.

"Living in towns costs money, Mr. Lucas." She thought about all the other things that cost money. Like cloth to make the children clothing and seed and shoes and pay for any hired man that didn't come from the jail. . . . Shaking her head to clear it, she said, "We get along. And that firewood won't stack itself, you know."

He touched two fingers to his temple in a sketchy salute. "Yes'm."

After a moment, as he threw pieces of wood into the wheelbarrow, she called to him. He raised his eyebrows in a silent response. "Do you think you're going to mind working for me?"

"There's nothing I can do about it right now in any case, Mrs. Landers. And it's not as though I have any urgent business elsewhere."

Chapter
Three

"Bart, Callie! Dinner!" Then Grace remembered someone else who would be interested. "Lucas! Dinner!"

The children, of course, would come scampering in from the ends of the earth for fried catfish and greens, on even a day as hot as this one had turned out to be, provided there was enough vinegar to drown the vegetables. They clattered over the scrubbed wooden floor, their eyes alight with hunger.

"Let me see 'em," Grace demanded.

Callie held up her hands. Pink and shiny. "All right, honey."

As soon as the food hit the little girl's plate, her golden head bowed. "God bless our daily bread," she said.

Bart held up his hands, a mischievous smile about his mouth. His hope, Grace knew, was always that she'd be too distracted to really look at them. She didn't have to look hard. Black streaks and mud clots and things she dared not examine decorated his hands—front, back and under the nails.

"Well?" she asked.

"Be right back." As if he were propelled by a powerful force, Bart dashed away. If he ever washed them right the first time, using more than a fingertip of water and a little fingernail's worth of soap, she'd drag him to the doctor lickety-split.

While putting a plate down as Bart came back, wetter all over than one would believe possible from just a hand-washing, Grace looked out the open kitchen door. No sign of Lucas. Maybe he hadn't heard her. But his ears would have to be made of wood not to hear her hollering.

She stepped out on the back porch. The heat mirage shimmered across the yard. Making a mental note to be sure the pigs had all the water they needed to make their cooling mud, Grace called again. "Lucas! Lucas!"

Recalling how she'd been taught to believe that a lady never raises her voice, Grace smiled. If only Chick had done as she'd so often asked and had an iron ring made that she could hammer, the way the townswomen did. At dinnertime, Ogden sounded like a blacksmith's convention, each household having a gong with its own particular tone.

Looking over her shoulder to be sure the vinegar jug was out of reach of the children, Grace stepped off the porch. The heat of the day hit her in the face like the blast she felt whenever she opened the door of her black cast-iron stove.

Where was that man? Lucas would have to learn that if he didn't come to dinner when it was served, he wouldn't get any.

That lesson, however, could wait. He'd worked hard this morning. Almost all the wood was gone from the middle of the yard, a job that would have taken her and the children the better part of a day. When the marshal came to collect Lucas tonight, she'd tell him that she wanted her hired man to come back the next day.

Grace went on feeling satisfied until she saw him.

He shambled between the wheelbarrow and the lean-to. Like a sleepwalker, he picked up a split log. Standing with it in his hands, he blinked down at it as if unsure of what to do with it. Then, slowly, he laid it on the stack. It rolled down. He bent and replaced it, no expression coming to his face, neither resignation nor exasperation.

Grace approached him slowly. "Mr. Lucas?"

She touched him on the arm and he shuddered. For a moment, he closed his eyes tightly. Looking down at her from his height, he said, "Mrs. Landers? What . . . ?"

He wiped his hands on his shirt, palms and backs both. Grace noticed that he left smears of blood behind. Horrified, she grasped his heated hands. "What did you do to yourself?"

Several of the nails that were already broken were now torn and one was split. Deep scratches scored the back of his left hand, while splinters showed like dashes beneath the skin of his palms. Furthermore, his hands were cold, cold in this heat.

She could feel him swaying. Looking up into his face, she saw him trying to focus on her but his lids were fighting to close. Without considering the consequences, she draped his arm around her shoulders.

"You lean on me," she said, walking him toward the house.

His body was hot, burning through the material of his shirt like a stove lid through a pot holder. She led him up to the porch, step by step, feeling his weight growing on her.

"Open the door, Bart," she called.

But the shambling man refused to go in. "Not the house," he mumbled. "Not the house. I promised."

"It's all right," Grace said. "I don't mind your going in. You're sick."

Bart shrank against the door frame as Grace tried again to get Lucas to go inside. "What's the matter, Ma?" he asked worriedly.

"Mr. Lucas is sick. I think he's been in the sun too long."

"Can I help?"

"Go take the coverlet off my bed. Then you'll have to run for Dr. Birkins."

Once again, Grace tried to take Lucas into the house. But he dug in his heels and she could not budge him. He was bigger and heavier than he looked. "Not the house," he said more clearly.

"Now look," Grace said. "You may be stubborn but I give Missouri mules ornery lessons in my spare time. So just go on in, would you, please?"

Every time she'd get a few steps forward, he'd stagger and they'd go reeling. Toby danced nervously under their feet, looking up into their faces as though asking the rules of this game. Once Grace actually persuaded Lucas to put a foot over the threshold, but he seemed at once to realize he was breaking his word. He tottered back. They nearly fell down the stairs that time. Toby barked, wagging his tail.

"Are they dancing?" Callie asked.

Naturally, her big brother took no notice of her question.

A bright expression coming into his round blue eyes, he waited until the grown-ups came close to the doorway. Then he called, "This way out!"

At once, Lucas turned and walked in through the door. He tramped through the kitchen as though on order. Grace tipped Bart a wink of congratulations and hurried to catch up to Lucas. He was making for the front door. She guided him to her cool room on the north side of the house.

She'd forgotten to open her curtains that morning. The simple calico kept out most of the sunlight, filtering the rest through the mostly dark red fabric. Lucas sighed when he reached the near-darkness.

"Sorry," he sighed, just before falling, a full-length sprawl, across her bed.

The cat let out a snarling yowl and leaped down from the bed as it bounced under Lucas's weight. She vanished through the open door.

Grace stood back, flicking the loosened hair out of her eyes, and took a long look at him. "I should have known better," she sighed. Impossible to leave him lying like this. For one thing, his dirty boots had landed right on her clean sheets.

"Should I go for the doctor, Ma?"

"Maybe you'd better. Though how we're to pay . . . Nevertheless, you run on into town. I don't like the look of that bruise on his face."

"Okay," Bart said, excitement creeping into his voice. "Boy, just wait till I tell Harry and—"

"Bart!" Grace caught him by the strap of his overalls. His brown body squirmed and then stilled. "Don't you stop to talk to any of your friends. They're too wild. You just run into town and come back with the doctor."

"Don't worry," he said with an impudent cock of his

head. "Harry's okay. So're the others. It's just them big Grupp boys—Win, Marv, Caleb. And they don't take no notice of a little kid like me."

He wiggled free and was gone. For a wonder, he didn't slam the door when he flew outside. Grace almost called him back. The rough Grupp boys might not have taken any notice of him before, but yesterday he'd spoiled their "fun" by fetching his mother.

Lifting up Lucas's feet to take off his boots, she gazed down at him. "Unconscious again. You have the darnedest luck, Mr. Lucas."

"Mama? Can Plowdy help?" Little Callie trailed her doll on the floor by one leg.

"No, thank you, honey." *It's just as well he fell on his face*, Grace thought. *I don't know if I could bring myself to get his pants off.*

"Is he gonna die?"

Shocked, Grace turned abruptly around. "Course not!" she said, instinctively denying any such idea.

"Daddy died. . . ."

Kneeling on the uneven pine boards of her bedroom, Grace held out her arms. Her daughter stepped inside her embrace. "Now, you know Daddy was very, very sick for a long time. Mr. Lucas just has a little touch of the sun. If he rests, he'll be fine. Do you remember when you had that cold last winter?" Callie nodded, her finger in her mouth. "You rested up and you were fine."

"Played with the clothespins."

"That's right. You played dolls with the clothespins. And I made you soup."

"Will Dr. Birkins give him pep'mint sticks?"

Grace chuckled at the hopeful light in her daughter's eyes. "Maybe, honey. Now you run along and play with Plowdy, all right? I'll take care of Mr. Lucas."

Standing up, Grace saw that he'd rolled onto his back, moving his head onto her goose-feather pillow. She decided she'd still leave his clothes on, though it was a shame they were so torn.

She wrung out a cloth in the tepid water of her washbowl. It wouldn't do to shock him by applying cold cloths, not yet. Laying the cloth across his forehead, Grace saw that his eyes were open.

"Are you all right?" she asked.

His hand moved among the bedclothes. Grasping hers suddenly, he clutched it in both of his. "You're a wonderful girl, just wonderful. So sweet and soft and sympathetic."

"Thanks," she said, trying to reclaim her hand. Something about his voice, the low, caressing tone, the intensity, played strange tricks with her insides.

"Oh, Margot . . ." He nestled his face into the pillow and sighed.

Grace jerked free and straightened up. "Margot. I'll remember that." Then she smiled and shook her head. "Which is more than you will, when you wake up."

Grace sat down on the bed and remembered the first time she'd seen him. The Grupp boys and the others had taken off and all that was left was a huddled bundle of rags at the end of an alley. Like everyone else, she'd assumed he was a drunk. But when she'd knelt down to pull his battered head onto her knee, no liquor fumes had assailed her.

She had thought him unconscious. A red mark showed on his cheek, the center bleeding. His beard had scratched through the bodice of her dress.

The town banker, Mr. Kent, had tried to urge her away. Blushing, Grace recalled that she'd defended the unconscious man when Kent had told her a drunken vagrant didn't deserve her help, that a few days in jail would be the proper conclusion for such a degraded creature.

"He's human, isn't he?" she'd asked. "Besides, he's not drunk."

Kent had been delighted to see the marshal. They'd whispered together, two men of the world united against the irrational female. Only when Wyman promised that the stranger would see a doctor before a judge did Grace get up. Besides, the man now known to her as Lucas had begun to stir, nestling closer to her bosom as though seeking refuge.

She'd been unable to get him out of her mind for the

rest of the day. It wasn't that he was so attractive, for she'd known nothing of that until he'd shaved. It was the unfairness of the situation. He was locked up while the boys who had assaulted him, even though everyone knew who they were, went free.

That was the only reason she'd gone down to the courthouse this morning. If the judge had let him off, that would have been the end of it so far as Grace was concerned. As it was, she was responsible for him.

She stood up and looked down at him. His shirt strained across his chest, his arms flung wide. The top button, unfastened, hung by a thread, and the rest were by no means secure.

"Doc Birkins will wonder if you're all dressed when he gets here," she said, as if Lucas could hear her. "And your clothes do need mending."

She lifted one of his slack arms and pried free the button that held his cuff closed. The edge of the cuff had frayed badly, the inner lining showing through the outer cloth. A scratch ran around his wrist. On the other cuff, the button came off in her hand.

After she twice drew back from tackling the buttons on the shirt, Grace rubbed her hands together as if she were cold. "Come on," she urged herself. "You haven't got all day."

His chest rose and fell gently to the rhythm of his breaths. Peering at his face, Grace saw that his eyes were closed and still. She took the cloth from his forehead, wrung it out again in the basin and replaced it. Chick had always looked vulnerable in his sleep, especially during his illness. Lucas, on the other hand, seemed more stern when asleep than when awake. A slight frown made his eyebrows draw closer together and the firm line of his mouth showed a resolute nature.

Grace shook her head, certain she was reading more into Lucas's expression than she should. She'd been fooled too often. A boy's spiritual look might result from thinking of his new slingshot. And the most vicious gossip she knew had a face like an angel's.

But these reflections weren't getting Lucas's clothes off!

Taking herself in hand, Grace began to unbutton Lucas's shirt. She held the placket edge by two fingers and, working gently with the fabric on the button-side, managed to slip the first two buttons free of their holes. The third button popped off by itself. She put it with the one from his sleeve in her apron pocket.

His shirt gaped open almost all the way now. Rich black hair grew in swirls over his solid, smoothly muscled chest, just as she had imagined. Her cheeks flushing, Grace tugged his shirt free from the confines of his waistband. After an interruption across his flat stomach, the hair grew low above his belt buckle. Grace tried not to look.

"It's nothing I haven't seen before," she said, her gaze inching lower.

But Chick had always been a few pounds overweight, carrying it as a roll of flesh around his waistband. And his chest had been enriched by only a few, sparsely scattered hairs. Of course, he'd had a gentle touch and a loving heart, she thought, with quick loyalty.

With the same two fingers, she took the end of Lucas's belt where it passed from the buckle to the keeper. She tugged lightly. Then she had to pull harder to free the smooth brown leather from the metal tongue of the brass belt buckle. There, it was free. Now for the row of silver buttons marching down the front of his undyed jeans.

Grace saw at once that her hands-off technique wouldn't work this time. The denim material, faded though it was, was still too stiff to let a button slip through easily. Grace wiped her sweating hands on her apron, and touched the top button.

Lucas stirred, a smile coming onto his face. He sighed contentedly, and rolled on his side. Wiping her shaking hands once more on her apron, Grace decided to give up on his pants. She could take his shirt, however, and replace those fallen buttons.

An hour later, Dr. Birkins came out of her room, closing the door behind him. Short and stocky, the doctor was on the shady side of forty with sparse hair on top and plentiful side whiskers. He'd seen his share of service during the war and sometimes his impatience with the ailments and complaints of civilians showed through his bedside manner. But no one could have been more compassionate during those long days of Chick's final illness.

"He'll be all right," he said, as Grace rose from her rocking chair in the sitting room to meet him. Looking over his glasses at her, Dr. Birkins frowned. "But don't you know any better than to let a man work in this heat without a hat on? 'Specially one with a lump like an egg on his head."

"I didn't think," Grace said weakly.

"More trouble comes in this world from folks not thinking than any other source. Well, it isn't all your fault, Mrs. Landers. That man in there is worn to a stub anyway. I told the judge a week in the hoosegow would do him good, like Saratoga for a rest cure."

"What did Judge Sterling say to that?"

"Sniffed and told me the court's not in the habit of providing leisure for criminals. Next I hear, our nameless friend in there is working for you."

"I guess it's all over town already then," Grace suggested, a blush sneaking onto her cheeks.

"Course. Now, if you'll give me his shirt, I'll get him ready to go."

Grace lifted the shirt that dangled from her fingers. "Go?"

"He can't stay here, Mrs. Landers."

"Why not? I'm responsible for him."

"Not that responsible. It's bad enough that . . ."

"Go on." He was bound to know all the gossip. His wife was Rena Presby's best friend. What Rena didn't hear, she made up.

"I won't deny that some folks are wondering what possessed you to interfere with this man's sentencing."

"It's very simple," Grace said. "I need a man."

Dr. Birkins's eyebrows rose as if to replace the hair missing from his pate. He sputtered. "You . . . you . . ."

Grace realized that an evil interpretation could be put on her words. Her blush intensifying, she hurried to add, "That is . . . Like Marshal Wyman said, a widow can't run a farm as well as a man can. I hate to agree with him, but he's right. And for the next thirty days, I have a man. He may not be much, but he's more than I've had for a long time."

"Oh, yes. Of course. I see." The shock faded from Dr. Birkins's eyes. Yet as he added some instructions for Lucas's care, Grace was aware that he still gave her some strange looks.

"Are you sure you wouldn't like me to keep him, just till he's over this incident? After all, we've got the room now that Junior's off to medical college."

"Thanks, but I can manage. Now, about your bill . . ."

The doctor shrugged. "Way I see it, the court oughta pay that. If he was staying at the jail, they'd have to stump up the two bits for a house call. I figure you're just taking over for the jail during the day, so I'll send the bill to Marshal Wyman."

"I appreciate that, Doctor." With a rueful smile, she admitted, "Right now I haven't got fifty cents in the whole house."

He put his hand in his pocket and opened his mouth as if to speak. Grace drew herself up, meeting his eyes with her own, pride shining in them. Clearing his throat, the doctor said, "Listen now, if that lump on the back of his head gets—"

"*Back* of his head?"

"Yes. Didn't he mention . . . ?"

"I only know about the bruise on his face."

"Darn lucky he didn't break his cheekbone. Those Grupp boys . . . Anyway, there's a nice lump on the back of his head too. If it weren't for his hat, he would have cracked his skull. But between the cushioning of the hat and a natural thickness—so to speak—of his occiput, he managed to get off with a beautiful lump. If it gets soft or more painful, let me know. Not sure there isn't some pressure building."

"Tell me, is that why he can't remember who he is?"

"Could be. Probably not, though. I talked to him in the jail yesterday, when I first attended him. He's a lost soul, Mrs. Landers. Brother Marill's the fellow to tell you about that kind of man, not a doctor."

He cleared his throat again to hide his display of a sensitivity usually hidden beneath a blustery manner. "How's that little girl of yours? No more of that cough, I hope."

"She's fine. She's playing in the other room."

"Good, good. And that Bart is a scamp and a rascal. Puts me in mind of my own boy. Junior could never sit still a minute either."

Talking of their children, Grace escorted Dr. Birkins to his runabout buggy. He stowed his black bag on the floor behind the high-curving dashboard. "Now, keep him quiet, if you can. If fever develops, keep up the cool cloths. A couple of light, nourishing meals and he'll be good as new in two days. But don't work him too hard the first week, unless you want him flat on his back again."

"I certainly don't!"

She felt a tug on her skirt. Looking down, she saw Callie, the little girl's face turned up toward her own. Dr. Birkins saw her at the same moment.

"There's my little girl," he said with a smile. "You wouldn't happen to know any little girls who like peppermint sticks, would you?"

Callie nodded emphatically.

"Who?"

"Me!"

She jogged from foot to foot while the doctor teasingly withdrew the awaited candy from his pocket. Grace looked skyward while Dr. Birkins brushed the lint off the red-and-white striped stick before giving it to Callie. Snatching it from the doctor's hand, she raced away.

Grace called, "What do you say?"

"Thank you," came back like an indistinct echo.

The adults chuckled. Grace said, "I guess Bart already wheedled his share."

"That's right. A scamp." Dr. Birkins climbed into his buggy and picked up the slack reins. His patient horse shook his shoulders and stomped, shifting his weight. But the doctor didn't give the signal to go. He hesitated before saying, "You ever have any more of those problems you told me about?"

"Which problems? I have a hundred of them."

"You know," he said, nodding toward where the children played in the shadowed doorway of the barn. "The lights and stuff you told me about."

"Not that I know of," Grace answered, crossing her arms, suddenly cold. "But I've been awfully tired lately, what with trying to keep the crops watered and . . ." She indicated the yard with a wave of her arm. "There could be armies marching across here during the night and I wouldn't wake up. Of course, it *looks* like armies have been marching through here. Sherman's armies."

"Well, my offer still stands. There isn't a ghost in the county that'll come around an over-and-under. And if it's *not* a ghost . . ."

"Thanks," Grace said, warmed by his concern. "I'll keep it in mind."

The buggy kicked up dust as the horse drew it out of the yard. Grace looked around her and sighed. So much to be done and now Lucas was laid up. At least the firewood was neatly taken care of. A pity the same couldn't be said for Lucas.

Grace went into the house. She'd check on her patient, and then start the soup she meant to make for dinner. Rapping on the bedroom door, she murmured his name, not wanting to disturb him if he were sleeping. No answer came. She turned the knob and crept in.

Her bed was empty.

Chapter Four

"Now where are you?" she asked the empty room. The bedclothes were crushed and tangled where his body had lain. She touched the pillow where his head had made a dent. Still warm. He couldn't have been gone very long.

Glancing into the sitting room, she saw his shirt where she had left it, draped over the arm of her chair. A picture came into her mind, of Lucas as she'd seen him last, half-naked, sprawled across her bed. He must be around somewhere, still undressed. What if the children should see him like that?

She picked up the shirt, noticing her needle still dangling by a thread from the button she'd been sewing on when Dr. Birkins came in. She knotted the white cotton thread and bit it short.

"Did you mend that?"

Grace turned around with a gasp of surprise, instinctively clutching his shirt to her breast. "Where have you been?" she asked shortly.

"Are you sure you really want to know?" His blue eyes challenged hers, his smile confident.

"The doctor said you should stay in bed. He says you've got a touch of the sun and a lump on the back of your head."

"And to think he went to school for years just so he could tell you that."

"Well, he did." She was unsure how to respond to his humor, if it could be called that. Standing in her sitting room, flaunting his half-naked body, Lucas did not appear in the least like the weak, ailing man for whom Dr. Birkins had prescribed rest and a low diet. On the contrary, Lucas looked wickedly healthy.

"Here," Grace said, thrusting his shirt at him. "Put it on, why don't you."

"Thanks for sewing on my buttons." Glancing at it, he said, "And for mending the collar and cuffs."

"It was nothing."

He took a step closer to her. "You didn't have to do that."

"Put it on," she said, a panicky tone coming into her voice. She had to curl her fingers to keep them from spreading out across his chest, to feel his rich hair prickling the palms. Suddenly there seemed to be not quite enough air in the sitting room. Feigning an interest in the water stain on the ceiling, Grace said, "Please."

"All right." He looked again at the shirt and then at her, a frown of confusion creasing his forehead. "But if I'm going back to bed . . . won't I be overdressed?"

"I think there's a nightshirt of my husband's in a trunk. I'll just go see." Grace stumbled almost blindly from the room. *Good heavens,* she thought. *Maybe I should send for the marshal. One of us definitely needs to be locked up. And I think it's me!*

The tiny box room off the kitchen was hot and airless. She found the trunk easily enough. As she opened it, a strong smell of camphor and cedar made her choke. Or was it the sight of all Chick's clothes, saved from the creditors?

She didn't know even now why she'd saved them. They'd be long out of fashion by the time Bart grew up, and they were doing no one any good hidden away here. But she knew there was one of Chick's old nighthirts here, for she'd worn it herself in the lonely days after he'd passed on. It had brought him close again, his scent and his personality somehow permeating the soft red flannel.

She dragged out the worn nightshirt, which she'd sewn herself when they had first been married. It had come down to Chick's knees.

Looking at it, Grace smiled. Whatever Chick's faults, he had had wonderful knees. She remembered how, a few months after their marriage, he'd blushed and squirmed when she'd confided her admiration to him. He'd argued that knees could never be beautiful. Daringly, she'd shown him her own. Had that been the night Bart was conceived?

Grace straightened suddenly and banged her head on the open trunk lid. "Ow!" she exclaimed, rubbing the top. It was a good thing she'd done it, though, she decided. Her brain seemed stuck in a rut of low thoughts.

She missed Chick at night, of course, but more his warmth on cold nights and the restful sound of his breathing on warm ones than the pleasures of the marriage bed. There'd been little of that after Callie had come, anyway. Who had the time or energy with two children and a failing farm? Then came Chick's illness and . . .

Counting it up, Grace realized she'd not known the pleasures of marriage for nearly three years. She couldn't even remember the last time, sure only that it had been quick and unsatisfying as so much of their later lovemaking had been. Too much anger and too many tears lay between them.

"Mrs. Landers?"

"Just a minute." She closed the lid of the trunk, determined to shut her memories inside with the medicine smell of the camphor. Brushing the moisture from her eyes, Grace came out.

"I hope this fits," she said, holding up the nightshirt.

"It'll be fine." He'd put his shirt on without buttoning it, so the sides hung open, emphasizing the flat lines and smooth contours of his body.

Grace stared past his left ear. "You should go lie down. The doctor said—"

"This was your husband's?" Lucas asked, taking the nightshirt from her hands. "Don't you mind my using it?"

"Not at all."

"But you've been crying." He drew his finger along the edge of her jaw and showed her the tear that clung to his fingertip.

Grace tossed her head away from his hand, stepping

back. Her eyes blazed up like a dying fire when new fuel is thrown on. "Mr. Lucas, I'll thank you to remember—"

"I can't."

"Try! Try to remember that you work for me. My tears . . . my feelings are none of your business."

"Yes, ma'am." He straightened up, though his smile was far from soldierlike. "What are your orders?"

"Go lie down. I'll bring you something to eat. And don't be so . . . so . . ." He just looked at her, a grin twitching his mouth, offensively appealing.

"Are you sure you're unwell?" she asked, suddenly suspicious. Maybe his lack of memory, his near collapse, were all just ploys for sympathy. Maybe he went around from town to town sponging off deprived widows.

"I'm sorry," he said, looking abashed. "Your doctor gave me some kind of painkiller for my headache. I think it's making me a little giddy."

"What kind of painkiller?"

"I don't know. Something in a red bottle. Looked like horse liniment."

"You'll be lucky if it wasn't. He probably meant for you to rub it on. Let me see that lump," she asked, still cautious.

Lucas started to bend down so she could see, but he clutched suddenly at the back of a kitchen chair. "Not a good idea," he muttered.

Grace was aghast by the sudden pallor of his face. How could she be so callous? "You turn right around and get to bed," she commanded. "The doctor said you had a thick skull but he wasn't sure those Grupp boys didn't do you more harm than he can tell."

"Grupp boys?" Lucas asked, groping along the hall toward her room. She thought it would offend him if she took his arm, but his hesitating progress distressed her.

"The ones that knocked you silly in the alley yesterday. When the marshal comes for you tonight, I intend to give him quite a little piece of my mind about them too. Imagine letting a bunch of savages run around loose in a respectable town!"

"You're . . . you're a firebrand." He swayed as he sat

down on the bed, the squeak of the wooden frame as noisy as that of her rusty gate. His eyes fluttered closed. Dr. Birkins must have helped him take his boots off, for she noticed for the first time that his feet were bare.

"Never mind me," Grace said. "Do you need help with that nightshirt?"

He shook his head and then grimaced. "You've been much too kind already." A thought seemed to occur to him. He half opened his eyes, the blue alive with merriment. "Don't try to take my trousers off again, okay? I can manage that too."

Grace backed up, out the door. "I'll leave you to it then," she said, her face burning. That was the last time she'd assume he was unconscious just because his eyes were closed!

Sitting down to her own midday meal, now entirely cold and unappetizingly congealed in her black iron fry pan, Grace tried to shut out the doubts that waited to spring upon her. They were sneaky little things. Entertaining one seemed safe—maybe the worry about how to scrape up payment for stud service for the red cow—and then before she knew it a whole host of worries and fears would surround her. They taunted her by day and tortured her at night, growing with every tick of the clock. She'd wake in the morning, searching for the gray hairs she was sure had sprouted in the night.

Now there was Lucas. *So far,* she thought, moodily chasing a limp green thing around her plate, *so far he's been more a burden than a blessing.* And just where was she supposed to sleep tonight?

That was the marshal's question too.

"What do you mean, he's staying? There's not enough room for all of you."

"There's plenty of room," Grace insisted. "I'm not throwing out a sick man and that's final. Dr. Birkins said—"

"That old woman? He could be bamboozled by a foxy baby, let alone a grown man." Reg gentled his voice and took a step up on the back porch, closer to Grace. "I'm just thinkin' of your good, Mrs. Landers."

"I appreciate that, Marshal Wyman."

"You know," he said, brushing the back of her hand lightly with his forefinger. "I'd sure like it if you could bring yourself to call me Reg."

She stood her ground, wishing the evening were not so perfumed by the honeysuckle. As if that weren't bad enough, the level rays of the westering sun softened and smoothed harsh reality, while the tiny fiddles of the cicadas tuned up for the songs of dusk. A quarter-moon was awake in the east, the valleys and craters clearly defined and yet with a kindly look, like a sentimental aunt peeping at a courting couple. A light breeze stirred Grace's straggling hair and tugged at her long calico skirt. The ardent look in Reg Wyman's eyes told her how this romantic mood of nature affected him.

Under the right circumstances, she might not have minded a pat on the hand and an offer of sympathy. At the moment, however, she did not feel at all in the mood for dallying, even if Reg did. Bart had kicked up holy hannah about washing behind his ears. Callie had needed extra hugs, turning whiny when Grace had tried to cut her good-nights short to see to Lucas, who'd woken up hungry as a hunter.

"I don't think it would be wise, Marshal, for you and I to start being on a first-name basis. Folks do talk so, you know. 'Specially about a woman alone."

"What about doing it in private? If nobody hears, nobody can talk," he said, turning his head slightly and opening his brown eyes wide.

"I don't do anything in private I'm not willing to do in public. Now, about Lucas—"

"Notice you've come to call him by *his* first name."

"So far as I can tell, it's the only name he's got." To divert his mind from his unsuitable jealousy, she told him about the name sewn in the lining of Lucas's coat. "He can't tell if it really is his name or not."

"And you tell me he's shaved?" He sighed as he put his mind back on official business. "Gotta get a look at him, so I can check his description against the posters. I wouldn't be at all surprised to find he's a wanted man. Stands to reason."

"Well, you can't see him tonight. The doctor said he needs complete rest."

"I won't bother him much." The marshal came all the way onto the porch. Without waiting to ask by-your-leave, he pushed on into the kitchen, his boots clumping on the wooden floor.

Grace followed him, her dander up. "I shouldn't let you in at all. Mind you keep your voice down. I won't have the children wakened."

"This way, isn't it?"

Unerringly, the marshal cut through the sitting room. Grace only paused to glance in on Callie. The little girl's whistling breaths were faint. Slowly, afraid of it creaking, Grace half closed the door.

She met Reg Wyman coming back, his face set in determined lines. "Don't you worry, Mrs. Landers. I'll catch him."

"Catch him?"

"Your man is gone!"

"Gone? But—" She held up her hand. "Wait a minute. Don't bother getting all overheated. He's around somewhere. He always is."

"But you said he was keepin' to his bed."

"Doesn't mean he didn't have to go out back for a minute, or something." The hot blood ran under Grace's cheeks at having to mention such a delicate subject. But the way Marshal Wyman's hand rested on the black grip of his gun, like a man ready to draw, troubled her.

She hurried to add, "I've looked for him several times today. He always comes back in a few minutes."

"If you say so." The marshal put his hand inside his vest and pulled out a black twist of chewing tobacco. Raising it to his lips, he met her eyes. With a sheepish grin, he put it back unbitten. Grace said, "Thank you."

On the sitting room mantel, the towered Gothic-style clock ticked steadily. With each tick, the room became darker. Muttering an excuse, Grace picked up the coal-oil lamp from the table and went into the kitchen. Lighting the lamp with a spill from the ashes in the stove, she sent a troubled glance out the window.

Where had Lucas gone this time? Had the whole day been some elaborate trick? She recalled how she twice thought he'd vanished, only to be proved basely cynical each time. Grace decided to try having more faith in Lucas. After all, if he hadn't run away while he was feeling himself, why would he go now, feeling poorly?

"I'm afraid I haven't much to offer you, Marshal," she said, bearing back the lighted lamp. "But if you'd like some coffee . . ."

"No, thanks, ma'am. Better I should keep my hands free."

"Yes, I suppose so. Do you mind if I sew?"

"Go ahead."

Pushing a protesting Georgette off Lucas's out-at-elbow jacket, she sat in her rocker mending the sleeves in the yellow lamplight. It was difficult to concentrate, knowing Marshal Wyman was staring down at the top of her bent head. Trying to keep her stitches neat and small, Grace wanted to snap at the marshal, to tell him to find something else to do besides hovering over her.

As if hearing her thoughts, the marshal began to pace. Over to the mantel. Back to her chair. Again and again, like a lion in a cage. Glancing up through her lashes, Grace expected to see him lash a tawny tail.

"I'm wastin' time!" he burst out at last. "I should be roundin' up a posse."

Faintly, but growing louder, Grace heard singing. She had excellent hearing—"Mothers' ears" as Chick used to say—and despite the marshal's blustering, she could pick out lyrics.

"Lovely Fan, won't you come out tonight, come out tonight, come out tonight? Lovely Fan, won't you come out tonight, and dance by the light of the moooon!"

Whoever it was had a singing voice like a cracked molasses jug. Poor Toby set up a howl from under the back porch, echoed by the rooster. Marshal Wyman heard it now too. He whirled around, heading for the front door.

"It doesn't work very well," Grace said, after he twisted and tugged at the doorknob.

With a muffled curse, Marshal Wyman flung around, hurrying toward the back door, his sharp-toed boots clattering. He stepped wrong on a rag rug and slipped, saving himself by a sudden twist of his hips. The glance he threw her was strangely savage.

As Grace passed Callie's door, she heard a soft call of "Mama?"

She paused only long enough to speak a word of comfort to the girl. "I'll settle Toby down, honey. Go back to sleep."

The dim silhouette lay down again. In the morning, Callie would remember nothing, having not really awakened.

Bart, on the other hand, would remember better. When Grace stepped outside, she saw Lucas in the yard, one hand flung upward toward the sky. He seemed to be pointing at the moon. As Grace came closer, she heard him making a speech, apparently to Bart, crouched at his feet.

"I tell you, my dear sir, that the prophecies of Verne will undoubtedly come true within the next one hundred years. A mere century, and man will walk on the surface of an alien planet! There may be some philistines"—the forefinger of his right hand pointed directly at Reg Wyman—"but I tell you that the dreams of our earliest ancestors will be realized. What can we do as citizens to bring this dream to fruition?"

"I dunno," Bart said.

"Hey, you!" said the marshal. He'd been standing a few feet away, as if turned to stone by Lucas's eloquence. Now he advanced and clapped his hand firmly over Lucas's upraised arm.

As if a switch had been thrown, the excitement and enthusiasm drained from Lucas's expression. He turned mild eyes on the marshal. "Yes? Oh, it's you."

"That's right. Stop all this ruckus. Where do you think you are, Congress?"

"Isn't this Mrs. Landers's farm?"

Bart scrambled to his feet. "Leave him alone. He ain't doing no harm."

"Ain't none of your business, boy."

"Bart, come here," Grace called softly. "Come on."

Dragging his feet in the dirt, her son came to her side. She laid her hand on his shoulder. "Weren't you supposed to be in bed?"

"I saw him heading out and he didn't look right, Ma. I didn't want him to get into trouble. And now the marshal's got him. Is he going back to jail?"

"It's all right," she said, looking down into his troubled eyes. "Mr. Lucas is staying here tonight. You can go to sleep."

"And you'll look out for him?" Bart asked. "I don't reckon he oughta be alone."

"I'll look out for him. You go to bed."

As soon as Bart went inside, Grace approached the two men. The marshal was talking fast in a low tone to Lucas. He didn't seem to be listening, though he nodded once or twice. When Grace came closer, Wyman turned to her.

"I'll be takin' him along now. He may not be back for a couple of days. I don't know how much Doc Birkins will be coddlin' him."

"No, Marshal. He's staying right here until he's feeling better. Can't you see he's a sick man?"

"Drunk's more likely. You keep some likker around here someplace, don't you? Most likely, he's gotten to it and drained the bottle dry."

"I resent—" Lucas said.

Grace interrupted, offended, "No, I don't keep a bottle around, as you put it. I wouldn't dream of it. And he's not drunk, any more than he was drunk yesterday." She looked anxiously up at Lucas. His eyes were dazed, half-closed. He swayed on his feet, like a willow in a high wind.

"Go into the house," she said, her tone gentling. "Go back to bed."

He shook his head. Making an effort that was plain to see, he focused on the marshal. "I'm not drunk. A . . . a touch of the sun, that's all."

Grace said, "You don't have to explain anything, Lucas. I'll take care of it."

A smile, both unshakable and happy, reassured her. "I'm not a child either, Mrs. Landers, slightly foolish though I look at the moment. I'll be very happy to go with the marshal, since that is the arrangement agreed upon by the judge, yourself and Mr. Wyman."

"That's more like it," Wyman said with satisfaction. "Come along quiet-like and it'll be better for both of us."

"Are you sure that's what you want to do?" Grace asked. "It's no trouble keeping you here. And it's what the doctor ordered for you."

"He oughta be in the hoosegow. I've said so right 'long."

"However," Lucas said, taking no notice of the marshal, "I will be back in the morning, as was also agreed to by Judge Sterling, Mrs. Landers and yourself, Marshal. I believe in honoring agreements, even ones I'm not a fully consenting party to, strictly speaking."

"You talk too much," the marshal said. "My horses are down by the road. You get along and wait for me."

"Wait a minute," Grace said, acceding defeat. There wasn't a lot of point in fighting for a man who wouldn't fight for himself. She could, however, protect him from the night air. "I'll get your jacket."

The marshal caught up to her in the sitting room. "Now be reasonable, Mrs. Landers. You're never goin' to get a full day's work out of him. He's sickly, that's what, if he's not downright crippled. And I don't know what lies he's spun you, but I can tell if a man can't keep off the bottle. It's his eyes and the way his hands shake."

"I can't say I've noticed anything wrong. Barring a touch of the sun, which any man could take. Especially one that has been hit on the head with a rock. Speaking of that, Marshal, just what are you planning to do about the Grupp boys?"

"There's not much wrong with them boys."

"Nothing wrong? Accosting a perfect stranger and throwing stones? And their behavior the rest of the time. I'm not a snob, I hope, but they really are getting out of hand. Why, Mrs. Birkins told me the other day she was afraid to cross the street until they'd gone, they stared at her so boorishly."

"They're just kickin' up their heels. Wild colts, you know, not broke to bridle yet."

Grace took a deep breath. Maybe the marshal guessed what was coming his way, for he began rapidly to back toward the door. "Guess I'll be gettin' along. If you really want this Lucas feller back in the morning, I'll bring him 'long 'bout seven. That'll give you a good long day . . . not that I figure he'll be much help to you."

"Thank you, Marshal." She handed him Lucas's jacket. "Until tomorrow."

The house was strangely quiet and lonesome after they'd gone. Sleeping children are little company. A cat and a dog, curled up together in front of a slowly cooling cast-iron stove, are no replacement for human companionship. After checking a last time on the stock, Grace sat in her rocking chair, listening to the cicadas and the beating of her own lonesome heart.

Chapter
Five

Lucas sweated. The hard bunk beneath him wasn't much more comfortable than a plank. And the accommodation in the jail didn't run to a pillow, a blanket or glass in the barred window. The hot breeze that blew whistling through it brought out more strongly the stinks of previous occupants, including, unless his nose deceived him, tomcats and mice.

Last night, somehow, he hadn't minded these things. After all, compared to an alley, the jail was a paradise of luxury. But today, he'd put his newly shaved cheek on the smooth linen pillowcase of Grace Landers, had smelled the honey fragrance of her hair that still clung to the down, had lain in the hollow that her body made every night in her mattress. Small wonder he couldn't recapture the pleasure of his first night in jail.

Halfway through an interminable night, Lucas abandoned the effort to sleep. He sat up and stuck his feet in his boots. He staggered to the barred cell door.

"Hey," he called softly down the hall to the deputy. He'd seen him briefly earlier in the evening when Wyman had shown the incoming man the prisoner.

The creak-creak of a rocking chair had pursued him all the time he'd been trying to sleep. A moment or two after he called, the sound stopped.

The leggy deputy was young for the job, not more than about twenty. His sandy hair was a little long, falling into his green eyes. The gun holster on his skinny right hip had nothing in it. Standing at the end of the hall, he said with a mixture of good cheer and caution, "Hey, yourself."

"Got any coffee going?"

"Sure do."

"How 'bout a cup?"

The green eyes looked him up and down while the angular jaw moved as if he were chewing the question over. "Well, I guess it'll be all right."

He brought it in a stoneware mug, the steam curling and feathering above the black, oily surface. "Hope you like it black. Ain't got no sugar or cream."

Lucas licked his dry lips. "Smells good," he said, reaching out through the bars.

"Oughta be. My ma grinds the beans herself." The deputy watched as Lucas sipped gingerly from the hot coffee. "It'll keep you awake, you know."

"Who can sleep?" Somehow, the hot night and the hot coffee seemed to go together. The sweat that broke on his brow was cooled at once by the breeze, hot though it was.

"Feel that breeze arising," the deputy said. "Funny, this time of year. Maybe there's a storm comin'."

As though in answer to his surmise, the jail shook with a distant rumble. "Yep," the deputy said, craning his neck to look out Lucas's window. "I could see lightning that time. A real whip-cracker."

Lucas thought about Grace and her children. He wondered if the roof of that old farmhouse was as leaky as it looked. Would she be racing around from drip to drip, pots and pans at the ready? Or would they all be cuddled together under her red-and-blue quilt, taking comfort from one another?

He wished he were with them. Even if they all stayed in their own rooms, at least he'd know someone else was there. Though he did not believe himself to be afraid of thunderstorms, he was the only prisoner in jail, and all four cells were empty and echoing except for him. He'd been alone for a long time. This was the first time he could remember feeling lonely.

"Much crime in Ogden?" he asked, desperate to fill the silence.

"Not much. Sometimes a drunk gets noisy, or once we had a robbery at Lansky's general store. Course that was in Marshal Sweeney's day."

"Was he marshal here before Marshal Wyman?"

"That's right. Matter of eight months ago. He's living in Santa Fe now, with his brother. Funny thing about— Hoo-wee, it's really comin' down now."

His words were drowned in the sudden rattle of rain hitting the tin roof of the jail. With resignation, Lucas saw that the water was driving in through the barred window, splashing on the uneven concrete floor in big drops. It wouldn't be long before the bed would be the only part of his cell not swimming.

The deputy noticed too. "Looks like the rain's coming in."

"Looks like it," Lucas said, matching the young deputy's laconic tone.

"Guess I could move you to the other side of the jail. Looks dry over there."

"I'd appreciate it."

"Course I don't know what Marshal Wyman'll say about it. He thinks we oughta be tougher on criminals."

"I'm not exactly a criminal, am I?"

"Course you are, or you wouldn't be here. I guess maybe you oughta stay where you are. Don't want to take a chance on your escaping."

"Look, uh . . ." The first violence of the storm had already passed on, leaving behind the steady roar of a heavy downpour. Some of the drops were hitting the foot of the bed. Lucas wished he could drag it to the other side of the cell, closer to the door, but it was chained to the wall.

"Jasper Crowley. Pleased t'meetcha."

"Me too. Have you heard anything about me?"

"Just what Marshal Wyman said. He thinks you remember a sight more than what you're sayin' you do." He eyed Lucas with blatant suspicion. "You done with that coffee?"

Lucas drained the last black drops from the cup. He handed it through the bars. Jasper asked, "Want any more?"

"Thanks, but listen to me first. Yes, I'm a drifter and

the court passed sentence on me. But I'm not the dangerous kind. I'm working at Mrs. Landers's place."

"Out on Lynch Road?"

"I didn't know it had a name."

"Oh, it's got a name for itself all right." He nodded grimly and censored himself. "I'll go get 'cha more coffee."

When he came back, Lucas had seated himself on the bed, the better to watch the pools forming. The deputy peered down at the floor. "Sure is comin' down."

He brought two cups this time. The men drank companionably, as if one were not behind bars and the other one free. They could have been old friends, sharing a quiet evening at home.

"So," Lucas said. "Been a deputy long?"

"Not long, mister. Couple of days. Matter of fact, you're my first prisoner. But don't think you can take 'vantage."

"Wouldn't dream of it. I'm really your first prisoner? I'm sorry for your sake that I'm not at least a murderer."

The lanky young man shrugged. "One of these days . . ."

"I guess you've got to have something to look forward to."

"Yep."

A silence fell between the two men as the water continued to come in. The low spots in the floor were already nice-sized pools. Soon they'd overflow and join together.

"So you're workin' out on Lynch Road? Mrs. Landers seems a real nice woman." The deputy yawned and scratched his shoulder.

"Yes, she is. Not everyone would have bothered to come down to the court for a drifter like me."

"I liked her husband too," Jasper said. "He always seemed to have time for everybody, even a kid like me. I mean, a kid like I used to be." He straightened to his full height and adjusted his holster without looking at it.

"He must have been a very likable man."

"Yep."

"What happened to him?"

"Don't know 'zactly. Some folks say it was the consumption; others guess he got blood poisoning or aholt of a bad can of something. Like green beans. My cousin Orville et some bad green beans once and like to have died." Jasper brightened up.

"Did he die?"

"Course not." Some of the air seemed to go out of his spine and he was curved over again. He had long arms that dangled limply at his sides, terminating in bony wrists and raw hands. Lucas realized the deputy was barely out of his teens.

"You saying there was something funny about this old marshal you used to have?"

"Whatcha askin' 'bout that for?"

Lucas shook his head to show he hadn't meant anything. "Just feel like talking, that's all."

"Oh. Well, Marshal Sweeney'd been here for a lot of years. Least ten. Funny thing is nobody even knew he had a brother. Course he was an awful closemouth son of a . . . Friendly, enough, just not a whole lot to say for himself."

"And he retired when Marshal Wyman came?"

"That's right. Matter of eight months ago, like I said."

Lucas wanted to ask if that was why Marshal Wyman seemed to enjoy his job so much, because it was fresh, but he didn't want to antagonize the man with the freedom to get to the coffeepot.

Jasper yawned again, his jaws nearly splitting. Lucas asked, "Are you supposed to keep an eye on me all night?"

"Course not. Just gotta keep you from 'scaping, that's all. Marshal Wyman says if you get out, it's my job to shoot you down, just like a dog."

"I see." Lucas hid a smile. He couldn't bring himself to be afraid of a boy with an empty holster. Jasper yawned again. Lucas heard the boy's jawbones creak. He asked, "Don't you find it tough being up all night?"

"I kinda like it. Nobody bothers you."

"Except for more coffee," Lucas said, returning his cup through the bars.

"To be straight with you," Jasper said, looking into the empty cups as if trying to read his fortune, "my working at night is harder on Ma. She's not used to being quiet in the mornings. Most days she just warbles all dang day. Now she's got to be quiet while I'm sleeping. I think it's weighing on her."

"If you want to take a rest in one of the cells, I won't tell on you."

"Couldn't do that," Jasper said with a rueful smile. "Wouldn't be right. 'Sides, I'm tryin' to teach myself . . ." He looked Lucas up and down. "Say, you wouldn't know anything 'bout this game they call 'chess,' would you? No, I guess not."

"I'm not sure," Lucas said. "Chess? It *sounds* familiar somehow."

"It's mighty interestin'. All these little pieces you shove around a checkerboard. Kings and queens and suchlike. My uncle sent me a set for Christmas last year, and I been worryin' away at the book that come with it."

"But you're not having much luck?"

"Can't hardly make heads nor tails of it. But I was figurin' if I could just find somebody who knows the game, the book might make a sight more sense."

"Well," Lucas said, the prospect of a long, damp night before him. "I suppose you could show me what you have and if I remember . . ."

Jasper rolled the barrel he used for a table down the hall. "Say, you can't play sitting down while your bed's clear on the other side of the cell, can ya?"

"I don't think so."

"Hang on a sec."

He came back with the key that unlocked the chain passing through the leg of the cot. "Don't know why they did that. Not like you're goin' to pick up the bed and whang me over the head with it. Not 'less I was inside there with you and I ain't." He passed the key through the bars and went back to get the board and the pieces.

Jasper set the game up while Lucas thumbed through *Hantley's Guide to Chess,* a pleasing pamphlet of a dozen or so pages. But when Jasper set the black king down on his square, the pamphlet fell from Lucas's hand. He reached out for the five-inch-tall figure.

Carved of some soft wood, the king's mustache and beard, his imperial crown, his scepter, had been brilliantly delineated by a master carver. He and his army had been soaked in some natural dye, possibly even blackberry juice, for his royal robes had a faint purple sheen. The queen showed dainty lace against her rounded breasts and had heels to her shoes, while the bishop wore a miter and an expression of suitable piety. But there was something about the king that Lucas felt drawn to. The far-off look in his eyes, perhaps.

The prisoner and the deputy played, with some false starts, until dawn. The moves seemed natural to Lucas, even the crab-wise motion of the bishops and the three-step slide of the knights. Neither man noticed when it stopped raining, or that the rising sun tried to shine through the lingering clouds.

As long as Lucas didn't try to remember *where* he'd played chess before, he had no problems. Once half a memory returned to him—an image of leaves floating down outside a round window—but a comet-flash of pain behind his eyes told him it would be wiser to concentrate on the game.

Only when a strange clang and rattle echoed off the naked walls of the jail did Jasper sit up and stretch. "Right interestin' game. Had a notion I'd take to it, once I learned how to do it proper."

"Seems to me you have a natural knack for it," Lucas said, rubbing his stiff neck. He looked off toward the office. "Is that the marshal to relieve you?"

"Nope. It's Wenonah." He tipped his ladder-back chair back on two legs to call out, "I'm in the back!"

He shot Lucas a frowning glance, as if measuring his quality. "She comes to clean twice a week. I don't want to hear no cracks out of you."

Stung by the young man's sudden change in attitude from friendly to hostile, Lucas asked, "Why on earth would I . . . ?"

Then he saw her. Even though she wore a shapeless

calico dress, not deerskin, and carried a mop and bucket, not a coup stick and painted shield, there was no mistaking her high cheekbones and dark coloring. The moment the Indian girl saw him looking at her, the light of curiosity went out in her cinnamon-colored eyes. She bent to put the bucket on the floor.

"Hey, there, Wenonah," Jasper said, getting up and sauntering over to her. "Let me go fill that bucket up for you."

"No thanks, Mr. Crowley," she said, in a low, even voice. "I've already done it."

"I'll let you get on with it, then. Say, this is a new feller. Visiting for a spell, you might say. Name of Lucas. Don't worry 'bout him none. He's harmless as a cricket."

Something about the way Jasper stood beside her, a defensive quality in his posture, told Lucas that the young deputy was interested in more than the way Wenonah cleaned a jail. Watching them talking, the girl returning brief answers to Jasper's talk, Lucas realized she was pretty, with the shine of youth on her skin and a half-smile curving her smooth lips. But when Jasper left the room, all her animation left with him, leaving her expressionless, almost sullen.

Lucas lay down on his cot, listening to the steady swish-swish as the girl mopped the floor. The sound was lulling and his eyes closed. It might not have been wise to stay up half the night playing chess, not if he meant to go back to Grace's farm today. Her image came up in his mind. The lamplight on her face. The wisps of blond hair escaping from her tight bun to curl about her cheeks. Her neat hands, and mouth that looked so sweetly soft . . .

He rolled onto his stomach. How long had it been since he'd had a woman? A long time indeed, if the mere thought of Grace Landers's lips could put him in this condition! Better to lie facedown for a while, so Jasper and Wenonah wouldn't get the wrong idea.

Replaying one of the chess matches in his head, he soon calmed down. Though the bed was still rock-hard, lacking even a stained pillow, Lucas found that if he rested his head on his bent arm, he could drift off.

* * *

"Why don't you just *drown* him while you're at it?" someone exclaimed in a carrying whisper. "The last thing I need is a hired man who's laid up in knots with rheumatism. Let me borrow that mop, Wenonah."

"I'll do it, Mrs. Landers. I didn't want to disturb the gentleman before. If Marshal Wyman will open the door?"

Lucas half opened his eyes. The sunlight dazzled off the bars of his cell, but it seemed to him that the jail was crowded. He glimpsed Grace, wearing a bonnet that looked like Wenonah's bucket, upside down. Behind her, ranged in ranks like soldiers, stood the marshal, the deputy, the Indian girl and some other woman standing at the back with a covered basket over her arm. They were all staring at him as if he were an exotic exhibit in a zoo.

He sat up, combing his hair back with his fingers. Giving Grace a smile, he wished he could be alone with her. And the basket, if, as he guessed, it had breakfast in it.

"Did you sleep well, Mr. Lucas?" Grace said, as if they were meeting in a hotel lobby.

"Fine," he replied in the same tone. "My compliments, Marshal Wyman, on your fine jail."

"Guess you've been in enough of them to know . . . ," Wyman muttered with a black look.

"And all the latest conveniences," Lucas went on, glancing at the inundated floor. "Even a shower bath."

Somebody chuckled. Marshal Wyman glared around but before he could speak, the lady with the basket said in a surprisingly merry voice, "Ain't none of you throng goin' to get out of the way so this poor soul can eat his morsel of breakfast? You got the keys, son?"

"Yes, Ma, right here."

Young Jasper hastened forward to unlock the cell door. His mother stepped in. She had the figure of a young girl, but a face of laughing maturity. More than a head shorter than Jasper, she didn't look as if she could have ever carried a child. Her dark brown hair had a very few silver threads gleaming in the heavy coil.

Opening the basket she put on the bed, Lucas saw that

Jasper had undoubtedly grown like a weed if this bounty was Mrs. Crowley's notion of a "morsel of breakfast."

Five biscuits still steaming in a bandanna, with a crock of butter and a cup of blackberry jam, half an apple pie, a pail of buttermilk, two hard-boiled eggs laid by a chicken that was first cousin to an ostrich, thick slabs of bacon crisply fried, and a toothpick.

"Jest enough to get a man started on a day," Mrs. Crowley said modestly when Lucas exclaimed at the feast. "Won't be no trouble t'fry up some ham an' eggs if you have a mind to fill up the corners. I'm only sorry I wasn't here yesterday. Had to visit a cousin over to Greenville. Hope that son o' mine did your vittles right?"

Remembering how much he'd enjoyed the scrambled eggs and bacon he'd eaten yesterday morning—his first decent meal in a long time—Lucas nodded at Jasper. "It was very good, but nothing compared to . . ." He spread his hands helplessly over the cornucopia that covered the foot of his bed.

"It's my job to feed the prisoners, when we got 'em. You don't mind, honey?" Mrs. Crowley said to Grace. "I know you and the judge fixed it up between you that you were goin' to have the feedin' of him, but . . ."

"No, I don't mind at all," Grace said, smiling. "Not if I can have one of your wonderful biscuits."

"Why, shore. If Mr. Lucas don't mind . . ."

"Not at all. Miss Wenonah, would you care for one?"

The Indian girl, mopping up the rainwater, glanced at him in surprise. "I don't . . ."

Marshal Wyman turned to his deputy. In disgust he said, "Seems the worse a feller is, the bigger fuss the womenfolk make over him. Come on, Crowley. We got us some wanted posters to look over. Mind you don't miss none."

"Humph," Mrs. Crowley sniffed. "Sour grapes. Never you mind him, Mr. Lucas. Just eat up."

While he wondered what to tackle first, the two women held a conference over his head. "Wait till that boy o' mine hears me over this," Mrs. Crowley said. "Leaving a man in a damp hole like this!"

"I'm sure it wasn't your son's fault. I'm afraid the marshal isn't too fond of Mr. Lucas."

"I been tellin' 'em for weeks they need to get some glass in these windows—and curtains. Lansky down at the general store's got in some of the prettiest Chinese flannel you ever seen for curtains. But them two keep goin' on about folks doing themselves an injury, as if folks didn't have better sense."

"Believe me," Lucas said, glancing up from buttering his second biscuit with the dull knife she provided. "No one could commit suicide so long as they had one of your breakfasts to look forward to. This biscuit, for instance . . . King's would turn slave for a taste of one."

Mrs. Crowley's girlish face pinkened. "Go on, I've been warned about smooth fellers like you."

"He's a terrible flirt. I've already learned not to trust a word he says," Grace said, giving him a comically censorious look. "But we can't let him come back to this place every night! It isn't decent."

"Now, if a woman would have had the building of it . . . ," Mrs. Crowley began.

"It's not so bad, for a jail," Lucas said. "So long as it doesn't rain."

"But can you count on that?"

" 'Specially with the whole state praying for it," Mrs. Crowley added. "Wenonah? Your aunt still takin' in boarders?"

The girl nodded. She hesitated before she spoke. "It would not be very much drier," she admitted, her white smile flashing at them all too briefly. "The roof hasn't been repaired."

"He could come and stay with us," Mrs. Crowley said. "Jasper could keep an eye on him and all, him being the deputy. And I'd know where my boy is at night."

Stuffed like a Christmas goose, Lucas wiped his mouth with the bandanna and began to repack Mrs. Crowley's split-willow basket. "You're all too kind, ladies. But Mrs. Landers's agreement with the judge—"

"Oh, please don't start talking like that again," Grace

said. "You went on about agreements and contracts last night till I thought I'd go wild."

Lucas studied her. There was something different about her this morning, something softer yet more teasing. He wondered if the marshal had been making her laugh, and was astonished by the spark of jealousy that shot through him. After all, he'd known her only a day. He had no more right to be jealous than he had to be aroused by the mere thought of her. He realized it was just as well she hadn't come to his cell alone. Her hair was a brighter gold than he remembered and her eyes a clearer gray. The rest of her looked just as he'd pictured her. Obviously, his memory was improving.

"All right," he said. "But I don't mind sleeping at the jail. In fact, I prefer it." He couldn't recall any religious teaching, but he felt sure that temptation would be easier to bear at a distance.

Mrs. Crowley glanced into the basket. "Here I was thinkin' you'd be hungry. Why, you haven't eaten a bite, boy. Not a bite."

Lucas tried to point out that the basket was considerably lighter than when he'd begun, but the older lady just sniffed. "Well, if you don't want it, there's plenty that does. Fer instance, there's a couple of growin' youngsters outside that could do with a second breakfast, if a mother can judge another woman's children."

"If you mean Callie and Bart," Grace said, "I'm sure they'd love a second breakfast. And a third."

Mrs. Crowley left the cell, still talking airily about how she preferred a man with meat on his bones, who could do justice to her fine vittles. Lucas let out a groan as he wondered how his waistband could take any more breakfast. He looked around and saw that Wenonah had somehow slipped away unnoticed.

From the way Grace backed toward the door, it seemed she had also noticed that they were alone. "I hope you're feeling better. Don't wory about coming to work today, if you're not up to it."

"I feel fine, except for a swollen stomach."

Grace laughed, a little self-consciously Lucas thought.

"Would you believe that the last few prisoners they had refused to leave because of her cooking?"

"Easily."

"One poor man ran right out to commit another crime, the minute they released him. Fortunately, they caught him in time. Mrs. Crowley says another one came and serenaded under her window until her husband had to get out of bed to convince him that she was happily married."

"What about you?"

"I beg your pardon?"

"I mean . . . where are you from? You can't have always been a farmer's widow. Besides, you don't talk like Mrs. Crowley."

"Oh," she said, shrugging. "My parents live in Sedalia. I was trained to be a schoolteacher until I married Chick."

"That explains a lot."

"Come to think of it, Mr. Lucas, you don't talk like the men around here either. Last night, for instance, you were talking about somebody named Vern. The only Vern around here is the barber and he wouldn't dream of going to the moon. He wants to go to Philadelphia for the Centennial celebration, but his wife won't let him."

"Centennial? What Centennial? You mean . . . the anniversary of the War for Independence?" The familiar throbbing began in his temples, a beating like distant drums.

"That's right." She stepped forward and caught his hand as it started up toward his head. "Do you remember something about the Centennial?"

Chapter Six

Grace saw the black terror in his eyes. He swayed, clutching at her. She thought of a childhood friend who suffered from vertigo, coming over dizzy whenever he looked down from a height. But could a grown man experience it standing on a floor? Unless the depths he stared into were the depths of his own soul.

She said his name, feeling as if she were calling him back across some vast distance. She put her hands on his shoulders to try and get him to look at her, not at the emptiness he seemed to see. His grip was strong, painful. Yet she bore it, for he didn't know he was hurting her. "Lucas?"

A gruff voice sounded from behind her. "What in tarnation . . . ?"

Then Reg Wyman yanked open the cell door, grabbing Lucas by his shirtfront, jerking him away from Grace. His powerful fist swung up, directed at Lucas's jaw.

Blindly, automatically, Lucas parried, catching the marshal's swinging fist on his left forearm. With a driving right, he sank his other fist into the marshal's slightly flabby stomach. Grunting, the marshal doubled up and staggered back, the air leaving his body in an audible *whoosh*.

The whole incident happened so fast that Grace hadn't even time to yell. She stood staring between the two men. Once again, Lucas had surprised her.

"Holy cats!" Jasper yelped from the doorway. He tried to help the gasping marshal straighten, but Wyman turned such a fierce glare on the deputy that the young man backed off fast.

"What happened?" Jasper asked.

"I think the marshal thought Lucas was attacking me," Grace said coolly.

"Was I?" Lucas asked. His blue eyes were spirited again, alive with good humor, and male wickedness. Grace knew she shouldn't respond, but that flicker of laughter spoke to her, tempted her. She managed to control her own face.

Unsmilingly, she said, "No, you weren't."

"Silly me."

"Re . . . resisting . . . ," Marshal Wyman said between gasps as he tried to force enough air into his lungs to speak. "Resisting an officer . . ."

"What was he supposed to do?" Grace asked. "Let you beat the tar out of him?"

Lucas turned to the marshal, trying not to let his satisfaction show. He knew he could take Wyman if he had to. "I am sorry, sir. I acted purely on instinct."

Wyman had made it to the bed, clutching with both hands at the mattress. He dragged himself on to it, still hunched over, his head dangling almost to his knees. The sharp gasps for breath slowed. Everyone waited for him to regain his wind.

Grace wondered if the marshal would arrest Lucas again, this time on a far more serious charge than vagrancy. What could she say to change his mind?

When he looked up at last, a grin of good fellowship lit his rugged face. Grace realized she'd been holding her own breath and let it go in a gusty sigh.

Still rubbing his middle with one hand, he extended the other to Lucas. He pulled the marshal to his feet, smiling in answer. They shook hands, Wyman saying, "Gol-darn it, I gotta admire you, Lucas. Ain't every man jack that can best me. Dang me if I even saw it comin'."

"I didn't even know I was going to do it," Lucas admitted. Then they laughed, the marshal holding his hand firmly against his middle as if it hurt him to laugh.

"Men!" Grace said pungently. It seemed to be the only thing for her to say. "If you're completely ready, Mr. Lucas . . ."

"Ready for what? You said—"

"Dr. Birkins says I'm not to let you work again without a decent hat. Are you coming with me to buy one, or not?"

"That's up to the marshal."

"Sure, sure, go ahead. But you gotta promise to show me how you did that a little later on." He dodged and feinted with his right fist.

"I'd be pleased to. If I remember."

They chuckled again, suddenly the best of friends, Grace didn't understand—and knew she never would understand—how two men could find such fellowship in a fight. Bart was the same way with his young friends. It must be bred in the male from the earliest moment.

The children sat on the open end of the wagon, kicking their bare feet as they ate from Mrs. Crowley's bounty. Grace saw that Bart had disobeyed her at least once about getting out of the wagon, for his feet were coated with the black mud that filled the street. As though to set off the tasteful color of his feet, Bart's mouth was smeared with rich purple jam. His red tongue wiped in a circle when Grace got out her handkerchief to clean him off. He did so well that his mother put the cloth back in her apron pocket.

Callie's broad-brimmed straw hat hung from her neck by its wide, worn ribbon. Grace put it back on her daughter's small head, giving her a loving but admonishing look. If Callie only knew how her mother had agonized when younger over her own freckles, she wouldn't risk them now. But she supposed Callie was still too young to care.

"Say thank you to Mrs. Crowley, children."

"Love you, they've thanked me already. Nicely raised kids don't got to be told." The older woman's sharp eyes traveled between the man and the woman. She smiled slyly. "I'll be more'n happy to have 'em over to my place if'n you got somethin' else to be doin'."

"We're only going to Lansky's to buy Mr. Lucas a hat," Grace said quickly, interpreting Mrs. Crowley's look as a suggestion of impropriety. She needed to cut off all such ideas before they grew into gossip and slander.

Knowing the general store stood in place of a museum, a candy store and Santa Claus's workshop for her children, she asked, "Don't you children want to come with us?"

Both children shook their heads. Bart moved what was in his mouth into his cheek, giving him a lopsided look, like a greedy squirrel. "No," he said indistinctly. "She said she's got a berry pie."

Mrs. Crowley chuckled, her tiny body rippling. "So I do. A great big one. And a jug o' fresh cream. You run 'long, Mrs. Landers. I know how to look after your young'uns."

Grace was aware of Mrs. Crowley's eyes on their backs all the time they were walking up toward the general store. She noticed as they walked that a lot of the women out doing their shopping stopped to stare at Lucas. Glancing at them, she saw that her opinion of his looks was being confirmed with every pause and every hasty double-take.

She hurried on, holding up her skirt to give her feet free movement. The sooner she shaded his handsome, if unshaven, face with a hat, the better for her reputation. "Don't go so slowly," she said over her shoulder to Lucas.

He caught her arm. "Don't be in such a rush," he said, acting like a brake. "I'll start to think you're ashamed of me."

"I'm ashamed of myself," she answered quickly. "I didn't have time to darn your trousers yesterday."

"Well, it wasn't for lack of trying."

Grace glanced up and saw that he was thinking of her clumsiness in trying to remove his pants. Heat rushed into her cheeks, but she said steadily, "I'm out of practice, that's all."

"Any time you feel like starting up again . . ."

She stopped on the boardwalk, ignoring the now open and interested stares of the bonneted and shopping-burdened women around them. "If I do," she said unwisely, "you'll be the first to know."

"Do you mean that?"

"Of course not," she said at once, dousing the optimistic light in his eyes. Meekly, she added, "The store's a little bit farther along."

She started walking again. He paused a moment, before following. Grace could smile, knowing he couldn't see it. Catching up, Lucas said, "So what's gotten into you this morning, Mrs. Landers?"

"I don't know what you mean."

"Yes, you do. Yesterday, you were . . . let us say . . . orthodox. Even cold. Today, however . . ."

"Yes? Today?"

"What is it?"

She stopped again and gave him her happiest smile, not the one she saved for company. "Very simple. Two words, as a matter of fact."

"They are?"

"It rained."

"Is that all?"

"All?" She gawked at him. "Is that all? Heavens, where were you raised? Don't you know . . . ? Rain is everything."

She waved at the street, running with mud. Everything else had a new-washed look, the colors bright and clear now that the summer dust had been laid. The white-washed buildings shone like palaces, and the green growing things, in both yards and untended lots, lent tranquility to the scene. Even the air was sparkling.

"Rain, Mr. Lucas, is the food on our tables and money in the bank. It's new curtains for the parlor and seed for next year's planting. It's . . . it's life to a farmer. You won't find a sour face in all Ogden today. Well, you saw how the marshal was. Even he didn't get angry when you hit him."

"Because it rained?"

"Because it rained. For the first time in six weeks."

Grace turned from him to continue on to the store. She saw Mrs. Birkins come out and glance her way. The doctor's wife stopped dead, her mouth hanging open. Then, she went back up the store's narrow steps and down again, as if she'd lost something. All the time, she kept darting little peeks at Lucas from beneath the brim of her overly ribboned bonnet.

Girding herself as for an ordeal, Grace approached.

"Oh, dear me," Mrs. Birkins said quickly, her thin cheeks flushing. "I've dropped my . . . er . . . my coin purse. Do you see it anywhere?"

Grace looked under the stairs, peering at the muddy ground in search of what she confidently guessed wasn't there at all. "No, I'm sorry. Maybe you dropped it inside?"

"Oh, no, I couldn't have. I haven't been inside yet," Mrs. Birkins said, with a nervous titter and a sideways glance at Lucas out of pale blue eyes. "I'm sure, though, I dropped it around here somewhere. . . ."

Grace decided to put the poor woman out of her misery. "You haven't had the chance to meet Mr. Lucas yet, Kay. Mrs. Birkins, Mr. Lucas. He's helping me out around the farm."

"I hope to see your husband later, Mrs. Birkins. To thank him for caring for me yesterday."

Mrs. Birkins visibly hesitated before shaking Lucas's offered hand. Grace expected to see her wipe her hand off on her full skirt. She dropped her hand as though she would, only just stopping before her fingers made contact. "I'm . . . I'm glad to see you're better."

"I imagine I'm not used to such hard work," Lucas said. "Mrs. Landers is a real taskmaster."

"Oh . . . yes. Is she? I mean . . . Oh, dear, where can that purse have gone to"

"Maybe you should check your basket," Grace suggested. She saw the corner of the brown leather purse sticking up from beneath the checked gingham cloth.

"Yes, there it . . . Good . . . I thought I'd . . . I didn't drop it after all." She stood on the steps, the purse in her hand but her eyes measuring Lucas from the tears in his jeans to the beard shadow he'd not yet scraped away. She never quite managed to meet his eyes, Grace noticed.

He said, "Let me open that door for you, Mrs. Birkins." The doctor's wife scooted inside the store as the small bell rang over Lucas's head. She kept an uneasy eye on Lucas behind her. Not so much as the hem of her skirt brushed against him.

As Grace followed, she heard him whisper, "I wasn't going to pinch her." She choked on unexpected laughter and had to turn it quickly into a cough.

Her eyes adjusted slowly to the dark interior. Though large windows abutted the door, the light that should have come through them was blocked and filtered by heavy curtains to keep the merchandise from fading. Every inch of the place was crowded with things to buy, half of which could only be reached by one of the Lanskys standing on a ladder or fumbling with a pole that had a hook on the end. She walked carefully, avoiding the big barrels and kegs that took up much of the floor space. A muffled "ouch" from Lucas told her that he had barked a shin or stubbed a toe on one of them.

She could hear Mrs. Birkins talking to whoever was minding the store today. "A paper of pins, please, and some corn plasters. Oh, and that last mustard I bought . . . there's something wrong with it."

"Now, how can mustard possibly go bad?" Mrs. Lansky asked, her hands on her hips and a world of skepticism in her tone.

"I'm sure I don't know. After all . . . you sold it to me."

Obviously, it would be sometime before Lucas could buy his hat. Grace found her way to the counter where a lamp glowed dimly, bringing up the sparkle in the jewelry in the glass case under her elbows. The smell of hot oil in the lamp mingled with the spices and fragrances for sale, many kept in the drawers of a revolving box beside her. Dimly, behind the counter, penny candies dusted with big sugar crystals twinkled more alluringly than the inexpensive jewelry.

"Where are you?" Lucas called.

"Right here." She moved the lamp, making the prisms at the bottom of its dark yellow glass globe swing and peal like fairy bells.

"It's like a cave in here," he said, suddenly closer. "I better take care not to lose my guide."

His warm voice sounded on a low intimate note, smoothly penetrating her ear. Maybe it was the illusion of being alone in the dark with him that made Grace shiver when he spoke. She turned around and found herself practically in his arms. The expression in his deep-set eyes was watchful and hungry.

Grace realized it hadn't been the sudden rain that was the sole cause of her happiness. Watered crops certainly weren't the reason she'd put on the most becoming of her two sunbonnets. And rain would never make her drive poor old Ulysses and Hercules with the speed she'd wrung from them this morning.

All these things she'd done and felt because she was going to see Lucas, a man she'd known for a single day. A disreputable man at that. A mysterious man who looked as if he wanted to kiss her, right here in Lansky's General Store.

Then he stepped back, and she could breath again.

It was just as well, for at that moment the small bell dinged again and Mrs. Rena Presby came in. Her petticoats rustled softly as she furled her parasol, the bright sunlight behind her silhouetting her figure.

She must have been blinded by the sudden darkness the way everyone who came in was. But being Rena, she stepped forward confidently. After nearly tumbling over a barrel and sending a small spittoon—empty thankfully—rattling across the floor, she thudded into Lucas.

"I beg your pardon," she said in her high voice. Some of the local gentlemen compared her voice to an angel's. To Grace, Rena's squeak had about as much music in it as her front gate.

"No harm done," Lucas said, steadying the woman with a hand on her elbow.

"Dear me, I thought it was Mr. Lansky standing here. I'm so sorry. I don't know *you,* do I?"

"I haven't yet had the pleasure."

Lucas's and Rena's voices contrasted like the two ends of a piano keyboard. Grace decided that she'd imagined the look in Lucas's eyes. Obviously that expression of longing had been made up equally of the darkness and her imagination.

For here he was, smiling down at petite Rena, his white smile lighting up the darkness. And little Rena, her artless face belying the fact that she'd buried her second husband last year, smiled back at him with her rosebud lips, letting her hand rest carefully careless on his sleeve.

It gave Grace great satisfaction to introduce Rena to her latest flirt. "Mrs. Presby, meet Lucas, the hired man I got out of jail yesterday."

"Oh, my," Rena exclaimed, her hand flying off his sleeve like a freed white dove. "How . . . how do you do?"

"He's fine now," Grace answered. "We're here to buy a hat."

"How nice for you. They have some lovely new lace caps in the back. Just right for a lady in your situation. You must have Mrs. Lansky show you a few."

One thing about Rena, Grace conceded grudgingly, you couldn't keep her down for long.

"The hat's for me," Lucas said.

"Really?"

"So I won't pass out a second time in the sun."

"But I should have thought you'd be used . . . But then, I shouldn't say such things. Who's ahead of you? Oh, it's Kay. I must just say good morning to her."

Her petite figure, outlined in a dress more nearly fashionable than any other woman's in town, moved with fair accuracy toward the rear of the store. Grace noticed Rena didn't have any trouble finding her way now, and she didn't think it was entirely due to her eyes having adjusted to the dark. She felt sure Rena had bumped into Lucas only because he was male, and a stranger.

"Who was that?" he asked in a whisper.

"The widow Presby."

"Widow?"

"Twice. At least."

"I noticed how you introduced me. Were you warning her?"

"She doesn't need any warning when it comes to men. It's the other way around," she said, lowering her voice even more.

She heard Lucas chuckle. "Thank you for your concern. I'll be careful."

"You better be. In more ways than one."

"You told me yesterday a widow has to be careful about becoming the target of gossip. I suppose Mrs. Presby worries about that as well."

"There'd be plenty to gossip about her life if she wouldn't start it all herself about other people's."

Lucas looked over Grace's head toward the dim back of the store. "She seems like a nice enough woman."

"Sweet as they come," Grace said and then muttered, "If I know her—and don't I just—she'll get attended before us too."

That was how it worked out. Though Mrs. Lansky knew who was next, and had even turned to ask Grace what she needed, Rena stepped in with her attention-getting laugh and said, "Just a few little things today, Mrs. Lansky."

Before the store owner's wife could appeal to Grace, that fluting voice had her scrambling all over the shop. "I didn't at all care for that Castile soap you recommended, Mrs. Lansky. What else do you have? Lubin's? Let me smell it."

"It's twenty-five cents a cake."

Her rippling laugh broke forth. "That doesn't matter. It's what will suit me. I have a very delicate skin."

"And a thick hide," Grace mumbled. Lucas laughed as if he couldn't help himself, and the two women at the end of the store glanced up from their consultation. "Hush," Grace said.

"What else have you?" Rena wanted to know. After smelling and pricing every other kind, from plain glycerine to a few cakes of perfumed soap ordered from Paris in a spirit of hope by Mr. Lansky's late father, Rena chose the Lubin's soap. "If I don't like it, I'll be back to change it. Try, try again, that's always been my motto."

"We got in some cologne to match the soap, Mrs. Presby, if you're interested."

"I never use perfumes," Mrs. Presby said as though Mrs. Lansky had offered to paint her with poison. "But if they make toilet water . . ."

"Right here."

"Excellent! And now, I need a new toothbrush, and some tooth powder, and . . ." The list took quite a while, as she changed her mind, would switch from lace goods to gloves in a twinkling, only to speak longingly of violet-flavored candies that Lansky's didn't carry, and then change her mind again. She insisted on a brighter light being brought so that she could match a swatch of lace she'd brought in, the only undertaking that Grace entirely approved of.

"And lastly," she said at long last, "I need some stockings."

"Cotton, lisle or wool?"

"Wool? In this weather? Silk, if you have it."

"No, I'm sorry. You'll have to go to the millinery shop for those."

That was news to Grace. But then, she'd never worn a pair of silk stockings in her life. She'd heard about them, of course. Only abandoned creatures, or very wealthy women, wore such things. She wondered if it was very wonderful to slip silk over naked skin. And what would a man think, as he slowly rolled the smooth fabric down?

Rena's voice brought Grace back to reality. "But I know I bought my last two pairs here, and they've worn so well. I wanted to buy a dozen pairs this time."

"Can't be us," Mrs. Lansky said, her voice showing how tired she was. It perked up a little at the thought of persuading this difficult customer to spend more money. Grace didn't blame her for that, especially as everyone knew Rena Presby paid in cash as soon as she received her bill. "We carry some very nice lisle hose. I daresay it couldn't be told from silk."

"*Some* people might not be able to tell. But as I say, my skin is so sensitive. One touch of anything rough or rugged and it just itches so. My darling Curtis used to say— I know," Rena said perking up. "You take a look and tell me if I bought these here."

"Mrs. Presby!" Mrs. Lansky revived with shock. "There's a gentleman present."

"I'm sure he won't mind turning his back. Will you, Mr. . . . er . . . Will you?"

"Can't I just close my eyes?" Lucas said, his voice warm and amused.

Rena tittered. "Naughty, naughty boy! I shouldn't trust you to keep them shut."

"You can trust him," Grace said. "Because I'm right here to make sure." She took Lucas by the arm and turned him around. He went quietly, showing his white teeth in a grin.

"I'm sorry it's taking so long," Grace said to him as they stood staring at a cracker barrel.

"Why are you sorry? It's not your fault."

"I don't think it's Mrs. Lansky's either. She's doing her best. But Rena . . ."

Lucas folded his arms across his chest. "That's a remarkable woman to find in a small town like this. Was she born here, or did she get lost?"

"She's already lost two husbands."

"To what?"

"I think they must have been worn out." She bit her lip, ashamed of letting her wicked side show. "That was uncharitable. Forget I said it."

From behind them, they heard Mrs. Lansky say, "That's our best lisle hose all right, Mrs. Presby. You can tell by the old gold stripes."

"That's impossible!"

By contrast, Lucas chose the first hat offered to him, which was just as well. The broad-brimmed, low-crowned straw gave him a dashing look, like a riverboat gambler. Not that Grace had ever actually seen one. But she'd heard her father and his friends tell tall tales on the front porch while she pretended to be asleep in the room above. They had described dashing men, sitting at their cards wearing just such hats, only made of smooth felt.

Mrs. Lansky showed some hesitation at allowing Grace to put Lucas's hat on her bill. Though Grace knew it was because the store owner's wife was afraid the hat would leave town when Lucas did, it still bothered her. She'd been shopping here for five years and always paid as quickly as she could.

As they exited, dazzle-eyed, into the sunny street, Lucas reached out to take Grace's elbow. "I don't want you to fall, Mrs. Landers. That street is awfully muddy."

Grace lifted her arm free of his touch. "I can manage a few steps, Mr. Lucas. I've been walking for more than twenty years now. Ever since I was a baby."

"Not much more than twenty years, I'd guess."

She gave him a disgusted glance. She was really going to have to take him to task over this constant flattery. Not now, however. Not with Rena Presby and Kay Birkins standing not a dozen feet away. Their tongues were running like bows at a fiddlers's contest.

Though she was in her late twenties, about the same age as Grace herself, Kay Birkins appeared washed out, as if she'd been dried in the sun for too long, but then any woman would look that way who stood next to Rena.

In addition to a figure that was a little too full on top to be in proportion, Rena had chestnut hair, caught up in flirtatious ringlets under a hat rioting with flowers, feathers and ribbons. Her gown was of lavender, which was the proper color, but the tight, fussy style was as far from half-mourning as one could get. Anyone who looked less like a widow could hardly be imagined.

When Rena Presby got a good look at Lucas in the full light of day, her pretty bow lips opened as though in a voiceless scream. With great presence of mind, she covered her suprise as though it had been a yawn. Rena's immediate reflex in the presence of any man was to flirt. She reached up with both hands to fluff her ringlets, making her breasts strain against the shiny silk of her dress.

Taking a second look at Lucas, Grace found that he was smiling warmly at Rena. Grace felt a little nauseated, especially when Rena laughed in that affected way, shaking back her ringlets so that they bounced and collided. Kay whispered audibly, "What are you laughing at?"

"I just had a funny thought. Too foolish to mention."

They nodded as Grace and Lucas passed. Grace pretended to be too preoccupied to see them, though she couldn't help being aware that they started gossiping again, twice as hard, afterward.

"What do you think?" Grace asked, stung by the way he'd returned Mrs. Presby's nod. "Isn't she the loveliest thing you've ever seen?"

"Exquisite."

"Everybody thinks so. At least, all the men."

"You know," Lucas said to the air above her head, "I wonder if all women ask questions when they won't like the answer. Of course, Mrs. Presley is lovely . . ."

"Presby," Grace corrected, feeling strangely comforted.

"Presby. Why don't you like her? It can't be jealousy over her looks. You have nothing to worry about there."

Grace stiffened at this blatant flattery. "Mrs. Presby and I are dear friends," she said. "I shouldn't care to say anything against her."

"It's a little late for that."

"I'm sorry I said those things. It was wrong. I'm glad the children weren't there to hear me. It's just that . . ."

"You'd like to be that extravagant?"

"No!" She stopped in the middle of the street and collected her thoughts. For some reason, she wanted him to understand. "She just takes everything for granted. Her money, her looks, her chances of getting married a third time, or even a fourth."

"Do you want to get married again, Grace?"

In her earnestness, she overlooked his calling her by her first name. "No. I'll never marry again. Not ever."

Chapter
Seven

"Mrs. Landers?"

Grace saw that Lucas wanted to ask her a question, perhaps even challenge her statement, as her parents had done. But someone else was calling to her from across the street.

"Who's that?" Lucas asked. "He looks familiar."

"That's Mr. Kent. He took over the bank from his father last year." He called her name again, cupping his hands into a tube so the sound would carry. When he saw he'd caught her attention, he motioned for her to cross.

"He looks familiar, but I don't think I know him."

"You might recognize him from the alley. I was speaking to his wife when Bart found me. She went to get him."

"Was everybody in town in that alley?" Lucas asked, pushing back his new hat with his forefinger.

"No. But it seems that everybody in town has heard about it. We're very capable that way."

Grace surveyed the street for a good place to cross. The mud, black and shiny, probably wasn't very deep, an inch or two at the most. A few dry areas stuck up above the slime. It was just a matter of choosing the easiest, cleanest way across.

"Maybe you should stay here, Mr. Lucas. I saw that your boots are about worn through."

"They'll hold up," he answered confidently.

"All right. Follow me."

She stepped off the boardwalk onto a slight rise. Her own shoes, with a stack heel and stout soles, carried her nicely through the thin skimming of mud over this part of the ground.

"It's not too bad today," she said, throwing the words over her shoulder. "Just step where I do." She walked around a pothole that cherished aspirations of lakehood. A little farther out, however, and she had to skip from hillock to hillock, teetering on the smaller ones. The bottom inch of her skirt began to suffer from the unavoidable contact with the mud.

"Not much further," she said, stopping to catch her breath in the middle of the street. She glanced back for Lucas, planning on an encouraging smile. He was not there. Blinking, Grace wondered if that pothole had been deeper than she'd thought. Had he fallen in?

He wasn't on the boardwalk either. Realizing what a foolish figure she must cut, talking to herself in the middle of the street, Grace started resolutely forward. She'd give him a piece of her mind when she saw him!

Dead ahead of her, grinning like a clown, stood Lucas. He twiddled his fingers at her in an idiotic wave. He couldn't have walked straight across; his legs were still clean.

Frowning at him, Grace didn't watch her steps. She strode to the next hillock and it wasn't there. Her feet slipped and slid. There was no way to save herself. She could only totter, waving her arms, trying to grab air.

As her feet went out from under her, her one thought was of Mrs. Birkins and Mrs. Presby. They were bound to be watching as she sat down hard in a mud puddle. "Damn!" she yelped, more from humiliation than fear.

Then Lucas's strong arm was around her. As if she weighed nothing at all, he swung her up into his arms. He was muddy now, the ends of his pants legs and the top of his boots indistinguishable in a single column of sludge.

Grace wasn't used to feeling as defenseless as a sack of potatoes. She didn't even dare to struggle for fear she'd plop into the mud. What frightened her though was that she *liked* it. She could have thrown her arms around Lucas's neck and been glad to hold on tight. His arms cradled her, yet she was aware of the controlled strength beneath his gentleness. It excited her.

She realized something in that instant. She wanted Lucas in the worst way. Wanted him with a longing that came right out of her baser nature, the animal part of herself that no decent woman ever acknowledged. This discovery shocked her so completely that she couldn't even thank him for carrying her.

"There you are," he said, setting her upright on the boardwalk. "Safe and sound. You know, that's what we should have done from the first. I'll carry you back whenever you want."

Grace couldn't say what was in her heart. How could she admit to him the low feelings that surged through her at his touch? She looked away, afraid Lucas would read the truth in her eyes, worried that he already knew.

The banker came rushing over to her. "Mrs. Landers, I'm so sorry," he said breathlessly when he reached them. "If I had known . . . I was only asking you to stay where you were while I came over to you. I never expected you to come to me." He glanced between Lucas and Grace, his thoughts obviously a jumble of conjecture and distress.

"Never mind," she said, surprised by the normalcy of her voice. "Now that I am here, Mr. Kent, was it anything important?"

"Come into my office," he said, leading the way with an anxious backward glance, as if to be sure she was following. Lucas walked beside her.

However, Mr. Kent stopped on the doorstep of his respectable brick bank and said, "Wouldn't you rather . . . I mean . . ." He dropped his voice to a whisper. "He *is* a stranger."

"Yes, he is. Will you wait for me, Mr. Lucas?"

"You're the boss."

Ignoring the fascinated stares of the young clerks, one even pressing his face against the brass grille to see him better, Lucas leaned against the door frame of Mr. Kent's office, his hat pulled low over his brow. Glancing back, Grace herself would have taken him for the lowest sort of desperado.

Her stomach still fluttered shamefully when she considered how ruthlessly he'd swept her up. So might a man abduct a woman from her own drawing room, carrying her up the stairs to who knew what end. Grace wished she might undo the two buttons of her suddenly too tight collar, but she worried Mr. Kent might misunderstand.

Grace followed Mr. Kent into his quiet inner office. He closed the door. The safe, made of black metal picked out with gold, stood on stubby legs beside his desk. Her own modest savings—twenty-five dollars—were in that safe, or so she hoped. The banker went at once to sit behind his shiny, perfectly clean desk.

Grace took the chair he offered, a smaller, lower version of his own. For a chair padded and upholstered in leather it was surprisingly uncomfortable.

Steepling his fingers before the bridge of his nose, Mr. Kent leaned forward, his elbows on his polished desktop. He studied her for a long time without speaking.

"Yes, Mr. Kent?" Grace asked. She felt as if she'd just lost a point in some strange game. "What did you want to see me about?"

He began tapping the tips of his fingers together. "We at First Fiduciary Trust are pleased to be the holders of your mortgage, Mrs. Landers."

"Glad to hear it." She found it difficult to concentrate, her thoughts still bound up in that startling discovery in the street. Had Lucas felt the tremor that had gone through her when he picked her up? She hoped he attributed it to natural alarm.

"Naturally, we'd like this situation to continue," Mr. Kent went on. "However, we must consider the future."

"Of course." Hastily Grace reviewed her loan payments. So far as she knew she'd always been right on time and exact to the penny, though she hated to remember the difficulty she'd had at times to scrape it together.

"There may come a day when you no longer wish to continue your attempts to farm. That being the case, why not consider—"

"That is not the case," Grace said, interrupting. "I have every intention of holding on to my farm for as long as I live."

Mr. Kent spread his hands. "Yes, *now* you may feel this way and it does you great credit. However, a young, and may I say attractive, woman like yourself may at any time form a new tie . . . that is to say, you may contract another marriage and then . . ." Perhaps the stormy look in Grace's eye made him abandon that suggestion. "Or you might wish to return to your parents' home. In that case, the offer I have been asked to put forward might very well be a welcome one."

"What offer?"

The banker brightened. "I have received a most generous offer for your property. More than enough to cover the mortgage, plus a desirable sum over that for your personal use."

"Why didn't this person come to me?"

Beginning to smile with more than professional warmth, Mr. Kent said, "Undoubtedly, this person felt that a lady in your circumstances is ill-prepared to deal with the legal 'nonsense' bound to arise out of such an offer. Not the sort of thing a lady should be bothered with anyway, in my opinion. Just let me show you the figures. . . ."

"Mr. Kent," Grace said, her dander starting to rise, "I don't think it's right for you to talk to me as if you were my Dutch uncle. I am neither a child nor mentally deficient, but in all things a *femme sole.*"

Young Mr. Kent, whose own wife would have no more tossed a legal term at him than she would a cream pie, sat in his comfortable chair and goggled at Grace.

She continued, "I can enter into contracts, pursue a business and sue at law. No man has any right to my profits or, let me add, my person. Even if, as you suggest, I might wish to enter upon a new marriage, the thought of giving up these rights to a husband is utterly offensive to me." She wanted to stamp her foot and snap "so there," but that would have been childish.

"As for the legal end of things, I shouldn't in any case take your advice. As you have made yourself an agent for the other party in this offer, I would take my questions to Mr. Lathman or Judge Sterling. But as I'm not remotely interested in selling my farm to anyone—let alone someone who doesn't want to give their name—the issue doesn't arise."

She stood up. Turning, she noticed that the door, which Mr. Kent had closed with a snap of the handle, was now slightly ajar. As she came out, Lucas walked away, to stare out of the barred windows. She wondered how much he'd overheard.

Mr. Kent could do nothing but accompany her to the door. "Don't you even want to know how much the offer was for?" he asked, abandoning his fatherly tone.

"What's the point?" Grace asked. "It can't be enough to change my mind. Good afternoon, and thank you for your trouble."

Her indignation carried her elegantly over the threshold but wasn't enough to take her across the muddy street. The thought of enduring Lucas's strength again was daunting. She stepped off the boardwalk to make her careful way back.

"Mrs. Landers," Lucas called, starting out after her.

She hurried along, leaping like a mountain goat from hummock to hummock. This course she charted more painstakingly than her first attempt. Yet all the while, the mud squishing and slipping, Grace was more aware of Lucas behind her than of her task. Hearing him swear softly at a stumble, Grace looked behind her. As with the mythological Orpheus, that glance sealed her fate.

Her foot went onto a spot that looked dry, a crust sealing the top. But the crust was no more than a finger thick. The mud beneath was as slick as grease. Her foot flew sideways and she fell, bouncing on one hip, jarring her teeth and rattling every bone. Her arm fell into a particularly juicy puddle, splashing mud up into her face and over her head.

"My God!" Lucas exclaimed, hurrying over, stepping in mud puddles with abandon.

Grace pushed herself into a sitting position. Using the back of her right hand, still relatively clean, she wiped the mud out of her left eye. She blinked down at herself. The right half of her body looked bandbox fresh. On the left, however, she resembled an Indian medicine man, daubed with mud to work a great earth spell.

"My God," he repeated. "Are you all right?"

When she spoke, the mud gritted between her teeth. "Fine," she said. "How are you?"

A giggle rose inside her, like a fizzing fountain. She tried to choke it down while she reached for Lucas's hand. Sputtering, she let him raise her to her feet, fighting hysteria, if that's what this laughter was.

He glanced up and down the road as though searching for help. Those women who were still shopping stood on the boardwalk, ready to gawk but not ready to risk the same fate that had struck Grace.

"I'm all right, really," she said, choking on her laughter. He patted her back as though to help her during a coughing fit.

Mud slid off her bonnet to plop on her bosom. Grace glanced down at where it had fallen and realized she couldn't tell the new mud from that already there. Pressing the back of her hand to her lips, she giggled helplessly.

"There, now, Mrs. Landers, we'll find some place to wash you off."

"I'm not . . . I'm . . ." The bubble burst. She broke out into roars of laughter, right there in the middle of the street. For Grace had realized how ridiculous her previous worry had been.

Yes, Lucas was handsome and desirable. Yes, it had been a long time since she'd been with a man. But she needn't worry that passion would overcome either of them. What man would want her, a matron with two children, at present dripping with blackest Missouri mud?

From the way Lucas glanced in near-panic at the women on the boardwalk, Grace could tell he was worried she'd lost her mind. Making a great effort, she controlled her ill-timed descent into merriment.

"We'll . . ." No good. Another balloon of laughter escaped her grip. She pressed the cleaner of her two hands to her lips and tried again. "We'll go to Mrs. Crowley's. She has a pump in her yard. I'll just stand under it and rinse off."

"But won't that ruin your clothes?"

Grace shrugged. "I wash them in water all the time. I don't wear silk, Mr. Lucas, or anything a little water could possibly hurt."

As they reached the other side of the street, Mrs. Presby and Mrs. Birkins came up to them.

"My goodness," Mrs. Birkins said. "You're so muddy."

"Am I?" Grace replied. Instantly, she was contrite, but a bubble of laughter escaped her again. "Yes, I suppose I am."

Another dollop of mud slid off her bonnet. Grace untied the strings and pushed the wilted thing off her hair. Some of the pins dropped out too, and a few stray locks fell down.

"You poor thing," Rena Presby said, standing well out of range of any stray splatters. "I feel for you. So embarrassing. Do you want to come to my house and get clean? I'll gladly lend you something old of mine to put on."

"Thanks, Rena, I appreciate it. But it's all right. Besides, my children are waiting for me at Mrs. Crowley's. I better go there first." She smiled broadly. "I don't know what they'll think of their mother."

"Oh, I'm sure they'll understand. . . ." Mrs. Birkins hurried to reassure her. "Children have such beautiful natures."

Lucas murmured, "Bart will probably wonder why you didn't get a bath at the jail."

Grace glanced up at him. The alarm in his sky-blue eyes had faded, to be replaced by a laughter equal to her own. For a moment, it was as if rushing time stopped while she looked into the eyes of a stranger and found a friend.

Before any of the ladies could notice and wonder, Grace said, "Well, I better get along before somebody sets me in the park as a monument."

"As a symbol of courageous womanhood?" Lucas asked outrageously.

"More likely as 'the price of folly.' Come on, Mr. Lucas." The surrounding ladies parted like soldiers on the parade ground as Grace went through them, her head proudly erect.

"Coming, Mrs. Landers." He tipped his hat to Mrs. Birkins and Mrs. Presby as he left.

Very quickly, he caught up to Grace. "One guess," Lucas said, "what the topic of conversation around Ogden's dinner tables will be tonight."

"I don't need to guess. I know." She didn't tell him that *he* was the only thing any of those women would be talking about, when out of earshot of their husbands and children.

"You know, I like this town." Lucas nodded at strangers as he passed them by. "Something always seems to be happening. Fights, beautiful women all over the place, mud baths in public . . ."

"I can't say I've ever noticed it being a hotbed of activity before, Mr. Lucas. And as for my mud bath . . ."

"I'd rather talk about the beautiful women."

"I've told you everything I know about Rena Presby."

"Who's talking about her?"

Grace glanced at him. He was looking straight ahead. "I suppose," she said carefully, "you've fallen wildly in love with Mrs. Birkins."

"No. Not her. Which way to Mrs. Crowley's house?"

When she smiled, she could feel the drying mud crack on her cheek. Grace said, "Turn past the jail and go down two streets. And we'd better hurry. This stuff is starting to harden up."

"If it gets too tough, I can always carry you again."

"No, thanks."

"I don't mind carrying a little freight, Mrs. Landers."

After a moment, she said, "I suppose it's Mrs. Crowley you've fallen for."

"That's right. Hit me like a ton of bricks the minute I saw her."

"You'll have to wait in line."

"Oh, I've got time. Thirty days, as I don't have thirty dollars. Thanks for the hat, by the way."

"My pleasure." This is what it should be like, she thought. A man and a woman should have this easy rapport, without any squalid issues raising a barrier of discomfort between them. A comradeship, pure and simple.

Of course, she was still boss and he her employee, how-ever temporary that arrangement might be. But that didn't exclude enjoying his company. As a matter of fact, a little shared humor would make it that much easier for Lucas to accept her management.

"Lands!" Mrs. Crowley said, throwing up her hands when she saw Grace. "These streets are a disgrace. I been tellin' the mayor so since time took its first tick."

"I hope Bart and Callie—"

"Love you, girl, she's been cuttin' out biscuits with me, gooder 'n' gold, and that boy of yours is enough to make a cat laugh. He's chopped my kindling all to flinders and pumped me up enough water to drown my garden under. Then he sidles up to me and 'lows how he's aiming to marry a gal jes' like me."

"Darn," Lucas said, "he's beaten me to it. I was going to propose myself."

Mrs. Crowley laughed, her whole body shaking. "If you decide to throw this one back, Grace honey, you toss him my way. Though he's big enough to keep if you ask me."

Grace didn't dare glance at Lucas, though she couldn't guess which she was more afraid she'd see—his laughter, sure to set her off again, or his compassion.

"May I stand under your pump and get clean, Mrs. Crowley?"

"Shore, but I reckon it'll take more 'n a pumping to get you washed up and respectable."

"I just want to be clean again."

After Grace had gone, Mrs. Crowley flicked her gaze over Lucas. "Seems to me how you could use a wash yourself. Take her out some of my soap and a couple of towels and get yourself duded up as well."

"Yes, ma'am," he said, snapping off a salute.

"An' don't be givin' me none of that sass. You're just as like to my boys as peas in a pod. Full of sass and vinegar from the day you first squalled."

"I wouldn't know."

"Take a mother's word for it. We know." She smiled with a mystery no man could begin to plumb.

Fresh white sheets flapped on the line between the back

windows of the frame house and the pump. The fence the Crowley's yard shared with the one next door seemed like a solid wall of heavy pink roses, nodding on their stems and filling the summer air with their intoxicating scent.

Grace stood beside the pump. She put her face into the intermittent rush of water, keeping her skirts from getting wet. She had to reach around to try to work the pump, and seemed to be having difficulty raising and lowering the curved metal bar.

"Here, let me do that," he said.

Startled, Grace looked up, her cheeks flushed with pink from the stimulation of the water. Lucas glanced between the wall of roses and Grace's complexion and couldn't see a shade of difference. Maybe the roses had the worst of it at that, for surely her color deepened when he stood over her.

She put her hands before the spout. When Lucas worked the pump, squeaking up and down, water gushed out. Catching it in her hands, she rubbed it all over her face, splashing the back of her neck. Her hair curled in wet tendrils, springing free of the tight bun, just about the right size to twirl around a man's finger.

"Keep pumping," she said, reaching out her muddy arm.

Working the pump more vigorously, Lucas sent the flow gushing from the pipe. As soon as the water hit Grace's white blouse, it turned it transparent. Lucas could see the beautiful lines of Grace's arm revealed as though by a sheer veil. Not a useless member, by any means, but one where strength and determination showed in the definition of muscle and bone.

Lucas had hardly an instant to admire her before Grace bent at a twisted angle and put her back under the flow. "Keep going," she said. "Boy, it feels good to be clean."

"If wet," Lucas said, surprised by the husky sound of his own voice.

"The sun'll dry me in no time. I'll do you next." She twisted around to look up at him. "Well . . . go on."

Despite the water splashing all around him, Lucas's

mouth was dry. He knew as soon as the water hit her back, her blouse would be totally transparent. Yet already he was bringing the pump handle down to send the water sluicing over her. He couldn't stop himself.

Chapter
Eight

"Of course, if you're not up for it," Grace said, beginning to wonder if this was a good idea.

"I think I can manage. After all, it's not that hard, is it? Just drive it in and keep going."

"All right, but I don't want you to get hurt. Dr. Birkins said you ought to take it easy at first. Go slowly, and if any funny feelings come over you, you ought to stop."

"Don't worry. I'll stop just as soon as you want me to."

"I think you better stop before that. I might get so absorbed in what I'm doing I won't think of telling you to stop."

Grace drove the cultivator forward, guiding it by two long handles. It was an old one that Mr. Hackiff had gotten rid of when he bought the latest model. He had sold it on the condition that she cook him supper every day for two months.

When Chick died, Mr. Hackiff, an elderly widower, had proposed to her within a week, on the strength of her cooking. When she turned him down in shock, he'd promptly married one of Mrs. Devin's four daughters and gotten fat as a prize hog in consequence. They had two boys now, with another baby on the way. Grace thought about the other children she'd never have now, and felt a pang as fresh as the day Chick died. She ruthlessly corrected the motion of the cultivator, forcing her mind back to the job at hand.

"Just keep it going steady," Grace said to Lucas, looking over at where he sat watching from a tree stump. "Ulysses knows what to do. All you've got to do is make sure you don't run over any of the corn."

"Sounds easy enough."

"It would be, but you see the blades are slightly twisted." She stopped the mule. Chick had meant to get around to straightening the blades but never had. Yet it worked well enough to roust up the weeds that grew between the rows of sprouting corn.

"I'm sure I can manage." He stood up and came to her. Lifting the leather reins off her shoulders, he looped them loosely around his upper body. "Like that?"

"Yes, that's . . ." With one of his hands on each of the wooden handles, Grace stood trapped between his arms. He hadn't shaved yet today. She wondered if his beard would sting or be soft against her cheeks.

Hastily, she turned her back. "Let me show you again."

"If you like. I think I saw enough the first time."

He breathed in the scent of her dark gold hair, for she hadn't put on another bonnet after this morning's chaos. Lucas could still see, when he closed his eyes, the way Grace's wet blouse had clung to her every curve. She hadn't noticed anything odd or amiss until a breeze had roused her breasts and she'd glanced down.

Lucas swallowed hard as he remembered the way her puckering nipples had pushed against the material, and her gasp of surprise as she covered herself and ran for the house.

She had wrapped up in one of Mrs. Crowley's voluminous shawls on the ride home, and hadn't said a word to him since that wasn't related to farming. Not even his joke about how he and Ulysses looked like brothers in their straw hats brought her laughing smile to her lips.

Grace wondered if he was thinking about that embarrassing episode at the pump. She honestly hadn't thought how white cotton turns transparent when wet, never having worn a wet shirt before. If anybody had seen her, they would have thought her the most abandoned woman in creation.

But only Lucas had seen her, and that was bad enough. Did he think she'd stood under the pump on purpose to tantalize him? She didn't dare glance at him to try and read his face.

"I'll show you one more time. It's tricky till you get the hang of it. Keep pulling to the right to make up for the drag of the crooked blades."

She reached out to grasp the handles and touched his warm hands instead. Jerking her hands away, she hastily said, "It's not that complicated. I'm sure you'll manage just fine."

"No, go ahead." He chirruped to the mule, as he'd heard her do. "Come on, boy," he urged as the mule flipped one black-tipped ear back in response to this new voice. "Let's go."

As Ulysses started his lazy walk forward, Grace made an urgent grab for the cultivator's handles. She couldn't afford to have even half a row ruined. This crop would see them through the winter, God willing.

"Like this," Grace said, holding her arms akimbo to hang on to the bouncing handles. "Just keep hauling gently to the right."

"I understand," Lucas said. He wrapped his hands over hers. He chuckled, deep in his chest. "Your hands don't feel much like a farmer's. You'll have to show me the calluses, because I don't believe they're there."

Grace couldn't pull her hands out from beneath the enveloping warmth of his without letting go of the cultivator. His arms were around her, so she couldn't get free. After a moment, she didn't want to be free, though she knew it was madness to think of the things she was thinking of.

Distracted, Grace stumbled out of step. For a flaring moment, their bodies rubbed together too intimately for strangers. She was outrageously aware of the firmness of his body behind her. She wanted to lean against him, encouraging this closeness. His arms felt so right where they were.

"Maybe I can straighten this thing out for you," he said, in a conventional tone.

Grace remembered that her peculiar attraction to this man was all on her side. He most likely didn't feel a thing when she was close to him. Probably even the sight of her body nearly naked behind wet white cotton hadn't aroused him a bit. After all, she wasn't a young girl with a firm shape and high breasts. She was a mother of two, with all figure flaws included.

"I'd be awfully appreciative it if you could," she replied, forcing her tone to be as easy as his. "Whoa a minute, there, ol' mule. Whoa."

The instant Lucas's hold relaxed, Grace slipped her hands free. When she turned, however, he didn't drop his arms to let her go. With the cultivator behind her and him in front, she had to wait for him to move. She lifted her chin and made her eyes as cold as she could manage.

"I wanted to say . . ."

"Yes, Mr. Lucas?"

"I want to say that no one will ever hear of today's little event from me. So far as the world knows, I took no notice of anything that might have been . . . revealed."

"Thank you, Mr. Lucas," she said with a dawning smile. He was a gentleman, no matter that he didn't know his name and address. "Now, if you don't mind . . ."

"Of course, that's just as far as the world knows."

Grace's smile vanished, drowned in confusion. "I hoped you wouldn't bring the matter up at all. I know it showed me in a poor light but I had never . . . well, the circumstances being what they were . . . I hope you'll forget about it completely. That is what I intend. At least, I'll try."

"Forget about it? How can I?"

"You've forgotten everything else, why not that you saw me . . . the way you . . ." She got flustered, unable to find a decent way to state the fact of her near-nakedness. "I hope you'll put it out of your mind. I intend to."

"My dear Mrs. Landers," he said, his eyes perfectly serious. "Don't you know you have a figure that would make Venus put on heavy mourning? Compared to you, nymphs look like old nuns. If I had the pens of a thousand poets, I couldn't do you justice. I certainly couldn't forget anything."

Shocked, Grace put her hands to her ears. Had he guessed that she was attracted to him? Was he using her embarrassment to dupe her into doing something about it? He might think that his work would be considerably easier if she made a fool of herself over him.

Sparking mad, she pushed violently at his chest. "Don't say another word!" she demanded, when he fell obligingly back. "It's bad enough you saw . . . what you saw. But to comment on it!"

"Only to you," he said, a laugh escaping him.

"Only to me! You shouldn't say such things to anybody!"

She pushed past him. Swinging around, she took a firm stand in the field, even in her fury careful not to step on any young plants. Fighting to control her voice and her flaming cheeks, she said, her hands on her hips, "This will never work out."

"It's not the end of the world," Lucas said, his sensational smile breaking out.

Grace refused to be charmed. "Unless you promise me this instant that you'll never even think about this morning, I'll have to tell the marshal to take you back to jail until your sentence is up."

"I don't see why you're so angry, Mrs. Landers. I'm only saying that I wasn't disgusted by what I saw. You were worried about that, weren't you?"

"Of course I wasn't! I don't care what you or anyone thinks about . . ." She couldn't say the words. She could only make circular gestures. Dropping her hands, she said, "I want your promise, Mr. Lucas."

"What do you want me to promise? That I won't think of you as a woman? You might as well ask me not to think about myself as a man. And I am a man, Mrs. Landers."

Grace stood her ground as he walked forward with his determined stride, though her insides quivered with suspense. What if he grabbed her and ruthlessly kissed her? Could she conceal her infatuation? What if . . .

Lucas didn't touch her. She didn't know if she was glad or sorry. He gazed down at her with his deep-set eyes, a troubled frown between his dark brows. "You see, I had forgotten that I haven't known you very long. Somehow, it seems as though we met a long time ago, not yesterday. I thought I knew you well enough to tease you. I was wrong. I'm sorry."

"Maybe I overreacted, a little."

"No, you were entirely right. You have my promise, Mrs. Landers. I'll never mention today's embarrassing incident again."

Without another word, or letting her reply, Lucas returned to the idle machine and mule. Grace watched him loop the reins over his broad shoulder. As if he'd been walking behind farm animals for years, he put his hands on the cultivator and called to the mule. He had no trouble keeping the blades straight or making stubborn Ulysses obey him. He made it all look so easy.

Realizing she'd gotten what she asked for, if not all she'd wanted, Grace watched him for a moment longer. She was ready to call out some words of advice if Lucas looked around. Really, however, she just watched the way his body moved under his clothes when he walked with that slow, strolling stride.

Realizing she was ogling him, she turned her back and went resolutely back to the house. Piles of laundry awaited her, and if she daydreamed about what hadn't happened in the field, dirty shirts wouldn't tell on her.

Watching the blades turn over the soil, cutting the encroaching weeds off at the stalk, was one of the most satisfying things Lucas could remember ever doing. Glancing behind him, he saw the darker earth turned up to the sky, worms and grubs displaced from their hiding places. A few blackbirds swooped down to claim their share of this plunder. Ahead, past the mule, harnessed off-center, Lucas could see many more rows to traverse, each one a source of achievement.

Thinking idly, Lucas pictured himself at the center of the world. The warm sunshine beating down gave him a sense of well-being, while the mild breeze might have been conjured on purpose to keep him from becoming too hot. All around him, busy nature went on, eating, sleeping, procreating, while he took his proper role by

cultivating this tiny plot of earth. He began to whistle the
tune that ran through his head.

When he saw the children, he wasn't sure how long he'd
been working, except that a dozen turned rows lay behind
him. The soothing motion of the hind end of a mule lulled
him into a state of half-waking, half-sleeping. Only on the
turns did he have to pay more than nominal attention.
He'd misnegotiated a couple until he'd figured out what
to do. The mule helped him by giving him a disbelieving
stare every time he tried it the wrong way.

Making the next turn, Lucas walked behind the machine in the direction of the house. He saw Bart and
Callie heading up the slight rise to the barn, several other
children following behind. They were closely attended by
Toby, his tail flailing at the excitment of this game. Lucas
would not have thought anything of this, if the children
had not been so obviously secretive.

Bart, for instance, kept glancing back at the house, so
absorbed in avoiding his mother's vigilance that he forgot
about Lucas. Callie walked on tiptoe, and even at this
distance, Lucas could see how often she put her finger to
her lips to caution silence.

Wiping the sweat from his forehead, Lucas decided to
finish this row and then see about getting a drink of water
for himself and Ulysses. While he was at it, he'd drift on
up to the barn. If the children were safe and not up to any
mischief, there wouldn't be any reason to call Grace.

As he peered around the half-open barn door, Lucas
heard Bart's voice. "An' right there from that cross-
beam's where they hung the worst of 'em all. Dodger
Caldwell. He was the leader, an' he swore he'd be back to
get his revenge, if he had to come back from hell to do it."

Shafts of sunlight filtered down through gaps in the
boards, the hay dust sparkling like sifting gold dust. Four
frightened children raised big eyes to the beam that Bart
pointed to. They were all young, none of them older than
Bart himself. Only Callie stood by, interested in nothing
but her doll.

One of the girls, her braids short and straggling, said in
a stuffy grown-up kind of voice, "Don't you know you

shouldn't say 'hell,' Bart Landers. 'Sides, ain't no truth in it! Ghosts and such is just lies. Ain't they?"

"I tell you it's *true,*" Bart said, fixing her with his earnest gaze. "Ask your pa if you don't believe me. Most of the old folks round town know all about it 'cause they was here when it happened."

"When what happened?" Lucas asked.

Six children screamed in terror, their piercing shrieks rousing the owls that slept high in the frame. The screams drowned out the startled who-ing, but owl pellets, ejected in disgust, pattered to the floor. The children ran out, their fright already turning to giggles.

Lucas reached into the rushing crowd and caught an overall strap. He hauled, bringing up Bart like a fish on a line.

"Lemme go," the boy cried, taking a swing at him.

Lucas set him down but kept a hold on his strap. He felt as if he'd caught a snake by the tail. "Calm down, Bart. It's me."

The boy reminded Lucas of Grace in the way he flared up and just as quickly calmed down. It must be something volatile in their blood.

"Oh, hey," he said in greeting, ceasing to wriggle. He gave Lucas a gap-toothed smile, the empty space new since this morning. "I lost a tooth," he announced proudly, poking the tip of his tongue through.

"Congratulations. What's going on up here?"

"Nothing much. You know."

"Who were those kids?"

The boy shrugged his thin shoulders. "Friends of mine," he said breezily. "I got another tooth about ready to go. See, I can twist it pretty good."

Lucas refused to follow this tempting conversational lead. "Does your mother know you bring your friends up to the barn?"

"Course she does. She don't care a mite."

"Sure about that? Shall we cut along and ask her?"

Bart squirmed one bare foot against the hard-packed dirt floor of the barn. "Well, she never said I *couldn't.* 'Sides, we don't do no harm."

"What was all that nonsense about hanging?"

"Ain't nonsense! See—" Bart began but was interrupted by his little sister.

"They want their pennies back, Bart."

Lucas stared down at the boy in mingled admiration and amusement. He hadn't realized he stood in the presence of a fledgling robber baron. "Do you charge them to come up here?"

As if the thing were self-explanatory, Bart said shortly, "Course. We got the only haunted barn for miles."

"Haunted?"

"Bart . . . ," his sister said, reminding him.

"Tell 'em to come back tomorrow."

Callie persisted. "They want their pennies back, seeing as how they didn't get to see the grave."

"Grave?" Lucas asked sternly. Suddenly this episode wasn't funny anymore. "What grave?"

Grace's children exchanged glances. Making up his mind to trust Lucas, Bart said, "Come on, we'll show you."

The entangling honeysuckle and creeping wisteria vines caught at Lucas's hair and clothes, holding him back. He wished he'd brought a knife to hack his way through the dense growth on the other side of Lynch Road. The children wriggled through with less difficulty.

The two littlest ones clutched hands and looked as if they wished they hadn't come. The other two swaggered and whistled, joking about their chances of seeing a clutching hand rising out of the dirt. Their troubled eyes, however, told Lucas that this bravery was the merest bravado. Callie brought up the rear without a word, while Bart led the way with Toby.

The two of them seemed to take a fiendish pleasure in plunging through underbrush and sidling between the narrowest of gaps. At least twice, Lucas could see a simpler way around the obstacles that Bart headed straight into. Giving the boy the benefit of the doubt, Lucas thought that maybe Bart couldn't see the easier way from his shorter vantage point. But he also considered it possible that Bart took the more difficult path to impress his "clients."

When they came to the clearing in the woods, Lucas saw that Bart knew his showmanship. Certainly they all felt they'd triumphed over long odds when they at last stood beside a low mound. Long and narrow, it lay in the shadow of a immense half-dead oak. The vegetation had all but covered the mound, yet by its contours it was obvious that it was man-made.

The children stood quietly beside the grave. Without their chatter, Lucas felt the deep silence of the woods. Not even a bird sang. Only the dead branches above their heads rubbed together with a mournful sigh, stirred by the slight breeze. That and the dog's somewhat asthmatic breathing.

"They buried him out here," Bart said, making everybody jump. " 'Cause he was too wicked to be buried in the churchyard with his men. They all was murderers but Dodger Caldwell was worst."

"He don't *walk*, does he?" asked the girl with braids.

"I never seen him," Bart admitted. "But there's lights an' stuff up to the barn at night. Noises too."

Callie, whom everyone had forgotten, said suddenly, "I've seen him."

"You have not!" the girl snapped, angry enough to start tears in her big green eyes. "I don't believe you, Bart Landers! I don't believe it's a grave at all." She kicked the mound with her neatly shod foot. She kicked again, sending dirt trickling down the side.

"Don't do that," Bart warned. Toby backed away from the grave and bayed from deep in his chest. The sound made the hairs on Lucas's neck stand up.

"Oh, who cares about it?" the girl said, giving a vicious dig with her toe. "It's not—"

One of the littlest children screamed. Under the girl's foot, something white gleamed.

In less than ten seconds, Lucas was alone.

After examining the thing that had been exposed, Lucas made his way back to the farm. A few puffs of dust hanging in the still air showed him that the other children had sped home. But where were Bart and Callie?

Grace stood in the shelter of the back porch, looking down at her skirt. As Lucas came nearer, he saw that Callie had run to the safety of her mother. She now clung to Grace with all her might, her face concealed in the folds of her mother's skirt.

"What's the matter?" Lucas heard Grace say.

Callie only shook her head and tried to climb up. Grace pried the child off and knelt down, putting her arms around her daughter. Callie promptly hid her face against Grace's shoulder and continued to shake in silence.

Lucas asked, "Have you seen Bart?"

"He ran into his room as if chased by a wolf. What's going on, Mr. Lucas? Have the children done something they oughtn't? They haven't been bothering you while you work, I hope."

"It's a long story. Maybe you can tell me part of it."

"Me?"

"What happened in your barn? Was someone really—"

He stopped, for Grace had held up her hand to silence him. She unfastened herself from Callie and stood up. "Have you and your brother been talking about the barn again? You know what I told you. Well, go to your room until you think you can do what I tell you. And tell your brother he's to stay in his room until he hears from me."

"But, Mama," Callie said, putting her head back, tears running back to mat her hair. "The ghosts might get us."

"I've told you—"

Lucas said, "I've heard that the more you talk about ghosts, the more they come around. If you never mention them, then they stay put."

"Oh!" Callie's eyes shone with understanding. She wiped the tears away and snuffled. "I won't ever talk about 'em again."

"Nevertheless," her mother added, "you will go to your room. March!"

"Yes'm." Stopping only to pick up the doll she'd dropped when she'd flung herself at her mother, Callie marched.

Lucas said, "They got a pretty bad fright in the woods. We looked at something Bart called a grave. The grave of someone called Dodger Caldwell."

"Dodger . . ." Grace sat down on the top step, as though her legs no longer supported her. "I had no idea they'd heard that old story. Oh, don't worry, Mr. Lucas. I don't know what Bart showed you, but it isn't a grave."

"Actually it is." He found that if he put his foot on the bottom step and his arm across his thigh, he could lean close to her. Close enough to catch the faint floral scent of her hair.

"A grave?"

"Well, a burial. I uncovered some of it, enough to see what it was. Some farm animal, I think. A cow or a goat. I'd guess it was somebody's pet. One of the kids disturbed the soil and a bone showed through. They thought it was this Dodger person."

"No, he's buried in the regular cemetery in town. It was the least folks could do. All of them are buried there."

"All of who? Bart seems to think . . ." Lucas looked up toward the barn, the freshness of its white trim and red body looking perfectly innocent in the strong afternoon light.

"Bart's right. They all died in my barn."

Chapter
Nine

"I told Chick we shouldn't have bought this place. It had a bad name, ever since the war. But it was going cheap—the heirs of the man who owned it didn't want it either."

"Somebody lived here then, afterward?"

"Yes, Calvin Enright. He owned it at the time too. But when he died, nobody wanted it. They wouldn't even come out to see the place." Grace glanced up at Lucas. "Don't worry. He died naturally."

"That's a relief."

His smile made her perk up. She still didn't like talking about it, but at least he didn't seem to be superstitious. None of his fingers were crossed. "It was the war, you see. After the war, not everybody was happy with the outcome."

"Some folks still aren't."

"I know. It's still not a safe subject for discussion, especially with the men who fought in it. Did you?"

Lucas shrugged. "I don't know. I guess I'm about the right age to have been a soldier."

"You don't look much like a soldier."

"Can you tell by looking?"

She cast her eyes over him appraisingly. Two days ago any reasonable cat would have refused to drag him in. Now, if she didn't look at his face, he resembled any other farmer who had to scratch for a living. His face, however, strong and chiseled, remained to give him away. He didn't look resigned to a hard life. The humor that always spoke to her sparkled in his blue eyes and defined his mouth.

Grace wondered again what he'd been before he became a drifter. Nothing ordinary, she was sure. He couldn't be thought of as an ordinary man. She knew lots of ordinary men. Not one of them had ever set her pulse to beating a tick faster.

She said, "Sometimes you can tell by the way they walk. The officers still march like they're in the army. Either one of the armies."

"And I don't."

"No, you walk like . . ." He walked like he owned the earth, even when he couldn't lay claim to any piece of it. But she couldn't look into his eyes and tell him that.

Dropping her gaze, she pleated a corner of her apron and said, "Anyway, some of the soldiers for the South came around here in '66. They'd been robbing and murdering people all up and down this area ever since the surrender was signed."

"And they came to Ogden? Were you living here then?"

"No, I still lived in Sedalia. We moved there soon after it was laid out in '59. I was born in St. Louis."

"And that's where you met your husband? In Sedalia?"

"That's right. He was living with his parents in Ogden when the raiders came. He never forgot a moment of that night." She didn't want to talk about the nights she'd held her husband, when the nightmares clutched him in their talons. "He told me about what happened."

"I'm surprised he wanted to live here, if he was that upset by what happened."

"As I said, the farm was cheap. We didn't have any money to speak of. We didn't want to live with his mother and be a burden." That wasn't the only reason she hadn't wanted to live with his mother. Grace would have taken a house where ghosts galloped up and down the stairs day and night rather than live with an "invalid" whose only illness was laziness combined with irascibility.

"At first," Grace said, "the town couldn't defend itself. The raiders came suddenly. About a dozen of them. They broke into the mayor's house first and kidnaped his wife and children. After that, they could do pretty much what they wanted."

Grace could imagine what it must have been like to have been the mayor's wife. To see guns pointed at the heads of her innocent children, to live every moment in the fear of death.

"Chick told me that the raiders promised that all they wanted was to rob the bank. Mr. Kent's father even opened the safe for them, to save them the trouble of blowing it up."

"Where was the marshal?" Lucas asked.

"Mr. Sweeney didn't have any better luck than the mayor. I never heard whether they caught him napping or what. Maybe things would have turned out differently if the law had been properly represented. I don't know."

"Did things get ugly?" He could imagine the scene with strange clarity. The restless townspeople, looking for a leader, hoping to pacify the thugs in their midst. The mothers, huddling with their children in darkened rooms, listening to the mutterings and shots, praying no bullets would strike a beloved husband or brother.

"They got ugly fast. Chick says he saw his uncle killed and heard some of the girls as . . . well, you know."

Lucas passed his hand across his forehead. "How old was Chick at the time?"

"Twenty-two. He always said there wasn't anything he could do. I think he felt guilty and that's why he always talked about that night."

"I wish I'd known your husband."

"Why?" Grace asked, looking up into his face. She saw that he was frowning and rubbing his forehead hard, as if he were getting another headache.

"I would have told him that he had nothing to be guilty for. What could he have done, what could anybody do, against armed and desperate men?"

"He knew how to fire a gun. He could have done something to stop it."

"He could have been killed for his trouble," Lucas said shortly. "Best thing to do is keep your head down in a situation like that. Yes, keep out of sight and hope it'll all be over soon."

He spoke in a strange, thick voice as if he were forcing

the words through a wall of mud. His face changed too, settling into lines Grace hadn't seen before. Lines of discontentment, of pride, and of impatience. He could never be less than attractive, but Grace saw that something base could shadow his good looks. He swayed, his hand over his eyes.

Grace reached up and touched his other hand. "Come here and sit down before you fall down."

Lucas sat down heavily next to her on the narrow step. "What happened next?"

Wondering if it was wise to go on, Grace said, "The raiders got drunk. They started down this road to lose themselves in the woods when they came to the Enright place, as it was called then. Some people still call it that. More folks call it Lynch Road Farm. Not a very funny joke."

"Go on. What did the townspeople do?"

"They came after them. Furious. Chick didn't know what made them change their minds and decide to fight. Maybe the mistreatment of the women. He followed along when they came out here. Mr. Enright had sneaked off to town as soon as the raiders were good and drunk, to tell where they'd gone to. Chick saw everything that happened. The raiders were too drunk to defend themselves."

Lucas stared at the barn. "So this great shoot-out at your barn that Bart was telling me about—the hundreds of raiders shot and twice that many hung—is just his fancy."

Dropping her voice to a whisper so there was no chance the children could overhear, Grace said, "That was the worst part. Chick says the townspeople shot the raiders in the legs so they couldn't run and then they hanged them."

"I can't say I feel too sorry for them." Lucas put his arm around Grace's shoulders and gave her a squeeze. When she stiffened, he took his arm away as if she'd suddenly glowed white-hot. "I . . ."

She smiled at him, realizing he only meant to be comforting. "Thank you. But I'm not upset. I don't believe in ghosts or spirits. It's not a pleasant thing to think about, that ten men lost their lives in your barn, but that doesn't mean there isn't a cow to milk and mules to groom and feed. Not to mention mice, cats and birds. They don't mind the history of the place, so why should I?"

"Because you're not a cat or a cow, Mrs. Landers. You're a woman." By his expression, Grace knew he was thinking again of reminding her that he was a man, not with words this time but with actions. She quivered, knowing his arm was behind her. One moment's weakness and she could be locked in a devastating embrace. The temptation to be weak was never so strong.

She fought and won. "Yes, I am a woman. But that doesn't mean I have to cower because of imaginary troubles. I have plenty of real ones. It's worry about my children and my livelihood that keeps me awake at night, Mr. Lucas. Not the moaning of ghosts and goblins. There's not a demon in the depths of hell more frightening than a mortgage payment."

The tension of the moment passed off when he laughed. "I'll back you against any demon Satan can put up, Mrs. Landers. Three-to-one odds."

"Thank you. I'll let you know when the bout is to be held." She stood up, giving her apron a tug to set it straight across her hips. "You still have that field to work, Mr. Lucas, though I thank you for watching out for Bart and Callie."

"My pleasure. Before you go . . ." Grace turned back. "What happened to the money?"

She shrugged. "Nobody knows for sure. After they cleaned up, everybody and his cousin Fred searched that barn. They thought maybe the money'd been buried when the raiders knew they weren't getting out."

"And they didn't find anything?"

"Not a penny. There were no signs of any fresh digging. They practically tore the barn apart looking for it." Grace shook her head. "It certainly would be something to see."

"Surely the money would be all rotten and mildewed by now," Lucas said. "Paper wouldn't last this long, not if it were buried."

"Paper? That money wasn't paper. Nobody trusted

paper money at the end of the war. Don't you remember . . . sorry. No, they got away with ten thousand in gold."

"Gold?" Once more he looked at the barn.

It was Grace's turn to chuckle. "Don't think I haven't thought about that too, Mr. Lucas. Course the money wouldn't be mine to keep. Mr. Kent's father made all those people's savings good out of his own pocket. It almost broke him. But it sure would be something to see it all together in one spot. Ten thousand in gold. I've heard gold never tarnishes, not even if you sink it in the sea."

"Didn't Chick look?"

"I think he may have. But he never told me about it if he did. Once he said that money with blood on it never did anybody any good."

"He was right. And yet . . . I wonder."

Hearing a call from inside the house, Grace said, "Wonder while you work, Mr. Lucas. If you please."

Grace looked at herself in the sitting room mirror, apparently to thrust loosened hairpins back into the tight knot of her hair. In reality, it was to give herself a good talking to. She knew she wouldn't be doing Bart any favors if she let him off the punishment he deserved. A mother alone had to be firm, or her children would walk all over her.

These words of wisdom sounded very familiar. Grimacing, Grace recognized her mother's voice repeating in her head. All too frequently, she'd find her mother's voice coming out of her mouth. "Sit up straight, mind your *p*'s and *q*'s, good girls don't wear pink on Mondays, never sing at the table, keep out of the night air . . ." She knew a million such strictures. Though she vowed not to say any of them to Bart and Callie, sometimes they slipped out.

Grace did her best to sift the foolish or superstitious sayings from the prudent. Every now and then, however, she would unwittingly reveal how her mother's early influence still lingered. The sayings her mother repeated about widows sometimes troubled Grace in her sleep.

Making a last face in the mirror, Grace crossed into her

son's room. When she knocked, a mournful voice said, "Who is it?"

"Old Dan Tucker. Who did you think?" Grace peeped in. Bart sat on the bed, his hands dangling loosely between his knees. Toby sat beside him, one paw on the boy's knee as if offering comfort. Boy and dog had the same miserable expression, though Toby thumped his tail at the sight of Grace. Bart didn't even look up.

"Are you going to wallop me?" Bart asked.

"You're getting too big to wallop." With a pang in her heart, Grace sat down beside her son. Remembering how comforting Lucas's arm had been, she put her own around Bart and gave him a squeeze. She usually refrained from showing him too much affection, knowing he had to grow up tough and strong. Maybe though she didn't need to be so restrained all the time.

"I'm sorry, Ma. It's just . . ."

"Did you really charge those children a penny to see the barn?"

"Yes'm," he sniffled.

"And they paid it?" She shook her head. Pennies must be plentiful in some houses.

"Sure," Bart said, brightening. "Most anybody round here would. Not everybody's got a haunted barn."

"But it's not haunted. You know it isn't. Come on, you've never been afraid to go in the barn."

"Course I'm not afraid," he said, puffing up his childish chest. "Least not in the daytime. I didn't used to be afraid at night either. But them lights . . ."

"Fireflies," Grace said with an assurance she didn't feel. Fireflies blinked on and off. The lights she'd seen had glowed steadily, only to go out the moment she came near.

Bart turned up a disbelieving face. His eyebrow rose high enough to tangle in his hair. "Yeah, fireflies. And them noises is just the cow kicking over her bucket."

"That's right."

"But if folks think it's haunted, they'll pay money to see it. I got twelve cents that way, showing it to the town kids in the spring."

"Twelve cents? You mean the twelve pennies I found behind the bureau was yours?" Bart nodded, a wash of red coming into his cheeks. "Why didn't you say something when I took it to pay Mrs. Lansky some of what we owe? I wouldn't have spent your money, though I might have asked you how you got it."

Bart gave a kind of embarrassed wiggle. Glancing down, Grace saw him smiling. She said, "You meant for me to find that money! Oh, sweetheart, we're not that hard up. You don't have to lie and cheat your friends. We'll be all right."

"I just wish I could find that ol' money box," Bart said fiercely. "I'd buy you a Singer sewing machine, an' a di'mond ring, an' skates an' a real Texas Bull Dog revolver with the pearl handle and the double-load cartridges. Aw, I'd even get Callie something."

Taken aback by this flood of generosity and even more so by the look of worship in her son's eyes, Grace said, "Thank you, Bart. But we don't need any of those things. All we need is . . . each other."

"But if I could find it . . ."

"We don't need it."

Grace put her arms around his skinny frame and hugged him tight. All the good advice she'd heard about how to bring up a manly boy faded from her mind. This is what he needed most: the loving embrace of his mother. He'd grow up soon enough to be rough, tough and full of anger at the unfairness of the world. Let him, for an instant, stay her baby son.

The instant was over all too quickly. Bart squirmed and Grace let him go. "So you're not mad at me?" he asked.

"Not too mad to make sugar cookies." His face lit up, only to fall when she said, "But you've got to give those pennies back to the children you brought up here today."

"Ma, they saw Dodger's grave!" he said, aggrieved.

"No, that's not what they saw. Mr. Lucas says it's an animal's grave. You just forget all about that. I don't want you going back out there to trouble it any more."

He frowned, his wispy brows taking on something of his late father's obstinacy. "An animal? But . . ."

"Yes, a goat or something. No, I don't know why it was buried over there, but leave it alone. It could have had some disease or illness that I don't want you or Callie to catch. And you're going to give up offering tours of the barn. There's nothing to see there, but plenty of work to be done." She waited and then prodded. "I want your promise, Bart Landers."

"Yes'm," he said grudgingly. Then his lips parted in his merry grin. "Say, you should of seen 'em all run when Dee kicked that bone loose!"

Rightly ignoring this, Grace took his chin in her fingers and looked into his mouth. "Bart, have you been losing teeth?"

He poked with his tongue at the loose one, making it flutter like a cellar door in a windstorm. "Put it under your pillow tonight and you'll have good luck. At least," she added quickly, "that's what your grandmother says."

Two hours later, Grace crossed the yard, a pail covered with a blue gingham cloth in her hand. Her cornfield was on the other side of a slight rise. Climbing it, she looked over to where Lucas worked the land. She dropped her gaze at once, only to raise her eyes again, overwhelmed by an irresistible desire to admire his body.

He'd taken off his shirt. The leather straps of the reins crossed his shoulders, accentuating the smooth ripples of his muscles as he gripped the handles of the cultivator. Black hair curled over his chest as far as his pectorals. The outlines of his ribs were clear under his skin, but she didn't for a moment think he needed feeding. He looked like the pinnacle of all things male, sleek and healthy. Looking at him unobserved, Grace remembered she was a woman in every sense of the word. A woman, moreover, who was lonely for a man.

She asked herself who would know, or care, if she and Lucas slipped off together. Within sound of the brook grew a shady tree, where the grass was thick and lush. Would it be so terrible to take Lucas there, to exchange a little pleasure? Grace forced herself to use a lawless word to describe the pictures in her head. Would it be so terrible to become lovers?

He'd seen her now, and waved, his grin inviting her over. Her insides lurched as she thought of him smiling down on her, the sun behind his head as he positioned himself above her. Grace tried to control her leaping pulse as she picked her way across the field to him.

Of course, she knew it was just a widow's fantasy, born out of loneliness and need. But if that was all it was, Grace asked herself, why did the thought of taking another man to her special place seem sordid and low? She couldn't, for example, imagine Reg Wyman lying on the grass beside her. She shrank from that picture as if it had been a threatened slap.

But with Lucas as the center of her fantasy, the idea seemed natural and safe. His arms were strong; she could see the muscles move in his corded biceps. Yet he had a gentleness she'd sensed from the first; there'd be nothing to fear in revealing all of herself to him.

When she reached him, Grace had a color in her cheeks that was not entirely due to the walk. "You're doing a wonderful job," she said, then wondered if she sounded too gushing.

"Thanks. It's not as easy as you made it look." He wiped his forehead with the back of his arm.

"I hope you're stopping often for water. It's not as hot as yesterday, but the air's wetter."

"If I don't stop enough, this old mule lets me know when he's ready. He stops dead and won't budge till I bring him some water." He shucked the reins off his shoulders.

"Mules are smart."

"Smarter than men, I guess," Lucas said, his quick smile flashing out.

"Sometimes," Grace conceded. Then she remembered her errand. "I brought you dinner," she said, handing him the pail. "It's not very lavish . . . I mean, to someone used to Mrs. Crowley's ideas of mealtime."

He lifted the cloth. "Looks just the ticket. For a while there this morning, I thought I'd never want to eat again. Funny how this work gives you an appetite."

"Yes, isn't it?" Grace tried to find someplace safe on

him to put her gaze. But his eyes were too full of laughter, his chest too tantalizing, his arms too suggestive. To stare past his ear was just possible except for a funny longing to nibble on it. Finally, striving to get herself under control, she stared at her own neatly buttoned boots.

"You know," Lucas said, "I don't know much about farming but this seems to be good land. The dirt's the blackest I've ever seen. Isn't that supposed to be a good sign?"

"Yes. And you're right. It is good. But . . ." She sighed.

"But . . ."

"There's only so much I can do. Marshal Wyman's right about that. I scrape along. I can't afford to hire anyone to improve the land; I can't afford to improve the land without hiring someone."

"Or borrowing them from the jail."

"I can't expect to find good hired hands there more than once in a blue moon."

His smile from a distance had been dangerous. Close to, full strength, it devastated her. Grace stammered, "I . . . better be getting back. The children . . ."

"You could sell out."

Grace shook her head. "Never. Besides, nobody wanted it before. Why would they want it now?"

Lucas shuffled his feet. "I beg your pardon for eavesdropping, but I heard that banker say someone had made an offer. Why don't you take it? Get someplace where people can treat you the way you deserve. See a little life."

"You mean where men can see *me?*"

"You don't like men?"

"Sure. Why, some of my best . . ." Grace saw something change in his expression. A warmth came into his eyes as they fixed on her mouth. Heat ran up under her skin, setting every corner of her body burning. Her breath shortened as she saw he had the look of a man about to kiss a woman. Her.

Her fantasies had leaped right to the culmination. She'd forgotten all about beginnings. Starting to tremble,

Grace understood how much she wanted Lucas to kiss her and how much the thought of his doing it alarmed her.

Her lips were so dry, she had to lick them. She saw the smoldering in his eyes leap into flame. He took a step nearer, his hand rising in the air as though to grip her shoulder.

Hating herself for being too cowardly to take what she wanted and damn the consequences, Grace stepped back hastily, almost tripping over a furrow. Lucas changed his movement to save her from falling. She flinched away from his touch, her balance restored.

Pressing her hand to her untasted lips, she said, "I could never sell the farm. It's the only thing my husband left the children."

His face fell at this rebuff. Then his expression hardened. He spoke with a light indifference that seemed somehow forced. "That's understandable. Seems a pity, though you probably know your own mind best."

Grace seriously doubted that was true.

Chapter
Ten

The next day, Lucas didn't come to work. Giving in to the children's whines, Grace cooked breakfast for them instead of waiting for him as she'd intended. She kept stepping into the sitting room to glance at the clock. Had she worked him too hard yesterday? Had he relapsed?

Reaching for the jam, Bart said, "Guess Lucas ain't coming today."

"Mama . . . ," Callie called. "Bart's stealing jam."

"Now, Bart," Grace said. "I gave you plenty."

He shot a glance of hatred at his sister. She put out her tongue, as little and pink as a kitten's. Catching sight of her, Grace said, "You shouldn't tell tales on your brother, Callie. And don't make faces either. You might freeze that way and have to spend the rest of your life with your tongue stuck out."

"Do it again!" Bart urged.

"Won't!" Callie said, just to disappoint him.

As the hour advanced and no Lucas appeared, Grace began to be less worried than irate. What could be keeping him? He had the rest of the field to cultivate, seeing how he hadn't gotten more than half done yesterday through being unused to the work.

Sending Bart out to fill the woodbox, Grace took Callie up to the henhouse to collect eggs. A hot mash had spurred the best layers to new efforts.

Callie had a talent for egg gathering. Her little warm hand stole under the hens like a lost chick. After fifteen minutes, Grace had a basketful of brown eggs, ranging from a creamy white to an egg that resembled a large acorn.

At the house, Grace separated the darker eggs from the lighter. "Do you want to go to town with me, children? We can sell these to Mrs. Lansky. She told me yesterday she can't get too many white eggs. It means walking, though. I'm not taking the wagon today. The mule is needed in the field."

To Grace's surprise, Bart didn't want to go to. "I'll stay home and clean my room, Ma."

She put her hand on his forehead. He didn't seem to be running a fever. Grace touched her own face. She wasn't hot either. Bart must have really said what she'd heard.

"Clean your room?" she echoed, incredulously.

"Shucks," he said, blushing. "Can't a feller try?"

Grace kissed him on his forehead, intensifying his blush. He went to his room, with the air of one who meant to do or die. Waiting till he was out of sight, Grace put the jam and yesterday's cookies out of his reach, even if he stood on a chair. Calling to him that she'd be back in time to give him his lunch, Grace left with Callie.

Of course, walking meant carrying Callie half the distance. Though the little girl was on the thin side for her age, there was no doubt that thirty-five clinging pounds got heavy quickly on a hot day. And it was getting hotter by the minute. In the distance, the air above the road wavered like water.

Grace's blouse clung to her, and beneath her calico skirt, her petticoats adhered to her legs. She envied Callie in her short wincey dress, her simple muslin drawers the only fabric between her and whatever breezes that blew. Grace didn't believe in overdressing her children, even if she could have afforded frills and furbelows. Callie never wore even a single one of the child-sized corsets her grandmother continually sent.

The woods thinned out as they came closer to Ogden. The town had grown just since Grace had come to live there, spreading out, stretching its boundaries. The railroad had come six years previously, running the track on the other side from Lynch Road. Grace remembered how excited Chick had been when it had looked, briefly, as if the railway would be buying their farm. He'd spent the money a hundred times in his imagination.

The town had half a dozen streets now, all running down to the railroad track. Vacant lots sprouted hotels, seemingly overnight, to house grain and corn buyers from back east. There was some talk of adding a theater. The town council seemed to think that it wouldn't be long before Ogden would take over as county seat from Bladesburg. Grace had been to Bladesburg once. She didn't think the other town had anything to worry about.

The streets had dried considerably, thanks to the heat. Grace walked up Main, Callie trudging along behind. Suddenly, she heard someone call, "Hey, lady!"

A youngish stranger, sharply dressed in a loud check suit and round derby hat, came puffing up to her. His thick ginger mustache blew with the force of his breath. "Sorry to holler like that, ma'am, but there doesn't seem to be a soul awake in this dead-and-alive town."

Grace drew herself up. "Is there something you wanted?"

"Yes indeedy, ma'am. Say, are those eggs?"

"Yes," she answered, glancing down. How anyone could mistake them for anything else was beyond her.

"Hard-boiled by any chance?"

Sure she was dealing with a madman, Grace glanced behind her to check that Callie was safe. She crouched in the dirt, drawing with a chance-found piece of stick.

"No, they're not hard-boiled."

"Damn! It'd be better if they were hard-boiled. Never mind. I'll take the whole basket for a dollar."

"A dollar!"

"Dollar 'n' a half?"

"Why do you want them?" Grace asked, prodded by unbearable curiosity.

The man, not more than twenty-two, talked fast, with a strange, nasal accent. "It's like this. There's no place to eat in this burg. There's hotels and stuff but not a single restaurant, 'cept that bean-burner down by the depot."

"Yes, I know, but . . ."

"I'm traveling from St. Jo to Denver, and the basket of

food I brought along is emptier than the bottom of an echo. Not a thing left but the salt. An' my inside . . . begging your pardon . . . is getting to be the same way."

"But eggs . . ."

"It's like this. I'll get some boiling water from the engineer—the whole train's a kettle anyhow—and boil up these eggs sweet as sweet. Then I eat like a king from here to the next town that does have a restaurant, or at least somebody cooking who doesn't think he's making a burnt offering."

With a smile, Grace handed him her basket. Since it seemed she was never to get more than a word in, she kept her reply brief. "Here."

"Thanks, you've saved a starving man's life." He pressed two coins into her hand. Taking the basket, he took off running for the depot. He cradled the basket under one arm like a ball. Spurred by the whistle of a soon-departing train, he put on a burst of speed, only to run into Lucas, coming up the boardwalk.

The stranger bounced off, one egg leaping to its doom from the back of the basket. Clapping his spread fingers over the remaining eggs, he apologized to Lucas. "Sorry, didn't see . . . Say, do I know you?"

Lucas grasped the other man's upper arm. In an eager, almost offensive voice, he said, "I don't know. . . . Do you?"

The stranger glanced at Grace as though looking for moral support. "I thought for a minute . . ." The impatient whistle screamed again, reaching into every house in Ogden. "No, I guess not," the stranger said, stepping away.

Lucas let him go. Grace came up to where Lucas stood. Together they watched the city slicker run for the train in his pointed toe shoes, his tight checked trousers making his legs look as long as a spider's.

"Friend of yours?" Lucas asked.

"No, I never saw him before. But he gave me a dollar and a half for those eggs. Even if I include the basket, that's a mighty fine price."

She glanced at Lucas, then stared in surprise. He wore

a natty blue flannel suit, the long body and straight-legged trousers making him seem even taller than he was. From the wings of his collar, a forest-green tie lent a dash of color and silkiness to his monochrome palette. Even his shoes were gleaming new, as was the suitcase in his hand.

He grinned under her incredulous stare. "What do you think? Makes me look like a respectable citizen, doesn't it?"

"You might be a banker," Grace admitted. "But how . . ."

"Mrs. Presby."

"Oh?" Grace drew back, the smile fading from her lips.

"Yes, she came to the jail this morning and told me that she'd run across some trunks of her late husband's clothes. Some things he'd hardly worn. She thought I should get some use out of them."

"Yes. She's such a thrifty woman."

"You sound like you don't approve," Lucas said, searching her face.

"Why shouldn't I? It doesn't matter to me." Grace coughed, trying to bring her voice back under control, for it had gone absurdly high, into a tone of pique. After all, it really wasn't any of her business if Lucas chose to get entangled by the wiles of Rena Presby.

She went on. "If you want to take off your clothes in . . . that is . . . It doesn't matter to me if you want to take clothes from her. Your old things were getting more and more shabby, though I don't see how you're going to work in those fancy things."

"She gave me two pairs of her husband's work pants, as well. We must have been about the same height."

"I'm sure you would have had a lot in common," Grace said.

She looked down at Callie, still playing in the dirt, utterly unconcerned with the mysterious affairs of the grown-ups. "Come along, Callie. Since that man bought the eggs, we don't need to go to the store. Tell Mr. Lucas you'll see him later. We will be seeing you later, I hope, Mr. Lucas?"

"As soon as I can change into my work clothes, Mrs. Landers."

"It would have saved time if you had changed at Mrs. Presby's."

Grace only meant to hint that he was wasting time that she needed him to spend at the farm. She was surprised by the hot blush that darkened Lucas's face. He coughed and rubbed the back of his neck. "That's what Mrs. Presby . . . I mean, she seemed to think I look better in these clothes."

"She's right," Grace said. "You look like a different person altogether."

"That's what I thought. It's funny. I don't ever remember wearing clothes like these, yet I tied my tie as if I'd been doing it for years."

"Maybe that's true. There's no way of telling. Unless . . . Did you remember something?"

Lucas shook his head. "Not a thing. Mrs. Presby insisted I should stay on to lunch with her, but I thought I should go. I knew you'd probably be wondering what happened to me."

"Oh, you should have stayed. Her Elvira is one of the finest cooks in town."

Grace didn't want to know what had happened at Mrs. Presby's beautiful house in the elegant end of town. At the same time, however, she found her head whirling with imagined scenes, ranging from the innocent to the lurid. Had Rena Presby been forward? Had Lucas disliked it as much as he was trying to make her believe?

"If you'd like to go back," Grace added, "I'm sure Mrs. Presby's offer is still open."

He glanced over his shoulder, a vaguely hunted expression coming into his eyes. "No, thanks," he said, with a slight shudder. "Cold bacon and beans with you is better than rack of lamb and spring peas at Mrs. Presby's."

"Oh!" Grace said, brightening. "I'm glad you think so."

"At least your food comes with an honest price—honest labor."

Grace wondered again what Mrs. Presby had been charging. She hadn't realized she was jealous until Lucas smiled down into her eyes, lightening her mood. "Why don't I walk with you to the farm?" he asked. "I can always change in the barn."

As they turned together and headed back up the street, Callie tagging along obediently, Lucas said, "I'll be glad to get out of these things. The day's too hot for a suit."

Some dust from a passing wagon hung in the motionless air. A dog lay in a narrow band of shade cast by a barrel, his tongue lolling out, his ribs scarcely moving. Above the town, the sun baked the color from the sky, leaving it so pale a blue as to seem white. From the buildings and the street, a glare bounced right into Grace's face. She stopped to adjust her bonnet, to shade her eyes.

"Come here, Callie." She lifted her daughter's hat by the strings that lay against her neck.

"I don't want to wear my hat," the girl complained.

Lucas said, "I'm wearing mine. I've learned my lesson."

Callie glanced up at him with a thoughtful expression. "Okay," she said, submitting to her mother's care.

As she straightened from this task, Grace saw Wenonah carrying a basket along the street. "She must be going to the jail," she said as the girl turned the corner.

"Who? Oh, Wenonah. She's an Indian, isn't she?"

"At least half," Grace said. "Sioux, I think."

"Jasper seems to think she's something special. I noticed how protective he is of her."

"Really?" Grace said, interested. "He was seeing the Fillmore girl for a while, till they had that fight at the corn shucking last fall."

Lucas was easy to walk with, for he neither strode along without a thought for her, nor dallied as if thinking she would never keep up without his help. His hand brushed her skirt sometimes as he swung it, a tantalizing reminder of his nearness. Grace debated taking his arm as they turned at the end of the street.

"Who are they?" Lucas asked suddenly.

Looking ahead, Grace stared in repugnance at the scene before her. Wenonah, her eyes cast down, had been blocked on her way by three mountainous young men. Dressed in raggle-taggle finery and cast-off hats, they were too big for whipping and too mean for it to do any good anyway.

Two of the behemoths stood in front of her, one pawing through the basket she'd been carrying. The other stood behind her, like a guard. All three wore the meaningless grins of dolts on holiday. A snatch of their conversation reached Grace and Lucas.

"Now, come on, honey, what say you an' me go back behind the livery stable and get friendly-like? You know you want to." The biggest and ugliest of the three Grupp brothers, Caleb, put his crooked finger under the girl's chin and tried to lift it.

Wenonah tossed her head free and said nothing. Her face, set in sullen lines, expressed her distaste and discomfort more forcefully than it would have with a twisted grimace.

"Why dontcha look at me?" he complained.

"Ol' Caleb's sure got a thing for you," the youngest said, with a foul snicker.

"Yeah, the thing in his pants!" the brother behind her said. The two younger brothers practically fell over laughing, but were quick enough to catch Wenonah when she made a sudden dodge.

Only when the Grupps put their hands on her did Wenonah struggle, wriggling to be free of their grip. She tried to throw off their hands, only to be tripped up and sent into Caleb's embrace. He bent her back over his arm, burying his face in her neck.

Wenonah still hadn't made a sound, though she flailed her free arm. Then her hand crept up to give his ear a violent wrench.

"Ow!" he hollered, letting her go. She fell to the ground and lay there without moving. "You bitch!" the biggest Grupp boy yelled, drawing back his booted foot to kick the girl.

Furious, Grace started forward, only to find Lucas holding her back. She turned her glare on him. If he told her to mind her own business . . . .

"The Grupp boys, I take it," he said, with a strangely tender smile. He touched his still purple cheek. "I think I owe them a little something for their trouble over me the other day."

Grace realized Lucas had taken off his fancy coat. Before she had a chance to warn him that his opponents were well known for their viciousness in close combat, he was advancing at a speedy lope. The smile he threw her was full of anticipation.

He yelled something as he ran closer to the little group standing in the middle of the street. One Grupp brother turned, his lips curling in a sneer—Lucas sent him flying backward with a swift uppercut to the heavy chin.

The second jumped in front of Lucas, his ham-hands spread wide to wrestle or strangle. A simple low reach and wrench and the chunky ruffian dropped to his knees, his hands clutching a tender piece of himself.

But Caleb, standing above Wenonah like a snarling cur above his meat, was greater in cunning than his brothers. He pulled a knife, a sharp, silver blade that flashed in the sunlight. His meaty lips spread in a confident grin as he weaved back and forth. His first words showed that he recognized Lucas. "Well, now looky here! If it ain't the rummy! Looking fine and fancy, too."

Wenonah, unnoticed for the moment, crawled painfully away on her knees and elbows, away from the contested ground between Lucas and the Grupp brother. Grace went to her at once, kneeling in the dirt. "Are you all right?"

Trying to rise, the half-Indian girl bit her full lower lip to stifle a cry of pain. "I must have hurt my wrist when I fell." She cradled it against her chest.

"Mama," Callie said, tucking herself against her mother's body.

Glancing up, Grace saw that Lucas and Caleb Grupp were circling each other cautiously as two cats. Win and Marv were still out of it. But Caleb had begun to feint with his knife, slashing at Lucas, who kept back, his eyes flicking as he searched for an opening.

"Callie," Grace said, "I want you to go get the marshal. No, wait. Mr. Crowley. Get Mr. Crowley."

For a moment, Callie stood frozen at her side. Then she

looked up into her mother's face. With a hopeful smile, she asked, "Is it all right if I run?"

"Yes. Run as fast as you can."

The little girl let out a war whoop she must have learned from her brother. Hiking her skirt, she ran like a cloud with a storm behind it. For a moment, forgetting everything else, Grace stared in amazement. She hadn't the slightest notion Callie could run like that. But she was glad of it. Even if help arrived too late, at least Callie wouldn't see the impending gutting of Lucas.

And that certainly seemed inevitable. Caleb Grupp was moving slightly closer with each dancing, mesmerizing motion of the shining blade. Did Lucas see? Grace didn't dare call out a warning, for to distract Lucas might be to confirm his death. She could only clasp her hands and pray, her eyes wide open.

Finally, when Caleb brought his hand down for the short, sharp sweep that would flay his opponent's stomach, Lucas made his move. Almost too quickly for Grace to see, Lucas caught Caleb's arm in mid-sweep and carried it forward under his control, not Caleb's. His forearm came down with crashing force on Lucas's thigh.

The knife fell, point down, into the dirt.

Caleb grunted in pain like a wounded buffalo. Lucas jabbed his elbow into the big man's windpipe. With a force Grace never guessed he possessed, Lucas tossed Caleb to the ground. Brushing his hands lightly, he gave her a half-wave.

Perhaps her expression warned him. Turning quickly before she could do more than squeak in alarm, he thrust the second brother down again when he would have risen. A mere glance sufficed to keep the third on the ground.

When Jasper Crowley got there, his speeding footsteps slowed in wonder. He pushed back his tall hat and scratched his head. "Well, I swan . . ."

"Swear all you want to," Grace called. "After you help me."

His forehead puckered with concern, Jasper came over at once to where Wenonah lay on the ground beside

Grace. "Are you all right? They didn't . . . Those bastards! Beggin' your pardon, ma'am."

"Don't mind me," Grace said. "I agree with you. I'm afraid she may have broken her arm."

"God Almighty!" he said. He bent as though he'd scoop the girl up in his arms. But she shook her head, her dusty braids swinging.

"No, I am all right. There's no need . . . I can go home alone."

"I'll go with you," Grace said.

"No, you must see to your daughter. I will be all right." Saving her right arm, the wrist swelling ominously, Wenonah rose to her feet. She wasn't tall, yet she had a certain dignity that not even rough handling could mar.

She stepped delicately around the inert figures of the Grupp brothers to speak to Lucas. Grace couldn't hear her quiet words of thanks, but she saw Lucas shrug them off.

Jasper said, looking in the same direction, "She shouldn't go home alone. It's not right."

"I doubt Lucas will let her go alone." Grace felt another pang of jealousy, as ugly as it was unexpected, when she saw Wenonah graciously accept Lucas's bent arm. The only reason she didn't lambaste herself for it was that she could see the same emotion in Jasper's eyes as the tall, handsome stranger went off down the road with Wenonah.

"Where's Callie?" Grace asked, remembering her responsibilities.

"Oh, my ma's got her. Don't you worry. She's a good kid. Course she threw a scare into me when she said Lucas was getting killed. I see she got it backwards."

He looked around at the crowd that had gathered, though the good people of Ogden kept well clear of the Grupp brothers, terrible even in defeat. "The marshal can't keep from locking them up this time," Jasper said, half to himself. "Not after a knife fight."

"What about Lucas? Won't he have to lock him up too?"

"I hadn't thought about that. I guess he will. Though

I'm sure Judge Sterling will let him out again, once he hears how it all happened. And I aim to tell him, Miz Landers, don't you worry about it."

He walked forward to gaze at the thrashed brothers. "Okay," he said to the crowd, "who wants to help me clean up this mess?"

Mrs. Crowley, who knew everything, knew where Wenonah lived. "But you don't want to be going out there," said the tiny brunette.

"Why not?"

"Don't you know about Chainy Town? How long you lived here, girl?"

"I know it's not the best part of Ogden."

"It's the worst part of Ogden. Lower'n a snake's belly and twice as tough." Mrs. Crowley shook her head. "I've tried to help that girl, I really have. I offered to have her come live here. Tried to tell her that it weren't charity, that she'd work. She turned me down real polite-like but she made me feel like I'd just slapped her. She's proud—proud as Satan. And that's a bad combination. My daddy used to say, 'Too proud and too poor shows kind heart the door.' "

"I don't know about that," Grace said.

Mrs. Crowley looked abashed. "There I go again. Golly, you figure an ol' gal like me would know better than to go shooting off my mouth like a cheap shotgun."

Getting precise directions from Mrs. Crowley wasn't easy. Chainy Town was literally on the wrong side of the tracks. It should have had the feeling of a bucolic retreat, nestled amid the noble woods half a mile from Ogden.

Instead, it was a collection of broken-down shacks, collected around four saloons, one on each corner. The nature of the place showed in the squalid street, the heaps of refuse and the air of neglect that breathed like a stale draft among the trees.

For the second time that day, Grace found Lucas coming from another woman's house. Only this time, he was angry. His breath came short and his dark brows were lowered so far that his bright blue eyes could scarcely be seen. His lips were compressed into a firm line, as though he held back words by force. He sped past Grace, giving no sign he saw her. She had to tug his sleeve to get his attention.

"You shouldn't be here," he said the moment he recognized her.

"I wanted to be sure Wenonah hadn't broken her arm." Grace glanced around. She saw only squalor. Not even a cat slinked by, and no dogs bared their teeth. Not even birds sang. The air was hot and thick, dragging on clothes and skin like a beggar's touch. The trees seem to huddle together warily.

Grace asked, "Where does she live?"

Lucas jerked a thumb over his shoulder. "Maybe you can talk some sense into her—I can't."

"Wenonah?"

"No, her aunt."

"I didn't even know she had one. Is she . . . ?"

"An aunt by courtesy, I'd guess. Not a very civil person."

"Did she swear at you?" Grace said lightly.

"Among other things, yes. Come on."

Following him, Grace said, "I can't believe Wenonah lives here! She always keeps herself so neat."

"You haven't even seen where she's living yet," Lucas said grimly.

Leaning drunkenly against the Brass Ball Saloon stood a two-story building. The windows showed broken glass, while the shutters hung at crazy angles. From the open front door, a stench of wet carpet and thousand-year-old cabbage poisoned the air. Grace didn't want to think about going in.

"Mrs. Crowley said she offered Wenonah a home with her. I wonder that she didn't jump at it!"

"It's probably because the old woman won't let her go. Of course, she offered to sell Wenonah to me for forty dollars."

"Sell?"

Lucas hadn't seen Grace angry before, not really angry. Her lips tightened as a blaze flared in her gray eyes, hard-

ening them as a blade is tempered in fire. Her back stiffened, and she raised her firm chin, as if daring a blow.

He followed her as she marched up to the boardinghouse, his heart filled with admiration and respect.
Something of her courage, the courage to follow her con-
victions wherever they led, passed to him in that moment.

Chapter
Eleven

Grace showed Wenonah her new room. Stooping to collect some of Bart's things off the floor, she said, "I'm sorry it's not larger."

The girl looked around at the square space, Bart's mess still scattered widely despite his best efforts. She looked at the collection of bird's nests and snake skins on his bureau. "It has a roof and a floor, Mrs. Landers; I don't ask for anything else."

Remembering the ugly room she'd found Wenonah in at her aunt's, Grace could only nod. "Of course, if you'd rather stay with Mrs. Crowley, I know she'd be more than pleased to have you. She said she's offered you a home before."

The girl stared out the window at the green trees. "Yes, she was very kind."

"Why . . . Oh, well."

"I couldn't," Wenonah said, her back very straight. "I couldn't be a servant in that house."

"I'm sure Mrs. Crowley didn't mean . . . and I hope you don't think that I . . ."

Wenonah's unpracticed smile had a furtive charm, her warm-colored lips revealing teeth whiter by contrast. "No. I don't think you took me in as a servant. And I know Mrs. Crowley would have treated me in all things as a daughter, but I couldn't live in that house, not with . . . him."

Enlightened, Grace patted the girl on the shoulder. It was like touching a block of wood. Her hand fell away, not shrugged off, but by no means encouraged to stay. Looking at the girl's pretty brown skin and smooth braids,

Grace wondered again at her keeping so neat while living under such dreadful conditions. But no matter how decently she kept herself, there would always be people who'd look at her merely as a half-breed, only slightly better than a dog. To be in love with a man she could never have must be nothing but torture.

Grace sympathized, not only with Wenonah's situation, but with her pride. There was no point in saying anything encouraging. They'd both know it would be nothing but a comforting lie.

"Bart's bed's kind of small for you, Wenonah. My mother-in-law's old bed is up in the attic. I haven't looked at it for a while, but I suppose it's still good. It should be; she told me often enough how much it cost. There's a decent mattress I can borrow from Callie's trundle bed."

"I wouldn't mind sleeping with Callie. It's not fair to Bart to throw him out of his room."

"It won't hurt him to sleep in Callie's room and I don't mind taking her in with me." She kept to herself the fact that Callie kicked like a mule in her sleep.

"All the same . . ."

"Anyway, things will only be confused for a week or so at the most. I'm taking the children to visit my mother soon. Her house is bigger than this one, and much cooler in the summertime. I remember . . ." Grace shook her head. "Never mind. Make yourself comfortable, child."

Bart didn't look pleased at all to be changing rooms. He shot Wenonah enough sharp looks to pierce her like a pincushion. Grace took him aside before supper. "You treat Wenonah like a guest in this house, young man, or you'll sleep with Toby on the porch."

"Can I?"

"Of course not." She didn't want him sneaking off to the barn to investigate any strange noises. Not even his own ghost stories would keep him in bed if he could find trouble.

"But what's she doin' here, Ma? How'd she get all banged up?"

"Never you mind. Just make her glad to be here, that's all I ask."

After his examination, Dr. Birkins had stated that Wenonah's wrist wasn't broken, merely badly sprained. As the girl picked up the wood box awkwardly with her left hand, Grace reminded her of what the doctor had said.

"You sit down and take it easy. Let Bart get the wood. And no . . ." She took the big blue bowl of biscuit dough away from her. "I can roll those out myself. Goodness' sakes, can't you act like a lady of leisure?"

Once again, the girl's smile came like a flash of light in a lightless room. "I have never tried."

"Well, here's your chance."

Sitting at the table, Wenonah looked around fretfully. She drummed the fingers of her left hand on the table, then stopped as if caught in a dubious deed. Her right arm was draped in a sling made out of a large white handkerchief. She pleated and unpleated the ends sticking out of the knot

Grace felt fidgety just watching her. She wondered how to ask a delicate question without hurting her feelings. Maybe it was best just to be blunt. "Can you read?"

"Yes. The nuns at the Indian school taught me to read."

Grace wondered how much pain was concealed behind that bare sentence.

"Good. There's a book in the sitting room. Walter Scott. I'd appreciate it if you could read to me while I work. I never get a minute to sit down with a good book these days."

The girl came back in a moment, her steps silent in contrast to the thudding noise that Grace endured from her children. "Quentin Durward . . . ?" Wenonah read, dusting the black-and-gold spine of the book.

"Yes. Just start from the beginning, will you? It's been such a long time since I started it that I don't remember half of what happened."

She'd bought the novel to pass the time during the long hours of the night with Callie nursing and Chick so queasy from his first illness. Since then, she'd scarcely had a minute to lose herself in fiction, not with life so hard.

When Lucas came to the back porch to tell Grace he was leaving, he could hear Wenonah, slightly hesitant, reading aloud. He paused to listen for a moment. Wenonah had a faint flavor to her voice, not really an accent, just a hint that English hadn't been her first language.

"Charles, surnamed the Bold, or rather the Au . . . Aud . . ."

"Let me see," Grace said. "Audacious."

"Charles, surnamed the Bold, or rather the Audacious, for his courage was allied to rashness and frenzy, then wore the ducal coronet of Burgundy, which he burned to convert into a royal and independent crown. The character of this duke was in every respect the direct contrast to that of Louis the Eleventh."

Lucas frowned as he listened, though not because Wenonah tripped over some of the words as she read them. Grace came to her rescue whenever she was truly stuck. The author went on at length about the differences between Charles and Louis, the shiftiest, foulest king France ever produced.

As she read, it was as if the words were unrolling inside Lucas's head. He *knew* what came next, as if he could see the page himself.

He pressed his hand to his hot forehead, fighting down the headache that had begun to pound behind his eyes. He saw a tiny picture of a long window, divided by lead lines into little panes of glass, a wall covered with crowded bookshelves, a large desk set at an angle to a vast fireplace with firelight dancing off ash-gray stone. Snow drifted past the window, but the boy lying on his stomach on a dark red rug never gave a thought to sledding or skating. He was lost in fifteenth-century France, a Scottish knight riding beside the fair Isabelle de Croye.

And someone disturbed him, walking in the library at his family home in . . . where? Who was it, standing above him, looking down on him with some elusive expression in his deep-set blue eyes, eyes like the ones he'd seen in the shaving glass this morning?

The tide of blood rose in Lucas's head, blinding his memory, filling his thoughts with pain. He reached out as if to capture some part of his past, struggling to save the tiniest fact to carry with him into this confusing present.

He liked to read.

That was the fact. Whoever he was, whoever he had been, he had liked to immerse himself in books. But what kind? As if the question opened a door, his head was suddenly thronging with characters from adventure novels. He sorted them out, remembering clearly where he'd met them. *Ivanhoe* and *Kenilworth*. *Journey to the Center of the Earth* and *Twenty Thousand Leagues Under the Sea*. *Moby-Dick*. Most of the works of the late Charles Dickens and all of Cooper and Dumas.

Lucas wondered what kind of a man he was who found so much pleasure in tales of derring-do and high adventure. Try as he might, he couldn't summon the memory of a single moralistic tale or improving work. He decided that he must be some dull clerk or contented family man, who only acted with decision and courage between the pages of someone else's imagined life.

But if that were the case, how did he wind up here? Why had he believed himself to be in the Dakota Territories? Where had he learned to fight? Deputy Crowley had pointed out when Lucas changed clothes at the jail that he'd dispatched the Grupp brothers with as much skill as if he'd been battling wickedness every day of his life.

Sighing, for every answer seemed to raise new questions, Lucas knocked at the back door. Wenonah's voice broke off in the middle of a sentence as Grace's quick footsteps crossed the kitchen floor. Opening the door, she said, "All done?"

A shaft of afternoon sunlight glanced off her richly colored hair, bringing up the glinting lighter blond highlights that framed her heart-shaped face. Her soft lips smiled up at him, her gray eyes warm. Framed in the doorway, she seemed an attainable dream, like a vision of home after six months of wandering.

Her smile trembled and faded when he didn't answer at once. Lucas realized he was staring. Hurriedly, he said, "Oh, the field? Yes, it's done. I've put the mule in the barn and I washed off the cultivator."

"Sounds like you've earned your supper tonight. I only

wish I had something better to offer you. You'll get plenty tomorrow, though."

"Why? What's tomorrow?"

"There's a social after church. Everybody brings something to contribute. About all I've got is buttermilk biscuits, but I'm bringing four dozen."

"Do you think I'll be welcome?" Lucas asked. "I mean, I'm not a regular churchgoer."

"After you thrashed the Grupp brothers? Everyone in town will want to shake your hand. Besides, how do you know you're not a church member? You could be a pillar of the community and a deacon into the bargain."

He chuckled. "I don't feel like a deacon." Then, suddenly daring, he added, "Not when I look at you."

A wash of color came into her too-pale face. She shot a glance over her shoulder at Wenonah, who studied a page in the book with an improbable intensity.

"Hush," Grace said, glancing up into Lucas's face. "That's no way to talk."

"Not to my employer, maybe, but to a beautiful woman, it certainly is. Someone ought to tell you that you're looking blooming this evening, Mrs. Landers. Aiding damsels in distress agrees with you."

"I didn't . . . You did it all." She stepped closer to him, dropping her voice so Wenonah couldn't hear her. "I wanted to tell you . . . I thought it was wonderful what you did. You saw the way everybody else just watched. God knows what those boys would have done to . . ."

"But you're the one who got her away from that woman." Lucas lowered his voice too. There was something tantalizing about whispering like this, more intimate and revealing than speaking aloud. So might two lovers whisper in the dark.

Grace shrugged. She'd just ignore what he said about the way she looked. He was only being nice. "It was just a matter of finding out what she really wanted."

"But only you would have guessed she wanted a new dress and a pig."

"That reminds me . . . I'd better get those things together. Do you think you can drive the pig all the way out to Chainy Town?"

"I think I can manage. And . . ." He swept his hand down her arm to grasp her hand at her side. "And you are beautiful, Grace. As well as brave."

He told himself he wasn't going to kiss her lips, just her hand. A simple congratulatory kiss, as a courtly gentleman to a lady. But when he touched his lips to the back of her hand and heard the sharp intake of her breath, he glanced up to see her eyes half-closed and felt the trembling of her hand in his.

Her lips looked so soft and delicious in the sunlight that no mortal man could have withstood their temptation. She didn't move as he tenderly brushed them with his own. Realizing Grace wasn't going to leap backward and chastise him for his impudence, Lucas put his hand on her waist and drew her closer. Another moment, he thought floatingly, one more moment in Paradise can't hurt anything.

Grace felt as if all her strength had drained out of her body at his touch. She had no more resolution than a leaf, blown by a soft breeze against Lucas's strong body. Then his breath warmed her into responding. She kissed him back with an intensity all the more eager for having been hoarded.

She forgot about her duties, and her responsibilities. Forgot that Wenonah sat just inside. Forgot that her children might appear at any moment. Repressed desires surged up in her. The gifted way Lucas played upon the exquisite sensitivity of her long-unkissed lips sent her sliding into a whirlpool of sensation. Whatever he had forgotten, he certainly remembered how to kiss!

His arms tightened around her as he sighed her name, turning her so she had to put her hands on his shoulders for balance. The shock of her body coming into total contact with his seared her from thigh to shoulder as though she'd embraced fire. She pushed away, clapping her hand over her mouth to stifle her own cry of astonishment.

Staring at him over the ends of her fingers, Grace saw that he looked back at her with equal amazement.

Quickly, however, his face relaxed into a reassuring smile. "It's not the end of the world, you know," he said.

"I've got to go milk the cow," she replied like a crazy woman.

Grace bolted from the porch, running down the steps. Only when she was halfway to the barn did she slow down. Even then, she didn't dare glance over her shoulder to see if he watched her. She didn't have to. She knew he did.

In the musty dimness of the barn, she stopped short and pressed her hand over her thundering heart. He really had just kissed her. Kissed her as she'd never been kissed before. And if that was a sample of what he could do with just his mouth, heaven alone knew what else he might have in store!

"My Lord, my Lord," Grace said distractedly. Her fingers were cold. She lifted them to her glowing cheeks. It had been difficult enough having a man on the place without this complication.

She'd never thought of herself as man-hungry, that unattractive term applied to old maids and widows. Grace knew she was guilty of applying it herself to Rena Presby. She'd always thought herself above Rena because the other woman was so obviously in the market for a third husband while she herself had determined never to marry again. Now she knew that Rena was at least honest, while she was the worst kind of hypocrite!

"Grace?" Lucas called.

Flustered, Grace grabbed a bucket at random and headed into Lola's stall. Only when she sat down by the cow's flank did she see she'd picked up the hen's feed bucket. "Shoot!"

She stood up and went to get the right one. She pushed past Lucas as if he weren't there. "Grace," he said again, a ripple of laughter in his voice.

"Wrong bucket," she said, picking up another pail.

He took it out of her hand. "You know you can't milk a cow when you're upset. You'll sour the milk."

"*Now* you're an expert farmer too?" She made an ineffectual grab for the bucket. Realizing she was losing her precious dignity, Grace stepped back and looked him in the eye. Only then did she remember how dangerous that was.

A man shouldn't have eyes as blue as the circle on a peacock's tail. He shouldn't be able to make a woman's heart turn over just by looking at her with half-humorous reproach. He shouldn't be so strong, especially when she felt so weak.

"Don't," she said, holding up her hands in defense. "I have to think . . ."

"What is there to think about?" he asked, taking her hands in his own. He held them lightly, swinging them a little between the two of them, like a rope bridge swaying in the breeze.

He smiled at her as if she were boundlessly entertaining and said, "It was just a kiss, after all. A nice, friendly kiss."

"Too friendly." Grace slipped her hands free, trying to deny she felt disappointed that he let them go so easily.

"Well, yes, maybe a little too friendly. Obviously, we need to practice to get it right. Maybe one more time and we'll have it exactly friendly enough."

"Handshakes are friendly, Mr. Lucas. Kisses are . . ."

"What? What are kisses, Grace?"

"Dangerous. Now, please. I have to milk the cow."

She realized he'd been advancing and she retreating ever since he'd released her hands. Now she stood in an empty stall with nowhere to go. The wall was at her back, the sides of the stall hemming her in. And Lucas stood before her, more dangerous to her peace of mind than a dozen Grupps.

The only thing to do was to be firm. She had to put him in his place, making it perfectly clear where she stood.

"Lucas," she began. Only it came out on a sigh, a sigh with a laugh behind it.

"Grace." He moved slowly, giving her plenty of time to evade him. Grace felt like a saint, captivated by a devil— an especially handsome and seductive one. Only who exactly was doing the tempting here?

She reached out to splay her hands across the firm contours of his chest, as she'd longed to do from the first moment she saw him without his shirt. At the same time, she tilted her head back, beckoning him nearer. Caution no longer appealed to her . . . he did.

Lucas put his hands on her waist and dragged Grace against him. He plunged into her waiting mouth with an abandon that he knew was too passionate, too soon. But she was so lovely and desirable, that he couldn't hold back. He felt like a starving man offered a single crust from a groaning banquet table. Who could blame him for snatching more?

She answered his hunger with a greed of her own. They clutched one another desperately, mouths meeting in an ardent dance. Grace dug her fingers into his shoulders, knowing she should be careful, that she would have to face the consequences of this moment. Then Lucas passed his tongue over the sensitive roof of her mouth. All her senses sang and she forgot the future.

Drawing back a scant inch, she sighed his name, and said, "Yes. Oh, my goodness."

Chick hadn't bothered much with kisses, except when they were first married. After a while, he was satisfied with a few dry pecks before moving on to what he termed "the heavy plowing."

Lucas, on the other hand, seemed to enjoy kissing for kissing's sake. Though his hands wove wonderful patterns on her back, and felt like heaven as they cupped her heavy head, he made no move to advance on the rest of her body. At first, she appreciated his restraint, then after a few more moments of bliss, Grace began to wonder why he didn't go further.

She pressed up to him shamelessly, her breasts flowering against his chest as she rediscovered the thrill of a strong male body next to her own. Her fingers moved to explore his neck, caressing the living strands of his waving black hair. "Lucas, please," she said.

His hands moved down over her skirt, lifting her up so she gasped as the full measure of his masculinity was revealed. "Like that?"

"Yes." She cried out when he found the spot in the side of her neck that sent sparkling pleasure flooding throughout her body. Heat spiraled and blossomed wherever he touched her, leaving her breathless. She kissed him hard, licking his lips as if she licked her own.

"Hey, Lucas!" someone called from outside the barn. "You in there?"

For a moment, neither of them understood that someone was about to break in on them. They were dazed by the sudden passion that held them enthralled. Only when the voice called again, more impatiently, did Lucas and Grace separate, so suddenly that it was as if each had thrown the other back.

Grace's lips stung; she knew they must be swollen from his fervent kisses. Her face flamed like a torch. She felt as if smoke must be spiraling from her clothes. Lucas was in better condition, though his hair was rumpled from her wandering hands and his expression was that of a man just run down by the noon express.

"It's Wyman," he said in a hoarse undertone.

"I . . . I know. You'd better answer him."

"Be out in a minute!" he called. "Grace . . . ," he started, reaching out toward her.

"No! We'll talk later. We have to talk."

"Hey, Lucas! Come on, man. I don't got all day."

Lucas didn't dare look at Grace another moment. She was as tousled and pink as if they'd just made love in the hay—which they would have done, if Wyman hadn't shown up at that exact moment. With a frustrated sigh, Lucas decided it was better that the marshal had appeared when he had, rather than in ten minutes' time.

The sight of the marshal, complete with a low-slung gun and a big bouquet of clove pinks clutched in his gloved hand, darkened Lucas's mood further. Wyman had walked out from town, as the dust on his boots showed. For the rest, his mustache was neatly trimmed and he wore a fancy gold-embroidered vest over his tan canvas shirt.

"Have you seen Mrs. Landers?" he asked, waving the bouquet.

"No, not for a while. Those for me?"

The marshal sniggered. "I ain't that kind."

Lucas compared himself to the marshal and came off

second-best, even if Mrs. Presby's late husband's work pants had no holes in the knees. He didn't own anything that wasn't his by charity. A black suspicion entered his head but he painstakingly dismissed it. No woman could kiss like that out of compassion alone. He ached to return to the sweetness of Grace's arms, but how could a prisoner rid himself of his guard?

Looking down at the house, Lucas saw someone move in the shadows under the overhanging eaves. "Give your flowers to Wenonah," he said. "She'll hand them over when Mrs. Landers comes back."

He started away from the barn, to give Grace time to recover her poise. His own desire had turned into an ache, which walking eased but only a little. He only hoped Grace realized that to come out of the barn after him would raise unwanted suspicions in Wyman's mind. Ever since they'd sparred at the jail, he had been genial. However, if he knew what he'd interrupted, that friendliness would evaporate like breath mist on a cold morning.

Wyman was charm itself to Wenonah, commiserating with her on her sprained wrist, while making it clear the flowers were not for her. He civilly hoped the girl would be able to attend the church social, and she said she wasn't sure.

On the way back to town, however, he said, "Maybe you can drop a hint in Mrs. Landers's ear, Lucas. She don't listen to me."

"What about?"

"She's storing up plenty of trouble for herself taking that girl in. Doesn't look right, nice little family with a half-breed living with 'em."

"I don't think Grace is likely to kick Wenonah out. I was there when— Damn!" Lucas stopped walking.

"What's up?"

"I forgot to get the pig. And the dress."

"You've got to dress a pig?" the marshal asked, his thick brows rising.

"It's a long story. Look, I've got to go back."

"Nope. Maybe tomorrow."

"Wyman . . ."

"Nope." The marshal tucked his hand under Lucas's elbow and towed him along. "I've got to be at a meeting of the town council in a little bit and I ain't got time to walk you out and back again."

"Then let me go alone." He saw the marshal was thinking it over. "Come on, Wyman. I'm not going to run out."

"Sure like to help you out, Lucas, but I don't see how I can. Don't care to be in contempt o' court—Judge Sterling charges mighty high for that."

"He won't know. Look, I give you my word."

Wyman laughed outright. "Last fella told me that was gone afore I said yes. Now, I don't want to have to draw on you so come on."

Lucas realized that nothing he could say would change Wyman's mind. He started toward town again, hoping Grace would understand. "It's going to be a little awkward, isn't it? I mean, the Grupp brothers and I all staying in the same jail. They didn't seem too happy to see me when I made out my statement."

"You don't have to worry about that."

"Why not? Am I sleeping somewhere else?"

"No, the whorehouse ain't got room—I checked." He laughed again, snorting.

"Then I guess I'd better sleep with one eye open tonight."

"You'll be safe enough so long as you stay in jail. I had to let the Grupp boys go."

"Go? After what they did?" Lucas couldn't believe the marshal wasn't joking.

"Well, what did they do? Try to make time with some little piece from Chainy Town? That's no crime. And as for you takin' 'em down . . . well, I managed to talk 'em out of charging you with assault. Took some doing too, I don't mind tellin' you."

"Thanks," Lucas said, still hoping this was some elaborate joke.

"Don't mention it."

Chapter
Twelve

Jasper Crowley waited a full hour after dark before letting Lucas out of jail. "I'll hurry back," Lucas said as he took the single step that was all the difference between freedom and imprisonment.

"Take your time; I got nothing else to do tonight." Jasper hung the heavy ring of keys on a nail within arm's reach of Lucas's cell wall. "Just lock it up again if I'm asleep or something when you get back. No point in letting Wyman know you've been out."

"I appreciate this."

The deputy shrugged. Unusual hostility still smoldered in his green eyes. Lucas had expected Jasper to rail against the marshal, but his anger had expressed itself by the ready way he had unlocked Lucas's cell door the moment he'd mentioned a task undone at Grace's farm.

"Watch out for them Grupp brothers," Jasper said. "They were talkin' mighty big against you for the way you cut 'em down. Seems you don't fight fair, Mr. Lucas, which means you didn't let them whip you to pieces."

"They got their licks in the first time we met. I don't think I owe them a second chance at me," Lucas answered, running light fingertips over his still bruised cheek. The color had already mellowed to a faint brown, nearly lost in his tan, but it still ached when he smiled. Funny how it hadn't bothered him at all while he was kissing Grace.

"You don't know them Grupps the way I do. I went to school with the younger two. Well, I went to school. Marv and Win sat in the back till the teacher said they were too big to go anymore."

"How old were they then? Ten?"

That brought a faint smile to the young deputy's lean face as he sat down in the marshal's well-sprung chair. "Just watch your back," he said. "I heard Caleb talking about carrying a knife from here on in."

"Did you tell the marshal that?"

"Sure, I told him. He told me not to listen to big talk, that I ought to know better, being from Missouri."

"Do you think he's from Missouri too?"

"Hell no. I don't know whereabouts he hails from. Can't you tell the difference between us by the way he talks? He's got some kind of a funny accent."

Lucas hadn't noticed. To him, Jasper and Wyman sounded about the same, a nasal quality he simply classified as "countrified." "What about me?" he asked. "Am I from Missouri?"

Jasper shook his head. "Nope, no way. You sound like . . ."

"Yes?" Lucas fixed his eyes squarely on the deputy.

"I don't care to hurt your feelings, Mr. Lucas."

"Hurt away."

"Well, sir, you sound like this actor that once come to town. They were only about three folks in their group and so everybody had to be more than one person. Whoa, but they had some strange 'uns. And this guy dresses up in a old bedsheet and plays somebody named 'Hamlet's Ghost.' That's who you sound like."

"Thanks. I think." It had been a long time since he'd read the history of the Melancholy Dane. Yet he could somehow imagine the part of Hamlet's father being read by a great dramatic actor, slightly gone to seed, whose only claim to adequate pay lay in his still-plummy voice. The picture was not encouraging.

"Thanks again," he repeated, still doubtful of the compliment. "I'll try not to wake you when I come back."

Jasper kicked his booted feet onto the scarred leather surface of the desk, narrowly avoiding the kerosene lamp. Crossing his ankles, he pushed the chair back at an angle until the top edge hit the wall. His posture slouching into comfort, he tilted the edge of his worn cowboy hat over his eyes. He began to breathe heavily.

Lucas reached the door before Jasper asked, still under his hat, "You say Wenonah's okay?"

"Just a sprain, the doctor said. She'll be good as new in a few days."

"Mighty beholden to you, Mr. Lucas. I won't be forgetting."

There rang in the young man's voice such gratitude and fellowship that Lucas went on his way strangely humbled. He had only meant to avenge his own wrongs, yet his impulse had won him a friend. A good and useful friend, if the ease with which Jasper had let him leave the jail meant anything.

Lucas wondered if Grace thought of him as a hero. He doubted it. Not after he had abused her hospitality this afternoon. Yet, he couldn't regret kissing her as he had. He'd wanted to kiss her in just that way from the first minute he'd laid eyes on her. But not even in his fantasies had he dreamed to meet with such an eager response.

He started whistling as he walked through the dark, a lively tune he seemed to know well. Its merriment reflected the state of his heart. A few short days ago, he'd been a drifter, lonesome and eyed with suspicion everywhere he went. Today, he had a friend, a job, some few possessions and he'd fought a good fight. Best of all, a beautiful woman had been warm and passionate in his arms.

"Not bad at all," he said, pausing to moisten his lips. Then he went on whistling, wondering all the while what tune this was, and where he'd heard it before.

Lucas stopped in the road outside of Grace's house to brush the dust from his pants. The scent of the honeysuckle was strong, the yellow-white flowers on the far side of the road reflecting the starlight. He combed his fingers through his hair before walking into the yard.

He'd have to see her, to get the dress she'd promised Wenonah's aunt, and wondered how she'd act toward him. Cool, he'd guess. Polite but definitely cool. She wouldn't want him to think that she was thinking about what had happened between them in the barn.

He looked with affection toward the dark building up the slight rise from the house. Then he stared harder, straining his eyes to penetrate the darkness. The moon was a mere fingernail crescent and the stars shed only a feeble glow. But the light that had shone out from the gaps in the barn door had been strong and clear.

It had also been very brief, a mere flash no more than that of the lightning bugs flickering like a thousand church candles in the leaves of the old apple tree. Maybe that's all it was. Nevertheless, he decided to take a closer look.

The hard earth was bare of twigs to crack beneath his feet but not of other things that might betray his presence. After he tripped over an axe handle, got entangled in the barrel hoop that Bart had been rolling, and trod on Georgette, sending her shrilling away like a roman candle, Lucas felt he had lost the element of surprise.

Yet, when Grace came out of the house, lamplight spilling around her, he shushed her natural exclamations. "There's somebody in the barn."

"I'll get my rifle!" she said loudly. She dashed back to the house. Lucas went on without her, hoping the scuffle would be over by the time she came back.

With delicate caution, Lucas pushed open the door. "All right. Come on out."

Only the silence of the night, alive with insect song and the cry of the nightjar, answered him. Feeling a little foolish, Lucas stepped over the threshold. The interior of the barn, all but lightless, seemed as huge and silent as a cathedral. It smelled of animals and hay dust. The cow shifted in her stall, her tail swishing against the wall seeming to echo like a gunshot.

"Lucas?" Grace entered the barn behind him. Instead of a black rifle, she held the bowl of a glowing lamp. The gentle light fell on her long, wavy hair that flowed over the tapestry shawl she held with one hand at her breast.

"Nobody here," he said. He noticed how her eyes fell

beneath his. To save her embarrassment, he turned away as if to continue searching the barn.

"What made you come up here?"

"I saw a light. Or maybe it was just my imagination. I don't know now."

Grace came to stand beside him, also peering about her. He caught the scent of jasmine and lemon. He realized her hair gleamed so bright a gold because she'd washed it. This was the first time he'd seen her without her hair scraped back into a bun. His hands fairly itched with the longing to stroke it and find out if it was as smooth and cool as it looked.

Sneaking a glance at her, he also saw that she wore a shawl because underneath she had on some sort of frilly top instead of her usual tight-collared blouse. Her elbows were bare, edged with white lace.

"It probably wasn't anything," Grace said, obviously hoping he'd agree with her.

"Probably not." He chuckled. "I blame Bart's ghost stories myself."

She gave him a wavering smile. "You should have asked Reg to keep you in jail. It's too new to have ghosts."

"Dead people don't bother me. It's the live ones that keep me up at night."

Perhaps she read something of his real meaning in his eyes, for when he stepped forward, his hand out, she backed hastily away. Her hand tightened on the gathers of her shawl. "Mr. Lucas, I just want to say . . ."

"You left off the 'mister' a moment ago."

"I'm sure I don't have to worry that what happened this afternoon will occur again. There was no reason for it to happen even once, after all. There can't be any reason for it to happen again."

"You mean, whatever curiosity we had about each other is satisfied?"

She seemed grateful that he understood so quickly. "That's it! It was just curiosity, wasn't it? And, as you say, it's satisfied."

"Well, my *curiosity* might be satisfied . . ." He knew that if he reached for her, she'd respond as powerfully as she had this afternoon. There was nothing in the world he wanted more. However, he wouldn't force her to give in to her lower self. "But there's more to this than just curiosity, Grace."

"Maybe so," she said, meeting his eyes steadily. "But curiosity is all that's going to be satisfied around here, Mr. Lucas."

Smiling, he dropped his hands in the act of reaching for her. He knew when he was defeated, at least for the moment. Only a cad would persist in pressing his attentions after so clear a rejection.

Yet he felt very strongly that Grace was hiding her feelings, as much from herself as from him. Maybe he'd have to keep his hands to himself, but it would be fun to go on teasing her, reminding her that, though their positions might be unequal, he was still a man and she a highly desirable woman. Maybe he was a little bit of a cad, too.

"Why did you come back, anyway?" Grace asked, walking away from him to pick up a mule collar that had fallen to the ground. She put down the lamp to use both hands.

Lucas came over to help her lift the heavy leather contraption onto a peg. He had to reflect a moment before he remembered. "Oh, I came back for that dress and pig you promised Wenonah's aunt."

"That was good of you. And of the marshal, to let you come back after dark."

"He didn't. Deputy Crowley let me out. I think he's not too pleased with the marshal right now. Not after he let the Grupp brothers go."

"He did what?"

"He let them out. He seemed to feel that no real harm had been done." He stepped back and looked at the collar. Rubbing the back of his neck, he said, "I could have sworn I hung this on the other side. . . ."

Grace grabbed his arm as a raucous noise split the night. Hens suddenly awakened, cackled and twittered, while a rooster let fly with a trumpet's clarion call. "He's down at the henhouse! Come on. Whoever's playing these games won't get away this time!"

"Grace! Wait—let me go first!" But she'd already run

out of the barn, her shawl flying to the ground. Without pausing or thinking, Lucas skimmed it up as he passed. Before he'd gone more than a dozen steps beyond the barn, he heard her scream with rage and disgust.

"Grace! My God! Grace!" he called, dropping the shawl, his heart almost ceasing to beat. Was some fiend strangling her?

He caught a glimpse of her waist-length wrapper, white as milk in the dim light. Her hands were over her face, her whole attitude one of deepest distress. But not a soul stood near her.

Wenonah and Bart, wild with excitement, ran out of the house at Grace's shriek. Toby loped along behind them. They ran full-tilt toward her, filling the air with broken shouts, only to stop as though they'd run into a brick wall. Toby shuffled backward so fast his back legs went out from underneath him.

"Pee-yew!" Bart shouted, instantly clapping his hand to his nose.

The breeze shifted and suddenly Lucas was inundated by a smell so foul, so pungent, that his eyes instantly filled with water. He wished he could breathe through his ears, rather than abuse his nose any further. "I guess it wasn't a ghost then?" he asked, squinting against the powerful stink of skunk.

"Very funny," Grace retorted. "Bart . . . back in the house. March! Wenonah, I'm going to need . . ."

"The vinegar jug," the girl said in a thin voice, obviously trying not to inhale. "Yes, I'll get it." She ran after Bart, too polite to hold her nose but patently glad to get away.

"What about me?" Lucas asked.

"You go . . . shut up the henhouse. I don't think he got away with any chicks." She advanced on him blindly, her face wet with the tears that streamed from her eyes.

Lucas dodged her, trying to shift around so that she was downwind of him. "Where are you going?"

"The creek, of course. I've got to bathe at once!"

"Wait. Wipe your face at least. You'll trip over something and break your neck."

"Just see to the hens, please, Lucas. I'll . . . I'll be all right." She sounded as if she were suffering from a heavy cold.

Shaking his head with commiseration, Lucas approached the small, narrow shed at the side of the barn. The skunk scent was strong here too, odorizing every breath, though it wasn't nearly as potent as in Grace's immediate vicinity. She must have received the full brunt of the cat-sized creature's defense tactic. The hens were still gabbling in alarm, while the rooster seemed to think it was morning.

"Hush, now," Lucas said to the male bird, who stood atop his harem coop crowing hoarsely.

Lucas opened the small door in the front of the coop, wondering if he was supposed to sing some sort of lullaby to put the hens back to sleep. They were milling about inside. One white-feathered hen, noticing the open door, made a dash down the studded ramp.

"Damn!" Lucas said, making a grab. Who knew a chicken could run so fast?

Keeping just enough presence of mind to close the henhouse door, to prevent a mass escape, he took off in chase of the white hen. It cackled like a madwoman as it swerved and dashed around the yard. Lucas began to wonder whether he'd need a special net.

Stopping to catch his breath, he saw a flash of white out of the corner of his eye. Spinning, he swooped up the creature, only to realize as his fingers closed on it that this animal had fur, not feathers.

With an indescribable yell, Lucas dropped the skunk, but not before he met with a blast of flatulence, the likes of which he'd never before encountered.

Grace plunged fully clothed into the smooth-slipping stream, unable to bear the smell of herself another second. The soft creek water flowed over her body like the breeze, the temperature as soothing as a bath.

If it weren't for the unholy reek she carried with her, Grace could have asked for no more pleasant diversion. The confusions that the day had brought seemed to drift away in the running water. She even gained a new perspective on those heated moments in the barn. Obviously, she simply needed to spend more time cooling off.

She only luxuriated for a few moments. Water alone would not remove the stench of skunk. Wenonah would be along in a moment with the brown jug of vinegar. In the meantime, she would take off her fetid clothes.

Grace struggled to push the cloth-covered buttons of her dressing sacque through the holes. She should have done it before getting wet, but that was past praying for now. Thank goodness she'd dropped her good shawl when she'd run out to the chicken coop. At least that wasn't spoiled. Chances were good everything she had had on would have to be buried and forgotten like a plague victim's grave.

Standing up, she wadded her sacque into a ball and flung it on the shallow bank. The creek didn't usually run this high in summer, so she was doubly glad of the recent rain. As she worked loose the fastenings of her skirt, she heard someone moving through the woods. For a girl with Indian blood in her veins, Wenonah moved more like a buffalo than a cunning deer.

"Over here, Wenonah!" Grace called. She desperately wanted to get a hold of that vinegar jug. Her skirt, heavy with water, followed her sacque to land with a liquid plop on the bank.

She had just wadded up her petticoat when Lucas appeared on the bank, jug in hand. "What are . . . ?" she began.

Then a whiff of him came toward her and she found herself laughing out loud.

"All very well for you," he said. "How was I supposed to know it was a double-barreled skunk?"

He too waded into the water fully dressed, the vinegar jug in his hand. Grace realized she wore nothing but her chemise and drawers, both of which were of white cotton. Fortunately, the night was quite dark, unlike Wednesday's blazing afternoon when she'd wound up under Mrs. Crowley's backyard pump.

Lucas must have been thinking of it too, for he said, "Nice night. I could wish for a little more light, though."

"I like it dark. You better get out of those things. They'll have to be washed too, before you can wear them again. Luckily, I've got plenty more vinegar down in the cellar."

"What am I supposed to wear in the meantime?"

"Surely Rena gave you more than one set of her late husband's things? Or you can always go back there and ask her for some more."

"I mean what do I wear when I get out of the stream?"

"Maybe Wenonah will be good enough to bring us a couple of horse blankets."

"I hope so," Lucas said glumly. "Right now I feel like part of a horse. The back part."

Laughing quietly, Grace reached out and took the vinegar jug from where it sat in the stream. Keeping her body under the water, she floated downstream over the smooth rocks that lined the narrow creek. Better for her peace of mind not to be too close to Lucas when he took his clothes off.

"What's the vinegar for?" he asked. "Wenonah just shoved it at me and ran back to the house. That girl can certainly move swiftly, can't she?"

"Wouldn't you?" Grace let that sink in. "The vinegar's to rinse away the skunk smell. But I don't understand how you got sprayed. They only have enough scent for one shot—or so I always heard."

"Maybe this was the mate to yours. I don't know. I mistook it for a chicken."

"A chicken? How on earth . . . Never mind." All the while, Grace had been hearing the plops of his clothes landing on the bank. Without thinking too much about it, she'd been counting down—shirt, pants, socks.

A shiver that didn't come from the water temperature passed through Grace. Lucas was naked and so was she, or very nearly. The night was dark. No one was likely to intrude on them. One thing a skunk's victim could count on was privacy.

But she knew she wasn't brave enough to seduce Lucas.

The consequences would be unavoidable. What if she got pregnant? And even if she didn't, how could she face two weeks of his knowing everything about her, from top to bottom and all points in between? It was difficult enough facing him with the memory of those searing kisses fresh in her mind. Grace moved a little farther downstream, licking the water from her lips.

"Well, I'm ready if you are," Lucas said.

"Huh?"

"Not that I think vinegar smells that much better than skunk."

"Oh, but you get to mix it with mud. That's the fun part."

"Fun? I seem to remember . . ."

"There's a big difference between getting muddy at home and in the middle of the street." It was a wonder he couldn't see her blush glowing in the dark.

She scrambled out onto the bank, pulling the jug up with her. There was plenty of mud by the bank, where part of it had crumbled away to make a low spot. She worked the cork stopper out of the narrow neck of the old crockery jug. Ordinarily, the vinegar made her wrinkle up her nose. Right now, though, she couldn't even smell it.

She poured it out into the small hollow and mixed up a smoothly glutinous mess. She began to spread it determinedly on her arms and chest.

"What are you doing way down here?" Lucas said quietly from above her.

Grace couldn't look—she didn't dare. So with hands that suddenly trembled she went on applying the paste. "I found a good place to make mud," she said, proud that her voice remained steady, despite knowing he stood there, naked.

"What do I do?"

"Rub it on all over," she said. "Be sure to glop it on thickest where he got you."

She felt his hands in the mud beside hers. She drew away quickly. "My husband told me once that he got sprayed right in the face. He was creeping through a cornfield, playing soldiers with some friends. Chick said he looked behind him to see if anyone was following him, and when he turned around the first thing he saw was the back end of a skunk."

Lucas chuckled. "What did he do?"

"Yelled, I guess. He told me the other kids let him win, sooner than smell him."

"I'm sorry I never met your husband. I think I would have liked him."

"He would have liked you."

"Really?" Lucas sounded pleased. She heard the squish of his hands once more sinking into the mud.

"Yes. Chick liked everybody. He never could refuse to offer a helping hand." Sometimes they'd fought about it, Chick's habit of giving more than they could afford. She tried not to dwell on those arguments, remembering instead that Brother Marill had told her Chick had stored up his reward in Heaven for the good deeds he'd done in his life.

Lucas said, "I have to admit, though. I'm jealous."

"Jealous? Of who?"

"Your husband. Strange, isn't it? To be jealous of a dead man."

She did not know how to reply. She thought of asking him why, but that way lay dangerous waters. Instead, she returned to the business at hand. The cool, juicy mud slipped and slid under her fingers as she spread it on her chest. Lifting her chemise, she applied the mud to her stomach, sucking in her breath sharply as her hand made contact with her skin.

"Are you okay?" Lucas asked.

"Fine!" she said, too quickly. "We better hurry up. I don't want the children to be alone for too long."

"They're all right. Wenonah's with them." His voice warmer than ever, he added, "You've been alone for a long time, haven't you, Grace? When did your husband die?"

"Two years ago. But you're wrong, if you think a woman with two children is ever alone. Believe me, one of them is always around."

"That's not what I meant, and you know it."

Grace began slopping the mud more quickly on her arms, wanting to get away from the allure of his deep sympathy. She'd noticed his wonderfully resonant speaking voice from the day they'd met. When compassion entered his tone as well, she came perilously close to hearing nothing else. Certainly the harsh voice of reason could hardly compete.

She reached around to dribble mud down her neck, making a little noise as she tried to bend her arm double.

Lucas moved behind her, kneeling on the ground. "Let me."

Before Grace realized his intention, he'd lowered the straps of her chemise so they fell in loops over her shoulders. Scooping up a handful of the mud, Lucas patted it onto her revealed skin. He began to rub the base of her neck with his thumbs. The rest of his warm fingers splayed over her collarbone in front.

She wanted to jerk away, but he held her gently yet firmly. "Wait . . ."

After a moment, the soothing motion of his hands began to relax her tired muscles. "Oh, my," Grace said, closing her eyes involuntarily. "That's . . . Oh, my, that's good!"

Finding herself making unthinkable noises beneath the delights his hands gave her, Grace pulled away abruptly. "That's enough. I don't think I got sprayed back there. . . . I'm just trying to cover all the possibilities."

"I'm pretty sure mine got me on the back," he said. "I turned away just as he sprayed me—but before I dropped him."

"Dropped him? You picked it up?"

"Remember I thought it was a chicken. Would you mind putting the mud on my back?"

Instinctively, her fingers curled in toward her palms. Touch him? Touch his naked skin? She couldn't! But on the other hand, he wouldn't be in this fix if it weren't for her. "All right," she said, pretending confidence, and felt or heard him turn his back.

Counseling herself to be calm, Grace dipped up some

mud. Hesitating, she tried twice to clap it on his shoulders and couldn't get her courage up.

"Don't worry," he said. "I'll try not to enjoy myself."

Biting her lip to keep from laughing, she flung the mud hard against his body with a sloppy whack.

"Hcy!" he said, starting up.

"Sit down and let me finish."

"Throwing it?"

"No. Here." She laid the next handful neatly on his other shoulder. Then, trying to control her shaking, she placed her palms against his skin. Rubbing lightly, she worked the mud in.

"A little harder," he murmured. "Purely for medicinal reasons, of course."

She obliged willingly. His back was a topography of muscles and hollows, his skin supple and smooth. Her hands slipped easily in the mud. Grace tried to think of something distracting, like the social tomorrow. As she continued her task, however, she began to feel as though she were slightly drunk. She wanted to do irresponsible, foolish things.

As her nails skimmed lightly down his noticeable ribs, Lucas groaned as though in pain. He grabbed her hands and pulled them around in front of him. Grace found herself brought hard against his back, the mud on both their bodies squishing together. Her hands held against his heaving chest, she could feel his heart's turbulent beat.

"That's enough," he said raggedly.

"Now . . . now we rinse off in the creek."

"Good. I'm ready for a cold bath." He let go of her hands and Grace moved away. Their bodies separated with a sound like a wet kiss. It made her laugh, nervously.

She smeared the goo on her face and over her hair, rubbing it in well. Glad again that it was dark, for she knew she must look a sight to frighten horses, she entered the water again, letting the half-dried mud on her body swirl away. Rising up, she sniffed at the crook of her arm. Her nose was used to the smell now, but she hoped that the pungency had faded.

"Now we rinse off with the plain vinegar and go back

and forth between it and the water until we smell human again."

"Ladies first," he said.

The stinging liquid was cold. She shuddered and shook as she held the jug high and let the stream hit her body. It was some consolation that Lucas suffered the same reaction.

After another rinse in the creek, Grace pulled a hank of her hair forward and smelled it. The fragrance of her shampoo was long gone, replaced by a faint hint of polecat. "One more time for me," she said.

"What do you say I go get the horse blankets?"

"Okay," she agreed eagerly. Anything to get him away from here and her foolish impulses. Her hands still tingled, remembering as if by themselves the feel of his body. At least, he hadn't realized how close she had been to writhing against his back like an abandoned wretch.

She had not counted on his coming back with the lamp.

"Oh, my God," she said as she saw the gleam bouncing among the trees. She couldn't snatch up her clothes for shelter; that would undo all the good of the vinegar and mud. Besides, nature itself revolted against touching those foul-smelling garments. Grace considered dashing into the woods and returning in the dark to the house, but with her luck she'd probably break her leg on a tree root or something.

Lucas came out of the trees, a blanket tossed Indian-style over his shoulder. Another one was wrapped around his hips, low-slung beneath the sprinkling of hair that ran over his lean stomach. She admitted silently that she was disappointed to see that he had covered his lower body. It was disloyal to think of Chick at this moment, Chick with his belt always slipping beneath his slight potbelly.

Grace clung to her dignity, glad of her chemise and drawers. The half-dry, clinging cotton stuck to every outline of her body, but at least she was covered. She knew the pitiless lamplight must show him everything. Nevertheless, she went on pretending he couldn't see anything. Surely he'd go along with the charade.

But his eyes stole her confidence. They lingered over

her contours even while he offered her the other blanket. "Thank you," she said stiffly.

"Can I help you?"

"I can manage, I think." She swirled the fabric around her body, catching it under her arms. The smell of mule was infinitely preferable to that of skunk, even sweaty mule. She gathered in the last corner and tucked it in over her left breast. Water dripped from her hair onto the blanket.

"You look like a Grecian goddess," Lucas said.

"I feel like a wet mess."

"Nobody would guess. I've noticed, Grace, that you do have a talent for coming through trials smelling like a rose."

"A rose is the last thing I smell like."

He laughed. After a moment, Grace laughed too. It was absurd to feel so easy with him now, when a moment since she'd been jumpier than a rabbit with a nervous twitch.

Smiling at him, she said, "I guess we'll just leave our clothes where they are for now. No creature in its right mind would bother them tonight."

"And tomorrow? Will you try to wash them?"

"Maybe I'll give them a few days," she said, wrinkling her nose. "Being even this close to them is a little much." Yet she was oddly reluctant to leave.

Lucas reached out and took her hand. Grace left it in his for a moment, then pulled away. He said her name in so low and caressing a tone that she swayed toward him without thinking. At once, however, she commanded herself and turned away.

"Grace," he said again. Two strides brought him next to her. The lamplight shown on his face, alive with serious purpose. "Grace, stop a minute."

"There's nothing more to say except good night."

"I have something else to say."

"I don't want . . ."

Then she was in his arms, his fingers entangling in the wet strands of her hair, his other arm tight around her waist. It was as if the blankets weren't even there. His body branded hers as he bent to kiss her.

Grace forced her head away from his restraining hand. Bowing her head, she flinched away from his embrace. Instantly, Lucas let her go.

"I can't," she said, not defiantly, but miserably. "I just can't take the risk, Lucas."

"If you mean pregnancy, I can—"

"No, I don't mean that. I mean . . . oh, a lot of risks. Like what people would say, and what they wouldn't say. And more . . . For goodness' sake, you don't even know who you are! You could have somebody waiting for you. A sweetheart . . . a wife."

"I've thought of that, Grace. All I can say is that I don't *feel* like there's someone waiting. If there was, if she was like you, I'd be straining every muscle to get back to her. I would be on my way already."

"But you don't know there's not. Don't you see? I can't risk falling in love with you." Even as she said it, she knew it was too late. Sometime during the last three days, maybe even when she'd first seen him unconscious in an alley, maybe when he'd piled into the three Grupp brothers without a second thought, Grace had fallen in love with Lucas, fallen past all hope.

Chapter
Thirteen

Callie didn't turn over when her faintly malodorous mother climbed into the big bed with her. But as if some hint carried across the border into her dreams, the little girl kicked out as soon as Grace got in. No matter where Grace lay, even at the extreme outside edge, Callie snuggled close and then kicked. Between those little feet in her side and thinking of Lucas, Grace hardly slept.

Sitting in the baking hot interior of the church, she found her head nodding, her plain bonnet sliding forward on her smooth hair. The perpetual buzzing of flies in the window seemed to sing to her of sleep. Brother Marill had a cold in the head, so his normally powerful tones were dull and monotonous. Just as Grace's eyes were closing inexorably, she saw Bart stealing his hand into the pocket of his Sunday pants.

Instantly, all her mother instincts came alert. She didn't know what he was about to do, yet she felt certain it was something she should stop. Therefore she was baffled when all Bart brought forth was a triangular piece of paper. It looked so harmless.

However, he peered around furtively as soon as the paper was in his hand. His instantly angelic smile when he caught her eye started those alarm bells ringing again.

"What's that?" she whispered.

In the pew in front of them, Mrs. Chasen, pious and elderly, turned her head and gave her an admonishing glance. She had already sniffed the air in a meaningful manner as soon as the Landers entered the pew along with Wenonah. This time, Grace raised her hand and wriggled her fingers in a little wave. Mrs. Chasen faced front again. Grace repeated her question, her voice so low as to hurt her throat.

"Just paper, Ma."

"Where'd you get it?"

"Lucas."

"What is it?"

"Just . . . trash."

Now Mr. Chasen, who was notoriously hard of hearing, turned to glare at them. Grace met his eyes steadily, her face intentionally expressionless. The Chasens had never had any children, so they had no idea what it was like trying to keep them still. Even Callie swung her feet and wriggled today.

Grace knew they weren't being too loud, for heavyset Mr. Dexter, next to Mrs. Chasen, didn't rouse from his sedate doze.

"Let me see," Grace said, holding out her hand. With a shrug, Bart handed the paper over.

It was cunningly folded. When Grace released it, it opened into a not unpleasing winged shape, like a stylized bird. She recognized it as a sheet of her best writing paper. It was blank on both sides. She handed it back to Bart. He gathered it together so it was once more a triangle. "Put it away," she said.

"It's just trash."

"Then throw it away."

Bart grinned impishly. "Okay." He raised his arm high and brought it down, releasing the paper with a snap of his wrist.

Instantly, an astonishingly loud pop disrupted the congregation. Women gasped in surprise while men started out of their seats. Reg Wyman leaped to his feet, his hand going under his coat for the weapon he'd left at the door. Nervous Lily Mae Foster shrieked and swooned against the stalwart shoulder of her beau. Mr. Dexter woke up with a loud snort, smacking his lips, and Brother Marill broke off his sermon to look out, his pinkish eyes confused. Chatter broke out among the parishioners, shocked surprise the main theme.

Grace grabbed Bart by the slack of his sleeve, tugging

him to his feet. With a whispered word to Wenonah to watch Callie, Grace began to hustle her son from the pew. Fortunately, they were on the aisle. Knowing everyone was staring and talking about them made her cheeks glow red as coals. "Dust that boy's jacket for him," Mr. Chasen advised loudly.

As she passed Lucas, standing at the back with Deputy Crowley to guard him, she met his eyes. The blue sparkled wickedly as he grinned. She wanted to challenge him there and then, but enough tongues were wagging.

When he winked, however, a bubble of laughter floated up from deep inside her. She smiled back at Lucas and had the satisfaction of seeing him blink. Bart towed her out through the half-open doors into the sunshine beyond.

Grace choked as she let Bart run down the church steps ahead of her. When she reached the bottom, she couldn't hold back her laughter. She knew people at the back of the church must have heard her. After the first burst, she managed to quash it down until she thought of poor Mr. Dexter and the look on his face—exactly like a trout frightened to the surface of a lake.

When she mastered herself, she crossed to where her son—never one to worry about the future—was teasing a beetle in the shade of the church's prized elms. Bart looked up without a care. Grace felt a little proud of that, for she'd never hit him yet, though a few times she'd lost her temper with him. She hoped her mother would remember her opposition to physical discipline when Bart and Callie went to stay with her in Sedalia.

"What was that thing?" she asked.

"Lucas calls it a popper. Gee, Ma, didn't it make a bully noise though?"

"Wonderful. When did Mr. Lucas teach you that . . . interesting novelty?"

"Yesterday while he was eating dinner."

"Anything else?"

"Sure, some dandy little things . . . I forget what you call 'em . . . but you twist up some paper and throw 'em down and they shake all over the place. We had to pitch 'em out a tree, though Lucas says a second-floor window's better. Lucas says—"

"I see I'll have to have a long talk with Mr. Lucas."

"If you want. Here he comes." Bart lifted his chin toward the church. The congregation sang the soaring finish of an old hymn, the wheezy organ drowning the words.

Grace turned, the box pleats around the hem of her best poplin skirt skimming the grass. Lucas stood on the church steps, shading his eyes against the bright sun as he looked for them. His smile when he saw her was half-shamed, half-hilarious.

She tried to be serious, but it was no good. Just seeing him made her want to smile. Only after she'd started toward him did she think that if he remembered how to make a boy's toy, he might have remembered other things. Why hadn't he told her?

They met in the middle of the green. "So I have you to blame," she said, knowing her eyes twinkled.

"Guilty as charged." He too seemed to be having trouble controlling his expression. His smile warmed her more thoroughly than the bright sunshine.

"Bart tells me you remembered how to make several interesting toys. I guess I don't have much writing paper left."

"Maybe not much. Do you mind?"

She shook her head. "I'm just glad something's come back to you. Have you remembered anything else?"

"I've been too busy learning new things to worry much about the old." He reached out and took hold of her hand, lightly playing with her fingers. "I haven't remembered any other women in my life, if you're curious."

"Why should I be?" Grace tugged her hand free. "Besides, I know of one."

"You do?"

"Yes. Someone named . . . Margot?"

She turned on her heel, hoping he'd follow. But before he'd done more than say her name on a note of exasperation, the church doors were flung open from within and the townspeople came streaming down the steps. The ladies were adjusting their hats and the men were tugging at their once-a-week suits. Children, their spirits more uplifted by the glorious weather than by any sermon, ran free over the grass. Bart was instantly the center of a crowd of youngsters, all demanding the secret of his "popper."

Callie ran to her mother, her beloved doll flopping behind her, followed more sedately by Wenonah. Grace saw Jasper Crowley tip the brim of his hat to the girl and her cool nod in return. Grace wished she could be as aloof toward Lucas as Wenonah was to the man she cherished.

Dr. Birkins and his wife came over to Grace, the doctor still sniggering in his mustache. "That Bart—a scamp to the end!"

"I felt for you so," Kay Birkins said. "Children can be such a trial."

"And such a pleasure," Grace added, patting Callie on the shoulder.

"Come on and get your basket," the doctor said to his wife, touching her elbow. "I swear Brother Marill's sermons seem twice as long when I know there's your fried chicken waiting at the end of it."

A slow, congested voice from behind them said, "I find that to be true myself."

With welcoming smiles, the three people turned to face the preacher. Brother Marill was a tall, rail-thin man whose black suit and stooped shoulders made him seem even more cadaverous. But behind his dour outside lay a warm heart and a profound understanding.

"I hope you'll be kind enough to save a piece of your chicken for me, Mrs. Birkins. It may be a little while before I can get to it. We seem to have every member of our flock with us today."

"Good preaching draws them in," the doctor said with a wink.

"I hardly think it's my preaching that has called them out. More likely, it's the social. The preaching's just an extra."

"I'm sorry about your cold," Grace said. "There's nothing worse than a cold in the summertime."

"Here's where we leave," Dr. Birkins said. "If a man won't take my advice when he pays for it, he sure won't take it at a church social."

"Doctor?" said Callie in a small voice.

The doctor leaned low. "Yes, honey-lamb?"

"Can I have some pep'mint?"

Dr. Birkins laughed. "After dinner," he said. "Wouldn't you like a drumstick first?" Callie bit her lip as she thought it over and then nodded. Dr. Birkins glanced up at Grace. "Mind if I take this little lady along?"

At her nod, he swung Callie up to his shoulder. "Do you know the story of the Frog Prince? Well, once upon a time . . ."

"Oh, Daniel," said his wife. "Not those old fairy tales."

"Hey, I've got to practice for when that boy of ours gives us some grandchildren, don't I? Though you're too pretty to be a grandmother," he added teasingly while Kay shook her forefinger at him.

"Once upon a time . . . ," Callie prompted.

"Oh, yes. Well . . ."

Grace looked up to share her amusement with Brother Marill. Only his long face was uncommonly serious. Taking both of her hands in his cool ones, he said, "I heard what you did for that poor vagrant. It was truly an act of mercy."

"Not in the least. I needed someone to work for me. And he couldn't refuse just because I couldn't pay him."

Brother Marill nodded and released her hand. "Nevertheless, you have a good heart, Mrs. Landers. Tell me, is the unfortunate fellow with us today? Perhaps a few words from me . . ."

Grace tightened the ribbons under her chin. Obviously Brother Marill, with no wife or daughter to give him the freshest gossip, hadn't heard of Lucas's transformation from a shabby beggar into the handsomest man in Ogden. How could she adjust his picture of Lucas without giving her feelings away? On the other hand, if anyone would understand her confusion it would be this gentle clergyman.

His next words were almost frighteningly to the point. "How long has it been since Chick left us?"

"It was two years ago in March." Where was Lucas? She didn't see him in the crowd. Maybe he'd gone to get the basket of biscuits from the wagon. Though she couldn't see Lucas, she accidentally caught the eye of Reg Wyman. He tossed up a hand in greeting and began making his way across the crowded green toward her.

"That's a long time to be alone."

"Well, I have the children," she said, and smiled remembering last night when she'd had a similar conversation. Even kindly Brother Marill would be shocked if he knew the circumstances under which she'd last discussed her solitary state.

"Children are a gift from God. But I wonder whether it is time for you to consider a new tie. After all, men and women were not meant to live alone."

"You live alone," she said, glancing up into his face. To her surprise, his skin was oddly flushed and he had some difficulty meeting her steady gaze. A dreadful suspicion seized hold of Grace. Brother Marill couldn't possibly be working up to a proposal, could he? No, it was impossible.

He opened his mouth, as though to speak, but fumbled in his pocket instead. Pulling out his white handkerchief, he jerked to the side and sneezed violently. Blowing his prominent nose with a vibrant blast, he sniffed and stuffed the hanky back in his pocket.

"Yes, I'm alone too. Mrs. Landers . . . Grace . . . it occurs to me that . . ."

"Great sermon, Marill," the marshal said, stepping between Grace and the preacher.

"Thank you; I'm glad you liked it," Marill said automatically. "Grace, if we could talk later . . ."

"Of course," she said, never so glad to see Reg Wyman before. As a result, her greeting might have been a little too enthusiastic. Certainly he seemed to beam after hearing it.

"That boy of yours needs a good scare," he said, after explaining that he hadn't really been all that startled by

Bart's little prank. "Should I tell him I'll throw him in my jail if he don't straighten up?"

"Please don't! I don't believe in frightening children into being good."

"Hey, hey," the marshal said, holding up his hands as if in surrender. "Just kiddin'. 'Sides, it's not like takin' a strap to the kid."

"Oh, I don't know," Brother Marill said. " 'Spare the rod; spoil the child.' "

"My ol' man beat me regular and . . . I mean, you're right, Marill. A lick of the strap now and again kinda gets a kid's attention."

Grace found it increasingly difficult to be mannerly while two ignorant bachelors discussed child-rearing techniques. Looking around, she saw Lucas standing near the trees. He laughed suddenly and she smiled until she saw he was talking to Rena Presby. She'd sat in the front of the church, fine as a peacock in a blue silk dress, her chestnut curls hardly hidden under a dainty hat no bigger than a teapot lid.

Grace instantly looked the other way and saw that Mr. Kent and his lovely young wife were coming up to say a few words to Brother Marill. Only the banker addressed Marshal Wyman first.

"Say, Reg, you've got to do something about Roy Summers."

"What's he done now?"

"He came in yesterday, demanding all the money in the family's account."

"Can't do nothing 'bout that. Law says that money's his."

Grace shook her head. Roy Summers was a town disgrace. He'd abandoned his wife and children to go live with a loose woman in Chainy Town. He was drunk half of the time and quarrelsome whether he'd been drinking or not. His poor wife, Glenda, worked her fingers to the bone with washing and cooking for strangers, anything to keep her four kids shod and fed. She saved every penny she could, determined to move from a shoddy boardinghouse to her own home. Then her wastrel husband would clean out their account anytime he felt like it.

"I know," Mr. Kent was saying, "I don't have any problem with giving him the money. It's that he wouldn't leave after I gave it to him. He just kept hanging around, sharpening that big knife he carries. He scared my poor wife half to death when she came to meet me."

"What can I do about it?" Reg asked, shrugging his shoulders. "He's got his rights."

"Could you come around next Saturday? Roy shows up about the same time every week."

Brother Marill said, "Perhaps I should be there too. After all, he should be brought to see the error of his ways. A man belongs with his wife and family." He gave Grace a melting look, blinking his pinkened eyes at her, but she hardly noticed.

"I doubt Glenda Summers would thank you for interfering," she said. "I'm sure she prefers he continue living with his doxy in Chainy Town to living with her."

"Why, Mrs. Landers!" Brother Marill said, shocked.

Grace turned with a jerk to Mr. Kent. "And you should have a problem with him taking that money! Mrs. Summers slaves for it, and he takes it to spend on that same doxy."

"The law says the money's his," the banker said, shrugging. "I can't go against the law."

"Who wrote that law?" Grace asked rhetorically. "Some man somewhere. Some man who never had his hands bleed from washing clothes in lye soap and washing soda. Some man who never had his back ache from hanging laundry or saw his children cry because their father has gone off with all the money again. Some law! It should be smashed for the cage it is!"

Mr. Kent glanced at Reg as if to defer to his greater expertise in dealing with hysterical women. "Well, now," the marshal drawled. "I don't say it's fair, but the world's not fair, now is it?"

"No, the world's not fair," Mr. Kent agreed. The preacher nodded.

For a moment, it looked as if one of the men would pat

her on the head and tell her to run along and play. Grace's hands and voice shook. "I get mighty tired of folks saying the world's not fair like that's supposed to make me feel better. Why isn't it fair? Because decent folks won't stand up to see that it is. Married women should keep our wages in our own hands. We should be able to sign a contract in our own right, without a husband or father's countersignature. We should have the right to sue for custody of our children and . . ."

Oh, what was the use? The men only shifted their weight uncomfortably, like boys eager to slip away from school to play.

Young Mrs. Kent grasped her husband's arm for protection and possibly reassurance. "But the Summers are just one family, Mrs. Landers. Most men aren't like that."

"Oh, no? Tell me, do you ask your husband for money?"

The pretty brunette glanced adoringly into her husband's face. "No, he gives me a weekly allowance for the housekeeping."

"And she does a fine job of keeping within her budget."

"Well, once we did quarrel a little . . ."

"Only because you'd been such a silly little juggins about that wallpaper." He smiled fondly down on her. "And if there's something special that she needs a little extra for, well, she lets me know what it is in the cleverest ways." He might have been speaking of his dog or cat.

"Oh, no, I never have to ask for money," Mrs. Kent declared again, but a little wrinkle had come into her smooth forehead, like the shadow of a cloud over a sunny day.

Grace shook her head again, more in resignation than anger. What had she been thinking? All the girlish fantasies she'd been weaving around Lucas were a waste of her time. She'd never marry again. To be another person's chattel, to have to dissemble and scheme to get what she wanted instead of just doing what she pleased—never again!

Looking around at the men, so uncomfortable when she spoke her mind, so easy when Mrs. Kent had shown her femininity, Grace said, "It's almost time to eat. You'd better get in line."

Excusing herself, she walked away. Mrs. Kent caught her up in a moment. "I felt so sorry for you," she said, dropping her voice to a confidential whisper. "I know what it is to be out of sorts. Is it that time of the month?"

About an hour later, after there was nothing left of the food except bones, even the children were too stuffed to run around. Fathers lay on the grass, their red or blue spotted bandannas over their faces. Boys leaned back on their elbows, their legs sprawling any old way on the grass, talking of this and that or just contemplating the sky. The littlest ones napped under their mothers' parasols, like baby birds beneath so many bright flowers.

The young girls wove listless daisy chains, while their older sisters counted petals according to the ancient prophecy—he loves me; he loves me not! Mothers washed dishes, packed baskets up or stood and talked, taking in the news of the town and offering good advice to those with the swollen midriffs and aching backs of pregnancy.

There'd be games later, songs and catches. Probably young Zachary Smoot would recite Emerson's "Excelsior" as he had when awarded a medal last year from the district superintendent of schools. And then they'd go home in the near-dark, Brother Marill's final prayer fading into the twilight, each family content or sorrowful in its own way.

Grace stayed apart from it all, even while Callie napped in her lap and Bart crept nearer to hear what the big boys were saying. Nearby, Wenonah shared a blanket with Mrs. Crowley, though Grace saw that the girl did not sleep, but watched Jasper, who sat on the grass and smoked his pipe.

And Lucas? She hadn't seen him since she'd made her outburst on women's rights. Now she could smile at her own earnestness. She might as well have saved her breath. Though many states in the northeast had long since passed laws protecting the property of married women, Missouri showed no interest in such legislation. Most of the states that had sided with the Confederacy, either openly or in secret, had delayed following the north in this. There'd been too many other pressing needs in the ten years since the war.

Once, before her marriage, she'd even written a letter to a state representative, indicating her dislike, after the newspapers reported sympathetically on his ridiculing of a similar bill. The man had never even replied. She'd not been too surprised when she learned that the measure had been buried under a load of derision.

And then she'd married. Chick had always been ready with a joke when she started to talk about politics or the drive to get women the vote. Wanting to please him, she'd soon stopped talking about it. Then the children had come. Her interest in politics had been smothered in diapers.

Callie moved restlessly. "Ma, I want to go home."

"Do you, sweetheart? They'll be playing games later on."

The little girl wrinkled her nose. "Baby games. Let's go home."

Wenonah sat up in an easy, graceful motion that Jasper seemed to fully appreciate. Grace noticed that his eyes never left the young girl, at least so long as she wasn't looking at *him*. She put her hand over the tight bandage on her right arm. "Yes," Wenonah said. "I should like to go myself."

Even Bart didn't seem too reluctant to leave. Apparently the dirty looks he'd been collecting from the grown-ups were more powerful than the admiration he'd found among the youngsters.

"Hey, where's Lucas?" he asked as he climbed into the back of the wagon.

"He doesn't have to come with us," Grace said. "It's Sunday. He can take the day off."

Grace wondered again what had happened to Lucas. Then she determined to put him out of her mind. If he was off with Rena Presby, that was none of her business. Just let him show up to work on time and do what she told him to do. If he got fresh, she'd soon put him in his place. There'd be no more passionate kisses in the barn or anywhere else. That was final!

Chapter
Fourteen

Two weeks later, early in the misty morning, Grace sat on the back porch steps, a worn tin bowl nestled in the swag of her skirt between her knees. Beside her was a basket of green beans. She snapped the ends off with crisp flicks of her wrist. In the same motion, she let them drop into the bowl. The task took little of her thought, except when she discarded any bean that didn't snap at a touch.

The scene she looked on had changed tremendously. She could gaze at her yard now with satisfaction. No longer littered with odds and ends, feathers and warped pieces of lumber, the grass had been cleanly scythed. The border ties once more marked the boundaries of her garden, which had never been so tidy. All the weeds had been pulled and the sprawling bean vines restaked to neat poles.

Grace wiped her hands on her apron and smoothed back her hair. She'd taken to getting up earlier in the day, for the heat had become so intense by noon that it was all she could do to move. The children felt it too, becoming listless and complaining ceaselessly. Poor Toby spent his days under the wagon, his tongue out. Georgette had disappeared down cellar last Wednesday and hadn't been seen since.

Only Lucas seemed unaffected now by the heat, as if his touch of sun had vaccinated him against more intense attacks. Grace had become almost used to the sight of him, laboring in the yard, his chest bare to the waist. Almost used, but not quite. She still couldn't trust herself to look anywhere but in his eyes when she spoke to him.

Despite that, she felt more at ease with Lucas since

she'd made her resolution. His ready humor, his sympathy and above all his willingness to work hard made him frighteningly indispensable. Grace had already begun to wonder how she'd get along without him when the time came, as it soon would, that he'd be free to go.

Reg Wyman had stopped escorting Lucas to and from the property a few days earlier. So when he appeared at the end of the drive mounted on his gray horse, Grace was surprised. "Where's Lucas?" she asked, putting the bowl of beans aside.

"Still asleep, I'd say," Reg answered, dismounting. He came up to the porch, his hat in his hand. Grace noticed that his hair was slick with brilliantine, and a waft of Florida water drifted toward her. He wore a fancy embroidered vest under his freshly pressed tweed coat. The only flaw in his dandyism was the long black gun he wore strapped to his right side. Even it, however, gleamed with oil and polishing.

Grace stood up, clutching the bowl to her stomach. Though his eyes didn't rake her as if he were stripping her naked in his mind, he always seemed to stand too close to her. She either must stand her ground, or be backed against a wall.

"What can I do for you, Marshal?"

"Lucas tells me you're off to visit your ma. You gonna be gone long?"

"I'm not sure yet. The children have been begging to stay in Ogden until after the fourth, but it's too hot."

"I've never heard Sedalia is all that much cooler."

"My mother's house is made of brick with a heavy slate roof. She's got some old oaks in the yard that shade it. It always seems cooler there. And there's a big fair every summer. I think the children will enjoy that."

"What about you?"

"Oh, I'll be back before then. It depends . . . there's so much still to do here. Lucas has been such a help, but . . ."

"There's plenty of folks who'd be willing to help you, if you'd give 'em a chance." He fixed his big brown eyes upon her with a warmly wistful expression.

"It's good to have friends," Grace said. Reg stepped up onto the porch and she backed up farther. Why could she never take his friendliness at face value? Why did she always feel uneasy when he was near? She felt uneasy around Lucas too, but that was different. She strove to keep herself under control, never fearing that he would lose his.

"Course friends sometimes have to say stuff they'd rather not. Like a friend would tell you what they're sayin' about you in town."

"Oh?"

"I don't pay talk much mind. I got too much else to be thinkin' on, but folks are kinda curious why you went and took on that half-breed gal."

"You may tell them from me . . . ," Grace began hotly.

Reg Wyman held up one of his hands, the bright studs on the back of his black leather glove catching the early light. "I know, I know. I ain't got no quarrel with you, there. Didn't I hire her to clean the jail? Not many would of done it, but I did. She's a pretty little thing—nice to have a piece of calico around the place. Being a lonely bachelor and all . . ."

Grace stiffened, warned by his softening voice and the brightening gleam in Reg's eyes. Brother Marill had never come around for their little "talk," perhaps frightened off by her vehemence at the social. If only it had served to alarm the marshal too!

"Speaking of Wenonah," Grace said, turning her head as if to listen. "I think I hear her waking up. I'll just—"

He reached out as though to block her between his arms. Grace gave him such a discouraging look that *he* backed away. He ran his hand over his mustache, smoothing the prickling hairs. "Ah, why you gotta be so unfriendly, Grace? Don't you know I . . . I'm crazy about you."

He reached out to grab her hand. His glove was hot and softened by sweat. Grace pulled loose, rubbing her hand to rid it of the memory of his touch. "Let's not start this," she said, meeting his eyes resolutely. "I'm not interested in anything but friendship. I thought I had made that clear."

"Oh, you didn't mean any of that talk at the social. I know your kind of woman. You put up a big front, pretending you're not interested just to draw the fellers in. It worked, honey; you don't have to pretend anymore."

Grace couldn't believe his conceit. She'd known he was fond of himself—his fancy clothes proved that—but that he would be so blind to reality as to think she was *flirting* when she'd meant every word she'd said passed all bounds.

"Look, Marshal—"

"Reg . . ."

"Marshal, please believe me when I say—"

"You need a man around, Grace. You've managed with Lucas, but he'll be gone soon. You need another husband. Why not me?" Once again he tried to catch her hand. Grace lifted it away, her forehead wrinkling.

"I don't need a husband," she said. "Thank you for the offer but I really don't think—"

"I've done more for you than you know."

"Have you really?"

"Sure. Just think how folks'd be talkin' if I let Lucas stay here at night, like he asked."

"When did he do that?"

"Sunday. He said he thought somebody'd been in your barn and asked if it was okay for him to sleep out in it. Course I told him to forget it. You don't have to thank me. I was just thinkin' of your good name."

"Thank you," she said sarcastically.

"My pleasure," he replied with a smile, her tone making no visible impression.

"And what about the noises in my barn?" Grace asked.

"You said yourself it's more'n likely a wild animal. Maybe it's a skunk or something."

Grace shifted uneasily at the mention of that animal, feeling as if an old wound troubled her. She'd had to bury everything she and Lucas had been wearing that evening. Not half a jug of vinegar had served to wash the smell out.

Reg Wyman slyly poked his gloved forefinger into her

side. Grace flinched away. He said, "You don't believe in ghosts, do you? But if you're scared, I'll be more than pleased to come out here while you're gone and keep an eye on the place. It'll be the least I can do."

"No, Marshal. That won't be necessary. I doubt I'll be staying with my mother for more than a night or two." She hoped she'd be able to stand it that long.

"But you're gonna be leavin' the little ones in Sedalia for a while, huh?"

"That's right. Mother can't get too much of their company."

"You know," Reg said, walking his fingers up her arm. "It's gonna be awful lonely out here without 'em."

Grace sidestepped around him. "Not at all," she said brightly. "Wenonah will be with me. And Lucas, of course."

"A half-breed girl and a drifter? That's not much company. I'll be happy to come up here any ol' time!"

As quickly as a striking snake, Reg had his arm around her waist, pulling her against him. Grace kept the bowl of green beans wedged between their bodies, while the marshal strained over it to attempt to plant a kiss anywhere on her face. Grace tossed her head, leaning hard against his restraining arm, trying both to remain untouched by the marshal's wet lips and to free herself.

"God!" With a violent twist of her whole body, she was free. The bowl crashed to the floor, bean pods skittering across the worn gray floorboards. Reg stumbled backward, his chest rising and falling in panting breaths and a queer glassy look in his staring eyes.

"Are you out of your mind?" she demanded, wiping her cheek with the back of her hand. Though he hadn't actually kissed her, she felt soiled. "I said no!"

The strange look faded in his eyes. She saw his Adam's apple rise and fall as he swallowed. "Grace, I'm sorry. I just thought . . . Well, you're so darn cold to me, that I reckoned you needed . . ."

"Needed what? To be mauled about like a common prostitute?"

A slow flush of red rode up from his collar. Grace

didn't think for a minute he was embarrassed; this was the red of anger.

"Yeah. Why not? If a gal won't when she's asked nice, why not?"

He came closer, one slow step at a time, his fancy spurs jingling on the floor. His fingers were crooked into claws, his lips drawn back from his teeth in a savage smile.

This time Grace didn't back away. She stood there, her eyes so angry she could feel them burn when she blinked. Her voice was little more than a growl. "Get the hell out of here, Marshal Wyman. Maybe I'll forget about this."

He caught her by the wrist. Enraged, Grace smashed him across the ear with her open hand. Reg Wyman let out a howl that brought Toby running around the end of the porch. The marshal staggered backward, clutching the side of his head. He turned his eyes toward Grace, and she'd never seen such hatred. A wild beast might turn eyes like that on an enemy.

Grace's teacher used to box ears to enforce discipline. Grace knew what overwhelming pain it caused. How her whole head would seem to ring like a bell, while licks of fire tortured her ears. Marshal Wyman must have been feeling all of that and more. Her teacher had never hit as hard as she could, as Grace had just done.

"Oh, go home," she said, just as she heard Wenonah calling. Grace went inside, slamming the door behind her. After a moment, she went to the window. Flattening herself against the wall, she lifted the curtain a hair.

She saw Wyman bend down and pick up something, his fancy hat most likely. When he straightened, she could only shut her eyes and press her face to the wall, for he hurled the tin bowl with all his strength at the window. The window shivered but the bowl bounced harmlessly to the ground. She heard Wyman swear viciously as he mounted his horse.

"Mrs. Landers?" Wenonah's soft voice vibrated with concern.

"I'm all right." She passed her hand over her forehead, not surprised to find sweat. Looking at Wenonah's anxious face, she said suddenly, "But listen . . . you're not to work at the jail any more. I know. Your arm is all healed up. But I don't want you working down there."

"But . . . Deputy Crowley would never let anything happen to me. And I . . ."

Grace took a deep breath and let it out in a sigh. She turned to the younger woman. "I don't have any right to tell you what to do, Wenonah. But if you'll be guided by my advice, you won't go back to the jail. You can find some other way to see Jasper Crowley, without going there."

Wenonah's eyes shifted from under Grace's gaze. "He hardly knows if I am there or not," she said, almost in a whisper.

Grace felt an impulse to tell Wenonah differently. It hadn't been mere politeness that had drawn the young deputy out to Lynch Road three times in two weeks. Nor would courtesy alone explain the bouquets of wildflowers and plates of his mother's fudge he brought each time.

It would be useless, however, to tell Wenonah about Jasper's feelings. Only he could do that. After what had just happened, Grace wasn't sure she'd vouch for any man. What had gotten into Reg Wyman? It was as if for a few moments, he'd become someone else. Did other men hide a dark soul under their cheery outside shells?

Wenonah said, "Breakfast is almost ready. I'll wake the children."

"No, I'll do that." Grace needed to see their sweet, uncomplicated faces. They'd hug her with no other motive but love. Bart might dissemble to get off extra work and Callie might play innocent to charm Dr. Birkins out of peppermints, but they'd never tear off their masks to reveal demons within.

Ever since Dr. Birkins had given his approval, Wenonah had worked both at the jail and in the house. Everything from the clock to the spoons shone with elbow grease, and the children's clothes were as clean as when they'd been new. Grace tried to stop Wenonah working so hard. It had been like trying to hold back a tornado. She felt guilty about all the work Wenonah did. Yet in a way, all the cooking and cleaning seemed to be healing the girl.

She spoke more and smiled more. The children adored her.

After breakfast, sure that Wyman was really gone, Grace went out on the porch to sweep away the spilled green beans. She was angrier now about the waste of good food than over Wyman's inexplicable behavior.

Lucas watched her vigorously attacking the porch floor as he came up. "Is it safe?" he joked.

Grace jumped about a foot and spun around, her hand flying to the base of her throat. When she saw who it was, she let out her captured breath. Even so, she was in no mood to welcome him. "Oh, it's you."

"Who were you expecting? Sitting Bull?"

"It's just . . ." She couldn't tell him that the marshal had proposed and she'd been so upset that she'd ordered him off the property. She went back to sweeping.

Lucas stepped up and laid his hand on the broom handle, effectively stilling her movements. Grace tried to go on, muscle against muscle, but she couldn't win. "What's wrong?" he asked. "You're obviously upset."

She couldn't tell him the truth. He and the marshal had been getting along so well. "It's just . . . I've got a lot to do yet if we're to pull out of here today. I mean, it's almost eight o'clock already."

"How far is it to Sedalia?"

"Half a day, at least. Providing the mules don't go lame or the wagon wheel doesn't break or Bart doesn't fall out of the back."

Lucas smiled. "You probably won't have to worry about the first two."

Reluctantly, for Lucas was far more mysterious than Reg Wyman, Grace answered his smile. His faded, a serious light coming into his eyes. Gently, he brushed her cheek with his work-roughened fingers. "Grace . . ."

She jerked away. "Goodness, what has gotten into everyone today?" Lifting the bristles off the floor, she shook them at him, ignoring his hurt expression. "You won't be the first man I've chased off my porch today, Mr. Lucas!"

"What do you mean?"

"Never mind." She swung the broom bristles to the ground again. "Just . . . get to work."

"All right, madam boss. What do you want me to do?"

"You can start by mucking out the stables."

Lucas's nose wrinkled. He'd done that smelly job last week and confessed that he was beginning to think much more fondly of that skunk.

"You might have to do it again while I'm gone, 'cause I don't know how long I'll be away." She glanced up at him, measuring as if for the first time his strength and his character. Once again, she liked what she saw, both with her eyes and her heart.

She said, more gently, "I'm leaving everything in your hands. I know I can trust you." She hastily added, "Trust you to look after things, I mean."

Perhaps realizing that the danger of making a second breakfast from broom bristles was past, Lucas once more took her hand. His thumb rubbed lightly over the back, arousing the nerves there. He hadn't touched her since the social, though sometimes his most innocent words could be loaded with double meanings. But he'd never tried to kiss her again. Sometimes Grace lay awake half the night wondering why. Was Rena Presby so alluring that Lucas couldn't think of anyone else?

Now he said, "Grace, are you sure you wouldn't like to change your mind and have me come with you? I'm sure Judge Sterling would agree to let me go, considering I'd be with my employer."

Longingly, she looked up into his blue eyes. There had been cornflowers that blue in the bouquets Jasper had brought for Wenonah. The deep, endless blue of truth would be the color of Lucas's eyes.

Perhaps she swayed toward him, some part of her wanting to drive out the memory of Wyman's staring eyes and hot breath. Lucas's hand tightened as if he'd pull her close. Then, however abruptly, he let go.

Grace blinked in surprise. Lucas had turned away. He combed his fingers back through his hair and sighed. She knew that sigh, having heard it from her own lips often enough in the past two weeks. It was compounded equally of wanting, frustration and willpower.

He said, "You've made it pretty clear how you want things, Grace. It's not easy for me to come here every day and not . . . do what I'd like to do."

She reached out toward him with both hands, wanting to change her mind. It was just as well his back was to her. Things would become impossible if she ran to him as she longed to do. Dropping her hands hopelessly to her sides, she said, "It's not easy for me, either."

"Grace!" He spun around, a bright, incredulous smile lifting the corners of his firm mouth.

She held up her hands again, only this time with her palms outthrust. "It's best this way. You'll be on your way soon, looking for whoever you may be."

"I don't care who I am now. I could be a farmer."

Smiling, loving him enough to tease, she said, "No, you'll never make a farmer." More seriously, she added, "There's too much of you unused here, Lucas. You're not the kind of man who could ever settle down to watching things grow."

"I could learn," he said without a trace of a whine. "Look how much I've learned already. I can already muck out a stable—never had a lesson in my life!"

She loved him for answering her laughter with his own. It would be so wonderful if he could stay. The children would love it if he could be a permanent part of their lives. But how could he be? she asked herself. They had no future because she couldn't possibly marry him.

"I've got to finish packing," she said as if it were some dire burden.

Grace stood it for as long as she could. Her mother did nothing overt to annoy her. On the contrary, she was sweet to her and couldn't be happier to keep the children for as long as Grace wanted to let them stay. Her father, as quiet as ever and far more gray, kissed her cheek and looked with warm concern into Grace's eyes. Apparently he approved of what he saw, for he nodded and left her to her mother.

Hardly had they been welcomed into the house, however, when it began. "Anything new?"

"Well . . ."

"How 'bout that marshal you wrote me about? Is he still coming around?"

"Sometimes. But I—"

"You know, if you wouldn't pull your hair back so tightly, you'd look a good few years younger."

"I like it out of my—"

"Look at your poor hands! I'll give you a nice piece of pumice—that'll get that real deep dirt out. There's nothing that puts a man off more quickly than dirty hands."

"Mother . . ."

"That Wenonah child seems like a nice girl. How old is she?"

Scenting a chance to turn her mother onto another subject besides her middle daughter's failings as a woman, Grace said, "About seventeen, I think. She's awfully pretty too, isn't she?"

"Is she really living with you now? That was kind of you, Grace, but is it wise?" Mrs. Landers gazed out toward the yard, where her husband and grandchildren romped, Wenonah looking on with a smile.

"Wise?" She knew her mother hadn't a prejudiced bone in her body, so it couldn't be Wenonah's mixed blood she objected to.

"Yes, dear. Someone so young and pretty might distract callers away from you."

"Considering that her whole heart is already—"

"Men will make these comparisons, dear. The mature woman of wisdom and character so often loses out to a pretty face. I wonder if a chamomile rinse would brighten your hair."

Grace wondered if she could leave before supper appeared on the table. However, she stayed for three days. Reminding her mother that Callie didn't need to wear a corset took up much of the second day, and rescuing Plowdy from the dustbin took up half the evening. The following day was occupied with explaining Lucas, Bart having let his name enter a conversation.

By some miracle, Grace managed to hide her true feelings about Lucas from her mother. She drove the wagon away after noon of the fourth day, having attended church with the family, and feeling as if she'd escaped the clutches of the Spanish Inquisition. All the turning and twisting she'd had to do to protect her secret love left her exhausted.

Her baggage was heavier by the addition of bottles of toilet water, her mother's own herb rinse for face and hair, three different kinds of soap and the promised pumice stone. She politely turned down the face powder and lip rouge. It wouldn't surprise her, however, to find them in her grip when she unpacked it later on this evening.

Grace and Wenonah stopped more than once on the road home, to picnic on the huge basket Grace's mother had packed, to sleep a little, to kick their hot feet in a swift running stream.

And Wenonah talked freely about her life. There had been more pain than pleasure in her seventeen years, though she remembered happier days when she lived with her mother and white father. Then he had died. Everything good died too.

"I know what that's like," Grace said.

"I know. That's why I told you."

Hours later, coming to a stop in front of the house, Grace shook the girl lightly by the elbow. "Wake up, honey."

Wenonah shook her head as if to clear it, and rubbed her palms over her eyes and face. "Did I fall asleep?"

"Looks like it. You go on in. I'll put the wagon and the mules up."

"I'll help. Only my foot's asleep."

"Can you get down all right?"

Wenonah nodded and stepped onto the spoke of the wheel. From there it was easy to reach the ground. She grimaced. "It's all pins and needles. But it's not too bad. At least let me get the picnic basket and the bags."

"Good thing Mother packed so much fried chicken," Grace said. "I certainly don't feel like cooking."

"Me either." The two straw cases safely on the porch,

Wenonah came back for the basket that had ridden under their feet. She looked up with shy admiration into Grace's face. "I hope you won't listen to what your mother said about me. I'm like you. I'll never get married."

"Not even if someone special asks you?" Even in the dim light cast by the lantern hanging from the whiffletree, Grace could see Wenonah's eyes fall.

"He never will," she whispered. She glanced up again, her smile forced. "So I will live in single blessedness—if that's the right way to put it. Perhaps I can go to school and become a teacher. I'd like to go back to the reservation and teach."

"Go inside," Grace said kindly. "Let me put the mules up and we'll have a nice talk about it. I was trained to be a teacher myself, you know."

Grace thought about Wenonah's future as she unharnessed the mules. Maybe she could scrape up a few dollars, or maybe Mr. Kent would consider sponsoring her, or there was always the owner of the paper, Mr. Flynt. He'd sent one of the Biederman girls through teacher's college three years ago. Maybe he'd be willing to help another deserving girl.

She dragged open the barn door and led the first mule in, one sweat-stained leather collar hanging over her arm. Putting the lantern in the middle of the floor and dropping the collar next to it, she led the mule to a box and tethered him on a lead. He began lipping at the hay in the manger. He'd need to be sponged down after his long journey. Grace knew just how he felt. She'd been sweating long before they'd left her parents' pleasant home.

Something nudged her in the small of the back. Turning quickly, Grace saw that Hercules had followed her and Ulysses into the barn. Grace tethered the other mule.

Taking up a bucket, she went out into the dark yard for water. Still thinking of Wenonah as she pumped, Grace wondered if she could interest Brother Marill in the matter. Maybe he could convince the congregation to sponsor the girl.

Carrying the heavy bucket in, she reached up for the currycomb and brush she kept on a shelf in a disused stall.

Before she turned, she heard a funny creak that she knew well. The ladder to the hayloft always creaked like that when Bart was trying to be sneaky. It wouldn't creak at all if he stepped boldly. But it couldn't be Bart tonight.

Grace stepped out from the stall into the circle of clear yellow light shed by her lamp. Anger and curiosity warred in her heart. "Just what the hell are you doing in—"

Pain exploded like a fireball in her head.

Chapter
Fifteen

Due to Mrs. Crowley's exaggerated ideas of what a dinner should be, Lucas was late. He'd been walking up to Grace's farm every evening that she'd been away. There was plenty of hay in the loft to make a comfortable couch. With the addition of a horse blanket, Lucas found himself sleeping in far more comfort than at the jail.

He'd walk back to the jail at about four in the morning, early enough to avoid Marshal Wyman. Lucas had asked openly if he could go up and keep an eye on things at Grace's place. The marshal had turned him down with a half-joking comment about setting a fox to watch a henhouse. Jasper, however, continued letting Lucas "escape" whenever he chose.

Tonight, under a faded moon in its final quarter, the barn looked very different from when the moonlight had made all as bright as day. The structure seemed to hunch sloping shoulders, settling down in the dark to some secret ceremony of its own. An owl asked a mournful question, like a sad and solemn priest.

He squared his shoulders and pushed open the squeaking gate, the path a faintly glowing white strand at his feet. Lucas turned as a light in the house changed all the shaded windows to opaque.

A voice called out. "Who is it?"

Light spilled out of the open porch door, silhouetting Wenonah. Lucas stood at the bottom of the steps, looking behind her for Grace. He realized anew how hungry he was for a sight of her. "You're back. How was the trip?"

"Oh, Mr. Lucas, it's you. I thought . . . The trip was fine," she said, peering past him even as he looked past her. "Mr. and Mrs. Landers are such nice people. Is there someone with you?"

"No, I came alone. Jasper doesn't seem to mind if I don't sleep at the jail. Where's Grace . . . Mrs. Landers?"

"She's at the barn, seeing to the mules. I could have sworn I heard someone out here."

"Well, the gate keeps on creaking, despite all the grease I've put on those hinges."

"It didn't sound like the gate."

"Maybe you heard that owl."

The girl's eyes glittered as she glanced up at him. "I can tell an owl from a man, Mr. Lucas. It's one benefit of my blood."

He'd never really noticed Wenonah before. She was quiet and seemed to bear patiently the blows of her life. Not many girls could go from unutterable squalor to comparative comfort with such calm acceptance. Yet, for a moment, Lucas heard something repressed in her tone, something held down by force but that still fought for freedom. She stepped silently back into the house and closed the door.

The barn at the top of the slight rise above the house no longer seemed to be brooding on ancient crimes and long-held secrets. Grace was there.

She'd be tending to the mules, or scratching the cow between the horns as she'd done while he was learning to milk. He doubted that Grace even knew how warmly she had smiled at him. The memory of that smile had kept his nights in the hayloft from being lonely. It sent him about his daily tasks with a new interest.

His heart lifting as he hurried up to the barn, Lucas could hope that Grace hadn't yet forgotten the kisses they'd shared. He could remember every moment as if it had just happened, and knew it would always be that fresh, no matter what else he might forget.

"Grace?" He stepped through the opening between the barn doors. The mules stood patiently in their stalls, still flecked with mud and bits of grass. A bucket lay on its side next to Ulysses's rear hoof, water draining away into the straw.

The barn seemed to ring with silence. Not even the animals made any noise, and the owls were out hunting. Lucas called her name again, stooping to pick up the bucket. It was so silent he could almost catch an echo of his call.

He saw that the ladder to the loft, dead center above the middle floor, was down. Had he left it like that? Lucas rubbed his forehead as he thought it over. Usually, he was sure, he moved it against the wall to keep it out of the way. Maybe Grace had gone into the hayloft. But in that case, why didn't she answer him?

Four stalls stood against the right-hand wall of the barn. In the first two, the mules nibbled hay. In the third, the family cow chewed cud. The fourth stood empty.

Lucas put his foot on a rung of the ladder to go up. Then some image returned to his inner vision, caught during that sweeping glance of the stalls.

Something black, nearly a teardrop shape, lay half-buried in the straw. Lucas took his foot off the bottom-most rung. His feet dragged as he walked those few steps. The black object resolved itself into shades of gray. A worn sole, patched in the center by no expert hand. The leather heel bore deep scratches as if the owner had been dragged.

"Grace?" He dropped to his knees beside her, his hand coming down as lightly as a hummingbird on her shoulder. She lay on her face, her cheek pillowed on straw. She was still warm.

The roaring in his ears sent a dark tide over his eyes. He couldn't see the woman lying in front of him. He couldn't see the blood that had poured from the gash across her temple, though he knelt in it, mingled now with straw and earth. A soft keening coming from his lips, he bent down over her, smoothing her matted hair, kissing her smeared cheek.

John Peyton Cobb came to himself, standing up, holding the body of a woman in his arms. But the woman's skin was fair, not dark. Her hair was a rich blond where it hung over his arm, not smooth red-black braids. Strangest of all, he no longer stood under the brilliant blue sky of a Dakota winter. The smoke from the burning *tipis* no longer sent columns rising to violate that sky. The whimpers and screams of the surviving Sioux women and children no longer echoed except in his ears.

And it was dark here. The soldiers of Fort Davies had attacked the peaceful camp in the early morning's mist, after a long night of drinking with the legislator from Connecticut. His rhetoric had so inflamed them that no one said a word against the suggestion they go "visit" the snow-covered Sioux camp. He'd followed them, his conscience awakening too late. He saw only the aftermath, and that had been too much.

John staggered under the weight of the memories that crowded his thoughts. Memories of bloodstained snow, of fire, of slaughter. Instinctively he clutched the woman more closely, so she would not fall. She murmured and he realized he did not hold a dead woman in his arms after all.

Letting her fall back a little, he saw her face and realized he knew her name. "Grace. Grace, can you hear me?"

She half raised her hand as though to touch the gash that marred her smooth brow. Already the skin had puffed around it, but the bleeding had slowed. She murmured again and let out a long sigh.

"You'll be all right. I'll take you to the house."

He didn't bother to knock. Grabbing the door handle with one finger, he jerked the door open, caught it on his heel as it swung back, and carried Grace into the house. The clean-scrubbed poverty of the place appalled him.

He found a room, with a rosy-globed lamp burning by a large bed. Placing the woman Grace on the red-and-blue quilted cover, he felt for a pulse in her left wrist.

"My God! What happened?" someone said from behind him.

John spun around. The lamp reflected red highlights from the high cheekbones and slightly prominent nose of the regal young Indian woman. Perhaps this *was* the Dakota Territory. Yet this young woman seemed to have the run of the house. He could remember no such girl at Fort Davies. The Indians there either lived out in the reservation or camped by the stockade wall if they were friendly.

"What happened?"

"I . . . don't know. I found her like this in the barn."

"I knew that couldn't be a ghost!" She came into the room to stare down at Grace. "That's a nasty cut. You better run fetch the doctor, Mr. Lucas. I don't like the looks of it. And though I hate to say it, maybe you'd best tell the marshal about it too."

"You should go," he said, standing very tall. He couldn't admit that he didn't know where the doctor or the marshal were to be found. "I will care for Grace."

"But, Mr. Lucas, I can—"

"Do as you're told, if you please." Her name drifted into his mind. He allowed himself to smile, that charismatic bend of his lips that had so often persuaded women to do his bidding. "Please, Wenonah. Don't argue."

Her nearly black eyes blinked in confusion. She said, "All right. But you'd better wash that blood off your hands. I wouldn't put it past Marshal Wyman to try and say you hit her."

With a last anxious look toward the woman on the bed, the Indian girl went out.

John turned his palms up. Drying blood glued his fingers together so he had to force them apart. He wondered if Grace Landers had suffered because of him, the way the Indians had. He winced with an inward pain, a pain of the soul.

The little room was stuffy, as if it hadn't been used lately. However, there was clear water in a pitcher on a washstand. A clean towel hung on a bar in the front. John poured some of the water into the basin set in the stand and dipped his hands in. The blood smoked and swirled through the water. Stained still, he picked up the fresh slice of yellow soap someone had put there—Wenonah? For Grace's use?

He washed. The soap slicked between his fingers, strangely roughened fingers. The blood gone, he could see where calluses had developed, where blisters had formed. They were no longer the hands of a man who drove a pen for a living. Glancing up into the small round mirror at the top of the stand, he saw a tan face, leaner than it had been when he last remembered looking at it, in a dirty chamber at Fort Davies where his lantern smoked so vilely he looked like a devil, peering through sulfur clouds. He had lost his bushy side-whiskers, making him seem younger, less self-satisfied.

He poured the foaming and bloody water away into the slop jar and dampened a cloth in fresh water. He could do little for Grace now, except clean the dirt and straw from the ugly wound. His hands trembled as he brought the cloth near. He stilled them by an act of will.

By concentrating firmly on the fact that he was doing her good, John wiped gently at the two-inch gash that ran from above Grace's eyebrow to her hairline. She moaned and turned her head restlessly on the pillow. As he worked, John frowned. If this was as primitive a country as he guessed from his surroundings, he doubted any competent physician could be found. Even if by some miracle the practitioner were not some clumsy drunkard, what hope was there that this lovely woman would not be permanently scarred by such a mark?

Finishing, he let out a shaking breath and realized he was frightened. Not that Grace's beauty would be spoiled, for dimly he realized that could never happen now, not in his eyes. Rather he was afraid that the spirit and beauty within would be lost forever. Always with an eye toward reelection, he'd visited, perforce, sad hospitals full of persons rendered imbecilic by similar blows.

John began to wonder what she could have hit her head on in the stall where he'd found her. The closest possible thing was a dirt-crusted shovel that stood against a wall. But how could Grace have struck her head on it? Perhaps he was wrong. He could not rule out the possibility of a mule having lashed out and Grace stumbling blindly to where she fell. Yet Wenonah had seemed to suggest that someone had hurt Grace intentionally.

He fought down the stunningly hot rush of anger that

thought invoked in him. To dwell on it now would do her no good.

Having cleaned her wound, Lucas dampened the cloth again and began trying to remove the crusting blood from her tangled hair, finding the tumbled pins. It was the only thing he could do for her now, except to whisper, "I hope you wake up soon, dearest. I'm lost without you. I wonder who you think I am."

She stirred and her lips parted with a slight smacking sound. Her lips looked dry. Remembering his military service, he took a second towel from the rack, dipped it in a little fresh water and then squeezed it between her lips. He saw the muscles in her throat work and was comforted.

It seemed an age before the doctor came. One look at his cheerful physiognomy and John guessed this was a man who knew his business. Always a respecter of competence, John stood aside, explaining how he had found Grace, while Dr. Birkins examined her.

"A nasty cut. But clean."

"I washed it. It had bled a great deal. But then I believe head wounds always do."

"Like a stuck pig as a rule. Her pulse is steady and . . . yes, yes. Satisfactorily strong. I'm only glad the children aren't here to see this. It would trouble them very much." The doctor glanced at Wenonah, hovering in the doorway. "Find Mrs. Landers's sewing box for me, there's a good girl."

"I have it here, Doctor." Wenonah stepped into the light, the little wooden box in her hands.

"Thread me a small needle then. And then you'd better leave. Mr. Lucas and I can manage the rest."

"Doctor, I . . . ," she protested.

But Dr. Birkins just looked at her over the golden rims of the round spectacles he'd put on. "Move that lamp a shade closer before you go. Now, Mr. Lucas. I'll require you to hold Mrs. Landers's hands down while I stitch. I cannot sew a fine seam with fists waving beneath my nose."

"Yes, I remember seeing men fight their doctors in the army hospitals."

"You remember . . . ? Never mind. Let us get on with this matter first."

After ten wretched minutes, the doctor pronounced himself satisfied. "I'm just as glad she stayed unconscious. I've been awake myself during suturing. It's not so much the prick of the needle but the long drawing of the thread through the skin that makes my teeth stand on edge."

"Shouldn't she wake up now?" John asked. "This sleep . . ."

"She's in no danger. Her pupils are not fixed. Let's give her some time to waken on her own." The doctor took off his spectacles and fixed his eyes on John, who saw that Birkins didn't need glasses to look into a man's mind.

The doctor said, "You wouldn't happen to have some whiskey in the house?"

"I don't think she keeps any."

"Oh, well." The doctor reached into his bag. "I just hate to drink my own if I don't have to. We'll go out onto the porch and have a sip. Wenonah'll keep an eye on Grace."

He tugged the cork out with his teeth and held the bottle up to judge how much was left. Then he took a healthy swig. Shaking his head, he said as he passed the bottle, "Fine stuff. I'll introduce you to the feller that makes it, if you want."

"I doubt Grace would approve." After swallowing, John coughed, feeling as if he'd absentmindedly drunk acid.

"Does your heart good, doesn't it?" The doctor took the bottle back. "What else do you remember?" he asked suddenly.

"Everything. Or nearly everything."

"Do you know who you are?"

John nodded but refused the whiskey bottle. The burning flavor reminded him too much of the liquor passed around the fire the night before the massacre.

"If you don't want to tell me . . . ," Dr. Birkins began.

"It's all terribly confused at the moment. You could tell me a few things, however."

"Do my best."

"What day is it?"

"June 25, give or take a few hours."

"June 25? 1876?"

"That's right. What's the last date you remember?"

"January 6. I was up north. This *is* Missouri? I remember her telling me that."

"That's right. Ogden, Missouri. About thirty-five miles west of Sedalia as the crow flies."

John strove to bring his memory down to the present. He couldn't picture all the places he'd been. Those six months were as dark as an abandoned theater. He decided not to try to remember that time. He knew he had wandered, had been hungry sometimes, had often shook with the cold. Far better not to try to recall all the miserable details. Instead, he would remember lying in an alley and a sweet voice defending him, while a gentle hand rested on his brow.

"I've been here two weeks," he said. "I've been working as a . . . farmhand. And Grace and I . . ."

The doctor leaned closer. "Yes?"

"She calls me Lucas. Everybody calls me Lucas."

"Is that your real name?"

"No. The only person I know named Lucas is my tailor."

"Take another swig of whiskey, my boy. It'll clear your head. No? Well, waste not, want not." He drank.

"Why did I lose my memory, Doctor?"

Birkins shrugged. "What's the last thing you remember as yourself? I mean . . ."

"I understand." In a soft voice, so the girl inside would not hear, Lucas told the doctor about the Singing Spring massacre. The red light of the lamp became the sunrise over a landscape forever blotted by blood.

When he was done, he felt the breeze cool the tears that lay on his cheeks. "I was too late to do anything. And it was all my doing. If I hadn't gone there, if I hadn't been so sure what I said about them was right . . ."

"Seems to me soldiers have done such things before, without your being there. Seems to me, they'll do it again. Maybe you remember all the fuss over that killing that went on at Sand Creek, must be twelve years ago now. The scandal took down a couple of officers as I remember. You weren't there. You weren't responsible this time either."

"I'm sorry, Doctor. I can't accept that these things just happen. Man's cruelty to man may be part of our ancient heritage, but I don't have to like it."

"Maybe that's why you forgot who you were, son. 'Cause you wouldn't believe that kind of viciousness was in you. From what I've seen of you—the way you've helped Mrs. Landers, the way you piled into the Grupp brothers when they were bothering Miss Wenonah—I'd say you don't have much to worry about. If you can forgive yourself for the bad you've done without forgetting that you've done it, you'll go a long way to doing good."

The doctor stuck the cork back in his bottle. He clapped John on the knee and said, "Better go check on my patient."

Sitting by himself, John thought of the things he hadn't told the doctor: his full name, his position in the legislature of his home state, his wealth. Though he now knew no wife waited for him, he did have family, most particularly a father. And there was a girl, or rather a blue-blooded, highly proper young woman, with whom he'd come to some understanding regarding their mutual future. He couldn't quite picture her face.

He heard the door open behind him. "Mr. Lucas?" Wenonah said. "She's awake. And she's asking for you."

Dr. Birkins held her left wrist in his fingers, watching the hand move on his watch. Grace lifted her other hand to John as soon as he entered the room. "I knew you'd find me," she said.

Kneeling by the bed, he touched her knuckles to his cheek and then pressed his lips to her palm. "You're all right. You're all right now."

As if she were a little embarrassed to be showing so

much emotion in front of the doctor, Grace withdrew her hand and glanced up at Dr. Birkins. "My head hurts."

"No surprise there, missy," he said. "That's a nasty ol' cut I had to stitch up. Now, I'm not going to bandage it. That wouldn't do your headache any good and I want the air to get to that cut. I'll be back in a couple days to take the stitches out. Till then, you take things slow. Let these two folks baby you a little."

John laid his hand over hers, silencing her instinctive protests. "Always follow doctor's orders," he said.

"This from a man who couldn't rest one day after being knocked down with sunstroke," Grace grumbled.

He smiled at her, saying, "I only give advice, Grace. I never listen to it myself." Then he sobered, "Do you remember how you hit your head?"

Her hand tightened on his. "No, I don't." Once again, she glanced up at Dr. Birkins. "Thank you for coming out."

"I won't say it was a pleasure. Pity your Callie isn't here. I just laid in a fresh stock of peppermint." He paused on his way out. "Now, you remember what I said. Lie up for a few days. If you're a good gal, you'll be able to go to the Centennial celebration with nothing more than a bruise to show for tonight's work. Otherwise, there won't be any dancing for you."

"I'll save you a waltz in any case, Doctor."

"I count on it. I'll just have a word with Wenonah about tending you."

He left the room. John got off his knees. "Will it bother you if I sit next to you?"

"I'd like you to." She raised herself up and rested her uninjured temple against his shoulder. Sighing, she murmured, "That's better."

"Do you remember what happened?"

Grace was silent for a moment. Lucas thought she'd fallen asleep. Then she said, "Yes. There was someone in the barn. I saw him."

"Did you see his face?" A flood of anger arose anew in his heart. That someone would strike down this woman—

his woman—filled him with such fury that it was all he could do to keep his voice steady.

"I don't think so. The lamp wasn't very bright. I remember a flash of something silver and then . . ." She raised a faltering hand to her temple.

He tightened his arm around her shoulders. "Don't think about it now. Just rest."

"Will you . . . ? I guess you have to be going back to the jail?"

John pressed a kiss to the tumbled hair just below his chin. "I'm not going anywhere. Are you hungry?"

"No. I'm not sleepy either."

"Shall I read to you?"

"Please."

He read *Quentin Durward* to her until her breathing became deep and natural. Then he went once again to the barn, a lantern in his hand. The mules still needed to be tended to, but more than that, John wanted to take another look at that shovel.

The dirt on it had only just begun to dry. But there was no disturbed earth inside the barn. John went outside and searched around the exterior. Standing puzzled for a moment, he recalled the earthen mound in the woods on the other side of Lynch Road. Stopping at the house to warn Wenonah to lock the doors until he returned, he crossed the road.

The dirt mound was undisturbed. It seemed to have doubled in the night, however. A new trench, five feet long and about two foot wide, had been dug beside it. The earth on the shovel was exactly as fresh as that on the new grave.

Chapter
Sixteen

When Grace woke up in the morning, her head hurt too much for her to even brush her hair, let alone force it into her usual restrained bun. The sight of her face in the mirror unnerved her. The white thread that laced through the purple bruise on her temple, the darker line of the wound itself, looked like something from Mary Shelley's *Frankenstein,* a novel of terror she'd read as an impressionable girl. Grace couldn't bear to look at herself another moment.

When the door opened, she put up a hand to hide the mark. But only Georgette wandered in. In a single elegant leap, the cat landed on the rumpled bedclothes. Grace extended her hand. Georgette sniffed her fingers and rumbled approval when Grace stroked her fur.

"Well, at least I smell all right."

She rested frequently during dressing, wishing that the world would stop spinning like a carousel out of control. When she bent to pull on her shoes, a wave of nausea flowed over her.

She grabbed the bedpost and leaned against it. For all she could tell, it too rocked up and down as though the whole house had upped anchor and gone to sea. A moan escaped her.

Lucas came in and instantly had an arm around her waist. He wore only his shirt and denim pants. "Little idiot! What are you doing out of bed?"

Though she clutched at him instinctively, she retained enough pride to say, "Don't call me that!"

"Sorry," he said, but he didn't sound convincing. "Let me help you lie down."

"I don't want to lie down. I've got things to see to."

"There's nothing you have to do except rest. That's what Dr. Birkins said. I intend to see that you obey him if I have to sit on you."

"Just who do you think you are?" Grace demanded. Getting mad only increased the throbbing in her head, but she didn't care. What did Lucas think he was doing, throwing his weight around like this?

"I'm your friend," he said. "And friends don't let friends walk around with scrambled brains."

Grace found herself with the backs of her knees pressed hard against the edge of her mattress. "Stop shoving," she said.

He tapped her shoulder and she sat down. "Stay there," he ordered.

"Look, Lucas, in case you've forgotten—"

"What an imperious thing you are, to be sure. I've never noticed that about you before, Grace." He gave her a smile that seemed saturated with odious self-confidence. "Now, sit still like a good girl and I'll bring you the breakfast Wenonah is preparing. Are you hungry?"

"Starving. But I'll eat in the kitchen. I've only eaten in bed when the children were born. I don't like it. It's too uncomfortable and you wind up sleeping on crumbs."

"On second thought," Lucas said. "I'll have Wenonah bring your breakfast. If I leave the room, you'll only get up."

"Darn tooting."

She watched him go to the door and call for Wenonah. When the girl came, Grace said, "Wenonah, will you tell this . . . this *man* that I've got to get up."

"No, I won't," she said, her smile mixed with anxiety. "Dr. Birkins said—"

"I'll have to have a long talk with Dr. Birkins. Confining a busy woman like me to her room! Doesn't he realize this place needs me?"

"What's wrong, Grace?" Lucas asked. "Don't you trust us to take care of things for you?"

Grace was in a mood to deny everything that came out

of Lucas's mouth. But one glance at Wenonah's worried face made her submit meekly to Dr. Birkins's orders.

When Wenonah went into the kitchen, Lucas piled every pillow in the house behind Grace's back. Then he sat down at the foot of the bed, clasping one knee in his hands.

"What are you grinning at?" Grace demanded.

"You." The affection in his blue eyes was too unabashed for her to meet them for long, but his next words brought her gaze back to his face, with a flash in the depths of her eyes. "Dr. Birkins said you had the hardest head he'd ever seen on a woman."

"Yes, I shall certainly have a long talk with good Dr. Birkins. What else did he say?"

"You're lucky to be alive."

Grace reached out her hand. "I know it."

He enfolded her hand in both his own, leaning forward. "I'm lucky you're alive. When I saw you up there, I thought . . ."

She felt his hands tremble. "Don't. I'm all right. A little crack on the head? I fell out of the tallest oak in town on my head when I was a child. Got right up and walked away too. Never even raised a bump."

"Children are more resilient than adults. Grace, I think someone tried—"

Wenonah pushed open the door with her shoulder as she backed into the room, a wooden tray in her arms covered with Grace's breakfast. "I didn't know what you'd feel like eating, so I made some of everything."

Grace reached eagerly for the cup of coffee between the eggs and the waffles. It was hot and strong enough to put heart in a corpse, let alone in a live, if sore, woman. She cradled the warmth of the cup in her hands while Wenonah put the tray across her knees. Then the girl said, "Oh, my! I left the coffee boiling!" and dashed out of the room.

Though she started eating with a good will, after the first few bites of eggs and ham, Grace quickly pressed her fingers to her lips. "I don't think I'd better," she said, when the nauseated fit had passed.

Lucas took the tray from her knees. "Try this dry toast," he said, handing her a slice. "Just nibble it for a while."

"I don't want to hurt Wenonah's feelings. You eat some of that up and we'll pretend I did it."

"I'd be happy to. I can't remember when I was last this hungry."

"Why?" she asked. "Has Mrs. Crowley stopped stuffing you like a Christmas goose?"

"I didn't have breakfast at the jail today," he said, spooning up grits eagerly. "As a matter of fact, I didn't even sleep there last night."

"You didn't?"

"No." As his fork dipped toward the eggs, he stopped to look into her startled eyes. "There was no point in letting Callie's bed go to waste."

"But Wenonah . . ."

"What about her?"

"Her reputation," Grace said, her voice sinking to a whisper. "If anybody found out . . ."

Lucas stood up and put the tray on the dressing table. Returning to her, he took the toast and the empty cup from her hands. Then he leaned down over her.

"There's not a soul in town," he said, "who'd ever link Wenonah's name with mine in a scandal. Not when everyone knows I'm wildly in love with you."

He kissed her, a mere brushing of lips as soft and brief as the sweep of a hummingbird's wing. Before he could straighten, Grace had twined her arms around his neck. The knowledge that Lucas loved her made her head spin more violently than if she'd been walloped by an anvil.

"Your head?" he murmured.

"Never mind it. I . . . ." The words she longed to speak, that she did not dare to say, were lost as she brought his face down to hers.

The swirling motion of the room steadied as his warmth enfolded her. Though he didn't hold her tightly or plunder her mouth, Grace could feel the strength it took for him to keep within bounds. It pleased her even as it frustrated her.

Lucas broke off first. "Remember, you're a sick woman."

"I forget when you kiss me," she said, blushing. He gave her a last kiss, at the corner of her mouth, then sat back.

"It's not just my head, either," she said. "My shoulders are sore and I've got a big scrape on my . . ." She met Lucas's eyes and invented a quick substitution for what she'd been intending to say. "On my back."

"Oh, your back?"

"That's right. My back."

They chuckled together. Then Grace tried to look severe. "What's gotten into you, Lucas?"

"How do you mean?"

"Maybe it's just this," she said, raising her hand to her forehead, though she didn't touch the tender spot. "But you seemed awful pleased with yourself considering you thought I was dead."

A fierce fire rose in his eyes. "Don't say that, even as a joke. Do you remember anything else about what happened last night? You said you saw someone in your barn."

"I'm sure it was a man. I remember seeing him against the light—it was behind him—and the person definitely had two legs."

"Good. That narrows it down." Though his tone was lighter, he still carried anger in his eyes. "We can rule out all one-legged people in Ogden."

Grace smiled at him, appreciating his attempt to ease her tension. Just thinking about that moment when she'd surprised the intruder sent cold chills down her spine. She didn't need Lucas to tell her how close she'd come to death.

"I mean," she said, "that if it had been a woman, I would have only seen darkness where her skirts were. A man in trousers lets light show between his . . . You know what I mean."

"I think I know too what that flash of silver you described might have been. The shovel."

"Did he hit me with the shovel?" she asked, trying to be brave.

"I think so."

"Oh, my God," she said. Very slowly, like a toppling tree, she leaned forward and buried her face in her hands.

In a moment, she found herself cradled in Lucas's arms while her tears soaked into a circle on the cloth under her cheek. Sniffling, she tried to sit up. But he held her to him, saying, "Hush, dearest. Just hush."

"I'm all right. I just can't believe that someone actually tried to . . . tried to . . . My poor babies!"

"They're all right," he said, his forehead wrinkling with concern. "They're in Sedalia with your mother, remember?"

"Of course I remember. But what would have become of them without me? How could someone be so cruel?"

"You must have surprised him. But surprised him doing what?"

"I don't know. He was just there! But I know one thing —he was no ghost. Ghosts don't use shovels."

"Oh, I think we can rule out ghosts and anything else supernatural. This much wickedness has to be the work of man."

"I'm afraid . . . afraid you're right, that is."

"Grace." He lifted her chin with gentle fingertips. "Grace, it's all right to admit to me that you're frightened."

"But I'm . . ."

"I'm frightened too. I have gained too much in the last two weeks to lose you now."

There was nothing to do but kiss him again. She told herself that it was just her bodily weakness that made her cling to him. But a secret side of her confessed that she had often wished for a strong pair of arms to hold her. Though she knew it was best to stand on her own two feet, a burden shared was still a burden halved. And she was so tired.

When her eyes closed, he laid her down on her pillows with a whispered blessing. Then Lucas tiptoed from the room. Grace smiled sleepily.

Yet despite her exhaustion, she found it difficult to rest. Questions crept slowly into her head and, once there, refused to be dislodged. What had Lucas been doing at the farm last night? How had he known where to find her? How did he learn she'd been hit with her own shovel?

A hideous suspicion slithered into her thoughts. Harder to budge even than the questions, this suspicion whispered in her ears, "Are you sure it wasn't Lucas in the barn last night?"

Grace instantly dismissed the thought as preposterous. She closed her eyes and settled down to sleep. Yet the whispers followed her across the border between waking and slumber. "Are you sure? Are you sure?"

A short while later, Grace woke from a troubled sleep. Thankfully, the pain *inside* her head had faded to a mere dull ache, though the outside was as tender as before. Nevertheless, this time when she got up, she could walk a straight line across her room without holding on to the furniture.

She'd entered the sitting room, making for her rocking chair, when she heard the jingle of harness and the creak of saddle leather. Peering out through the curtains, Grace saw Marshal Wyman ride up. With the shadow of their last meeting between them, Grace didn't feel strong enough to meet him, though she knew herself to be a coward.

He didn't dismount from his pale gray horse. The skirt of his coat lay flicked back over his thigh, leaving his long gun exposed to quick fingers. "So you're here," he said.

"That's right." Lucas stepped down one stair from the porch to stand facing the marshal.

"That's a violation of your parole, you know. Judge Sterling ain't going to like it."

"The judge is going to have to lump it. And so are you."

"Is that right?" Wyman seemed taken aback by the harshness of Lucas's tone. Grace too was startled. It was as though an immovable boulder had spoken.

"Absolutely. I don't move one foot from this property unless Mrs. Landers accompanies me."

"Mrs. Landers? She ain't here, is she? I thought she was in Sedalia." His brown-eyed gaze passed over the house.

"No, she came back last night."

"Is that right? Reckon I better have a word with her. I mean to tell her what you been saying. Maybe she'll have something to say about your ideas."

"She's resting inside."

"Resting? In the daytime? That don't sound like Mrs. Landers. Go on and get her."

"I told you . . . she's resting."

"Look here," the marshal said, shifting on his saddle. "You're starting to get me riled. You bring Mrs. Landers on out here pronto. I want to see her."

Grace put her hands on her hips, letting the curtain fall swinging against the window. Wyman was becoming outrageous, giving orders on her place like this! If he needed another sharp lesson, she was more than willing to give it to him.

As she stepped into the kitchen, she heard Lucas say, "There'll be no more nights when this place is unguarded."

"Haven't been all that many lately anyway, now have there? You see, I know that crazy deputy of mine's been letting you out at night. I'm minded to bounce him unless you be sensible."

"I can't help that," Lucas said. "Crowley will have to take his chances. I'm not leaving this place. And that's my final word." He turned and stepped again onto the porch.

The marshal's right hand lifted slowly to come down solidly on the exposed butt of his gun. "I can make you come along with me, you know."

"You can try."

The marshal pulled his gun, his hand moving so quickly all Grace could see was a blur. Then the ugly blue-black steel was in his hand, held with an air of negligence. "If that's the way you want it—"

Grace pushed open the door so violently that it rebounded against the wall. "Put that gun away! There'll be no shooting on my farm!"

Wyman stared at her as she emerged into the sunshine. Grace put up a hand to shade her sensitive eyes from the glare. She also half concealed the hideous bruise, for she felt that Wyman must be staring at that. She said, "What do you want, Marshal?"

"I . . . I want you to hear how your hired hand's been talking."

"Well?" Lucas stood before her like a guardian. Proud that he loved her, Grace took her place beside him.

"He's talking like he owns the place. 'Sides, he didn't come back to the jail last night. I gotta take him along with me. I'm purely goin' to hate having to force him to go."

Grace stepped in front of Lucas. "Listen, Marshal. The judge said I'm responsible for this man by daylight. In case you haven't noticed, it's daylight now. So never you mind about him."

"Get behind me, Grace," Lucas said, putting his hand on her shoulder and moving her out of his way. Only then did Grace realize that the marshal could have put a bullet through her to get to him.

Perhaps the marshal realized it too. He shoved the gun back into the holster. "If you folks want to make me go get a warrant, I sure will."

"You do that," Lucas said. "It won't make any difference."

The marshal spit, and wheeled his horse away. As soon as he was out of the gate, Grace gathered her skirts and started down the steps.

"Where do you think you are going?" Lucas asked, jumping off the porch to catch her.

"To hitch up the wagon, of course. We'll get to the judge before him, don't you worry about that!"

He caught her by the arm and swung her off her feet, one arm behind her knees. Doing an about-face, he started back toward the house.

"Have you gone crazy?" she demanded.

"I'm saving you from something more dangerous than mud this time, Grace."

"Put me down. Don't you know they'll throw you in jail for keeps? I've got to get to the judge first."

"You're going back to bed and that's the only place you're going."

She wriggled out of his arms. Her feet hit the floor with a bang that raced through her spine and leaped out the top of her head. Her knees buckled.

Lucas caught her as she sagged. "Stubborn woman," he muttered.

"Darn right," she said on a sigh against his powerful shoulder.

His lips moving in her hair, he said softly, "I'm stubborn too. And stronger than you are. So please do as you are told for once in your life. Besides, I sent Dr. Birkins to see the judge last night."

"You what?"

"We thought it would be best to get *his* permission for me to leave the jail at night, especially as the marshal had already refused. I don't intend to let Jasper have any more trouble than he has right now."

"And you and the doctor decided all this last night?"

"That's right. Don't bother to say thank you, Grace; it's the least—"

"The least you could have done is asked me if it's all right for you to stay here." She pushed away from his enfolding arms. "This is still my place, isn't it? Marshal Wyman is right; you are acting as if you own it."

"Go on," he said. "You're not really mad. Besides, you were in no condition to ask about anything last night."

"Did it occur to either of you that I might not want my business spread all over town?"

"Who's going to talk about you?"

"Just everybody. Half of them probably think you beat me. They already think we're . . . that we mean something to each other."

"Bless my soul, gossip's right for once." His smile was so intimate that she found herself blushing.

He said, "Grace, Dr. Birkins won't tell anyone about what happened. No one except the judge. You don't have to worry about gossip."

"Lucas, the doctor and the judge are the biggest gossips in town. And what they don't say, their wives guess. And everyone is going to wonder . . ."

"Wonder what?"

She looked into his eyes, all her doubts rising to the surface of her mind. "What were you doing here last night? How did you know I was in the barn? When did you find out about the shovel?"

He frowned at her, as his eyes changed from hurt to angry. "In a moment, you'll be asking me whether I'm the one that struck you down."

Grace didn't answer. She couldn't even bring herself to meet his eyes after that single glance. She didn't know which would be worse—to hear the truth, or to hear him lie.

"Grace, you don't mean it," he said, with a half chuckle. He went to gather her in his arms, but she stepped away, her outthrust hand between them. He stopped as if he'd run into a wall.

"I want to trust you, Lucas. But how can I? For all I know, you could have been lying since the day you came here. Maybe you never even lost your memory. Maybe . . . Oh, I don't know," she cried suddenly, tortured. "Don't you see I don't dare trust you? I have to think of the future. What if you . . . ?"

"What if I did try to kill you last night?" he asked, snatching the unspoken words from the air as though from her lips. "Grace, listen to me. This is just the bang on your head talking. You know you had strange things going on at the barn months before I came here."

"I know," she said, slowly drawing her hand out from his. "But you could be working for someone in town. Someone who thinks there really is raiders' gold buried in my barn."

"You don't believe that."

"I don't know what I believe anymore. If only you could tell me who you really are."

"I can."

"What?"

"Last night, when I thought you were . . . The shock made me remember. My real name is Cobb. John Cobb."

"A nice name," she said coldly.

"Thank you. I was named for my mother's father."

"And you just suddenly remembered this last night? Out of the clear blue sky, as it were?" She saw his face change from composure to surprise.

"You don't think I'm lying about *that?* For God's sake, Grace, I thought you'd be happy. I'm not just some drifter. I have a name, some position in life."

"Oh, I am happy. Delighted. Now I know for sure I can't trust you."

Chapter
Seventeen

"Did you need something, Mrs. Landers?" Wenonah asked, drying her hands on a towel.

"Yes, I need to be doing something."

"What?"

"Anything. Anything but lie there staring at the ceiling for another minute."

Grace stood in the kitchen doorway, fully dressed except for her shoes. She couldn't quite face bending down to put them on. Even less could she face the mirror this morning. Her bruise was no longer confined to her forehead, but had blossomed down her cheek. She'd only been able to chew her breakfast on her right side. However, the swelling had gone down overnight.

Entering, Grace saw that her kitchen was spotless. Even the stubborn grease stain on her linoleum floor, the last improvement Chick had made to the place, was gone. The old pine table that served as countertop, dirty-dish collector and, at times, children's fort, had been scrubbed so that it looked brand new, and store-bought at that. On it stood her beloved blue bowl, the dough within it rising under a checked cloth.

She uncovered the bowl and looked around for the board she used for rolling out. Wenonah hid the rolling pin behind her back and asked, "Do you remember what you told me when my wrist was sprained?"

"No, but I'm afraid you do."

"You told me to act like a lady of leisure. Now it's your turn. Give me that bowl back."

Reluctantly, Grace handed over the large piece of cobalt-blue pottery. "I wonder if you remember how fidgety you were when you couldn't do anything."

Wenonah's shy smile appeared. "I've never been much of a one for idle hands."

"Me either. What are you making that smells so good?"

"Molasses cookies. My mother's recipe."

"Your mother's?" Grace didn't want to ask the question that popped into her head, but she hadn't known Indians *made* cookies.

"Yes. She was adopted by a white family for a while."

"Only for a while?"

"She ran away from them. Not because they were cruel to her, but because she belonged to her tribe, not to them."

"But she married a white man."

Wenonah shrugged. "That was love."

Protecting her hand with a towel, she opened the heavy cast-iron door, highly embossed with vines and improbable flowers. A waft of heat caught her right in the face, yet released also the warm scent of cookies. Squinting against the heat, Wenonah reached in and pulled out a tray filled with crisp brown rounds. Slinging the tray onto the table, she said, almost to herself, "I bet even his mother can't beat my cookies."

"Oh, so that's who they're for," Grace said.

"I don't know what you mean." Then she said, slightly defensively, "Well, Jasper might come by today. And if he really has lost his job . . ."

"You'll console him?"

Wenonah nodded, a fugitive dimple appearing in her cheek. Grace knew that if Jasper asked Wenonah to marry him, all the girl's talk about remaining single would fly out the window. No unmarried woman ever baked cookies for a single man without some hope in her heart.

Grace put her arm around the girl's shoulder. At first, Wenonah stood stiffly, but then it was as if Grace embraced one of her own children. "I'm sure your cookies will make him turn his nose up at his mother's. And if not . . . then he's a bigger fool than I ever took him for."

"He might not even come today."

Smoothing Wenonah's disheveled hair, Grace said, "You know, you're old enough to start putting your hair up. Maybe a love knot on the back of your head, or a few ringlets. One thing's sure, you won't need to add any false hair."

"Do you think I should frizz?"

"I wouldn't. That's so bad for your hair. A girlfriend of mine once burnt hers off doing that." She patted Wenonah's shoulder. "Shall we try a few styles later on today? I think I have a few old copies of *Harper's Bazaar* around. I've been keeping them until Callie's old enough to care about her appearance—though I think I have a long wait ahead of me."

They talked for a while about hair, and clothes, and whether tight-lacing was really necessary. Then Grace said, "I know. I'll go pick some strawberries and we can have some after lunch."

"Oh, but Mr. Lucas said . . ."

"What did Mr. Lucas say?"

Wenonah pressed her lips together firmly.

"Go on."

"He said I shouldn't let you leave the house."

"Picking a few berries will neither make nor mar me, Wenonah. And so you may tell Mr. Lucas. Really, that man is getting to be a genuine tyrant. I'll have to have a little talk with him about this Centennial coming up. Maybe he hasn't heard about the Declaration of Independence."

Her arm looped through the berry-basket handle, Grace left the house, shading her face with her broadest-brimmed straw hat. Though the temperature outside made the overheated kitchen seem like a cool oasis, Grace couldn't complain about the weather. No clouds dared to challenge the sun, yet the earlier rains had blessed the lands with lush grass. The scent of the wild honeysuckle rolled across the road, breast-high. It hardly seemed possible that any evil had touched her last night.

Next to the barn, the pasture where the cow and mules grazed had a rich look. Even in bare feet, Grace climbed the fence as nimbly as a child. Holding her skirt up, and watching where she stepped, she crossed the pasture, only to climb the fence on the other side.

"Grace!" she heard Lucas call as she started over the split logs. She paused on the top to give him a careless wave.

Beyond the fence, she'd planted bare-root strawberry plants, culled from her mother's garden the day she married Chick. She'd kept them in a bucket of water, splashing and spilling with every turn of the wagon's wheels. They hadn't slept a night here before she'd sent Chick out to dig a spot for them.

Now the low plants sprawled all over the ground behind the pasture. The jewel-like fruits were safe here from the clumping hooves and greedy tongues of the farm animals, though the birds were always competition. Yet the birds weren't the main reason Grace rarely got to eat the strawberries she nurtured with such care. However, there were plenty of ripe ones now, after four days without the children picking all the best. Not that they'd be deprived. Her mother's garden overran with lush fruit.

She'd just chosen a spot with many berries within reach of her arm when Lucas appeared above her. "Grace, are you out of your mind?"

"I don't think so. Watch where you're stepping, please. I don't want any of these little runners crushed."

"What?"

"You're standing in my strawberry patch. Are you going to yell at me, or help me pick?"

He crouched down beside her. "I saw you go over that fence. Don't you think it would have been wiser to go around?"

"The only time I've ever gone around is when I was pregnant."

His gaze became subtly warmer. "I wish I'd seen you when you were pregnant. I've heard that a woman is at her most beautiful then. You must have been very beautiful."

Grace blinked at him in surprise. Was he serious? "I

suppose so, if you find fat, crabby women with prickly heat beautiful."

"Oh, surely not . . ."

"Oh, definitely yes. Callie was born in August. Do you know how hot it gets here in August? If you were sticking around, you'd find out."

"What do you mean, if I were sticking around?"

He put his hand on her cheek and tried to make her look at him. Grace tossed her head. "You know who you are now. Soon as your time's up, you'll be heading back to where you belong."

"I haven't made up my mind about that yet."

Now it was her turn to ask what he meant. "You've got family, don't you?"

"Just a father now. My mother died when I was a boy."

Her heart went out to him, but she reined it in. "He must be worried about you. You've got to let him know you're all right, not dead in a ditch somewhere."

"Yes, I should probably let Father know." Looking off into the woods, he said, "I'm not sure I want to go back to the life I had before. To the person I was before."

Puzzled, Grace stared at him. She'd never seen him look troubled before. Except for his headaches, Lucas had always seemed so happy-go-lucky, taking things as they came. She supposed it was hard to think about the future without a past.

"Who were you?" she asked. "Who are you?"

They must have looked like fools, she thought, to anyone who might see them. Lucas still gazed off into the distance, while she had put one hand down in the dirt to balance herself while she tried to see into his face.

When he turned, she was taken aback by the depth of sorrow in his eyes. "Don't ask me," he said. "Don't make me tell you."

"All right," she said. He evidently didn't believe her. "No, really, it's all right." She touched his hand fleetingly. "I won't ask any questions. Except one."

"What's that?" He spoke slowly, as if afraid of what specter she might raise.

"Should I keep calling you Lucas, or do you prefer

John? I've never been too fond of that name—a little too plain—but I'll try and get used to it, if you want."

The tension left his shoulders and face, leaving him more like the man she knew. "Whatever you want. I've gotten used to Lucas. But I'd answer to 'Hey, you,' if you were calling me."

"Seems to me you know a little bit too much about smooth-talking to be the Lucas I know."

"I'm just saying all the things Lucas has been thinking. He has been keeping his hands to himself, but his thoughts have been roaming."

"You ought to put them on a leash."

Happy that the miserable look had faded from his eyes, for she'd been horrified by the strength of her wish to comfort him, Grace reached for a brilliant red berry half-hidden beneath saw-bladed leaves. Too tempting to resist, Grace popped the sun-warmed fruit into her mouth. The taste, rich yet sharp, nearly made her swoon. "The best!" she sighed.

Glancing up, she saw his gaze fixed on her mouth. She swallowed quickly. "Here," she said, pushing the basket toward him. "Help me pick, or you won't get any later."

"Any what?"

"Any strawberries, of course. What else . . . ?"

He moved closer, still on his knees. A quickening of excitement started in Grace's breast, a tingle that ran over her, raising gooseflesh wherever it touched. With as much effort as if her arm were too heavy to lift, Grace raised one hand to fend him off.

Instead, it slipped around his neck. "Grace," he said, his arms going around her waist. He snugged her against him and bowed his head to kiss her lips.

At his first gentle nuzzle, Grace went up in flames. It was as if every part of her body had been waiting for his return and rejoiced. Though her mind might cherish reservations, her body obviously had no doubts. It felt so right; the sun on her back, the man in her arms and the lingering flavor on her lips.

"Strawberries were never my favorite," he murmured, as he raised his head. "I may change my mind."

Grace was not in the mood for courtly compliments. "Please," she said, touching her lips to the corner of his mouth.

His indigo eyes growing somber, he obeyed her unspoken command and slanted his mouth over hers. She clung to him, meeting his force with her own. They tried new holds, new pressures. The delights he'd shown her in the barn came back to her, intensified by the weeks of waiting.

Grace quickly noticed, however, a difference in Lucas. He'd been skillful before, but now he had a gift of ingenuity that left her gasping. He roamed her face, being so careful to avoid any painful spot, yet arousing everywhere he caressed. The bruises had no chance to distress her, swallowed up as they were in the overwhelming flood of delight. She panted and sobbed, when he nibbled the tender lobe of her ear, his breath tickling. Closing her eyes, she let her head fall back, exposing her throat to his lips.

"Lucas, I . . ." She couldn't bring herself to plead with him again, but she felt as if he were driving her along toward some precipice. A thrill of fear went through her, as she wondered dimly what he must think of her abandonment.

He didn't hesitate. She quivered as he tasted the soft skin of her throat, feeling the brush of his dark hair against her face. And when his hand came up to cup her through her blouse, she felt powerless to move away. At the back of her mind, she knew they were far enough away from the house not to be seen by anyone. It seemed somehow natural to be making love in the full light of the sun, not in the shameful darkness of her room.

Lucas worked free the tiny shell buttons that ran from her high collar to her waist. She didn't help him, but she couldn't bring herself to stop him. Grace's nails curled into her palms as he pushed aside the open edges of cloth and breathed, "God, Grace. You're so beautiful."

She dared to glance down at herself, to try and see what he saw. Her skin, never exposed to the sun, gleamed as white as cream in its rays. The low embroidered edge of

her chemise did nothing to conceal the top half circle of
her pink nipples.

The sun showed too much, even the faint silver lines
that marked her skin. She tried to shield her breasts, a
shiver of shame rising. "They're too big," she said. "Two
children . . ."

Gently Lucas pushed her hands away. "No, they're
magnificent."

He smoothed down the edge of the white chemise and
then cupped her breast, lifting it free of confinement.
Grace watched his face anxiously for any sign of distaste.
She saw only a yearning desire that conquered her self-
consciousness.

The first touch of his lips there woke all the desire she'd
worked so hard for so long to repress. She ran her fingers
through his hair to hold him there. Lucas drew the tight
tip into the heat of his mouth.

Grace began to feel a familiar, long-lost commotion
building inside. Tiny cries broke from her. He didn't stop
as her fingers sought for a grasp on his shoulders. He
didn't stop though her hips moved recklessly against his.
He didn't stop until she lay limply in his arms.

His body was solid against her when she lifted her head
off his shoulder. As embarrassed as a deflowered virgin,
Grace couldn't quite meet his intense eyes. "I . . . Oh,
dear."

It was impossible not to be aware of the tumult within
him, while his heart drummed furiously beneath her ear
and his breathing came as fast as a runner's. She knew
what he wanted.

To tell the truth, she wanted it too. However, now that
the insane moment had passed, the doubts she had came
crowding again into her head. How could she give herself
to him fully when she couldn't be sure he was who she
thought?

"Lucas, don't think me a tease, but I . . ."

He moved ever so slightly away from her, just enough
to look down at her unhappy expression with laughter in
his eyes. "I don't intend to ravish you here," he said.

Tugging her shirt together, he said, "Well, not any more than I have already."

Grace thought she hadn't a blush left. She was wrong. "But what about you?" she asked, knowing how much she betrayed. But for goodness' sake, he couldn't think Bart and Callie came from a cabbage patch. Not after seeing her half-naked anyway.

He shrugged, a little painfully perhaps. "I've managed to live through the last two weeks without exploding or going crazy."

"The last two weeks? But you didn't even try . . ."

"You didn't want me to try. You made that clear after our little visit from the skunks. But I took the liberty of continuing to think about you, Grace. I couldn't stop myself from imagining you. Though I have to admit, the reality is more amazing than anything I dreamed of."

Softly, Grace said, "I want you too."

He touched her cheek, his thumb caressing her lower lip. "You want Lucas, Grace. Part of me *is* Lucas. But until you're comfortable with the rest of me, I won't ask you for any more than what you've already given me. Though I have no idea how I'm to sleep now. Every time I close my eyes, I'm going to see you in this strawberry patch. Only you're far sweeter than the berries."

Grace couldn't bring herself to confess that she'd remember these moments always as well.

They returned to the house, taking at Lucas's insistence the long way around. As they carried the overflowing basket between them, Lucas made her laugh at his foolish story of a boyhood accident with a loaded table. "The conjuror at my birthday party had made it look so easy. Whisk! Not a glass rattled."

"However did he do that?"

"I haven't figured it out from that day to this. But it certainly didn't work for me. I'll never forget that crash." Catching sight of her skeptical face, he said, "Or at any rate, I'll never forget it again."

"Do you remember everything now?"

"Yes. Bits of it clearer than others. I know there's no wife waiting for me, though I . . ."

"Yes?" She took on the full burden of the basket.

"I had an understanding with a girl. Clarissa Hazelforth. Her father's a crony of my father."

"I see." Grace began to walk faster, her bare feet digging into the soil.

"No, you don't." He stepped in front of her. "I'm not in love with her. I've never been in love with anyone before, not like this."

"You kiss a little too well for me to believe you."

She tried to step around him. He blocked her. "I haven't been a saint, Grace. But neither have I been much of a sinner. No woman has ever complained that I mistreated her, or that I have ever been less than generous."

"I'm not interested," she said, knowing she lied.

She managed to make her way around him. She'd gone only a few steps when she turned to fling a question at him. "Who's Margot?"

"Margot? Ah, Margot," he smiled reminiscently. "Just a girl I used to know."

"I'm not interested."

He walked behind her up to the house. "Of course, there's always Mrs. Presby . . . ," he mused, loudly enough for Grace to hear.

She told herself she shouldn't ask, that it was just stoking his pride, but she couldn't keep her lips sealed over the words. "What about Rena Presby?"

"Hum? I was just wondering if she'd be the right person to advise me."

"About what?"

"About the proper courting gift for a certain woman."

"Courting gift?"

"Some little token of affection is customary when a man starts thinking seriously about a woman."

He stood before her, smiling in the sunshine like a giddy god, his black hair shining with those teasing red gleams. His smile was both tender and proud, though his eyes were solemn. She couldn't treat his statement as a joke.

He said, his deep voice more thrilling than ever, "I hope you'll marry me, Grace. I want to prove to you that you can trust me. I can't think of a better way to show that I'm planning to 'stick around,' can you? Besides, I love you."

Temptation sprang up as though the devil himself stood beside her, showing her the earth and all its wonders. She seemed to hear a voice whispering, "say yes, say yes," and she didn't know if it was the devil or her best angel.

It was obvious that Lucas came from wealth. All that talk about fancy birthday parties hadn't been lost on her. Marry him and it was possible that she'd never know another day of worry or trouble. All she had to do was give up all her rights.

"Let's not talk about this now," she said, taking refuge in weakness. "I shouldn't have spent all that time in the sun."

Instantly, he came to her side. "Here I am, thinking only of what I want and not of you. Lean on me, dearest. I'll take care of you."

That was exactly what she was afraid of.

She separated from him at her bedroom door, pleading her weakness. His dark eyes dwelled on her with such loving concern that she felt ashamed of herself for pretending. She should just tell him bluntly that she'd never marry him and that would be that. Only she was very much afraid that he would have powers of persuasion even more fascinating than those he had so far shown.

Grace looked at herself in the mirror, her spilling hair and misbuttoned blouse telling their own tale. What had gotten into her? She had never behaved so wantonly before. Chick would have called the doctor to her if she'd ever hinted at wanting to make love outdoors, in daylight!

Yet she admitted here, in the privacy of her room, with only her mirror for witness, that something in her had always demanded the honesty of love in the light. Grace was torn between knowing she'd done the right thing in stopping Lucas from proceeding, and regret that she had stopped him.

She couldn't stay in her room for long. First of all, she hated anything that looked like sulking, and secondly, a delicious smell soon floated through the air, beckoning her out as though she'd been hypnotized.

Lucas was already seated at the kitchen table, though he started to his feet the moment he saw her. His smile held an intimate knowledge as Grace sat down.

"You're spoiling me," she said to Wenonah, as the girl laid a filled plate before her. "I can't imagine how I'll ever be able to face my own cooking again. I've always wanted to be a better cook, but my husband never cared much for fancy dishes."

Lucas said, "I'm a plain man, myself."

Grace hardly looked at him. She put a forkful of creamed fresh peas and new potatoes in her mouth, and sighed blissfully. "Mine never taste like this!"

"It's how I season them," Wenonah said shyly. She had just seated herself when a knock sounded on the porch door. The girl's hands went instantly to pat her hair. Grace regretted not having taken the time to help her experiment with new hairstyles, as she had promised.

Yet Jasper didn't seem to see anything wrong. He came in, wiping his feet conscientiously on the rag rug before the door. "Are you folks just sitting down? I can come back. . . ."

Lucas pushed back the fourth chair from the table. "Have a seat," he said. "There's plenty."

Then Grace had to glance at him. This was still her house, wasn't it? But she turned a cheerful smile toward Jasper. "You're welcome, Mr. Crowley."

He stared at her. She remembered what she looked like and ducked her head. Quickly scooping up one of the light and airy liver dumplings on her plate, she tucked it into her mouth. Keeping the unmarked side of her face toward the young deputy, she said, "Wonderful! Be sure and try some of these. Wenonah made everything. My dumplings always come out like lead sinkers."

Wenonah had already filled a plate for Jasper. He looked down at the overflowing plate before him and gave Lucas a lopsided smile. "Looks like my ma's ideas of how to feed a man are spreading."

"That's not the only thing that will be spreading if I keep eating like this."

The two men grinned and picked up their forks. Wenonah ate in silence, flicking doting glances at Jasper. The moment he would put his hand out for something, whether it was salt, pepper or the homemade onion sauce, she reached it first and passed it to him with a smile.

Grace said, hinting on Wenonah's behalf, "Are you looking forward to the dance next week, Deputy?"

"Yes, ma'am, but you can't call me deputy no more."

That broke Wenonah's worshipful silence. "Were you discharged?"

Lucas said, "I hope you haven't gotten into trouble on my account."

The young man shook his head. "Nope. It's just that the marshal started jawing at me 'bout this and that, and I wasn't 'bout to sit still for it. You got any more of this here cornbread, Miss Wenonah?"

After everyone was stuffed, Wenonah stood up and said, "I'll get dessert."

"Oh, no," Jasper groaned, sitting back from the table and patting a hand comfortingly against his stomach. "I couldn't take another bite. What have you got?"

She brought out the hulled strawberries, lightly dusted with sugar, and the filled creamer. Jasper sat up, all thought of refusal dismissed. "Strawberries? Where'd they come from? My ma can't ever get hers to fruit more'n once and even then they're too small to see, practically."

He stuck his fork into the plumpest in his bowl and ate it with more speed than manners. Wenonah said, "I'll be happy to pick you some to take home to her, if you'd like." Then she glanced belatedly at Grace for permission. Grace nodded and winked.

For herself, she found it unexpectedly difficult to eat the delightfully ripe fruit. Every sweet, fragrant bite reminded her of those delirious moments when Lucas had awakened feelings she'd thought long buried. Try as she might to keep her eyes from turning his way, sooner or later she'd look, only to find him studying her.

When the last heart-shaped fruit had disappeared from the table, Grace said, "I'll help you clear, Wenonah."

"No, let me," Jasper said. "Ma'd purely skin me 'live if I didn't help with the dishes."

"I've got a better idea." Grace stood up and collected the basket from the sink. "You and Wenonah go pick some berries and Lucas can do the dishes."

"Wait a minute . . . ," Lucas began.

Shyly, Wenonah said, "I'll show you where to go, Mr. Crowley."

"Thanks." He unfolded his long legs from beneath the table and held open the door for the girl.

Grace rose up in her seat so she could see out the window. Jasper walked beside Wenonah. As Grace watched, he scooped the basket out of her hand. His lanky leanness well matched Wenonah's willowy yet rounded form.

"You're shameless," Lucas said, collecting the dishes. Grace looked up at him, alarmed. "As a matchmaker, I mean."

"I'm not so bad. I don't throw everybody together, but if they happen to be people I like, well . . ."

"Of course, you wouldn't have to work too hard to bring those two together. She's wild about him—it's written all over her."

"The question is . . . can Jasper read?"

Unable to be idle while another person worked, Grace picked up the clean bucket she used to fetch water. Lucas looked askance as she lifted it. "I'll get that for you."

"No, it's all right."

"Now, you're not going all the way out to the pump . . ."

Shaking her head, Grace turned to the well-rubbed black iron stove that stood against the wall. Putting the bucket on the floor, she turned the little brass spigot on the front of the stove and steaming hot water ran out into the bucket.

"I didn't know you could do that!" Lucas said.

"Every modern convenience supplied."

Grace carried the water to the sink. After checking for

potato peelings or strawberry hulls, though Wenonah would have never let one escape the slop pail, Grace poured the hot water into the sink. "Now you can wash up without waiting for water to heat up on the back burner. It was the one thing I insisted on when we bought this stove. The rest of the house can go to rack and ruin, but I can't stand having dirty dishes around. Draws mice, among other critters."

"Are you telling me, or warning me?" Lucas asked with a twinkle.

"I'm just making conversation."

"I thought maybe you were telling me what I have to look forward to. No dirty dishes and no mice. Sounds like the perfect home to me."

Grace saved herself from answering by looking for the soap. By the time she found it, she'd recovered her senses enough to say, "Scrape the plates into the slop pail, please."

"You say the sweetest things," Lucas said with a grin. "You almost turn my head."

She had to giggle a little at that, though she quickly suppressed it. As he scraped and she turned back her sleeves to start washing, she was taken aback by how natural it seemed to be doing indoor chores with him. Just as it had seemed right to be doing outside chores together. She caught herself up, and wondered when she'd lost her objections to Lucas coming inside the house. Had it been as long ago as the visit from the skunks?

As they worked, he asked her how her trip had gone. "I didn't have the chance to ask you before," he said, making no reference to the reason for this oversight.

"Oh, well, you know. Relatives."

"If you'd said that to me last week . . . Are they very difficult people, your parents?"

"No, it's me. I get itchy after I'm there a few days. Mother doesn't seem to remember that I'm an adult. She actually asked me if I'd washed my neck one morning! Thank goodness the children were already outside, or I'd never live it down."

"Maybe she misses having her own children around. Are you her only one?"

"No, and the rest of my family still lives in Sedalia. They're all happily married, with increasing families. My little sister Eloise had her first, a boy, a couple of months ago. She brought him along to church. He's as cute as a bug."

She'd held her new nephew for a few moments as he was being passed around from family member to friend, the anxious mother hovering. Grace had tried hard not to feel the maternal longing called up by the squirming bundle of infancy against her breast. Bart and Callie were wonderful children, but there was something secret and spiritual between a mother and infant, something that lessened or was lost as the child grew older. Only sometimes now, when Callie clung to her before sleeping, could Grace know that feeling again.

She washed while Lucas, a half apron snug around his lean hips, dried. "Missed some," he said, sending a plate back.

"Where?"

"Right there." He held the wet dish with one hand and pointed with the other.

"I don't see anything," she said, peering closely.

He kissed the back of her neck. Startled, Grace jumped. She knocked the dish from his hand and it smashed on the floor.

"Now look what you've done!" she cried, as tremors flooded her body. How could one slight caress cause this much disruption in a sensible woman?

"I'll get it," he said, kneeling to collect the heavy shards of ironstone. He looked up at her, his eyes glowing like sapphires. "This is about the right position."

"For what?"

"To propose to a lady."

"You did that already." Grace curled her fingers against her palms to keep them from wandering to touch his hair; it looked so alive and shiny.

"I know. You haven't answered me yet."

She looked down at her hands, wrinkled by water. "I . . ."

The noisy steps of booted feet on the porch interrupted her, and Jasper's voice came through the door, "Then I dropped my badge on his desk and strolled on out."

Jasper held the door open for Wenonah. The girl had a happy glow about her that was unmistakably that of love. "I don't see how you could have done anything else," she said. "A man has to have pride or he's no man."

Lucas gathered up the pieces of plate and put them on the table. He met Grace's eyes as he returned to take up his dishcloth. The expression in them said clearly that the moment was only postponed. She was glad, for she shrank from hurting him, as her flat refusal must inevitably do. She didn't care to imagine how much it would hurt her.

Jasper didn't stay long, only stopping to thank Grace for the strawberries. "It's nothing," she said. "You saw how much we've got out there."

"Well, don't be surprised to see me out this way again right soon. Ma's bound to want some more."

"Just leave me enough to take to the picnic on the fourth and I won't grudge you a bushelful."

The moment he stepped off the porch and out of earshot, Wenonah turned to Grace. "He asked me, he asked me!" she said, her white teeth showing in a smile so broad Grace had to look twice to be sure it was really Wenonah.

"Asked you what, honey?" It couldn't be marriage. Not so soon. Then she glanced at Lucas. He hadn't known her half as long as Wenonah had been cleaning the jail.

"Why, to the dance, of course. I didn't think he was going to, but then he did. He put the last berry in the basket and then he asked me."

Lucas murmured, "There's just something about that strawberry patch. . . ."

"That's wonderful!" Grace said to Wenonah, after aiming a sketchy kick at Lucas's ankle. "I told you he liked you."

The girl's smile faded. A troubled wrinkle creased her forehead. "I can't go," she said.

"What? Why would you say that? Of course you'll go."

"But I don't have anything decent to wear. I can't go looking like . . . like the girl who cleans the jail. But that's all I am. Just the half-breed who cleans the jail!" Her long-lashed eyes filling with tears, Wenonah whirled around and dashed for her room.

Grace and Lucas looked at each other. "I could make one of my dresses over for her," Grace said. "But my things aren't any better than hers. I already gave away my wedding dress."

"We could buy her something."

"What with? No one will give credit on piece goods."

Lucas looked worriedly down the hall. The house was not soundproof. The girl's wracking sobs could be heard plainly in the kitchen. "I never knew being a fairy godfather was so hard."

"It's not easy for a godmother, either. If only I could lay my hands on some real money. . . . Eggs!"

"Eggs?"

"That man, the other day . . ." She began counting on her fingers.

"Grace, what are you talking about?"

"You remember, the day you got all those fancy new clothes."

He rubbed his hand over his lips and coughed. "Mrs. Presby is a very generous lady."

"I'll say. But do you remember that man who almost ran into you? He thought maybe he knew you."

"Okay . . . Yes, I remember. In the loud checked suit."

"He said that there was no food on the trains. That there was no place to buy a meal in Ogden. He bought all the eggs I had and only wished they were cooked."

"So what are you going to do? Sell hard-boiled eggs to train passengers?"

"Eggs-actly." She was off to the henhouse before he had a chance to register that she had actually made as vile a pun as he had ever heard. His shout of laughter followed her a few seconds later.

Chapter
Eighteen

In the end, it was Wenonah herself who went every day to wait for the trains. Though she did not tell him her reason for working there, Jasper Crowley waited with her, walked her back and, on occasion, drove off male passengers who thought she might consider selling something besides eggs and new-made bread.

After four days, Wenonah hurried home from the dry-goods store, a brown paper parcel tucked under her arm. She burst into the house to unroll a length of dotted swiss. "Can we do it?" she asked Grace.

"We'll give it our best try."

They even stayed home from church that Sunday to labor on it, taking innumerable stitches as tiny as elf footprints. Lucas looked on in wonder, then went to water the garden. When he came back, they hadn't moved, only their painstaking hands waving over the cloth, the thin needles glistening. He got used to eating hastily prepared and often cold food. Only when Jasper stopped by the house—which he did more and more often, on less and less excuse—did Wenonah stop working.

The morning of the Glorious Fourth was clear and still, dry and hot as the inside of an oven's firebox. Lucas came into the kitchen from Callie's improvised room, to find Grace already sitting there, an empty cup between her hands.

She blinked vaguely at him when he picked up the coffeepot and shook it. "More please," she said, holding out her cup.

Pouring out the black, fragrant brew, he asked, "What time did you go to bed last night?"

" 'Bout two-thirty."

"Two-thirty? You shouldn't be drinking coffee; you should be under the covers."

"It's finished."

"The dress?"

Grace nodded wearily. Putting the cup down on the table, she dropped her head onto her folded arms. "She looks like a dream in it," she said, muffled.

"Do you think it's worth it? All that hard work. Nearly going blind sewing by lamplight. Was it worth it?"

Grace rolled her head to one side and gazed up at him through that eye. A tired but elated smile curved the side of her mouth. "When you see her in it, you tell me if it was all worth it."

Slowly, she sat up, rolling her stiffened shoulders to work the kinks out. "You remember when we took that mud bath?" she asked. She reached across her chest with her right hand and started rubbing her left shoulder. "Would you mind . . . ?"

"Gladly."

The slight pain that accompanied this massage was soon lost in the pleasure of having tired muscles and sore bones eased by his masterful hands. Grace let her head loll back and forth as he massaged her back through her thin calico-print wrapper. Her hair fell in foaming curls over his arms.

"Grace?" he said. The tone of his voice, more serious than the moment required, alerted her. "Grace, will you give me your answer today?"

She straightened up, her shoulders as tense as though he had never touched them. "Answer?"

"Don't tell me you've forgotten the question."

"No. I can't tell you that."

"Well? Between all those eggs boiling and all your sewing, I think I've been about as patient as a man could be. I know you've had a lot on your mind."

"I wondered why you hadn't asked again," Grace said. She stood up, moved away from him. "I appreciate your forbearance. More than I can say."

"Are you going to give me an answer sometime soon?

I'm just curious." The affectionate humor was seeping back into his tone.

Grace looked him full in the eyes. "I'll give you my answer tonight. After the dance."

He drew one finger over the back of her hand, a slight gesture that still had the power to rouse her. "Why not tell me now?"

"Oh, Lucas. I'm just too tired."

A flash of disappointment crossed his face. "All right. You sit there. I'll make breakfast."

"You?"

"I'll have you know I'm the best waffle cook in Connecticut!"

"Connecticut?"

She never had asked him the questions that teemed in her brain, though sometimes it was a toss-up as to which problem would drive her insane first—the question of marrying him or the question of Lucas's past. Sometimes she'd lie awake, as tired as she was, and wonder. Was he a murderer? A bigamist? Or just a ne'er-do-well? Was he really responsible for her fast-fading bruises? However, she respected the pain that had been in his eyes when he'd asked her not to demand answers from him.

"I know I saw a waffle iron back here," he said from the pantry, his voice muffled.

"Look behind the butter churn," she called.

"Aha!"

"Sssh! Don't wake Wenonah. The more sleep she gets the better. The dancing will probably go on half the night." She yawned just thinking about it.

He came out, the black iron circle in his hand. "Now prepare yourself, madam, for the finest waffles in America."

"You better throw some more wood on the fire to get that grid hot enough."

"You just sit there and watch. Now, where's the flour?"

While he was scooping out flour with his coffee cup, Grace asked, deliberately casual, "So you're from Connecticut?"

"That's right. New London. It's a whaling port."

"Are you a sailor?"

"No, though I've sailed for my college against Harvard."

That didn't get her anywhere. "How old are you?"

"Aren't there any eggs around that *aren't* hard-boiled?"

"Just under the chickens—if you're lucky."

"I'll go see." As he started outside, he said, "Thirty-two, but most people think I'm older. Or they did, when I wore a noble pair of side-whiskers. I'm thinking of growing them again, but I'm not sure how my future bride will take to them."

She didn't answer the question that lit his eyes, except with a sour expression. He laughed as he trotted down the steps.

When Lucas returned with the eggs, Grace was no longer seated at the kitchen table. The sound of dripping water drew Lucas's attention to the hot-water reservoir in the front of the stove. He turned the spigot down tight and mopped up the water.

A murmur of women's voices, broken by a giggle, told him that Wenonah was awake and the serious fussing of the day had already begun. Nevertheless, he made waffles and called Grace and Wenonah to the table. He politely ignored the girl's curl papers, sticking out from her head like tiny flags, and didn't ask why she ate breakfast with her hands encased in white cotton gloves.

Two hours later, as they left the wagon at the edge of a big meadow on the north side of town, Lucas caught Grace by the arm and let Wenonah get a few steps ahead. He asked, "How did you do that?"

"Do what?"

"That." He nodded at the young girl. "She's stunning."

Grace felt a pang of jealousy, quickly extinguished beneath a surge of pride. "Yes, she turned out pretty well."

Under a tiny hat that seemed to be held down by gravity alone, half of Wenonah's rich hair was caught up in a knot on the back of her head. The rest, soft and wavy like a spaniel's ear, fell in what looked like negligent disarray but was really carefully arranged. The plain dress accentuated her lush figure, making the most of a flat waist and high breasts. A bustle tossed and waggled enticingly on her backside. Two slim ankles in glossy high-button shoes were displayed to advantage under the ruffled edge of her skirt. Heads turned as she walked by, and Grace enjoyed the attention Wenonah received as though it were her own portion.

Lucas wrapped Grace's arm through his. "Yes, she's going to break hearts today. I feel as proud of her as if she were my own daughter. But may I say, Mrs. Landers, that you cast every other woman into the shade?"

"You haven't seen any others yet," Grace said, pleased. She lightly touched her new hairstyle, designed to hide the pink line and faint bruising across her brow. She felt a little strange, no longer pulling her hair back into a tight bun, and hoped people wouldn't think the change was on Lucas's behalf.

"I'm not likely to see any other woman," he said in a low voice that thrilled her. "There's only one woman here who can catch my eye."

All around the edge of the lushly grassy meadow, townspeople were spreading blankets and greeting friends. Everyone was there, even a few of the younger folks from Chainy Town, dressed in their Sunday finery.

In the first five minutes, Grace was stopped half a dozen times by friends, some whom she'd not seen since the last Fourth of July. Many lived in outlying farms. Though all were lifelong friends of Chick's, they greeted Lucas with warmth when Grace introduced them. He soon had the men chuckling and the women blushing.

Grace was proud of him, and jealous too. He looked too handsome in his natural linen suit, a maroon silk tie calling up the colors in his striped shirt. Grace took his arm possessively and was warmed by the smile he gave her in return.

Mrs. Crowley and her family had spread their blanket in the shade of one of the magnificent oaks that grew on the border of the meadow. Planted by the first settlers to shade a church burned to the ground by those raiders who met their end in Grace's barn, the trees were a symbol of the permanence of Ogden.

Grace and Lucas didn't need Wenonah's pleading looks to persuade them to stake their spot close to the Crowley's.

"Well, hello there!" Mrs. Crowley, with her usual generosity, was opening several baskets stuffed with good things. "Haven't seen you two for a while."

"I've been trying to get through some chores I've been putting off, now that Bart and Callie are out from underfoot."

"Lord, don't I know about that! You'd think now that mine are all grown up I'd have a chance to get a few things done, but they're just as much in the way as ever. Ma, do this. Ma, have you seen that—"

"Ma!" Jasper stood above his mother, chagrin pulling down his mouth. "Don't make us sound like babies, okay? Hey there, Miss Wenonah." He pulled off his hat and stood turning it between his hands.

"Hello. Isn't it a lovely day?"

"Mite hot." The heat sent a shimmer through the air. "You look awful cool, though."

The girl dropped her head, but looked up at him shyly. "Thank you."

"Mr. McFee's set up a tent if you'd care for a sip of somethin'."

"Jasper!" his mother cried. "A saloon keeper."

"Shucks, ma. He's got lemonade and nothing but."

Grace nodded in answer to Wenonah's pleading look. "Don't dawdle, though. The parade will be starting soon." She added, "I don't know how long our food's going to keep in this heat."

"Long enough," Mr. Crowley said, from under the brim of his hat. This was the first time Lucas had seen him. He was a man no bigger than his wife. However, where she was all energy and spunk, he had a lazy, contented look. He lay at full stretch on the ground, his hat over his face. Soon his suspendered chest rose and fell gently.

His wife glanced at him fondly. "There he goes. Oh, don't bother lowering your voice, Mr. Lucas. He won't wake up till it's time to eat."

Not even the parade woke Mr. Crowley. Grace, however, went with Lucas to observe closely. Where or how the town had created so many children was beyond her. They seemed to spring up from the ground as though someone had wildly sprinkled child seeds last spring. Bright sashes and rosettes of red, white and blue decorated their clothing.

How much Bart and Callie would have enjoyed the thrills of dressing up and marching! Grace felt a pang of guilt at depriving them. But when she saw how red the little faces were and how quickly the decorations became limp and shabby under the merciless sun, she knew she'd done the right thing to send them away.

"There's the marshal," Lucas said, nodding in that direction. "He's a popular fellow."

"That's the town council he's talking to."

Marshal Wyman, brilliant in an orange silk vest under a dark brown suit, strutted up to the improvised platform at the far end of the field. Grace saw him shake hands with the mayor and Judge Sterling. There were bright smiles and some clapping on the back from those members of the town council up for reelection in November.

The local band—drums, a violin, an accordion and Mr. Lansky on the tuba—struck up a lively, familiar air, good for marching. The proud, excited mothers harried their children into line. Breaking into a chorus of "Dixie Land," the children began to march around the field. Their fathers, just as proud, stuck their hands in their pockets and their chests out.

"Dixie?" Lucas asked. "Who's Centennial is this, anyway?"

"I forgot you're a Yankee." She smiled to take the sting out of the words and explained, "They switch the one they start with every year. They'll sing 'The Battle Hymn of the Republic' next. Then come the speeches."

"Let's not stay for those. I've heard quite a few."

"Oh, you have to hear the speeches. How will you know what to argue about with the other men?"

"I'm not interested in talking to men," he said, snugging her against his side. Grace enjoyed the feel of his strong arm, but only for a moment. With a hasty glance around to see who had noticed his bad behavior, she pulled away.

Only the part of the crowd directly in front could hear anything the speakers said anyway. Lucas amused Grace by mimicking the speeches they could not hear. She was astonished by how often he said something stirring right before the crowd cheered the official speaker.

"How do you *do* that?" she asked.

"Practice. Now he's saying that 'tyranny shall never more put out its hand over this fair nation. Washington . . . Jefferson . . .' I doubt he'll mention Lincoln. Not with this crowd. Definitely not Grant, either."

The young girls, fair in their sweetness, walked arm in arm, giggling when any young man came too close. Some of the more savage youths had gotten up an impromptu baseball game that had their mothers clicking their tongues, sure their sons would drop down dead from such exertion in this heat. Showers of laughter, snatches of songs and at least one fistfight enlivened the game.

Grace continued to encourage Lucas to enjoy himself, not to feel that he had to stay by her. But he refused to investigate any of the amusements unless she came too. Throughout the day, he was as attentive as a newly married husband. He hovered. If by some chance he was called to join a group of men, Grace had only to look around for him to have him make some excuse and return to her side.

He arm wrestled the blacksmith to win her a trumpery fan, and lost. He cheered her on when she foolishly entered the pancake flipping race, and lost. The three-legged races did not tempt them to participate, which was just as well considering that Wenonah and Jasper beat the field to the finish line by an ample lead.

"We're a fine pair," Grace said laughingly, returning to the blanket. "We can't win to save our souls."

"I don't mind a few temporary setbacks, as long as I win in the end. Maybe I should take another whack at the blacksmith."

"No, don't," she said, pulling him down beside her. "I

have an interest in how much work you can do, after all. I don't want my hired hand laid up with a broken arm."

"Grace! You do care." He reached across the blanket to the picnic basket and tossed a strawberry into his mouth.

Mrs. Crowley said, "That reminds me. Thank you so much for that basket of strawberries you sent home with Jasper. I just love 'em to death. I'd eat 'em morning, noon and night, if I could get 'em."

"Anytime you want some, just let me know," Grace said. "Or I'll be putting up preserves soon. I'll be happy to let you have a few jars of jam."

Mr. Crowley snorted in his sleep and muttered on a longing sigh, "Jam . . . jam. . . ."

His wife lovingly nudged him with the toe of her shoe.

The two groups shared the contents of their baskets. Afterward, Mr. Crowley was not the only one to doze and dream away the heat of the afternoon. All around the meadow, sleeping forms lay in uninhibited attitudes. Not even the young children found the energy to dash around in play.

Sitting with her back against the tree, Lucas's head on her thigh, Grace thought about her own children. The traditional family outing to a local swimming hole must be well under way by now. She hoped Bart and Callie were enjoying themselves with their many cousins.

Lucas opened his eyes. He looked so different upside down, but still handsome enough to set her heart fluttering. He said, "I'm sure they're fine."

She smiled down on him, deep affection shining in her eyes. "How did you know I was thinking of them?"

"You're a good mother. What else would you be thinking of?"

Grace lifted her shoulders slightly. "You."

He caught her hand with sudden passion. She withdrew it at once. "Not here. Go back to sleep."

"Who could sleep?" But he closed his eyes.

The approach of evening, even if the sun had only slightly dipped behind the trees, revived the citizens. The fathers slipped off for a bit, those who lived nearby, to tend the livestock. Some mothers returned with them, to be sure the stove hadn't set fire to the house. There were still plenty of adults to tame the wilder spirits among the small fry. Gallons of home-churned ice cream helped cool heads as well.

Wenonah volunteered to go home and see to things. Jasper wasn't about to let her go alone and offered to drive. His younger brother went along as a chaperone.

Mrs. Crowley watched them go and said in a confidential undertone to Grace, "They'll make a match of it."

"You won't mind?"

"Mind? Not a bit. She's a good girl and we could use a few more brunettes in the family." She passed her hand over her own still dark curls. "Course I'm not in any hurry to lose my boy. Besides, we promised each of the children a team, a sow and a cow. The way things are now, we could maybe manage the cow."

On the other side of the meadow, behind a canvas sheet pegged out on the ground, the band, mugs of beer set down by their feet, was tuning up. Mrs. Crowley nudged her husband. "C'mon, Mr. C. They're starting the dancing."

"So soon?" He sat up, stretching. "Seems they start earlier and earlier every year. They can't be done speechifying yet? Figure ol' mayor's got another two hours in him, easy."

"Well, they're starting to play."

Lucas looked up at Grace. "Do you dance?"

"When I get the chance."

"Here's your chance."

He stood up and pulled her to her feet. He said warmly, "I bet you're a great dancer."

"Try me and see."

Along with all the other couples, Lucas and Grace headed hand in hand for the improvised dance floor. When the first notes came from the band, however, Lucas stopped, his face creased in pain. "What is that?"

" 'Camptown Ladies.' I think."

The band stopped. Once again the violin player, the teller at Mr. Kent's bank, counted four. They started again, but it sounded no better. By mutual agreement, the players all had a swig of beer. When the downbeat was given again, the music roared out. Not sweet, not fancy, but clear.

"Let's go!"

The canvas kept down the dust, but the heat made McFee's stocks of drink dwindle quickly. Lucas learned to be careful when he went for refreshment, for the moment his back was turned, half a dozen men would importune Grace for a dance, leaving him impotent on the sidelines with two full glasses.

Once Grace's partner was limping when he brought her back before the end of a number. "I hope you'll finish this one with me," she said to Lucas after freezing the other man with a glance. He limped off while Grace sipped her lemonade.

"I'll be happy to," Lucas said, noticing her snapping eyes and high color. "Do you want me to pound him into jelly now or after our dance?"

She dimpled delightfully. "There's no need."

"What did he say?"

"I'm afraid you've been very bad for my reputation." Her dimples faded as she looked around. "I may have to kick a few more ankles before the evening's over."

"No, you won't. Unless you want to kick mine. You're not dancing with anyone else but me."

"Oh, no?"

"No."

He frowned so uncompromisingly that Grace found herself agreeing just to see his eyes lighten. She realized how very far she had fallen. If only she hadn't fallen in love.

The night had finally begun to creep across the sky. Grace looked up into Lucas's eyes, the same color as the deepening blue above her head, and said, "Let's make this our last dance tonight. I think my shoes are worn through."

"All right," he said, turning. The band was about ready for another break and they'd drifted into some slow song with a dreaming rhythm. All around the floor, girls laid their heads on their partners' shoulders.

Lucas brought Grace a little closer. The clean scent of her hair as it tickled across his mouth made him feel half-drunk. They'd already proven how easily their bodies fit together whenever the band played soft and slow like this. He wanted to prove how well they'd fit when they were alone.

Grace realized that her nearness was doing things to Lucas. She couldn't bring herself to break the connection between them. To tell the truth, she was enjoying having his arms about her again. Let the world make what it pleased about the sight of a widow dancing so intimately with her hired hand. She refused to trouble her head.

"Let's go home, Lucas," she murmured.

"I'd like that."

She stopped moving. Giving him a smile that made him feel as though his blood had gone mad, she left the dance "floor." He saw her pause to tap Jasper Crowley on the shoulder. The two young people started apart guiltily and Jasper's apology was cut short by something Grace said. Wenonah nodded. The two went on dancing, closer than ever.

On the drive home, the sun sent up streamers of fire into the sky, brighter than any fireworks. Lucas lifted her down from the wagon seat, and let her slide slowly down his body, Grace's skirt catching and bunching against his belt buckle. She looked into his eyes and saw there such hunger that her mouth went dry. Though she knew she'd given him every hint that she wanted him, Grace still felt a little shy.

He whispered, "I'll go take care of the mules."

"I'll come too. I'm not taking any chances with you."

Ulysses and Hercules had never been tended and turned out to pasture so quickly.

Lucas and Grace kissed in the middle of the yard, surrounded by the dizzying scent of wild honeysuckle. She caressed the sides of his neck with her fingers as she opened her mouth under his pressure. The moment his tongue touched hers, Grace was lost. There was no further point in embarrassment or restraint.

"Grace," he said, half laughing, putting his hands on her shoulders to fend her off. "It's all right. We've got plenty of time. Take it easy."

"Oh! Yes, I'm . . ."

"Let's go inside. I'd like to make love to you in your bed for a change, not in the barn or the strawberry patch."

He lit a candle at the stove and carried it back to the room. She stood in the middle of the circular rag rug, her blouse already halfway unbuttoned to show the smooth white rise of her breasts. Her hair fell in tousled waves, a gleaming golden cape about her shoulders. With the candlelight, the shyness returned to her eyes, yet she tossed her head proudly and met his gaze.

He barely managed to set the candle down on the dresser, his hands trembled so much from the flood of desire that filled him. The flame flickered in the tiny breeze that entered the open window. The few steps he had to cross to her were a vast gulf between himself and all he longed for in this world or the world to come.

"Grace," he said as he swept her into his arms. "I love you."

The huskiness and need in his voice broke down her final barriers. She said, "I love you too. God knows I do."

His mouth possessed her utterly. Now he showed no technique, no finesse. He took her and she gave herself willingly. Grace heard herself making noises of such wanton intensity that she could hardly believe they came from her throat. But they seemed to please Lucas no end.

"That's right. Oh, sweetheart!" He slipped his hands, warm and rough, inside her blouse and looked down. Grace had threaded a bit of Wenonah's red ribbon through the lace at the top of her chemise. This slight vanity made him smile. "Is that for me?"

"For you?"

"A red ribbon round a gift is traditional." He bent and kissed the ribbon, then wandered to tease the hard point pushing against the fabric.

Grace caught her breath as he blew gently on the spot

he'd dampened. Her nipple tightened almost unbearably. He glanced up into her face and smiled before taking it into the heat of his mouth. Her knees were quivering. She wanted to ask him if he'd like to move to the bed, but that would mean he'd have to stop this sweet torture and she couldn't bear that.

Her hands restless, she clutched his shoulders as waves of shattering pleasure swept over her. A tenseness began to twine within her. She couldn't stand still. Grace began to move her body in a very ancient way.

Lucas straightened, sweeping off her blouse and pushing her chemise completely off her shoulders. Bare to the waist, her eyes dazed with passion, she was the most glorious thing he'd ever seen. He stared openly.

"Aren't you going to take something off?" she asked.

He ran his hand back through his hair, a satisfied smile curving his lips. "Sure. Whatever you want."

Putting his arms around her, he sought out the three wooden buttons on her hip and pushed them through their button holes. As the skirt puddled around their feet, she laughed and said, "Not my clothes. *Yours.*"

She stepped out of her skirt. Clad in nothing but her foaming petticoats, she sat down on the edge of her bed. Fortunately, her shoes had elastic sides so she could kick them off easily. Grace realized that she'd dressed herself that day with forethought. She wanted this to happen. She needed him now.

She looked up at Lucas, standing in front of her, but who still had made no move to undress. "Well?"

His wicked smile undid all her confidence. "I helped you," he pointed out. "Fair's fair."

Taking up her courage, Grace kneeled on the bed. Not meeting his eyes, she reached for his maroon cravat and tugged on the slippery material. Pulling it free, she glanced up. "Go on," he encouraged.

His collar popped off, to fly across the room. Neither of them laughed. Fumblingly she worked at his shirt buttons, frowning in concentration. "You've undressed a man before," he stated.

"Never," she admitted. "Chick was always in bed before I got there. Chores, you know."

His eyes narrowed but Grace had no feeling she was the cause of his ire. "Now's not a good time to talk about Chick, Grace."

"I guess not."

Finally, all the buttons were undone. "Touch me," he said, pulling off his shirt to let it fall carelessly on the floor.

The crisp hair caught at her fingers. It abraded and aroused her hands. Grace yearned upward to press her lips to his. He stepped closer to the bed, his arms folding around her.

Again, as their kisses deepened, Grace found herself moving mindlessly against him. His scent, so warm, so male, surrounded her. His chest, furred and firm, brushing the sensitive tips of hers was easily the most tantalizing sensation she'd ever known.

Stockings, petticoat and drawers all took time to remove. But Grace didn't begrudge a moment. Everything that she revealed of herself, Lucas found a way to lavish with sensual attention. Naked, she helped him off with his boots and felt no shame as his heated gaze wandered over her. But when it came time to take off his belt and his pants, she froze. He seemed to understand and removed them himself. Then he turned around to face her.

Though it was indeed no time to think of Chick, she couldn't help making the comparison, which was no comparison at all. She might as well have been a virgin again, for the sight of Lucas set her heart to fluttering and her stomach to shivering, just as they had the first time she'd become acquainted with the full duties of marriage. In a way, it was even worse. For she knew now what would happen.

She jerked her gaze away. She tossed back the covers on the bed and lay down. Having come this far, she would go on. Maybe he'd hold her afterward. "All right. Come on."

The mattress squeaked as he complied with her sugges-

tion. Grace waited for him to climb on top of her. Instead
he turned on his side, his arm curled above her head.

"Just like that?" he asked.

She heard the smile in his voice and looked at him in
sudden surprise. "I don't understand."

"Neither do I. You went from being very sweet and
incredibly sultry to—"

"Was I?"

There was something close to sorrow in his eyes. "I
wish your husband were here for two minutes. I'd like
to . . . Well, he's dead and gone so I'll try to forgive
him."

"What on earth have you to forgive him for? Besides, I
thought you said you didn't want to talk about Chick."

"I don't. Not at all. But it seems as if I have to. Grace,
when you and he made love . . ."

She closed her eyes and sighed resignedly. "Yes?"

"What did you do, exactly?"

Grace realized that Lucas must remember everything
about his past except how to actually complete the act of
love. Although, considering the way he kissed and
touched her, it seemed very strange that he should have
forgotten that.

"Well, we would just . . . He'd kiss me a couple of
times, then we'd . . . just do it."

"Just do it?"

Funny that the smile was in his voice again. She opened
her eyes to see him smiling down at her with such un-
speakable tenderness that she felt tears prick her eyes. "I
don't suppose he ever did this."

Once again, he closed his lips on the softened peak of
her breast and teased enticingly. The slow heat of longing
began to rekindle within her. "No," she whispered. "Not
after the babies came along."

"He didn't know what he was missing. Sweeter than
honey." He tasted the full underside and drew provoca-
tive lines with his tongue. Then he returned to her waiting
mouth and plundered it. The combination of his gentle
hands and wild mouth drove her insane.

She hardly noticed when he glided one hand down over

her slightly rounded stomach. He lifted his head a little to ask, "He never did this, either?"

He touched her so fleetingly and grinned at the look of utter surprise on her face. He skimmed the hidden cleft and felt her vibrate as every part of her jumped to attention.

Teasing, he lightly drew his fingers over the smooth skin of her thighs and over her dancing stomach. Then again, he dipped lower, his touch slightly firmer. She rolled forward a little against his hand and stopped, a flood of shame in her cheeks. "No, that's right," he said. "Let me know what you like."

"Wait," she said, a tone of pleading entering into her voice despite herself. "Don't do that. It's . . ."

"A sin? Nothing that we do together is ever wrong, Grace. Not so long as you like it, and I like it." He began to move his hand.

She tried to tighten up, tried to resist the delectable feelings he brought to life. But it felt too good. She lost all restraint, all the hurt pride she'd hoarded.

Grace shattered against his hand, her spirit all but leaving her impassioned body. "Oh, God," she sighed as the tempest passed. "Was that what it's supposed to be like?"

Lucas laughed, a sound of pure delight. Then he kissed her. "Don't you know?"

"No."

"Then I'll show you again."

With surprising strength, Grace caught his wrist. She met his eyes with laughter in her own. "Show me later. Now, I . . . I want you."

She brushed her hand over him, reminding herself that she wasn't really a virgin. She knew some things that only a once-married woman could know. Lucas shuddered, then pressed her hand closer. Her touch was a little too mild. "I won't break, you know."

"I guess granite doesn't break." She tried to squeeze and failed to make an impression. Yet the way Lucas let his head fall onto the pillow and the ragged edge of his breathing told her that she'd managed to impress him.

Abruptly she found herself on her back, Lucas above her. "Now?" he asked, his voice hoarse.

"Please." She tried to smile with trembling lips.

He wrapped her in his arms and held her against his pounding heart. A moment later, they were one.

Chapter
Nineteen

Grace lay in a snug languor. Her whole body felt as light as air, only Lucas's hand on her stomach keeping her from floating away. Though tired, she did not feel like sleeping.

Searching herself for some sign of guilt or remorse, she learned to her surprise that she felt none of those things. Her heart belonged to Lucas already; she couldn't regret giving him the rest.

She sighed, a long, contented sound. Beside her, Lucas stirred. His thickly lashed eyelids opened and he looked for her at once. The smile he gave her spoke of a purely male pride in his prowess, yet a proportion of humor saved him from arrogance. "Happy?" he asked.

"Mmmm," she sighed, stretching. His gaze dropped to her bosom rising high as she lifted her arms. A gleam came into his eyes. He walked his fingers over her stomach, stepping up her rib cage.

She caught his hand and gave him a banteringly severe look. "What do you think you're doing?"

"Just browsing." Then his voice dropped into its deepest, roughly sincere register. "You're the loveliest woman I have ever seen in my life."

The harshness of his voice convinced her he meant what he said. Pleased, she let go of his hand. But instead of touching her breast, he touched her cheek. Turning her face, he kissed her with toe-tightening tenderness.

"By heaven, I love you. You're the woman I've needed my whole life. Someone brave and yet kind. Gallant and funny . . ."

"I'm not funny. Chick used to say I had no sense of

humor at all." She saw his face change and asked anxiously, "Do you mind my talking about him? I mean, he is the children's father."

"No, I don't mind. He was part of your life. I can't expect you to forget about him. Just try to pick your times. I don't want to hear about him when we're in bed."

"Well, I don't mind hearing about your past."

"My past?" His brows came together.

"Yes. Who is Margot?"

He chuckled, shaking the bed. "Margot was a . . ."

"Lady of the evening?"

"What? Lord, no! She was my nurse when I was a small boy. She's French. I still receive the occasional letter from her but my French deserted me long ago. I have to get someone at the office to translate for me."

"Lucas?" Thinking about what this information revealed about him, Grace drew her nails lightly over his back. He caught his breath as gooseflesh arose.

"Slightly lower and to the left. Ah, that's right." He sighed in absolute satisfaction. "What a woman."

"Lucas, are you rich?"

He looked into her gray eyes, so close to his own. "No," he said, and saw for an instant a flash of relief that confused him. "I'm paid a decent salary, but I'm not rich. But my father is."

"I'd better get up and start supper," she said, pushing at his shoulder.

"I'm not hungry. Well, not for supper anyway." He kissed her again, pressing her into the pillows. She kissed him in return, but absently.

"What's the matter, Grace?"

"Nothing. Would you like me to scratch your back some more?"

"Another time. What's wrong with my father being rich?"

"When you say rich, do you mean comfortable? Like the Kents?"

"No, I mean rich. Like the Vanderbilts. You've heard of them?"

"The people in *Harper's* who give those big fancy parties in New York City? With the mansions and steam yachts and jewels?"

He chuckled again at this conglomeration. "Yes, that's right. Though I've never been to a party with a steam yacht."

"Oh, God," Grace said, struggling to sit up. She felt a roil of nausea in her stomach.

"What's wrong?" He propped himself up on his elbow.

"Oh, nothing! Nothing, except you're from one world and I'm from another." She twisted to look at him, lying at his ease among the crushed and tumbled bed linens. "What are you doing here?"

"Right now? I'm enjoying the view." He ran his hand over her smooth ivory back. "Your skin is as soft as milk. Tell me, have you ever made love standing up?"

She couldn't miss the fact that his interest had shifted away from their conversation. It rather leaped to her attention. "Of course not," she said shortly. "That's impossible."

His smile became wicked. "Not impossible. Just . . ."

"Besides, you've had your fun."

"My fun?"

He sat up and caught her around the waist. Falling back onto the bed, he cradled her against his chest. "What do you mean . . . my fun? Grace . . ."

"Don't you think it's time we got up? There's chores . . ."

"Why are you trying to close me out, honey? We're happy together, aren't we? If you're having second thoughts about what we've just done, tell me." The torment in his tone struck to Grace's heart.

"No," she said at once, looking up into his deep-set eyes. She smoothed the frown away from his forehead with gentle fingertips. "I love what we've done. I'd like to do it again. . . ."

"That's right . . ."

He kissed her again, more urgently than before. His arms dragged her to him without playfulness or any mild quality. He kissed her as though he'd compel her to recognize that nothing mattered but this. Grace understood and didn't blame him for his ferocity.

She caught fire from his fire. There were still issues to be disputed between them, yet she couldn't resist the powerful feelings that he called into life with his every touch. She decided to take whatever Lucas wanted to give her, knowing how short a time they had. Sooner or later, he would go back to the life he'd forgotten. Then she would become just another memory.

He made love to her with almost savage yearning, insisting she take the pleasure he gave her. He didn't stop until she threw herself on him, demanding he finish what he'd begun. She could tell how ready he was, and knew her own desires had slipped completely out of her control. She wasn't the woman she had been. She had no modesty left and delighted in losing it.

He lay beneath her, his hands clasping her waist. His eyes regarded her with an intense flame, like the bengali fire of blue fireworks, in their depths.

"Grace, when are you going to marry me?"

Dazed and bemused by the powers he'd unleashed, she still retained sense enough to say, "I'm not."

"What?"

She tried to speak as matter-of-factly as though they were discussing crops. "I'm not going to marry you. I'd rather live in sin. Like now."

"Don't joke. You've got to marry me."

"Going to make an honest woman of me? I'm tired of being honest. Being bad's more fun. You showed me that." She moved her hips, trying to complete their lovemaking.

"No."

"What?" she exclaimed, unable to believe this.

"No. We're not going to do that. Not until you agree to marry me."

"That's . . . You don't mean that."

"Yes, I do." His face showed nothing but determination.

Though he'd just given her such pleasure that her body still trembled from the power of it, Grace's soul de-

manded the total fulfillment of a man and woman together. Her teeth ground in frustration as she tried to
reach behind her. But he held her hands. "No."

"Are you crazy?"

"I think so." His smile was grim. "But that's the way it's
going to be."

Somehow he made his way from beneath her. She
stared after him in shock and restless amazement. The
sight of him, still proud with unfulfilled desire, made her
hunger more intense. He began pulling on his clothes,
refusing to look at her.

Grace felt a rush of anger under her skin. He couldn't
treat her like this! Swinging her legs over the opposite
edge of the bed, she grabbed her drawers off the foot-
board. Glancing up to shoot a hard word at him, Grace
froze, instinctively covering her breasts with her arm.

"Lucas!" she yelped.

"Grace, I'm not—"

"There's somebody out there!"

"What?" He spun around to stare out the open window. Like her, he saw a bobbing light moving in the barn.
"We'll catch him this time!"

"I'll get the gun."

"Gun?"

"Chick's shotgun. Lord, what did I do with the ammu-
nition?" She went to the dresser and began to rummage
through the drawers. "I put it out of Bart's reach, but
where?"

Lucas had already twitched the calico curtains closed.
"Get dressed first," he said. "I'll go see what's going on."

"No, don't," she cried, clutching his arm. "Remember
what he almost did to me."

He smiled like a tiger showing its teeth. "That's why I'm
going out there."

Grace snatched her blouse from the floor and dragged
on her skirt any old way. Leaving her blouse hanging
open, she tore through the dresser drawers until she came
up with a waxed cardboard box with a blue lid. Her hands
shook when she took off the top. The long buff-and-brass
cylinders bounced and scattered on the floor.

Condemning them to Hades, Grace scrabbled up two. She ran for the gun stashed on iron hooks above the kitchen door. Snapping open the breech, she jammed the shells home, the brass ends gleaming up at her. Slapping the shotgun together, she ran out the door. "I'm coming, Lucas!"

Only the faintest breeze moved in the yard. Overhead, the stars glittered in the cold bath of the Milky Way, a foaming torrent of light that shed little clarity on the earth below. Grace held the long shotgun low against her hip, ready in her hands, one gripping the stock, the other supporting the wooden barrel casing. She called again for Lucas.

The silence lay like a blanket over the farmyard. What she wouldn't have given to hear Toby's familiar yap, or Georgette's inquiring mew. Even the cackle of a sleepy hen would have been preferable to this endless silence, her ears straining to catch any sound.

A twig snapped, louder than a pistol shot, and Grace threw the shotgun to her shoulder. "Who's there?" Her voice came out high.

"It's me."

"Who's me? Talk fast. I've got a gun."

"It's Reg Wyman." Standing in the entrance to the barn, he cast a dim shadow in the starlight. Grace squinted, trying to penetrate the darkness, but kept both barrels pointed at where she guessed his chest would be.

"What the dickens do you mean by coming onto my property in the middle of the night?"

"Now, Grace, you're not still mad—"

"Where's Lucas?"

"I haven't seen him." He moved forward. A stray beam of starlight showed the badge on his chest, a gleam of silver.

"I didn't hear your horse," Grace said.

"I walked up from town. They're about ready to start the fireworks."

"They're not the only ones. What are you doing here?"

"I came to check on your barn. With everyone down to the celebration, I figure maybe somethin' would happen

here tonight. All the excitement gives the louse we're after a chance to get clear away."

Obscurely, the all but healed cut on her forehead began
throbbing. She was no longer surprised by the intensity of
Lucas's headaches. To almost remember, to have some
fact on the tip of one's mental tongue, would give anyone
a headache. Her own head pounded as though half a
dozen Indians beat her eyeballs like drums.

"Did you find anything?" she asked.

"Nothin' but . . ."

"But what?" Her arms were aching from holding up the
heavy shotgun.

"Don't know how I can 'splain it. You got to see . . .
Maybe you can tell me if this is right or not. I ain't all that
familiar with your barn." His voice faded.

"Where are you?"

"I just stepped inside a second. You better take a look."

"I'll get a lantern."

"I've got one in the barn. Come on."

Grace, feeling a sudden coldness, realized her blouse
still hung open. Content that it should be dark until she
was decent, Grace leaned the shotgun against the porch
steps. She headed toward the barn, hastily buttoning her
blouse. Where was Lucas? She called his name again
without reply.

Hesitating in the doorway, she said, "Marshal? What
did you find?"

"Over here."

"Where?" She took one step in.

Every instinct shrieked alarm. She dodged reflexively as
something swished through the air at her head.

The blow fell across her back. Instantly, her right arm
went numb to the fingertips, while a crying pain broke in
her shoulder blade. She staggered forward, dazed and
confused, fearing a second strike out of the darkness.

Half-turning, her brain screaming a demand to *see,* she
glimpsed a figure coming toward her, arms raised above
his head. Something silver caught the starlight. Grace realized that what she'd seen before had not been the

shovel flashing down to strike her, but the star shining on Reg Wyman's chest.

Like a frightened animal, she tried to run, to burrow in the straw until the danger passed. She stumbled away, avoiding his second swipe less by effort than by chance. As she ran into the dark, her hands out before her, she heard him coming behind her, whispering ceaselessly.

"I'm sorry, Grace. I'm sorry. But I can't find it. I've looked and looked. You've got to tell me where it is."

She could hear him now, stumbling around just as she was, only on the other side of the barn. She thanked heaven that he'd lied about the lantern. A single gleam of light would have meant her capture. She heard the rustle as he kicked among the hay, still whispering, swearing now, promising vile tortures if she didn't instantly appear.

She kicked something long, like loose lumber. Something that flinched from the kick. Crouching down, she reached out with blind fingers. "Lucas?" she croaked in the tiniest possible voice.

Her hands fluttered over him. His mouth was bound with a strip of cloth. Horrified, she started working at the gag but he tossed his head to prevent her. She understood. There was no time. Wyman was too close at hand.

She leaned down to brush a kiss over his forehead, her thanks rising to God that he still lived. For one instant, she'd been afraid . . . Smelling something strange yet familiar, she pushed the hair off Lucas's forehead.

Her hand came away wet. With blood? Horrified, she sniffed her fingers. The distinctively oily smell of kerosene made her recoil.

Feeling around gingerly in the straw bedding, she touched a shard of broken glass. Beyond that, the twisted frame of a lantern, smashed, lay in a pool of oil. Wyman must have struck Lucas down by crashing a lantern over his head.

She listened for Wyman. The cow gave her peculiar little grunt, the sound she made when she wanted her ears scratched. Wyman must be standing beside her. "Grace!" he shouted suddenly.

She couldn't help startling. Her knees rustled the straw. Wyman heard. "Aha!"

Afraid that Lucas would be hurt if she were found near him, Grace scuttled back toward a stall without rising. Just as she reached it, however, she realized that she would be trapped there once Wyman started searching this side of the barn. She moved cautiously and as silently as possible along the long side of the barn, toward the door. Her little sounds were lost in Wyman's loud swearing when he didn't instantly find her.

Her eyes had adjusted to the dark. Searching, she saw that every gap between the boards let in a beam of starlight. The open entrance to the barn shed a bar of gray light across the barn floor. She'd never be able to get out without Wyman seeing her. She couldn't bet her life and Lucas's on reaching the shotgun before he caught her, not while her long skirt hampered her legs.

If only she'd left her blouse open! Then she wouldn't have put the gun down. So much for modesty, she fumed. She glanced down at herself. Her white blouse glowed faintly in reflected starlight while her skirt was so black she looked truncated. Her hand stole to the trio of buttons at her hip.

Her skin glowed as white as her blouse, but without her skirt she could at least run. She'd defy a hummingbird to beat her to the porch.

She waited, shivering with nerves, while Wyman hunted around the prostrate body of her lover. Once she heard Lucas groan as the marshal swore viciously. A dull thud told her Wyman had kicked him. Tears came to her eyes, tears of anger. She'd reach that gun now, or die trying.

She heard Wyman move off, toward the back of the barn. She listened hard, knowing she had to be sure he was as far from the barn door as possible. She prayed to God to clear all stones, sticks and holes from the path her bare feet would take. A fall now would end all her hopes for a tomorrow.

Her ears pricking like a cat's, she rose to a crouch. At the back of the barn, something fell with a rattle that made her jump almost out of her skin. Using that spring-loaded leap, she ran out.

Instantly, she heard a savage curse and the pounding of boots behind her. She burst out of the barn, lurching down the slope, ignoring the shooting pains of stubbed toes and cut feet. Everything loomed strangely in the darkness. Black shadows looked solid, blending with the darkness. The friendly glow of a candle shining through the porch door led her unerringly to the house, so far away.

She could see the dark shotgun like a sturdy branch against the light side of the house. Another three yards . . . Already her hands were crooked to catch it up. She could almost feel the resistance of the trigger, almost feel the weight in her hands as she swung it around to—

She went down, a crushing weight on her back, panting breaths in her ear. His hands fumbled with hers; she felt the bite of thin rope as he bound her wrists together.

Wyman rolled her over. She came up bucking, fighting to free herself of the oppression of his body, beyond thought, a snarling beast. He slapped her, forehand and backhand, jarring her teeth, setting her head to throbbing.

She shuddered, went still and stared up at him straddling her. His head and shoulders were a mere shade against the brilliant sky, but his violence confined her like a cage.

"Tell me where it is," he screamed. "Tell me, or I'll—"

"Where what is?" Though it tore at her throat, she kept her voice low, afraid that a loud word would set him off in a storm of violence. The smell of his hair oil choked her. She knew that if she lived, the odor of Parma violets would always remind her of imminent death.

"The gold, bitch. You're the only one who knows."

"Me? I wasn't even here when—"

He raised his hand as though to strike her. He said sharply, "The old man said you knew. That your husband told you."

"Chick didn't tell me anything."

"Don't lie to me or I'll . . ."

He got off her, and forced her to her feet. Dragging her by the elbow, he marched her up the hill to the barn. He didn't seem to notice her sketchy attire. Grace realized he'd never wanted her, even when he'd kissed her. She wasn't a woman to him, just a means to an end.

Wyman pushed her down beside Lucas. Kneeling, he grabbed her ankles. She kicked, trying to free them from his grasp. "Don't try it," he said. "Your lover'll pay for it if you do."

"He's dead."

"No. He's awake. But he'll soon wish he wasn't."

"What are you going to do?" Grace panted.

"I'm going to use him to make you tell me where the gold is." His tone was nearly normal now. She noticed that his country twang was gone, false like his good humor, a mere tool to make people like him.

"I don't—"

"Do you think I don't know how you feel about him? Everybody was talking about you today. I didn't expect you to return until late tonight. I should have remembered that lovers do strange things." He walked toward the entrance, saying, "I'll need light."

"Reg . . ."

He took no notice of her despairing cry, but went out, his head full of black thoughts.

Lucas made noises in his throat as if he were trying to speak. Remembering the gag she'd felt, Grace rolled toward him, coming to rest with her back to him. Some of the broken glass crunched and stabbed beneath her. Reaching up awkwardly with her bound hands, her right side pulsing with pain, she tugged the gag from Lucas's mouth.

"Glass," he whispered. "Broken glass."

"Are you lying on it?"

"Cut me free."

"I might hurt you."

"Not compared with what he'll do." She could hear the grin in his voice.

How could he smile at a time like this? She fumbled up a piece of glass wet with oil, slicing a finger. The pain hardly penetrated, her hands already swelling from being bound. Lucas rolled over, so that their hands were close together. Grace couldn't hold the triangular shard very well. She knew she was cutting him as well as the cord.

"Hurry" was all he said. "He'll come back soon."

"He's crazy. I don't know anything about gold. He said some old man told him Chick knew where it was and had told me."

"I know about the old man."

"Who? How?"

"He's buried in your woods."

"What?"

"Keep going."

Grace sawed on, though she wasn't even sure by now that she still held the piece of glass. Her fingers were numb. A strange buzzing ache crept up her arms, like pins and needles but a thousand times fiercer. The oil seemed to be in her mouth as well as her nose. She could taste the bitterness.

Facing the entrance, she saw the approach of the tiny flame that meant Reg Wyman's return. "He's coming back," she said, starting to panic. "Lucas, I love—"

"Me too. Try to keep him talking. Tell him anything you want."

"But I don't know anything." She repeated it as Reg Wyman came up to where they lay. Half closing her eyes, for the light of even this single candle was dazzling after the dark, she said earnestly, "Chick never said anything to me about gold. And he would have spent it if he knew where it was."

"He better not have spent it," Reg said. "It's mine."

He set the candle down on the floor, making his shadow leap up like a demon of darkness. With a chill of horror, Grace saw that he held one of her kitchen knives in his hand. He held it up and tried the edge with his thumb.

"Sharp enough to kill a pig," he said and smiled. She could see another man behind the face she knew, as though some horrible monster had put on a mask in the image of Reg Wyman.

"Won't you listen to me?" Grace pleaded.

"There's only one thing you can say I want to hear. I think I'll cut off one of his fingers first. Starting with his little one on his left hand. Then one at a time, until you tell me—"

"Wait!"

"That's better. What?" His eyes were wolfish in the light, neither cruel nor laughing, but nothing human either.

"I only know part of it. Maybe you know the rest."

"What do you know?"

"He did say that . . . that the barn would make our fortune one day." That had been when Chick had decided that they should go in a big way for dairy cattle.

"Yes?"

"And that . . . that . . . he'd see me living like a queen before he died."

"Go on." He licked his lips and leaned toward her.

Remembering the shovel, she said, "And he never wanted anyone to disturb the floor. I wanted him to dig a waste trench down the middle and he wouldn't hear of it." That was true enough. Chick had been full of schemes to make cleaning the stalls easier, but he'd never gone for the simplest of them all.

"That can't be right," Reg said, staring out at the middle of the barn. "The old man said it wasn't—"

Lucas's bindings snapped like a pistol shot. He sprang to his feet and took Reg in a tackle around the middle. The knife went spinning into the night beyond the candle.

Wyman's hands and feet were free while Lucas's feet were still bound and his hands dead from lack of blood flow. But Wyman fought for money while Lucas fought for love and life.

They fell together, Wyman underneath. Lucas pulled out the long gun the lawman wore, only to have it knocked from his hands. Still on top, Lucas pounded him, in the face, in the stomach. In the dim light, Grace saw that Lucas's hands ran with dark blood. Wyman heaved upward, throwing Lucas back, and dove at him with killing blows.

Grace fought with her own bindings, desperate to get

free. Nothing would stop her this time from gaining the shotgun.

The two men rolled over and over, their grunts and the deadly thud of bones striking bones louder than she would have believed possible. They didn't speak, only snarl, two wild beasts struggling for mastery.

The candle fell, kicked by flailing feet. With horror creeping over her flesh, Grace saw that it fell into some straw. Instantly, the straw began to burn. That was enough to strike fear into the heart of a farmer's wife, but the straw was soaked with kerosene from the broken lamp.

"Lucas!" she called in desperation. "Lucas!"

They'd disappeared into the dark. She could still hear them, panting now, no breath to spare for curses or boasts. Blind and deaf to everything but their hatred, they fought madly.

The hungry flame began to devour what it touched. The heat flared up, making her squint and draw her legs up. Tears stung her cheeks as the damp straw underneath made choking smoke. She must crawl to the door, creeping on stomach and knees like the lowliest snake.

So slow! So far! And no way to help herself. If the knife had but fallen closer to her, but she didn't know where it had gone. Sobbing with the pain of her cramped limbs, Grace wormed her way over the dirt floor. She'd traveled this ground a hundred times a day, yet she'd never realized how far away the door was from the stalls.

Then the two men, somehow come to their feet, careened out of the darkness, still locked together in battle. They fell over Grace, making her cry out in agony. Then she cried out in fear, for Wyman came up off the floor with the knife clutched in his hands.

Lucas crouched, prepared to take the lawman's spring. But then Wyman turned his head very slowly to the side, as though he were trying to watch Lucas and still see where the heat that scorched him came from. He saw the leaping flames, now licking the wooden support. "No! No, it's mine!"

Like a madman, he danced in rage, screaming obscenities at the fire. Behind him, the cow had begun to panic, rolling her eyes and yanking on her headstall. Her terrified mooing vied with the rising stridor of crackling flames. Smoke swirled in the air, reaching out like a ghost to smother and choke.

Exhausted, Lucas dropped to his knees beside Grace. A trickle of blood came from his bruised mouth, and beneath his cut eyebrows his eyes were weary. Grace thought he was a wonderful sight. He scooped her up and held her against his chest, her hands dangling, still tied, behind her. "Come on, Wyman. There's nothing you can do now."

"Help me put the fire out," Wyman said, coming around to block their way. "You can have the old man's share. Just help me."

"It's impossible!" Lucas said, raising his voice over the increasing roar of the blaze. "This barn's kindling wood! Let's go!"

"No, it's mine!" He lifted the knife in the air, the flames seeming to run down the shining blade. "Help me, or I swear I'll kill her."

A new voice said over the cacophony, "Put the knife down, Marshal. I got you covered."

Grace saw Jasper standing in the opening, a shining six-gun in his hand. He was hatless, and looked very young. But his eyes were sober and his hand did not shake. "Drop it," he repeated.

"But she knows! She knows where it is and won't tell me."

"I swear," Grace said, coughing. "I swear I don't know."

His eyes rolling as wildly as the maddened animal behind him, Reg Wyman glanced at the fire, at the couple before him and at the boy with the gun. A strangely calm look came into his battered face. Grace saw him as he might have been, had nobility been a greater part of his nature.

"This is where it should end," he said, the hysterical note passing from his voice. It was as if he spoke to himself. "They all died here. I've been living on borrowed time."

He turned, raising the knife in the air for a stabbing stroke. Slowly at first, then breaking into a run, he headed for Jasper. Grace waited for the young man to shoot, but at this moment, his hand trembled. She realized he'd never shot anyone before. Closing her eyes, she couldn't even scream a warning.

The blast that shattered the air was never made by any pistol. She opened her eyes in amazement. Wyman lay face up in the dirt, blood seeping through his shirt. He twitched and lay still. A cloud of gunsmoke rose as though it were Reg Wyman's spirit, floating to join the smoke of the burning barn.

Lucas ran past the body, carrying Grace in his arms. As he sat her down in the grass, the blessed cool, sweet air of night surrounding her, she saw Wenonah standing beside Jasper, the heavy, smoking shotgun still cradled in her hands.

Chapter
Twenty

They could do nothing to save the barn. Jasper and Lucas managed, however, to blindfold the cow, walking her safely past the flames, and to return for the lifeless body of Reg Wyman. They moved Jasper's horse and buggy into the road, and tied the mules nearby for company. For the rest, the orange glow of fire against the night sky would soon bring help from town.

Her bonds cut, Grace took Wenonah into the house. As they walked down the slope, the girl began to shake with sobs. "I . . . I killed him!"

Forgetting her own pain, Grace put her arm around Wenonah's shoulders. "Shush, now," she crooned. "Shush. Don't speak of it now. Don't think of it now."

The water in the reservoir was hot enough to make coffee. While it brewed, she brought out a shawl to tuck around the girl, who shivered now with shock. Grace took a moment too to put on a skirt.

While Wenonah rocked back and forth, her sobs quieting, Grace unbound the thick black hair and began to brush it, the regular motions soothing to broken nerves.

She said, "When I was a little girl, my mother would brush and brush my hair whenever I was upset. She'd sing to me too, just any little song."

"My . . . my mother would sing too."

"Did she?"

The girl's voice lifted in a rhythmic chant, unlike any lullaby Grace's mother would recognize. Wenonah's voice never went above a whisper, but her rocking slowed, her gulps becoming less frequent. Grace kept up the smooth, heavy strokes through the black cloud that was Wenonah's hair.

When the coffeepot began to seethe, she put a cup of the warm brew, heavily sweetened, into Wenonah's hand. She nursed the warmth more than she drank. "I'm sorry about your barn."

Grace shrugged. "It was old. I'm just glad to be alive."

"What did Mar—"

"We'll talk about him later. Are you all right now?"

Her brown eyes turned away. "Yes. Thank you."

"My pleasure. It's only to be hoped the roof of the house doesn't catch too." She could hear at least one of the men stomping around up there now, undoubtedly wetting down the shingles with buckets. "Are you all right now?" she repeated. "I should go help them."

Wenonah's teeth chattered on the rim of the cup, but she answered again with a dull "Yes."

Thinking Wenonah needed a few minutes to herself, Grace went out. Smoke hung in the air like the dun clouds of a battle, while the burning barn shed the red light of the day of judgment over the yard.

Beside the house, Jasper reached up a bucket of water to Lucas and then turned to go fill the second one. Grace was there first, bringing a pail that sloshed and slapped water with every step. "I guess the barn's hopeless."

Jasper nodded and wiped sweat out his eyes with his sleeve. Handing up the bucket, he said, "Help'll be here soon, but we can't stay. You ain't heard the news."

She ran back and forth with the bucket. "What news?"

"It just came over the wire. The Sioux wiped out General Custer and most of the Seventh Cavalry."

"When?"

"A couple of days ago. Someplace near the Bighorn river. In the Dakotas. They announced it from the speaker's platform. I thought I should get Wenonah out of there. Folks were lookin' at her kinda funny."

"Hurry up!" Lucas called from above their heads. Grace looked up. His face was all marks and bruises, his eyes swelling closed.

"Come down," she said. "If it burns, it burns."

"Get more water, Grace," he shouted back. "I'll save you this much, if I can."

"Come down," she said. "We've got more trouble."

Jasper explained to Lucas in fewer words even than he'd used to Grace. Despite the battering he'd taken, Lucas caught on quickly. "And now she's shot the marshal. They'll think it's an uprising."

"If only *I* had shot him," Jasper said, giving the stiffening body in the path a dirty look. "But I never shot anybody afore. Seems like I just couldn't make my fingers pull that trigger."

Grace wasn't wasting any breath on the late marshal. "Listen," she said, touching the young man on the arm. "Can you take Wenonah away someplace? I mean, do you—"

"That's what my ma wanted to know." He looked her in the eyes. "It's all I want outta life, Mrs. Landers. To take care of her forever."

Proud of him, Grace said, "All this about Custer . . . I don't understand, but it'll blow over sooner or later. And you've got enough credit in this town to keep people from talking, as long as you're married to her."

"That's just what my ma said."

Lucas pushed his fist into Jasper's shoulder. "If you already have the good advice of two ladies, then why are you hanging around here?"

"Gotta get Wenonah's stuff, don't we? And we would of been hightailin' it out of here a while ago, but for . . ." The two men grinned at each other, the firelight turning their faces for a moment into some primitive masks. Grace wondered if the horrors of the night would leave her and Wenonah as unmarked as it seemed to leave Jasper and Lucas.

"I'll help Wenonah get ready. Lucas, start thinking of a good story to explain all this. I think it's best if we say these two were never here."

"I haven't seen them."

Grace hardly had time to bundle a few loaves of bread and half a dozen boiled eggs into a basket, before Wenonah came out, her few possessions packed in a valise. "I don't know how to thank—"

"There's no time, dear. Besides, I should thank *you.*" Grace put her arms around her tall young friend and held her close against her mother's heart. Suddenly, Wenonah gave a convulsive sob.

"There now," Grace said, patting her back. If she started crying again, they'd never get away in time. "Don't worry; Jasper will take good care of you."

"No, you don't understand." She looked into Grace's eyes, her own spilling over with tears. "I'm so happy! I shouldn't be, with so much wrong, but I am!"

"Then that's all that matters. Forget about the rest of it. The only thing that matters is that you and Jasper love each other and be strong together. You'll write and let me know where you are?"

"Yes. As soon as we're settled. And . . . thank you."

Not ten minutes after the young couple drove away, the first of the townspeople arrived. The hand-drawn fire engine arrived soon after, drawn by the burliest men in town. As had Lucas and Jasper, they saw at once that extinguishing the barn was a pointless task. They focused the steam-pumped water on the house in steady sprays.

The women who had come with their husbands stood about with wet sacks, ready to slap to extinction any stray spark. Those children who'd tagged along with their parents seemed to think a barn fire was just another firework for their amusement. Most of them didn't notice the dead man, with the knot of concerned citizens standing over him.

"A darned shame," said Judge Sterling. "He wasn't the worst peace officer we've ever had." He patted his pockets, and then nodded his thanks when Dr. Birkins handed him a flask.

Young Mr. Kent asked, "You say he was after the raiders' gold?" Kent looked up at what was left of the barn. The inner supports had collapsed with a great crash and spray of sparks twenty minutes ago. In his staring eyes was something of Wyman's greed.

"That's right," Lucas said. His face hurt but not as

badly as his sides, where the marshal had rabbit-punched viciously. He had a presentiment that he would ache worse tomorrow than he had after his first day plowing. His wits, however, were still wide awake.

"Seems strange to think of all that gold and money sitting up there, with no one the wiser," Dr. Birkins said. "Just think what it would have meant to Chick and Grace too."

"Oh, I don't think it was ever there," Lucas said. Every face swiveled to meet his, this statement drawing their attention away from the corpse.

"Jasper Crowley told me about your former marshal . . ."

"Sweeney," Judge Sterling supplied.

"That's it. Sweeney. He said Sweeney had brought Wyman into town when he wanted to retire."

"Yeah, just goes to show no man's a true judge of character," Birkins said and then muttered an apology to Sterling. The judge dismissed his excuse with a wave of the doctor's flask.

"I think Sweeney knew more about Wyman's character than he let on," Lucas said. "Jasper also told me that Sweeney only stayed in town a week after Wyman came."

The judge said, "He left me a note, explaining that he wanted to slip away on the quiet. No public thanks or anything. As I remember it, he didn't tell anyone he was going to visit his brother in Santa Fe before I got that letter. Hell, I didn't even know he *had* a brother in Santa Fe and we'd been playing poker every Thursday night since Hector was a pup."

"He wasn't much of a one for talking about himself," the doctor added. "I heard he left his lodgings in the middle of the night to avoid a fuss. That'd be just like Sweeney."

Lucas hated to destroy these men's memory of their friend. He thought about not mentioning the body in the woods, but feared that someday someone else might be blamed for a crime that lay on Reg Wyman's soul, wherever it was.

"I think he left in the middle of the night to avoid

Wyman," Lucas said. The three men stared at him, their mouths hanging limply. "Sweeney hadn't ever talked about retiring before Wyman came to town, right?"

"He said to me once that he couldn't wait to draw out his nest egg and buy a farm somewhere," Mr. Kent mused. "But there was never more than fifty dollars all together in his account."

"It's a serious business in these parts to slander somebody who's absent," Judge Sterling said.

"He's not that far away," Lucas said grimly. "He's buried in the woods."

Once again, he amazed the others. In answer to their breathless questions, he said, "Because there are letters in his pocket that identify him as H. O. Sweeney. And those initials on a cigarette pouch in his breast pocket. I 'found' him one afternoon while playing with Mrs. Landers's children. They don't know about it being a real body."

"So how do you figure Wyman here killed him?" the doctor asked.

Lucas told them about Wyman's threat to start removing fingers until he got what he wanted. "When you dig for Mr. Sweeney, watch out for four of his fingers. They're not exactly where they're supposed to be."

Young Mr. Kent reached out and grabbed the whiskey flask from the judge. After he choked and coughed, he said, "But you said the money isn't in the barn. Wyman thought it was and under those circumstances—"

"Under those circumstances, a man must tell the truth?" Lucas asked.

"Not ol' Sweeney," the judge replied. "Not if he thought there was a chance of getting out with the gold and his skin. I know how good he used to bluff me. But you're saying that once Wyman heard what he thought was the truth—the circumstances being what they were—he killed Sweeney and buried him out there."

"That's the way I reconstruct it."

"You wouldn't happen to be a lawyer yourself, now would you?" the judge asked, looking at Lucas with narrowed eyes.

For the first time, he failed to meet that steely gaze. "I have had a certain amount to do with the law, yes."

Dr. Birkins said, "There'll have to be an inquest on both these bodies. But don't worry, Mr. Lucas. I think I can speak for the judge when I say there's no doubt you won't be tried for murder."

"I appreciate that. One trial in my life is enough." They seemed to have accepted wholeheartedly the story of how Wyman came to die. He and Grace had clung as closely to the truth as possible. The marks on his and Grace's wrists bore silent witness to their having cut their way free from confining bonds. Grace had readily agreed that he should take the blame, promising with her first smile since this evening to come visit him in prison.

"So where's the gold?" Mr. Kent asked.

Lucas lifted his shoulders in a shrug. "I haven't the faintest idea.

"And why did Wyman think Sweeney knew where it was, anyway?" the doctor asked.

"I can answer that," the judge said. "I remember the raid like it was yesterday. I'll bet you a plugged nickel to a greenback that Sweeney was in on it."

"In on it?" Birkins echoed.

"He was about the last person to get here. The hangings had already started." Now it was Judge Sterling who couldn't meet Lucas's eyes. "I wasn't a judge yet, you know."

"I didn't say a word."

"I thought at the time it was kinda funny that those fellas would hole up here, what with half the town after 'em. Maybe they were waiting for somebody. Like Sweeney. Kent?"

"Yes, sir?"

"Did your father talk to you about that day?"

"Almost never. But he did say that the raiders took the money, not Sweeney."

"But what did they do with it?" Lucas wondered. "Let's say that Wyman was on that raid. He escapes the lynchings, or went off in a different direction from the others, but he knows Sweeney is an accomplice. He comes back . . ."

"Why such a long time later? It's been ten years."

Lucas shook his head. "This is all conjecture. But he comes back, blackmails Sweeney into taking him in and makes him agree to show him where the gold is. But Sweeney slides out. Wyman catches him, tortures and kills him. But Sweeney lied. Wyman has to stay in Ogden to find the money. That would explain why he was courting Grace. As her husband, anything on this farm would belong to him."

"He made an offer to buy the place at least twice," Kent admitted. "She always refused."

"She would," Lucas said. He turned to look for her. She was handing out coffee to the firefighters. As though she could feel his glance, she lifted her head and gave him a little wave and a heartbreakingly brave smile.

Judge Sterling said with decision, "I reckon we'd better search Wyman's personal belongings and his office. Maybe there'll be some facts, 'stead of daydreaming."

Grace and Mrs. Crowley had no need to thrash out what had happened. A raised eyebrow, a half smile and they could return to their tasks, confident that each approved of Jasper and Wenonah's flight. Gold and sudden death were of less importance than an elopement.

Now that the barn had collapsed, the men turned the fire engine's pump on the mass of burning wreckage. A wagon was detailed to carry Wyman's body to town, and the judge agreed that tomorrow they should dig up the late Mr. Sweeney and convey him to Dr. Birkins for an autopsy.

When all the townsfolk had gone home, Lucas sat on the porch steps. Grace leaned her head on his shoulder, grateful for the moment to lay off her burdens. "Strange day," she sighed.

"I never asked if you were all right."

"Oh, well. I've been better."

He squeezed her shoulders in the circle of his arm. "You were so brave. I was shaking in my boots the whole time."

"Me too." They met each other's eyes and smiled. Then Grace again put her head on his shoulder. She didn't care that he reeked of smoke; she smelled the same.

He said, "I suppose the animals will be all right in the field for tonight at least."

"Yes. They'll do for the summer, if I can come up with some kind of shelter in case of rain. After harvest, I'll have to take them to be sold. I think I can get a good—"

"Sold? Why?"

Though she tried to be matter-of-fact, Grace's voice trembled the slightest bit. "No barn, remember. I can't let them freeze. Mr. Hackiff has always wanted my mules—"

"You can build another barn."

"Why didn't I think of that?" she said, then contritely added, "I'm sorry. I shouldn't be snide after all you've done for me tonight." She kissed his cheek briefly then snuggled against his side once again.

"Can't your parents lend you the money?" He felt her head shake against his shoulder. "The bank?"

"I don't have a thing to stake against a loan. The bank practically owns the place anyway."

"Then what will we do?" A scalding tear soaked through his shirt. "Grace?" he asked, looking down at her honey-blond hair, fallen into uncombed hanks. A ragged sob escaped her.

"It's . . . it's just been such a long time since I heard 'we.' "

Lucas embraced her closer still against his chest and let the hot rain fall on him. His own emotions nearly slipped their reins when he thought how close he'd come to never looking into her steady gray eyes again. He tilted her chin back and kissed her quivering mouth.

Her tears soon stopped. She found herself cradled on Lucas's lap, his arms around her so tightly that she almost couldn't take a breath. Yet somehow she didn't mind how hard he squeezed. He was solid and real, and she thanked God for his deliverance.

Soon though, she asked, driven by curiosity about the informal inquest in her yard over Wyman's body, "Why did Wyman think I had the gold?"

"Never mind that now," Lucas said. "All those questions will be answered in good time."

"I hope Wenonah and Jasper—"

"I don't want to talk about them either."

"Well, what do you want to talk about?" She glanced up to see a subtle smile tugging at the corners of his mobile mouth. Her heart began to thud in a quickened rhythm.

"I don't want to talk at all."

"But you said you wouldn't—"

He kissed her with a desperate intensity that left her shaking, breathlessly clinging to him. "That was before I almost lost you," he said, his voice deep and ragged. "Why do you think I was fighting him so ferociously?"

"You wanted to get free. . . ."

"No! I wanted to kill him for daring to put one hand on you! I wanted to strangle him, to smash him to pieces! I never knew I could feel like that about someone."

He stood up, keeping hold of her hands. Grace rose willingly. "Now," he said boldly. "Now all I want is to make love with you and show you—"

"I want that too," she said boldly. "More than anything! But wouldn't you like to wait till tomorrow?" She touched his contused cheek with gentle fingertips. "Those bruises are even more impressive than the first ones you had."

He caught her hand and kissed the palm, favoring the cut side of his mouth. With a twinkle in his eyes, he said, "I've got to make love with you now, Grace. Tomorrow I'm going to be too sore."

"Are you sure?"

"That I'll be too sore?" He put his hand to his side and winced. "No doubt about it."

"I mean are you sure you're not too sore already?"

"I'll make every effort. No doubt about that either." He began to lead her inside. "Unless you're . . ."

Despite the cuts on her wrists from the rope and on her hands from the glass, Grace shook her head. "I'll make every effort too."

Within five minutes, they'd forgotten every ache but the one for each other.

* * *

In the morning, a dreary drizzle added a pall of gloom over the blasted scene in the yard. But at the same time, each drop contributed to the dousing of the steaming pile of rubble that remained of the barn. Lucas, climbing out of bed without waking Grace, did chores and then walked into town to send a telegram, wincing every step of the way. Meeting the judge outside the telegraph office, he accompanied him up the stairs to Dr. Birkins's office.

The doctor came out of the inner room, closing the door behind him. However, Lucas got a quick glimpse of the deteriorated body on the table. It wasn't the first time he'd seen it, but he was not eager to see it again.

Dr. Birkins pulled down the handkerchief he'd tied around his lower face. "Got any whiskey, Judge?"

"Bad, was it?"

Birkins wiped his lips and nodded. "Yes. But it's definitely Sweeney. I set that broken leg for him myself."

"I guess that confirms it."

"Confirms what?" Lucas asked.

"All the stuff you were spouting last night is pretty close to the facts, so far as I can figure," the judge said sternly.

"You found that out? How?"

"We searched Wyman's rooms last night. Among other things we found a wanted poster. The name was different, but the face was the same. His real name was Hayes, wanted in towns south of here for raidin'. He didn't even have the bad excuse of being an ex-Confederate. He was just a black-hearted son of a bitch, wanted for everything from robbery with violence to spitting on the sidewalk. I don't reckon Sweeney was his first murder, either."

Lucas said, "He hid that side of himself from everyone but Grace."

"What's that?"

"Nothing. It's over and done with. Do you know where he's been since the raid?"

"Yep. Spent ten years in a federal penitentiary. And he was lucky not to have been hung for some of the things he'd done. He escaped 'bout five weeks before he showed up here. And we went ahead and made him marshal! What the hell were we thinkin' of?"

"Now, be fair," Dr. Birkins said. "He was a good marshal."

"Not really," Lucas said. "He did keep letting the Grupp brothers out of jail."

"They must've reminded him of himself at that age," Judge Sterling fumed. "I telegraphed the governor this morning, telling him we need a new marshal lickety-split. And the new one had better bring those boys up before me within the first week of his gettin' here or he'll be in worse shape than Sweeney!"

"So you think Wyman definitely was one of the raiders?" Lucas asked, bringing the important question up again.

"The wanted poster didn't show his mustache or his sideburns. As soon as I saw it, I recognized him. I should have; he was the one that held *me* up."

"Now then, Judge," the doctor said, giving him back the flask. "Ten years is a long time. Folks change."

"It's just the thought of that hyena laughing at me all this time! You see, I swore I'd never forget him, that I'd see him twisting in the wind. Well, at least I seen him dead."

"What about Sweeney?" Lucas asked the doctor.

"Considering that Sweeney introduced him to the town as an old friend, that he never let on about Wyman's past, I guess it's pretty conclusive. The poster we found was dated from Sweeney's time as marshal so we figure he must have known."

"Wyman blackmailed him, then?"

The two professional men shrugged. "I think this old world's well rid of both those bastards," Judge Sterling said. "Let's get 'em both underground quick so I can get back to important stuff, like fishing."

Rain fell for two days. Lucas and Grace spent most of the time in bed, only rising to take care of the animals, protected under a coppice of dogwoods. They ate when they were hungry, slept when they were tired, and often reached for each other. Some horse liniment had worked wonders on bruised skin and punished muscles.

Grace was lying facedown on the mattress while Lucas kneaded the creamy white liniment well into her naked back. The fragrance of peppermint, strong and gaspingly fresh, drove the last remnants of smoke out of her room. Sighing, Grace said, "Don't stop."

"Don't worry. Of course, there's not that much more to do. I've done your back and your legs. Your arms and your feet."

His strong hands stroked down over her smooth skin, rubbing and relaxing, pressing and releasing. Grace ground her whole body against the mattress, it felt so good.

She reached behind herself to trace her fingers over his hair-rough thigh. "I'll do you in a minute."

"Do what to me?"

Hiding her smile against the pillow, she said mock-severely, "Rub you down, of course."

"Could you rub me up instead?" He leaned forward, the mattress shifting and creaking under his weight, and kissed the corner of her mouth. Grace rolled over leisurely, raising her arms to lock around his neck.

It was a long, slow, drugging kiss that made her crave more. She'd never wallowed in luxurious carnality before. Strange that the more Lucas touched her, the more she longed for his touch. A single look from his hungry blue eyes could turn her heavy with longing. A simple kiss made her a wanton, with no will to resist. In place of willpower came a sense of invention that seemed to delight him. His enthusiastic response to her audacity proved how much.

The Saturday after the fire dawned bright and clear. The ground squelched underfoot when Grace went out to milk the cow, but the sky above shone a cloudless blue. A merry breeze rifled the grass and the mules positively capered as they came down to the fence to greet her.

Only the great pile of ash and charred wood showed what disaster had struck here. Though the barn had not been large, the square of scorched earth where it had stood looked enormous, a vast black patch like the footprint of a giant demon.

Lucas came out of the house as she came back with a pail of milk. She stopped to fill her eyes with him. Fresh from a bath, he wore his work pants, the suspenders hitched over his bare shoulders. Though he still bore the signs of his fight on his body, she saw only the smooth contours of his shoulders and the slim, wholly masculine waist and hips. Would she ever look at him with dulled eyes, or would this little leap of her pulses always greet the sight of him?

Right now, he looked puzzled as he ran his hand through his thick, damp hair. "Grace?" he called. "Do you hear something?"

"Like what?"

"Like . . . like a band?"

Down Lynch Road they came, a rolling mass of people. The children skipped and danced to the lively march the four-piece band played. Women carried picnic baskets so heavy it took both hands to lift one. And with the men came wagonloads of lumber and long toolboxes.

Confused, Grace looked from side to side as the crowd came to a halt before her gate. There was a rattle of confused talk. Then Brother Marill stepped forward. The tall man blinked when he saw Lucas and Grace standing hand in hand, but he said, "Mrs. Landers, the ladies church auxiliary think that . . . Well, here . . . I mean to say that . . ."

"Oh, let me, Gilbert." Rena Presby, dressed simply in a blue calico frock, stepped forward. She smiled dazzlingly and took the preacher's arm. "We all feel that you should have a new barn, Grace. So we're here to raise you one."

Grace put her hand to her cheek in astonishment. She hadn't expected anything of the sort. She glanced at Lucas, who grinned down at her and whispered, "It's what you wanted, isn't it?"

Grace threw her hands wide. "Well, come on in!"

A new spot was chosen, far enough away from the burned barn that they didn't need to clean up the site, but near enough to the house to be convenient even in the depth of winter. The runoff wouldn't poison the well in the spring. The flies would be fighting a prevailing summer wind all the way to the house.

Kept by the coddling concern of her friends from doing anything constructive, Grace sat on a rise and watched the work progress. She saw Lucas, a white shirt covering his muscles, working with the other men, accepted by them all. Until that moment, she hadn't realized how deep he was in the confidence of the town fathers. Sterling and Birkins, Marill and Kent, all the members of the town council, stopped to talk to him, and she could have sworn they were asking his advice.

By the time they stopped work to eat, the frame was already up, assembled in four pieces and then raised. Next, one team would begin work on the roof, while the other nailed up clapboards. On the grass, the men laughed and joked with each other over their clumsiness and mistakes. Grace went to join Mrs. Crowley.

"Seems a 'coon's age since our last picnic," she said.

"A lot has happened," Grace agreed.

Mrs. Crowley turned her brown eyes toward Lucas. He sat in the center of a group of men, all eagerly discussing the most recently revealed details of the Battle of Little Bighorn. Grace saw he looked seriously troubled, almost angry. She missed what Mrs. Crowley said next, until she was recalled by the white paper the other woman held out.

"They're married," Mrs. Crowley said, not giving Grace a chance to read the letter from Jasper. "But they'll be back in a few weeks, after they visit some of our cousins down in St. Louis. My boy sounds happy as a dog with two tails."

"I'm so glad."

"But listen . . ." Mrs. Crowley leaned closer. "Jasper wants me to find out if you're willin' to sell him this place. What with you takin' up with that handsome feller over there, Jasper figures you might be willin' to let it go at a short price."

"I suppose everyone is talking about me," Grace said.

"Pretty much. Them that aren't talking about Wyman, Custer or the preacher."

"The preacher?"

"Didn't you notice how Rena called him 'Gilbert'? If ever a woman set her cap for a man, she sure has. But she's got her work cut out for her, I'll say." Mrs. Crowley laughed, crossing her arms over her stomach. "A more drifting, heedless creature never put on his pants one leg at a time."

"They're a handsome couple. They're both so tall."

"Yes. You can almost forgive her for her dress making her eyes so pretty. Calico! That's a first. She'll take to wearing a sunbonnet next." Sobering, Mrs. Crowley said, "You think about my boy's offer. He says Wenonah's taken a real fancy to the place. And o'course we'll help 'em out with the price."

Grace rose to her feet. "I doubt I'll sell, but thank him for the offer."

She walked down to the gate, after catching Lucas's eye. Though she needed a few minutes alone, talking with Lucas was the same as talking to herself. She could say what she meant without dissembling, going straight to the heart of the matter.

He was in the act of walking toward her when the most expensive buggy in Carter's Livery Stable came tooling down the road. She recognized the horse as Carter's best mare, but the man holding the reins was a stranger. He wore a black suit and his tall hat reflected the sun with the gleam of silk.

Lucas hadn't noticed the fancy equipage yet. He had eyes only for Grace. One touch of her cool hands would ease this gnawing guilt. Was the battle with Custer in any way a retaliation for the massacre he'd been responsible for?

A voice, clipped and sharp, said, "You are Mrs. Landers?"

"That's right. What can I do for you?"

"You can direct me to my—"

"Hello, sir." Lucas said, standing beside Grace on the inside of the fence.

On the other side, looking as neat as though he'd stepped from a picture frame, was a tall man with silver-gray hair. His shoulders were not bent by his sixty years, but he gave the impression they were held straight only by ceaseless discipline. Bright blue eyes looked at Lucas from a remarkably unlined face, chalky white from long hours behind a desk.

Lucas turned to his beloved. "Grace, I'd like you to meet Ames Bickford Cobb. My father."

Chapter
Twenty-One

Grace looked in vain for the two men to embrace, to pound each other's backs, to give glad cries. She waited even for them to shake hands, as many men seemed to prefer expressing their feelings by crushing each other's fingers. But they merely sized one another up, like two slightly hostile strangers.

"Won't you come in?" she asked, feeling it behooved her to be gracious.

Mr. Cobb didn't so much hesitate as seem to ask himself whether entering would lower his esteem in his own eyes. Surveying the happy people in her yard, he asked, "You are having a celebration?"

Lucas said, "The people of Ogden are building Grace a new barn."

"Oh, yes?" He watched as young Phil Chandler chased a shrieking Millie Bates with a bucket of water. "I see."

He opened the gate and entered the yard. Grace had more pride in her place than she had the first time Lucas had seen it. Her hand slipped into his, which had been roughened by all the work he'd done. If his father had shaken hands with his son, perhaps the stern expression would have passed from his forehead and eyes.

"Your son has been a big help to me," she offered.

"Indeed." The man could quell enthusiasm with a single word.

"That's right, Father. I forgot to mention in the telegram I sent you that Grace is my employer. She bailed me out of jail and put me to work. See that garden? That's mostly my doing. Completely overgrown with weeds when I came here."

Grace turned a mocking frown up to her lover. "That burned-down barn is mostly your doing too, remember?"

"Oh, no. There I had plenty of help." He put his arm around her and squeezed. Grace lost her breath not from the pressure of his arm but from the look of adoration in his eyes.

"You'll be interested to learn, John," his father said, taking no notice of their banter, "that Senator Jayston was most pleased by the news of your approaching return. That replacement of yours is worse than useless. He's dangerous to the party."

"Father, I—"

"And of course Clarissa Hazelforth sends her warmest wishes. Her father is in Europe with his second wife, or I would have brought word from him as well."

Grace said, "I think I'd better . . ." but Lucas's arm tightened to keep her by his side.

"Father, you might as well know . . . I have no intention of continuing my understanding with Miss Hazelforth. I'm going to marry Grace."

Lucas had received his eyes from his father. The same dark blue irises lived in both faces, the lids similarly shaped and lashed. But Lucas's had never blazed with such cold fire. A chill fell on the warm afternoon, so golden until this moment. Mr. Cobb's gaze traveled slowly from his son to Grace and back again, and she felt her heart ice over.

"This, I take it, is Grace."

She realized that everything Lucas had said had bounced off this man as though he wore armor-plate. He hadn't heard a word about the farm or seen the obvious affection between herself and his son. Only when what had been said directly touched him or one of his plans would he pay attention.

Straightening under that cold appraisal, she said, "Yes. I'm Mrs. Chick Landers. This is my place. These are my friends."

"Mine too," Lucas added.

"I see we have much to discuss, John. If Mrs. Landers will excuse us . . ."

"No, sir. Whatever you have to say to me, she can hear."

Mr. Cobb turned his head to take in the noisy crowd about them. The roofers had begun laying full-cut boards across the rafters of the new barn, their hammering vying with that of the men pounding nails into clapboards and framing. The wives were packing up the leftover food while the children got in the way.

"And is it also for everyone else to hear? Or may we have some privacy?"

Mentally reviewing everything she had in the house, Grace offered Mr. Cobb refreshment as they went into her sitting room. "I know how hard it is to get some decent food on a train. Is there anything I can offer you? Some coffee, maybe? Or a piece of my burnt-sugar cake?"

The slightest line of puzzlement came into Mr. Cobb's forehead. "I ate excellently well on the train, Mrs. Landers. I always do. Let us not stand on ceremony."

He waved his hand toward her settee. Beginning to prickle at his high-handedness, something else he'd passed on to Lucas, she sat. Only then did the men take seats as well, Lucas close to her side.

Yet he didn't look at her. He watched his father. Something wary in his expression reminded Grace of those stressful moments in the barn. Was he waiting for a weakness in the other man that he could exploit? Grace felt colder than ever. She crossed her arms over her breasts, rubbing her upper arms to allay the goose bumps.

Lucas told his father all that had happened to him since coming to Ogden. He skimmed over what he remembered of the months he'd been wandering, as well as the cause of it all. Grace knew from his frequent glances at her that he wanted to spare her feelings. Furthermore, he told Mr. Cobb the revised version of what happened to Wyman. Wenonah's secret was still safe.

"It seems I have much cause to thank Mrs. Landers," Mr. Cobb said. But thanks were not forthcoming. His thin lips parted in a smile that would have been charming, if she had not been so worried. "Mrs. Landers, do you know who my son is?"

"Not any of the usual things, no. But—"

"He is John Peyton Cobb, the rising young state legislator from Connecticut."

"I didn't know that. But it doesn't surprise me. I knew he had to be something important." His hand crept over hers and she grasped it tightly.

"He has been missing, presumed dead, for months. Everyone believed he died of exposure in a sudden snowstorm. I believe quite a few Indians perished at the same time."

"Is that the story you've invented?" Grace jumped when Lucas spoke. His voice was like the sudden crack of a whip against the calm imperturbability of his father's.

"It is the truth, is it not? What should we say? That John Peyton Cobb, promising Republican legislator, disappeared after a bloody, drunken massacre of red women and children?"

She shot Lucas a glance. He still didn't look her way. His face was set now in hard lines. He looked older, more like his father. The grip of his hand on hers was punishingly strong, but she bore it uncomplainingly.

"Is that the truth?" she asked.

Lucas answered. "I tried to stop it. But, yes. It was all my fault."

"That I don't believe. It couldn't be all your fault."

Swiftly, he lifted her hand and gently kissed her fingers. He shook his head over the white pressure marks he'd put on her skin, and laid her hand once again in her lap. "What else, Father?"

Before Mr. Cobb could speak, there was a rattling knock on the porch door. "Hey, Lucas!" Mr. Kent yodeled. "Come on out here and tell us where you want the stalls!"

"Lucas?" his father asked.

"Yes, sir. That's what they call me around here."

"But Lucas is your tailor's name." For the first time, Mr. Cobb showed signs of shock.

He shrugged. "One name is as good as another.

Though I have to say I've gotten rather fond of Lucas. The woman I love calls me that."

"Come on, man! They're going to put 'em in any minute!"

Grace met his worried look. "You'd better go."

His hand rested a moment on her shoulder as he gazed at his father. "I'll be back in a few minutes."

She watched him go, torn between pride in him and chagrin for herself. He was wealthy, handsome, smart and brave. He'd made a name for himself in the wide world. What was she by comparison?

"Kindly give me your attention, Mrs. Landers."

"You have it, sir."

"This is your house?"

"Yes, sir. I own it—or rather I pay the mortgage on it."

"You are a widow, then? Are any of those outside your children?"

"No, none of them are. But I have a boy and a girl. They are visiting my mother." She smiled happily at the thought of Bart and Callie. Before too much longer she'd be with them again. How angry they'd be with her, when they heard all that had happened while they were gone. She did not, however, think they'd miss Reg Wyman. Bart especially had never much liked the "lawman."

"Mrs. Landers, I won't shade the truth from you. My son is a very important man. He is well liked in the party and has a happy talent for drawing warring factions together. It has been difficult of late in the party. Much petty squabbling between the Liberal Republicans and the men, like myself, who support Grant, for instance."

"But I've heard that Grant's administration is utterly corrupt."

She saw a ripple of surprise pass over his face and knew she'd astonished him. He hadn't expected a country woman to know anything about politics. He coughed and tried to bluster, "Certainly not! His administration is simply doing its best to encourage a free marketplace. That is what has made this country strong, Mrs. Landers."

"You were speaking of Lu—your son."

The red stain faded from Mr. Cobb's thin cheeks.

"There is to be an election in the fall. I have every hope that Grant will be reelected. He will undoubtedly remove from office some of those persons who have flirted with abuse of their position. He will look about him for honest men to take their places. It is not inconceivable that John will be among them. He himself is not up for reelection this year."

"That's just as well," Grace said. "Considering how long he's been gone, that is."

"Exactly! Precisely my point. He must reestablish himself. Whether he goes to Washington or not is immaterial. He must reestablish himself as quickly as possible as a solid and trustworthy man of the party."

Suddenly, he crossed the room to sit beside her. Seizing her hands, he said roughly, "Can you help him do that? I think not. What will you do for him? Offer the men with money burnt-sugar cakes? Can you run a great house? Can you be a gracious political hostess? Can you entertain their wives, learn their secrets, promise them more than you will deliver?"

Grace snatched her hands away from his hot, dry touch. "No, I cannot."

"No, you cannot. Clarissa Hazelforth can. Her father has money, power and influence. He's offered them a house in Georgetown as a wedding gift. She was born to be a wife for a man like John. Could you be the wife of the President of the United States, Mrs. Landers?"

"I don't understand you, Mr. Cobb." She drew away. "You thought he was dead. But all you can talk of is politics. Don't you care that he is alive?"

He changed his tone, trying perhaps to force some feeling to rise. "Naturally, I was most concerned when I heard nothing from him. The last word I had was more than six months ago. He wrote me a letter to inform me that the committee he'd joined—a federal committee—to study the question of the Dakota gold fields was progressing as we'd hoped."

" 'As we'd hoped'?" Grace echoed.

"I have worked as hard as John himself to put him

where he is. Naturally, I derive some benefit from his position."

"Naturally." Grace realized that the man she loved was not the man Mr. Cobb knew as his son. Lucas as part of conspiracies and plots? Lucas as a political warrior? Unthinkable. What was John Peyton Cobb like? Did he relish the power and influence as much as his father did? Was he as conscienceless?

"When no further word came," Mr. Cobb continued, "I can say fairly that I was most distressed. Yes, most distressed. As indeed was Miss Hazelforth. She had already set the wedding date and I believe had even made plans to go to Paris to purchase her trousseau. Naturally, she felt her disappointment most keenly."

"Yes, I imagine it was hard to give up Paris."

Mr. Cobb frowned forbiddingly. "Such flippancy is most unbecoming, Mrs. Landers."

"That's why I love her, Father." Lucas came into the room, his britches dusty around the knees. He gave Grace his most heart-stopping grin and stood over her. "It won't work, sir. I love Grace too much to consider letting her get away from me."

"What are you saying?" Mr. Cobb demanded.

"I like being a farmer."

"Madness! I knew I should have brought Dr. Davies to take a look at you. He said you might be suffering from delusions. He has an excellent sanatorium in New York. A few weeks of rest there and your mind will clear."

"My mind is clear, sir. I've just lost my taste for all the biting and scratching that goes on in politics. If I come back, it will be to help the people that elected me."

"That's more reasonable," Mr. Cobb said, the first true smile Grace had seen from him crossing his lips. "Mr. Hazelforth and the gentlemen of the board will be delight—"

"No, not the railroad kings and the robber barons. They only paid money to see me elected. I mean the farmers, the fishermen, the sailors who can't work anymore. They're the ones who elected me."

Mr. Cobb's jaw worked fiercely. Yet his tone when he

spoke was mollifying, even soothing. "Yes, of course, John. I know just how you feel."

Lucas chuckled and Grace tilted her head to look at him. "He's humoring me," he said to her. "You do that with patients suffering from brain fever."

His father's carriage became even more imperial. "You will do as you are told, John!"

"No, sir. I'll do as I please. I'm not afraid of you anymore." Mr. Cobb looked as shocked and angry as if he'd just been slapped.

"I always have been, you know. One of your famous chilling glances, a few hard words, and I always came into line. Not anymore. I've been through a lot since I saw you last. Battle, murder and sudden death were the least of it." He let his gaze fall on Grace. She blushed as though they'd touched intimately.

Mr. Cobb spluttered impotently.

Lucas went on, still smiling, but his eyes entirely serious. "I was always afraid of losing your love, sir. I think you do love me, somewhere in your heart. But I have learned I can live without your regard; I could never live without Grace."

"Do you mean to throw over your entire life, your career, for this . . . this . . ."

"Careful, Father." Grace saw Lucas's eyes turn as cold as the older man's. "Be careful what you call your future daughter-in-law."

She stood up, standing between the two men. "I haven't said I'll marry you yet, Lucas."

"But you will . . ." His tone admitted no doubt.

"Your father has brought up some points I haven't thought over yet. He's right about some things."

"A woman of sense!" Mr. Cobb exclaimed with an ironic twist to his heavy brows.

"I wouldn't know how to go on the kind of society you keep. I'd always be on the outside, doing the wrong thing, though maybe Bart and Callie would fit in eventually."

"I'd help you every step of the way," Lucas vowed. "Besides, do you think charming a political bigwig is any different from making your mules go where you want them to? You've dealt with all the difficult jobs here, Grace. Connecticut will be a snap to a woman of your skills."

Mr. Cobb said, "It sounds as though you've made up your mind to come home and do your duty, John."

"Only if she comes with me. If not, I stay right here."

"Your father is right about that too. You have a duty in Connecticut. You can't just slide out of that."

"Grace . . . ," Lucas said, taking a step toward her.

She said quickly, "I'll get a shawl. It's starting to get chilly out. Then I'd better go see how my barn is coming along. There's a good hotel in town, Mr. Cobb; the Gilmore Arms. I hear they've even got a bathtub in the cellar. Lucas, Mr. Kent can tell you where it is, if you'd care to see your father settled."

"I've already bespoken two rooms at that hotel, Mrs. Landers," Mr. Cobb said. Turning to his son, he added, "I trust there will be no objection if you sleep in a hotel tonight instead of a jail cell."

"I have someplace to sleep, Father. Don't be concerned about me. I daresay I shall lie more comfortably tonight than you will."

She gave a regal nod, to show that she was finished with them, and disappeared into her room. She didn't need a shawl, for the cold she complained of was within her heart. Mr. Cobb was right. She had none of the advantageous attributes of a political wife. When all was said and done, she was just a hick.

By the time Lucas came back, the barn stood complete, right to the weather vane on the top, a fine copper rooster. Grace found herself standing next to Mr. Kent. With his sleeves rolled up to show his slightly sunburned forearms and his usually neat hair falling in his eyes, he looked like just another farmer. He said, "Do you suppose it really is buried on your land?"

"Is what . . . ? Oh, the money."

"My father all but went under making the loss good. I certainly feel that if that money were here, it would be morally mine. Any honest court of law would—"

"I agree."

"You do?"

"And if it were here, you'd be welcome to it."

"You sound as though you are sure it's not here."

"I've been thinking it over." Grace squinted up at her shining new weather vane and thought of all the misery gold could bring, even the rumor of gold. "I don't think the gold is here. I have a couple of reasons, including common sense. How could drunken men come up with a hiding place so clever no one could find it? They only had minutes before the vigilantes arrived to shoot 'em or string 'em up."

"Stranger things have happened," Mr. Kent said. A light of greed danced in his eyes.

"I suppose. But the real reason I know the gold isn't here has to do with you, Mr. Kent."

"Me?" He touched himself on the chest.

"When Chick and I bought this property, we got it for a song, as the saying is."

"Yes, I remember drawing up the paperwork."

"Well, Marshal Sweeney was around then, in town. Chick and I were the only bidders at the auction. Nobody wanted the place, 'cause it had a bad name. If the money were here, and Sweeney was in on the secret, don't you think he would have bought this farm? He'd want to keep a close eye on that money. He never made such a bid, did he?"

"No, not that I recall."

Grace laid her hand on Mr. Kent's arm and looked him in the eyes. "It's not here, Peter. I don't know where it is. But it's not here."

He nodded ruefully, without speaking. The hot light of greed in his eyes faded. Hearing his wife's voice, he sought her out in the crowd. "Enjoy your new barn, Grace," he said as he moved off to join her.

Grace paid little attention for the rest of the day. When the barn was complete, they called for a speech and she said all she should, forcing enthusiasm into her tone, for her heart was dead. She knew that Mr. Cobb would spend every moment of time with Lucas, pounding in words like responsibility, obligation, trustworthiness. How could a little word like love stand against all those long, hard words, especially when she couldn't even promise to marry him?

When Lucas came back that evening, he toted a heavy volume in each hand. Setting the books down on the kitchen table, he wandered over to the stove to lift the lid of Grace's big stew pot. "What's this?" he asked as a savory odor floated up with the steam.

"Ham hocks and bean soup."

Dusting the potato peelings off her hands, she reached out to turn one of the books he'd put down in front of her. It was a thick, black book, with gold lines highlighting the spine.

Opening it, she read "Commentaries on the Law of Married Women, Vol. I. Joel Prentiss Bishop" in thick black ink. A signature "Nathaniel Sterling" sprawled under the copyright date of 1873.

"What's this?" she asked.

Lucas picked up the books and carried them out to the sitting room. He said teasingly, "Ham hocks and bean soup."

It was not until late that night, as they lay curled together in her bed, that he said, "You know, I have to go back."

"I know."

"But it won't be forever."

"Of course not." A forlorn hollowness grew inside her chest, where her heart used to be. Tears pricked her eyes. She fought to keep her voice steady, glad her back was against his chest so he could not see her face.

Lucas said, "I should be there for the opening session. There's a recess before Christmas; I could come back then."

"We'll always be glad to see you."

He lifted up then, and lay her down between his arms. With his thumbs he brushed away the wetness that creased the outside of her eyes. "I will come back, Grace. I swear it. And we'll write—"

"No. Don't write."

"Why not?"

"I won't answer."

"Grace . . . ," he said, hurt.

She lifted her arms, twining them around his neck. "Don't talk any more. Make love to me now, Lucas."

Chapter
Twenty-Two

Christmas passed without Lucas. The windblown banks of sparkling snow crept to the bottom of the windowsills. In the new barn, the animals lay more snug and warm than the people in the house. The children loved it, of course, taking turns sledding down the slope on a sled made of barrel staves, coming in with streaming noses and glowing cheeks, to drop snow on clean-scrubbed floors. They puzzled over why their mother did not scold, but only held them tight for a moment before giving them hot soup.

The snow covered the burned patch at the top of the slope, settling over the encindered beams and blurring not only the concrete evidence of that night, but also Grace's memory of it. When spring came, ash-loving weeds appeared, and wildflowers. Honeysuckle twined over the ruin, doing its part to efface the unsightly blot.

Wenonah and Jasper returned to Ogden with the spring. They'd been living in St. Louis. Wenonah told Grace, "I don't know how people stand it. Everybody's in such a hurry. Why, if you stop on the street, they push you to get out of their way."

"It's good to have you home again."

The porch door stood open to let the spring breezes and bright sunshine into the stuffy house. Wenonah had come to help with the spring cleaning, her hair tied up and a print wrapper around her dress to protect it. She looked charming. Grace, attired similarly, did not think so of herself. It required the freshness of youth to carry off such a haphazard style.

"Here, let me do that," Wenonah said, putting her hand

on top of the loaded wood box that Grace was trying to drag into the middle of the room.

"You can help," Grace allowed. "I want to clean behind it."

Bending together, the two women tugged the box out a few inches. "Thanks."

"Well, Mother Crowley said I wasn't to let you do the heavy work alone. She thinks you've gotten too thin."

Grace, passing the scrub brush up and down the baseboards, said, "Oh, I needed to lose a little weight. It doesn't come off the way it did when I was your age."

"You're not ninety," Wenonah protested.

"Do I sound ninety? Even if I do, after two children, you'll be glad to lose a few pounds. Besides, I don't know what it is lately, but food just hasn't been something I've felt like bothering over. If it weren't for the children . . ."

"I 'spect it's just the time of year." Wenonah wrung out the rag and dipped it in soapy water. The black soot over the stove would come off, after three or four scrubbings.

"I'm too old for spring fever, too."

Out in the yard, Toby barked in a high pitch, a particularly gladsome sound. Grace instantly looked up, craning her neck to see outside. All she saw was Bart and Callie playing a boisterous game of tag. Hoping Wenonah hadn't noticed her eagerness, she went on attacking the baseboards.

When would she get over this ridiculous feeling of expectation? Lucas wasn't coming back. She had to learn to accept that. After all, she'd known what would happen when he left, all his chivalrous promises aside.

As though she'd read her mind, Wenonah asked, "I wonder how Mr. Lucas is getting along now."

"Perfectly well, I'm sure. I told you what an important man he turned out to be."

"Yes. Have you had any letters from him lately?"

Grace pressed her lips together hard. Nearly every day someone asked that question. She should be used to it by now. That sharp pain, like a knife run into her heart, should cease sometime soon.

"No, I haven't heard from him. His last letter came at Christmastime." It had explained why he wouldn't be able to come. She had never answered it. She told him she wouldn't, unable to bear the inevitable dwindling of his letters and the halting phrases he would seek to free himself of his unfortunate love affair.

"I'm sure he must be busy," Wenonah said.

"Probably." There'd been no slow tapering off in the letters. She'd received the one at Christmas and that was all. She kept it still beneath her pillow, crumpled now and tearstained. Every time she changed her bed she vowed to throw it on the fire. It had always found a last-minute reprieve.

Grace passed a cloth over the spot she'd washed. The window curtains flapped in the spring breeze on the clothesline. She'd mix up a good brew of vinegar and water to wash the windows, though the smell of vinegar brought back a certain night. . . . *Concentrate on the task at hand,* she told herself for the millionth time since he'd gone.

"A good scrub with a sheet of newspaper and these windows will shine. Then all I have to do is blacklead the stove."

Jasper had taken out the stovepipes earlier that day to knock out the accumulated soot. Though the floor would need to be scrubbed again after all their work, she'd already been over it once. Jasper had been careful but had left a trail of black grit from the stove to the door.

"I want to thank you and Jasper for all your help," Grace said.

Wenonah shrugged her thanks away. "Mother Crowley won't let me do a hand's turn in her house. She waits on me, hand and foot, when it ought to be the other way around."

"She's happy to have you. A daughter at last."

"But I won't ever learn how to run a home living with her. She won't even let me watch her work! The minute I come in, it's 'Here's a glass of lemonade,' or a slice of something, 'sit down, put your feet up.' "

"Sounds good."

"I hate to think what she'll be like when I tell her I'm pregnant."

"Wenonah!"

"No, no," the girl said, grinning. "I'm not. Not yet. But I have hopes."

Grace shared the girl's smile, though once again she felt that clutch at her heart. After Lucas had left, she'd been a week late. Her disappointment when at last she started again had been as bad as anything she'd suffered. Though an illegitimate child would have confirmed all the gossips' spicy stories, she would have had something of Lucas to keep with her. She'd even gone so far as to consider names.

"What are we going to do next?" Wenonah asked, easing her back.

"The sitting room, then right through the bedrooms. I'll whitewash that wall you're working on tomorrow. The chimney smoke came through a chink in the masonry in the sitting room and marked the wall in there too. Thank goodness I never wallpapered it like I wanted to. Smoke must be very hard to remove from wallpaper."

"I'm sure Mother Crowley knows how to do it."

"Probably." She eyed the big stove. "You know, I think I'll wait to blacklead that until tomorrow too. I want to get the big jobs out of the way first."

"I've never shined up a stove before. Is it hard to do?"

"Not if the blackener is soft. You've got to rub it in with a lot of elbow grease and—" Toby yapped again. With an effort, Grace kept from looking out. "And if it's dried up, there's no way you're going to do a good job. Some people soften it up with lard when it dries. But then, when you fire up the stove, your house smells like burning lard."

She glanced at Wenonah to see if the girl was paying attention to this housewifely wisdom. A strange stiffness in Wenonah's position and the way she stared in amazement out the door gave Grace pause. "Are you all right? You look as if you'd seen a—"

"Not a ghost." The voice was masculine and heartstoppingly familiar.

Grace whipped around so fast she almost fell. A pair of

strong hands grasped her ribs just below her breasts and held her steady. She looked up into the face she'd seen so often in her dreams, nightmares that tortured her by forcing her to crawl the vast distance between Missouri and Connecticut.

She closed her eyes and shook her head to clear it. Impossible that Lucas should be here, smiling down at her in joy. But his hands were hard and real against her body. Her fingers, still wet with soapy water, closed on the rough tweed of his sleeves. His familiar scent surrounded her, overlaid by a faint lemony fragrance and smoke. She recognized it as lemon furniture polish and tobacco and knew he must have come straight from the train to her side.

"Lucas, Lucas!" Grace sobbed his name against his lapel.

His fingertips, rough despite soft living, tilted her face back. "Glad to see me?"

His lips slanted over hers in a kiss that held all the hunger and loneliness of nine empty months. The porch door closing softly behind Wenonah only made Grace open her eyes for an instant.

Grace buried her face again in his chest. He felt more solid than the last time she'd had her arms around him. His fancy tie had a diamond stickpin thrust among the folds. She tried to draw back, out of his arms. They tightened around her as though he'd never let go.

"You've grown very fine," she murmured.

"And you're too thin. Turn my back for five minutes . . ."

"Five minutes!"

"And you stop eating. You'll have to gain it back. I'm not taking a skinny woman to wife."

"Lucas, I . . ." She wanted to tell him that nothing mattered now, that she'd live with him in an igloo on an iceberg if he'd only stay.

"Hush." He traced the shape of her lips with the pad of his thumb, his eyes intent as he refreshed his memory. A slow fire began to burn inside Grace, bringing to life all her withered dreams.

They kissed less desperately, as they came again to realize the completeness of their bond. Then Grace nipped him lightly and he smiled over her mouth. Pulling her with strength to mold her against his body, he said, "By God, I've missed you."

They dueled in love play, tasting each other, already aroused. A loud cough outside broke them apart, but Lucas kept his arm around Grace's waist while they turned.

Wenonah stood there, her eyes averted. With a smile in her voice she said, "I've just had a great idea. Why don't I have Bart and Callie sleep over at our house? You know Mother Crowley'd be tickled to have them. . . ."

"Bart and Callie?" Lucas said. "Oh, no. They can't go. I have Christmas presents for them. And for you too, Wenonah."

As though conjured from the ground by those magic words, Bart and Callie came tearing into the kitchen. "Did we do it right, Lucas?" Bart asked. Without waiting for an answer, he turned to his mother. "He told us to be real quiet while he snuck on up here, and we did too. Callie wanted to tell you he was here, but I kept her quiet."

"Let me get my grip," Lucas said. He removed his gaze from Grace with a reluctance she could feel. She stared after him, taking an instinctive step forward in protest when he walked out the door. She felt that if she took her eyes off him for an instant, he'd retreat back into her dreams.

Wenonah stepped over to her. "Uh, maybe you want to fix your hair?"

"My . . . ?" She caught a glimpse of herself in the reflection at the window. Snatching off the gaudy kerchief that covered her hair, she dashed to the bedroom.

When she came out, the others were all in the sitting room, holding packages. "Come on, Ma," Callie said as soon as she saw her. "We're waiting for you."

"Yes, we are," Lucas said. Grace took the hand he held out to her and in two steps was clutched again to his side. She oohed appropriately over the harmonica for Bart, and the matching clothes of velvet and lace for Callie and her doll.

"I'll get Plowdy," Callie cried, and ran to her little room.

"She doesn't carry her as much," Grace explained in answer to Lucas's glance. "My mother convinced her she could manage alone."

"Oh, Mr. Lucas!" Wenonah said, opening her box. Fold after fold of icy blue satin exploded softly upward from between sheets of tissue. Standing up, Wenonah shook out the dress. Of the very highest style, with foaming lace and intricate draperies, it was a dress to fuel dreams of dances and parties. Wenonah hugged it to her breast.

"You'll need help to put that on," Grace said.

Unable to take her eyes off it, the young woman said, "Oh, I'm not going to *wear* it."

"You'd better," Lucas warned. "Or Jasper will be terribly disappointed. I saw him at the railroad station and told him about it. Some men wouldn't appreciate another man giving their wife a new gown."

But Wenonah only smiled and packed the dress again in the box. "I'll go set the table. I swear you brought enough food in those baskets for an army."

"It's a late Christmas feast. I've been planning it for quite some time." Lucas looked into Grace's eyes. Meeting that deep blue gaze, that she'd thought never to see again, brought tears to blur her vision.

Wenonah said, "Come on, Bart. You can help me."

The boy looked at his mother and grinned. "Sure thing, Wenonah."

In her ear, Lucas said, "Don't you want your present?"

"I have it," she answered, brushing her hand down his sleeve.

"No, that's what I want." He raised her hand to his lips, kissing each finger, giving a bite to the plump pad of her thumb. Grace made a tiny noise in the back of her throat and his eyes caught fire.

Settling back on the settee, he drew her over to him, patting his thigh. "Sit here. I want you as near me as you can be."

Self-consciously, Grace took her place. "I'm too heavy," she said after a moment, trying to rise.

"You? A strong breeze would blow you away." He tucked an arm around her to keep her where she was.

Grace turned toward him and kissed him, pushing her fingers through the soft strands of his hair. She'd forgotten how dazzlingly handsome he was when she came this close to him, forgotten the exact depth of his eyes, the gentle abrasion of his shaven face against hers. Though she had believed she remembered every detail, his reality overwhelmed her. Even while their lips met, tears dripped from her eyes.

"Hey, now," Lucas said, when the drops touched his cheeks. Wiping the beads away from her eyes, he demanded, "What's this? Aren't you glad to see me?"

"I missed you so. . . ."

His voice deepening, he said, "I tried to write to you, but you were right about that. Letters aren't enough. Every time I'd try to put on paper what I felt, I'd just throw the pen across the room and howl at the moon. It didn't stop me from thinking about you every hour of the day and night, though. My servants thought I'd turned werewolf."

"Just show me."

Their kisses burned away the loneliness as though it had never been. Grace found it difficult to keep her hands from wandering over Lucas's shoulders and back. She forced herself to recall that her children could enter at any moment. The power of his arms and the impelling strength of his body were heady magic, sweeping her away.

Finally, he broke off. His breathing came fast, his eyes darkening. "I still haven't given you your Christmas present."

"It's waited this long . . . ," she said, pressing her lips to his once again.

He drew back, a smile quirking his lips. "You'll like this. It's something I made myself."

Reaching into his breast pocket, Lucas brought out a sheaf of papers, folded lengthwise. "Here you are. With the compliments of the Connecticut State Legislature, the governor and your humble servant."

Grace saw that the documents were closely printed in black ink. Whether from the poor light or the nearness of Lucas, she could hardly make out a word. She gave it back to him with a slight shake of her head.

He grinned. "Just like a woman. Give her everything she wants in a neat bundle . . ."

"What is it?"

"A proposal of marriage, of sorts. You wouldn't marry me because it meant giving up more than you'd gain, right?"

"Wrong."

"Well, this is—" He shook his head as though he heard a buzzing in his ears. "What?"

"That was why I wouldn't marry you before. But it's not why any longer."

"You have a new reason not to marry me? Let me know what it is. If I can push through this piece of legislation, I can push through another."

She put her fingers over his mouth. "Do all politicians talk so much?" He nodded behind her hand, then began to suck gently on a finger. Grace closed her eyes as rivers of hot sensation ran up her arm. She tried to form words. "I can't say I'll marry you now because . . . Oh! Because you haven't asked me yet."

He swept her back, so she lay almost at full length on the settee, her legs still over his. Leaning down, he said, "I'm tired of asking, so I'm going to be a tyrant instead. The way I've arranged things, it's my last chance. Grace, you're going to marry me. You'll marry me ten minutes after we get off the train in New London if I have to drag you up to the altar."

"Yes, I will," she said, unwontedly submissive. "And then ten minutes after that, I'll drag you off to bed." She caught him and pulled him down for a kiss.

A piping voice cried out, "Yuck!"

Grace sat up, much disheveled, and waved at her daughter. The little girl's nose wrinkled. "You were kissing him!"

"That's right," Lucas said. "I'm going to be your new dad."

"Oh, that's okay then." Callie lifted her doll. "She wants to try on her clothes."

Some time later, sitting down to the delicacies that Lucas had brought with him, Grace looked around the table and said, "Everyone is so fine, I feel like the drudge of the family."

"I'm not fancy," Bart said with pride.

"You're fancy enough for me," Grace responded. "Why don't you say the blessing tonight?"

"I think Lucas ought to do it," the boy said, then looked uncomfortable. "I guess I should start calling you Pa, huh?"

"Lucas is still okay, if you'd like to use that instead."

Bart gave a shy grin. "God, bless this food before us. Pass the potatoes, please."

"Short but to the point," Lucas said. "Son, I'm afraid you have no career in politics ahead of you."

"Speaking of politics," Grace began.

"Not at the dinner table, if you don't mind."

"What did you mean by compliments of the Connecticut State Legislature?" In answer to the mock-annoyed roll of his eyes, she said, "Well, it is my present, isn't it?"

He rose from his seat, his napkin still in his hand, and went out of the room. Coming back, he handed her the papers.

Grace's dinner sat untouched as she read with a frown of concentration. As she finished the first page, she gave a gasp of amazement.

"Lucas, did you . . . ? But this is wonderful!"

"What is it?" Wenonah asked.

Grace began to read aloud. " 'In the case of marriage on or after the twentieth of April, 1877, neither husband nor wife shall acquire, by force of the marriage, any right to or interest in any property held by the other before, or acquired after, such marriage, except as to the share of the survivor in the property, as provided by law.' "

"A provision I hope we won't have to use for years and years. And years," Lucas said.

Grace continued, her voice shaking with excitement. " 'The separate earnings of the wife shall be her sole property. She shall have the power to make contracts with third persons, and to convey . . .' " Looking up, she met Lucas's eyes. "You did this. . . . You wrote this. . . ."

"Not all by myself," he said, reaching across the table to take her hand. "I had help from some very good men. Men I used to have nothing in common with. But we worked together to hammer out a compromise with some of the tougher birds in the House. I had a little more reason than most of them to pass this bill. I really couldn't see any other way to get what I want most in this world."

"Oh, there was an easier way," Grace said, gripping his hand hard. "All you had to do was leave me for a little while."

"Never again," he vowed. "Never again."

Callie leaned closer to her brother and whispered, "He's going to be our daddy."

"It's okay by me, if it's okay by Ma."

Lucas said, "The only drawback is that this law is only good in Connecticut. It may be years before a similar Act passes the national Congress. We're going to have to live in Connecticut. Will you mind?"

Grace shook her head; her heart too full to speak.

Wenonah said, "I don't understand everything. But does this mean Jasper and I can buy this house?" When Grace said she wouldn't sell it to anyone else, the girl said, "I can't wait to tell him!"

By the end of the meal, Callie had begun calling Lucas "Pa," giving a delighted giggle every time he answered to it. Bart talked man to man about what kind of games the children of Connecticut played and seemed relieved to learn that there would be little for him to learn on that head. Wenonah refused to let Grace touch a dirty dish, and she noticed the girl gave everything she touched a proprietorial pat.

The children were eager to visit Mrs. Crowley, Bart saying, "She always cuts her pie slices just my size." Waving good-bye as they and Wenonah drove off in the wagon, Grace said to Lucas, "I hope I'm doing the right thing. This place hasn't always yielded the greatest profits. Though last year's harvest was enough to pay off most of my debt at Lansky's."

"Thanks to your hired man," he said. He put his arm around her waist, his hand flat and warm against her stomach. "Thanks to him, I hope to have a different sort of harvest next year."

"Do you want to have a baby right away?"

He stopped nibbling her ear long enough to say, "I'm already a father, but I'd like to see how I do with babies."

"You're already a father?" Was this some part of his past he'd remembered after leaving Missouri?

"Of course. I have two great kids, a boy and a girl. Or at least, they will be mine in a few days. You read how we have to wait until the twentieth to get married?"

Relaxing against him, her last fear at rest, Grace said, "Oh, *those* two children."

"Sure." Lucas took her by the hand and led her through the house. "I never kept a harem, Grace. I'll have plenty to do keeping up with one woman. One very special woman."

"What about your father? He'll never approve of me."

"I've been working on him. Sooner or later, he'll come around. We'll keep trying until he does. A grandchild will make the difference, if Bart and Callie don't worm their way into his affections first. I've seen him envy other men for their descendants. He'll come around."

Reaching her bedroom, he said, "But enough about Father. Let's talk about something else."

"Talk? Is that what you call it?"

He began to work free the buttons on her blouse. "I've been longing for this moment for nine hideous months. Believe me, I've counted every hour of each one."

"Me too," Grace said shyly.

Much later, as they lay together in a tangled mix of sated desire and growing peace, Grace whispered, "Ask me one more time."

Beneath her cheek, his breath caught, stopping the rise

and fall of his chest. His hand stilled where he lovingly stroked her back. In a deep voice that thrummed beneath her ear, he asked, "Grace, will you marry me?"

"Yes. Yes. I will."

Epilogue

John Peyton Cobb knew the moment his wife left the ballroom. Though Grace had done her duty and he his by their guests, having had only a single waltz together, he'd kept an eye on her and her partners. Amazing how jealousy could still stab him deeply, despite their year and a half of marriage, despite knowing she loved him with her whole soul.

In her ball dress of old gold brocade, about the color of her hair, the low square bodice of this year's fashion displaying the most evident of her charms, he really couldn't blame his old friends and enemies for being attentive. But all the same, he saw green every time someone took her into his arms.

She'd gone in the direction of the library. Opening the big oaken door, John saw the book room, whose image had come back to him so often during those peaceful days in Missouri. Here was the window, as tall as the wall, divided into tiny panes of glass. Here were the books, cases of them, the warm gaslight reflecting off their spines. There was no fire tonight, for it was August and the dancers were complaining of the heat.

His father's voice sounded. "How the devil did you know I had an ace?"

"Just one of those things," Callie said, gathering in the cards. Her little toes showed beneath the hem of her robe as she leaned forward in the too-big chair. "Another hand, Grandfather?"

Mr. Cobb threw an oversized ten dollar bill onto the tabletop. "You're a cardsharp, missy, and you'll get no more of my money."

With a coquettish smile, Callie picked up the money and tucked it into her nonexistent cleavage. "We'll play for love then. And I won't cheat, I promise."

They looked up as John came over to the table. "Does your mother know you're still up?"

"I said she could stay and keep me company awhile," his father said. "And she's all but cleaned out my wallet!"

Ruffling Callie's feather-light curls, John said, "I remember when you were content to play for candy. Who taught you to play for money?"

Mr. Cobb coughed guiltily. "Have to make the game worth the candle, my boy. Or, at any rate, the gas."

"It's all right, Father," Callie said. "I always put the money in the collection plate on Sundays."

"At the rate you're going," he said, "you'll build a new spire all by yourself. Now, you'd better get off to bed. It's late."

Callie scrambled down from the chair and kissed each man on the cheek. "Thank you for letting me win, Grandfather." The older man looked embarrassed, unable to meet his son's eyes. She said, "Come on, Bart. Father says it's bedtime."

John looked around for his son. From behind the wings of an enormous armchair, Bart said, "After I finish this chapter."

"What are you reading?"

Bart hardly glanced up from the page. "It's the one that man you introduced me to in Hartford gave me. Mr. Clemens. It's really good."

Callie came up to the chair. "I thought you said reading is boring. You said you only wanted to play baseball."

"I can't play baseball, dum-dum. It's dark out." He turned over the page, his concentration returning.

"Don't read too long," John said. "You've got church tomorrow morning."

"Huh? No, I won't."

Callie left to go to bed. Mr. Cobb stood up and stretched, taking a cigar from his inner pocket. "I think I'll step outside and blow a cloud. Care to join me?"

"No, thank you, father. I'm looking for Grace."

"She popped her head in a little while ago. Didn't disturb the game."

"Sorry, sir. Listen, Senator Graham was asking after you."

The older man shrugged. "Nobody wants to talk to a man whose party is out of power."

"Actually, that's not what he wanted to talk to you about." He saw the proud set of his father's shoulders and sighed. Ever since Grant had lost the presidency, Mr. Cobb had been moping. "You know, he's on the board of Darrington College. He mentioned there's an opening. I think he means to sound you out as to whether you'd care to take the position."

"Darrington . . . Darrington? I'm not familiar with that school."

"It's a college for women."

"Oh, that." Mr. Cobb waved his hand dismissively, the lighted cigar tracing patterns in the air. "I'm not in favor of higher education for women."

"You could be helpful to Callie, seated on a board like that."

"She won't need my help," Mr. Cobb said, his resentful face softening into a smile. "She'll probably steal a diploma, or charm it out of the professors. Of course, now, if more girls were as smart as she is, colleges mightn't be such a bad idea. Keep the girls under control for a little while longer, before releasing them on unsuspecting husbands."

"Sounds like you and Senator Graham have a lot of ideas in common. You should talk to him, Father."

Grumbling, Mr. Cobb agreed and went out.

"Remember, Bart, not too late."

Bart, still deep in *The Adventures of Tom Sawyer,* merely waved his hand toward his stepfather.

On the other side of the library door, John found his father's longtime butler, imported in his salad days from England, passing by. "Anyone looking for me, Parsons?"

"No, sir. It's going splendidly. I've overheard some of your guests saying that this is the finest ball they've attended in years."

"Keep the champagne flowing and they'll soon say it's the party of the century."

"Yes, sir."

"By way, don't let Nanny wake up Master Bart tomorrow. If he misses church, tell her I said it was all right. I'll tell his mother."

"Very good, sir. She is in the nursery, I believe, sir."

"Thanks, Parsons. Remind me to tell Father that you're due for a raise."

The music followed him as he climbed the winding stairs to the third floor. Laughter floated through the house, the sounds of gaiety and merriment. Even here, where only family and servants came, flowers in profusion graced the tables in the hall. Grace had wrought these changes, making his father's huge, dark house into a home.

The nursery was at the back of the house, where the baby's cries couldn't disturb anyone else. Yet, John had often heard her door latch click as she left her bedroom at night, knowing as if by magic that little Adam needed her.

She stood above the crib, the lowered gaslight falling on the multitude of tucks and pleats in the bustle of her ball gown. It lit up the nodding aigrettes in the shape of honeysuckle blossoms, white diamonds and yellow, tucked into the crown of her hair. He'd given them to her on their first anniversary. She'd cried.

"Everything all right?" he asked in a low voice, coming into the nursery.

She turned with a smile, putting her forefinger to her lips, pointing the other one toward a half-opened door. Sonorous snores from the room beyond told him that Nanny was soundly sleeping in there.

John came to look over her shoulder at their sleeping son. Four months old, he slept with the concentration that in future years would be reserved for play. He lay on his round stomach, his baby fist pressed against his cheek. His black hair stood straight up, as usual.

Grace slipped her hand into her husband's. "Sleeping like a log," she whispered. Tugging, she drew him out of the room.

"You know," she said, in a more normal tone as she closed the door, "Bart and Callie never slept like that. They were up every hour and would come awake if a fly settled on them. Adam seems a lot happier than either of them were when he's awake too."

"He must take after me," John said. "Because I'm a happy man these days."

"Are you?" She stopped outside his bedroom door.

"Of course I am. I have everything a man could want."

"Do you?"

He faced her then, bewildered. "Of course."

Reaching out, she adjusted the white rose in the lapel of his cutaway coat. "You look very handsome tonight, Mr. Cobb," she said.

"And you're magnificent in that gown." Her breasts looked as white as doves above the rich gold of her dress. He tried not to look at them. "But, Grace . . . don't change the subject. Do you have any doubts that I'm happy?"

"No, but I don't think you have everything you want."

"You don't think I'm dissatisfied. You couldn't. Everyone downstairs was envying me. I have the most beautiful wife in the world, wonderful children, a solid future . . ."

"Do you think you'll like being Speaker?"

"Don't change the subject. Besides, I haven't been re-elected yet."

"But you will be. The wives are all sure of it. Even Mrs. Anderson-Finch said you were sure to be, and you know she hasn't let her husband vote Republican in twenty years."

"Grace . . ."

"I know, don't change the subject. It's just I . . . don't think you have everything a man could want out of life."

"What else is there?"

For answer, she came closer, her delicate perfume surrounding him. Her hands were no longer the rough, chapped hands of a farmer's wife, but smooth as cream. When she brushed her fingers over his lips, they were like flower petals.

"Grace . . ."

They melted together into a kiss. The music from the ballroom was very far away. John tried to draw back, but she held him close, one hand tangling in his hair. She pressed closer against him. Her dress outlined her form, as was the fashion, so there was little between him and her heat. And thin dress trousers did nothing to hide the effect she had on him, the effect she always had on him.

Slowly, reluctantly, he stepped back. He saw the disappointment in her trembling, downturned lips. "John . . ."

"We should return to our guests. . . ."

She caught his arm. One thing hadn't changed and that was her strength. "What is the matter?" she demanded, her eyes sparkling with anger. "You haven't been near me since the baby came. At first, I appreciated it. But it's been four months, for goodness' sake!"

"Longer than that," he muttered.

"Yes, longer than that. Much longer. And I appreciated that too. There's no doubt that in the last two months of pregnancy the last thing you want is a man. But for goodness' sake, John, how much longer were you intending to wait?"

Before he could answer, she said, in a lower voice, "It's me, isn't it? I'm just not . . . I mean, *three* children will do that, no matter how hard you try to stay . . ."

"No, no," he said, pressing her hands to his heart. "Grace, it's not you. I find you to be more beautiful now than the first day I saw you. And then I thought you were the most beautiful woman I'd ever seen in my life."

"You didn't remember your life," she said, starting to smile.

"Any man with eyesight would have thought the same," he said, dismissing her quibble. "If I haven't . . . The reason we haven't made love in a while is that the doctor said we shouldn't."

"I beg your pardon?"

"Dr. Gilling said I shouldn't trouble you for at least six months. That you wouldn't want me to." The words the bearded doctor had actually used had included "demon lust" and "vile congress."

Grace let out her breath in a gusty sigh. "Well, of all nonsense I ever heard! He told me that too, and I told *him* what I thought of that idea! Fiddlesticks!"

"Fiddlesticks?"

"Nothing but. He seemed to think I'd be happy to learn I wouldn't have to 'do my duty,' as he put it, for such a long time. He even hinted that he'd be happy to tell you I couldn't be bothered until after Adam was weaned. Well, I told him to save his breath. But now that I hear he talked to you anyway, I'm tempted to march down to his office tomorrow and give him a piece of my mind. Of all the unholy nerve!"

"Hush, Grace," John said, tucking his arm around her waist. Happiness flowed through him. "You'll wake the baby."

"It just makes me mad to think that I've been worrying all this time that it was me, when it was that blasted, interfering old—" The rest of her diatribe was lost on his lips.

After a moment, she gave herself up to the delicious sensations he aroused. Standing as close to him as possible, she gave a delightful wiggle and slipped her hands under his coat. The cool silk of his waistcoat contrasted with the heat of his body. She matched him kiss for kiss, opening her mouth to urge him on when he held back, still fearful of hurting her. Then his passion, so long denied, took over. She knew she had nothing more to worry about.

Drawing away a little, she said teasingly, "Our guests?"

"They'll never miss us." The doorknob turned under his questing hand. Their lips met and they fought again a heavenly duel as he closed and locked the door.

"But, John . . . ," she said.

"Call me Lucas," he said, knowing she would anyway. Alone in their room, as they loved, she always called him that.

An hour later, as the strains of "The Last Waltz" were played so faintly it might have been a song in a dream, Grace stilled her hand that moved softly across his chest.

"We really should get up to say good-bye, Lucas. We are the host and hostess after all."

"Father will take care of things."

"Yes, but . . ."

"If anybody asks, we'll just tell them the truth. We were too busy making love to be polite."

Grace turned to face him. "Well, I cannot tell a lie. . . ."

If you enjoyed this book, take advantage of this special offer. Subscribe now and...

Get a Historical

No Obligation

If you enjoy reading the very best in historical romantic fiction...romances that set back the hands of time to those bygone days with strong virile heros and passionate heroines ...then you'll want to subscribe to the True Value Historical Romance Home Subscription Service. Now that you have read one of the best historical romances around today, we're sure you'll want more of the same fiery passion, intimate romance and historical settings that set these books apart from all others.

Each month the editors of True Value select the four *very best* novels from America's leading publishers of romantic fiction. We have made arrangements for you to preview them in your home *Free* for 10 days. And with the first four books you receive, we'll send you a FREE book as our introductory gift. No Obligation!

FREE HOME DELIVERY

We will send you the four best and newest historical romances as soon as they are published to preview FREE for 10 days (in many cases you may even get them before they arrive in the book stores). If for any reason you decide not to keep them, just return them and owe nothing. But if you like them as much as we think you will, you'll pay just $4.00 each and save at *least* $.50 each off the cover price. (Your savings are *guaranteed* to be at least $2.00 each month.) There is NO postage and handling—or other hidden charges. There are no minimum number of books to buy and you may cancel at any time.

FREE

Romance
(a $4.50 value)

Send in the Coupon Below

To get your FREE historical romance and start saving, fill out the coupon below and mail it today. As soon as we receive it we'll send you your FREE Book along with your first month's selections.

Recipes from the heartland of America

THE HOMESPUN ❧ COOKBOOK ❧

Tamara Dubin Brown

Arranged by courses, this collection of wholesome family recipes includes tasty appetizers, sauces, and relishes, hearty main courses, and scrumptious desserts—all created from the popular *Homespun* series.

Features delicious easy-to-prepare dishes, such as:

Christmas Salad

1/2 pound cranberries	1/4 cup nuts
1 large red apple	7/8 cup sugar
(cored, not peeled)	1 pkg lemon-flavored gelatin
1 orange rind	3/4 cup warm water
(most of white removed)	Pinch of salt
Pulp of one orange	

Put cranberries, apple, orange rind, and nuts through food chopper. Add sugar and orange pulp cut in pieces. Let stand 2 hours. Dissolve the lemon gelatin in warm water. Add salt. When it begins to thicken, add fruit. Mold in ring mold or individual molds. Make leaves out of a thin sheet of lime-flavored gelatin that has been molded in shallow pan.

A Berkley paperback coming February 1996